HATTER M

LOVE
OF
WONDER

VOLUME FIVE

Dedicated to Barbara Marshall
for daring to leap into the first puddle.

HATTER M

LOVE
OF
WONDER

VOLUME FIVE

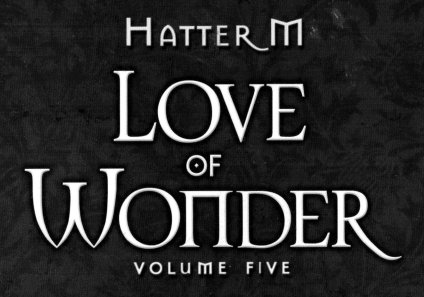

Written by Frank Beddor & Liz Cavalier
Art by Sami Makkonen

AUTOMATIC
PUBLISHING

Hatter M: Love of Wonder
Volume 5

Writers
Frank Beddor
Liz Cavalier

Art
Sami Makkonen

Cover Art
Vincent Proce

Letterer
Tom B. Long

Mirror Keeper
Lucas San Juan

Code Breaker
Kelly Contessa

Logo Design by
Christina Craemer

Interiors Designed by
Tom B. Long

The Looking Glass Wars ® is a trademark of Automatic Pictures, Inc.
Copyright © 2014 Automatic Pictures, Inc.
All rights reserved.

Printed in Korea.

ISBN: 978-0-9892221-6-7

This is not the story of a Mad Hatter

"One can never "fall" in love, you must rise to its level of consciousness. Love is not a feeling, it's a state of MIND!" – T.C. Carrier

Thank you

Crystal Gazers, Mirror Skryers,
Looking Glass Diviners and Prismatic Oracles

Contents

The Quest

The Rest

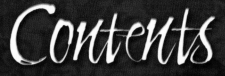

Who Are We?

The Hatter M Institute for Paranormal Travel is a devout assemblage of radical historians, cartographers, code breakers and geo-graphic theorists pledged to uncovering and documenting through the medium of sequential art the full spectrum journey of Hatter Madigan as he traversed our world from 1859 – 1872 searching for Princess Alyss of Wonderland.

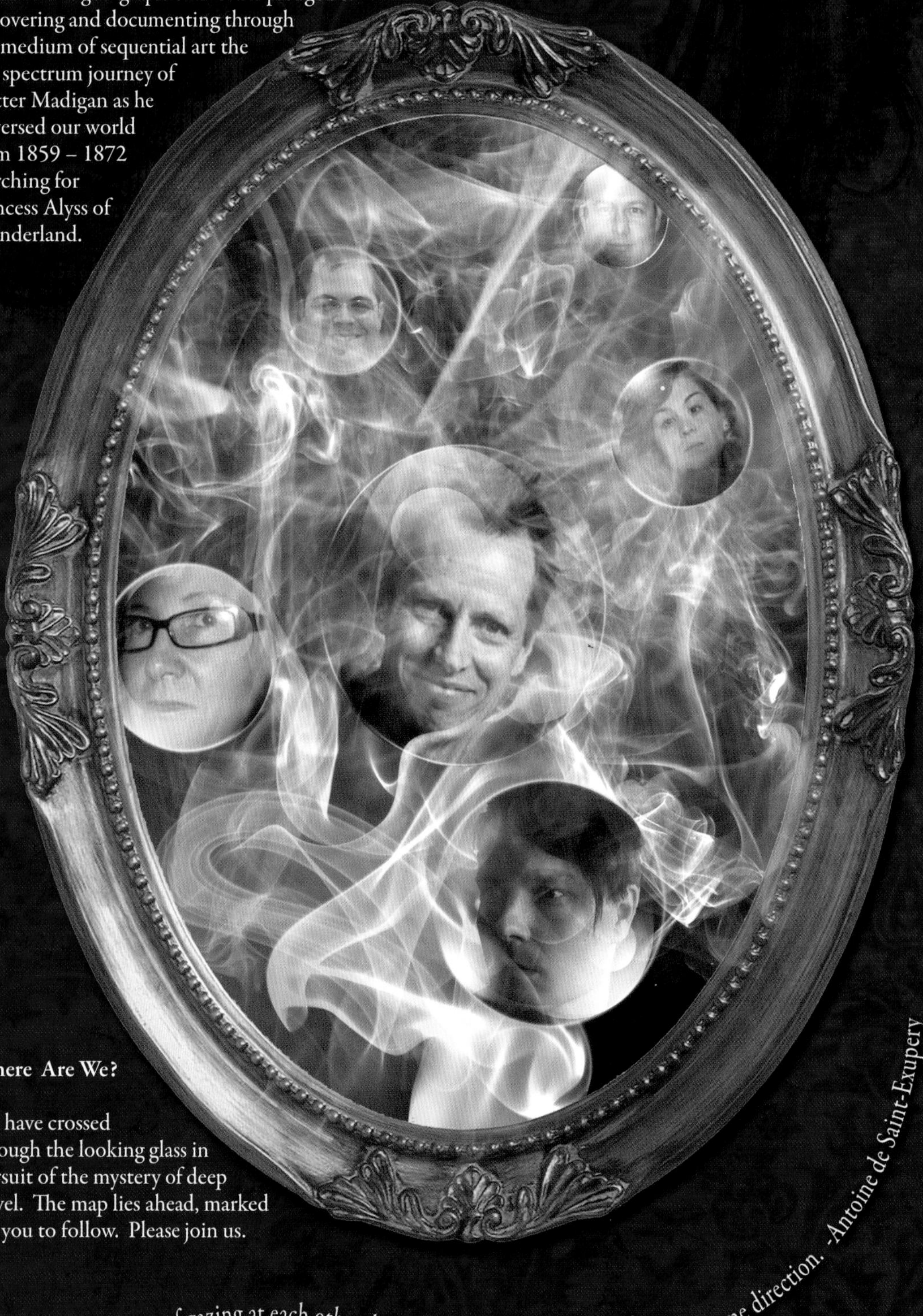

Where Are We?

We have crossed through the looking glass in pursuit of the mystery of deep travel. The map lies ahead, marked for you to follow. Please join us.

Love does not consist of gazing at each other, but in looking outward together in the same direction. -Antoine de Saint-Exupery

Introduction

The 13th Year and the 11th Hour

Our time on this reflected stage is fast ending. Tick Tock!
The journey is complete, the map has been drawn and now
it is your turn to discover the way back to Wonderland.
The final volume in Royal Bodyguard Hatter Madigan's
search has finally cracked open and awaits your keen perusal.

After a decade of investigating this mysterious traveler the
metaphysical gates opened wide and the Love of Wonder came
to us at break neck speed, pushing the limits of the space-time
continuum and our ability to channel and articulate what you
are about to receive. We ran as fast as we could to keep up with
the revelations and evidence of this epic crusade and now we
deliver it to you with the hope you will take up the cause and
continue your own search because this story never ends, it
only pauses.

To help you along on your journey we leave you with
these thoughts.

When you wish to travel through a puddle focus your mind
on your destination before you arrive.

The truth cannot stay hidden forever. At some point, just like
the sun, it will appear.

The future is being IMAGINED now. Who in the world will
you become?

Love is conscious. If you are looking for Love, Love is looking
for you.

Remember, it's all energy and it's all in your head.

With Love,

Hatter M Institute for Paranormal Travel

"One love, one heart, one destiny." - Bob Marley

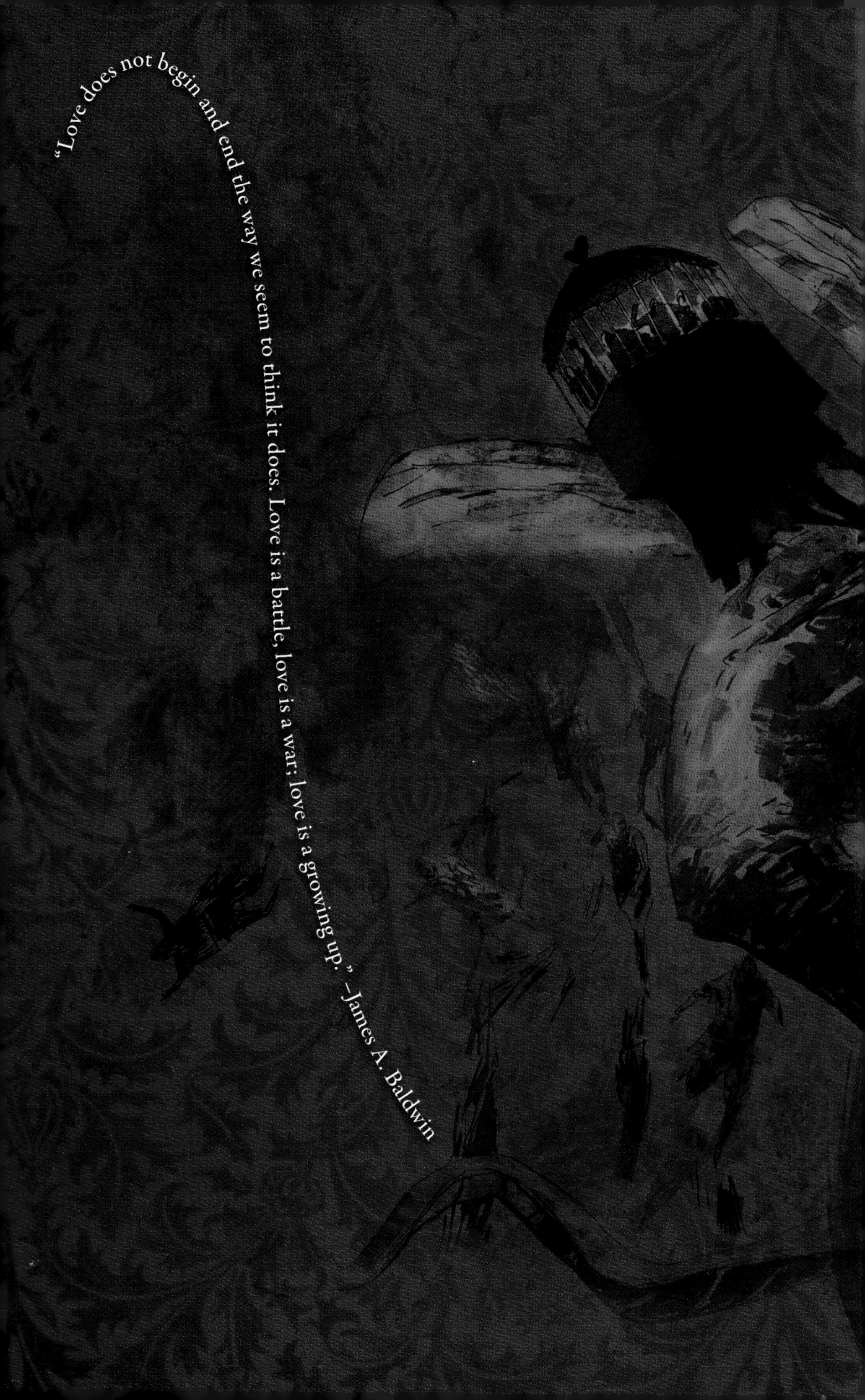
"Love does not begin and end the way we seem to think it does. Love is a battle, love is a war; love is a growing up." –James A. Baldwin

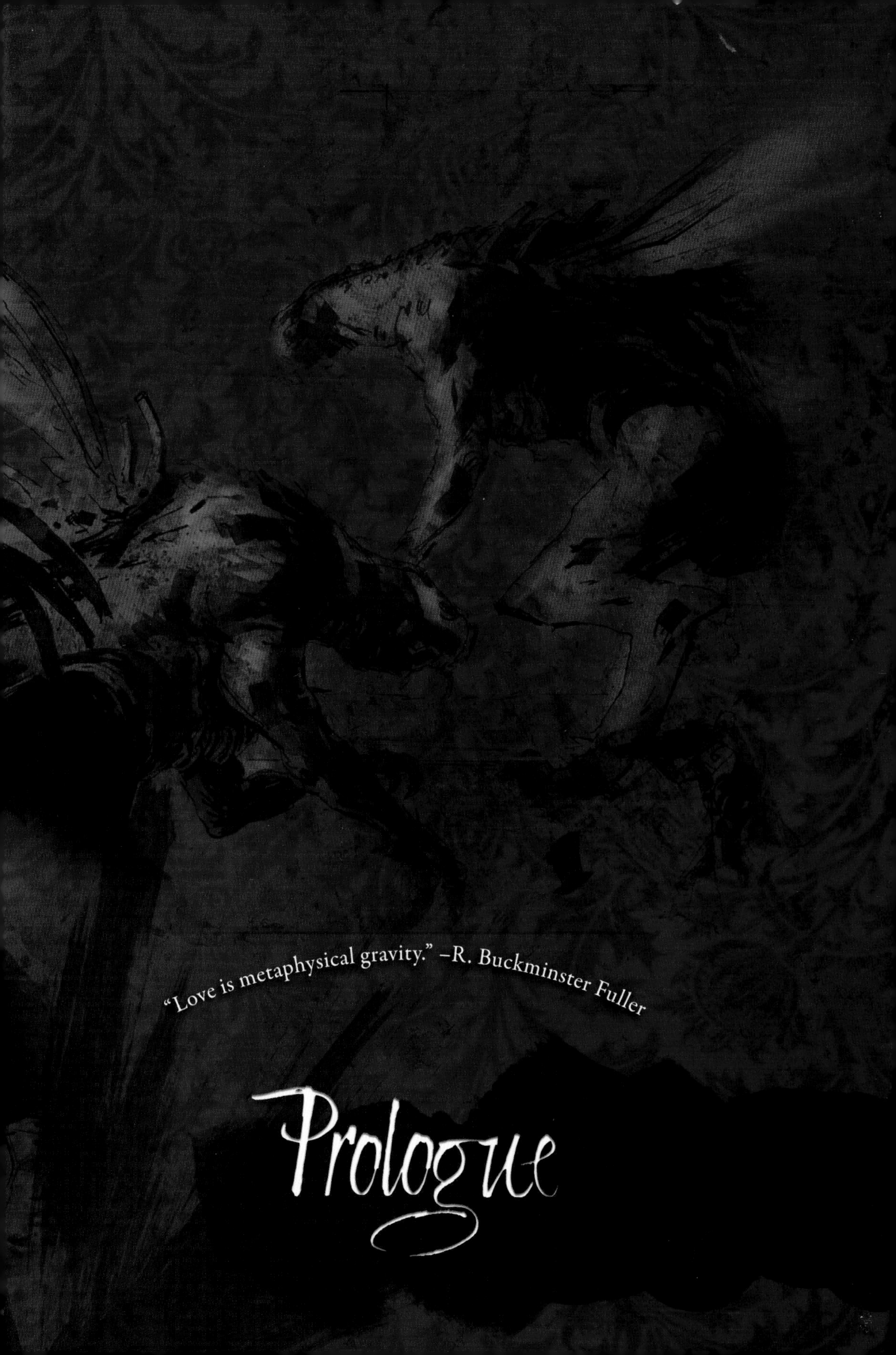

"Love is metaphysical gravity." –R. Buckminster Fuller

Prologue

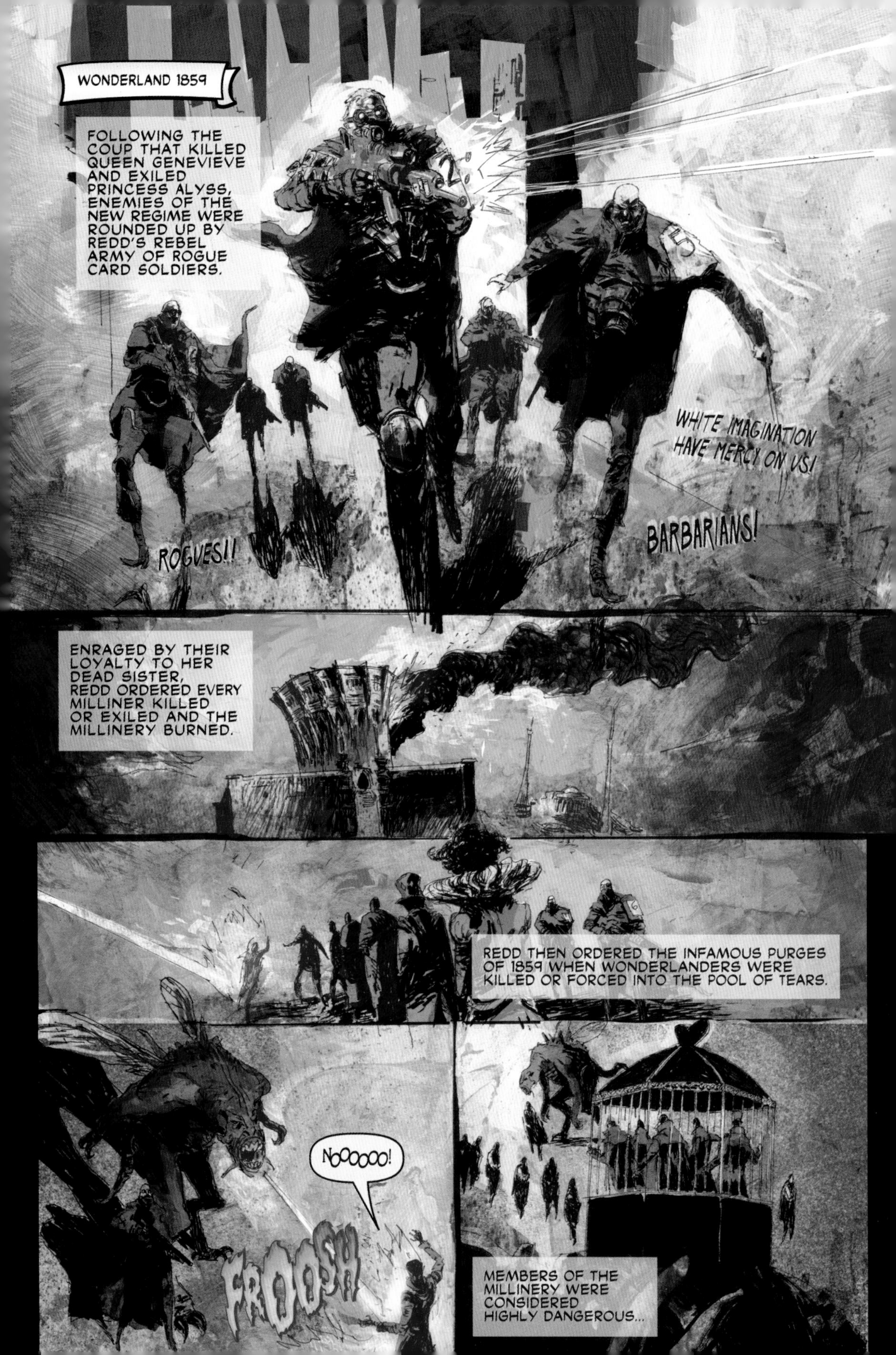
WONDERLAND 1859
FOLLOWING THE COUP THAT KILLED QUEEN GENEVIEVE AND EXILED PRINCESS ALYSS, ENEMIES OF THE NEW REGIME WERE ROUNDED UP BY REDD'S REBEL ARMY OF ROGUE CARD SOLDIERS.
WHITE IMAGINATION HAVE MERCY ON US!
ROGUES!!
BARBARIANS!
ENRAGED BY THEIR LOYALTY TO HER DEAD SISTER, REDD ORDERED EVERY MILLINER KILLED OR EXILED AND THE MILLINERY BURNED.
REDD THEN ORDERED THE INFAMOUS PURGES OF 1859 WHEN WONDERLANDERS WERE KILLED OR FORCED INTO THE POOL OF TEARS.
NOOOOOO!
FROOSH
MEMBERS OF THE MILLINERY WERE CONSIDERED HIGHLY DANGEROUS...

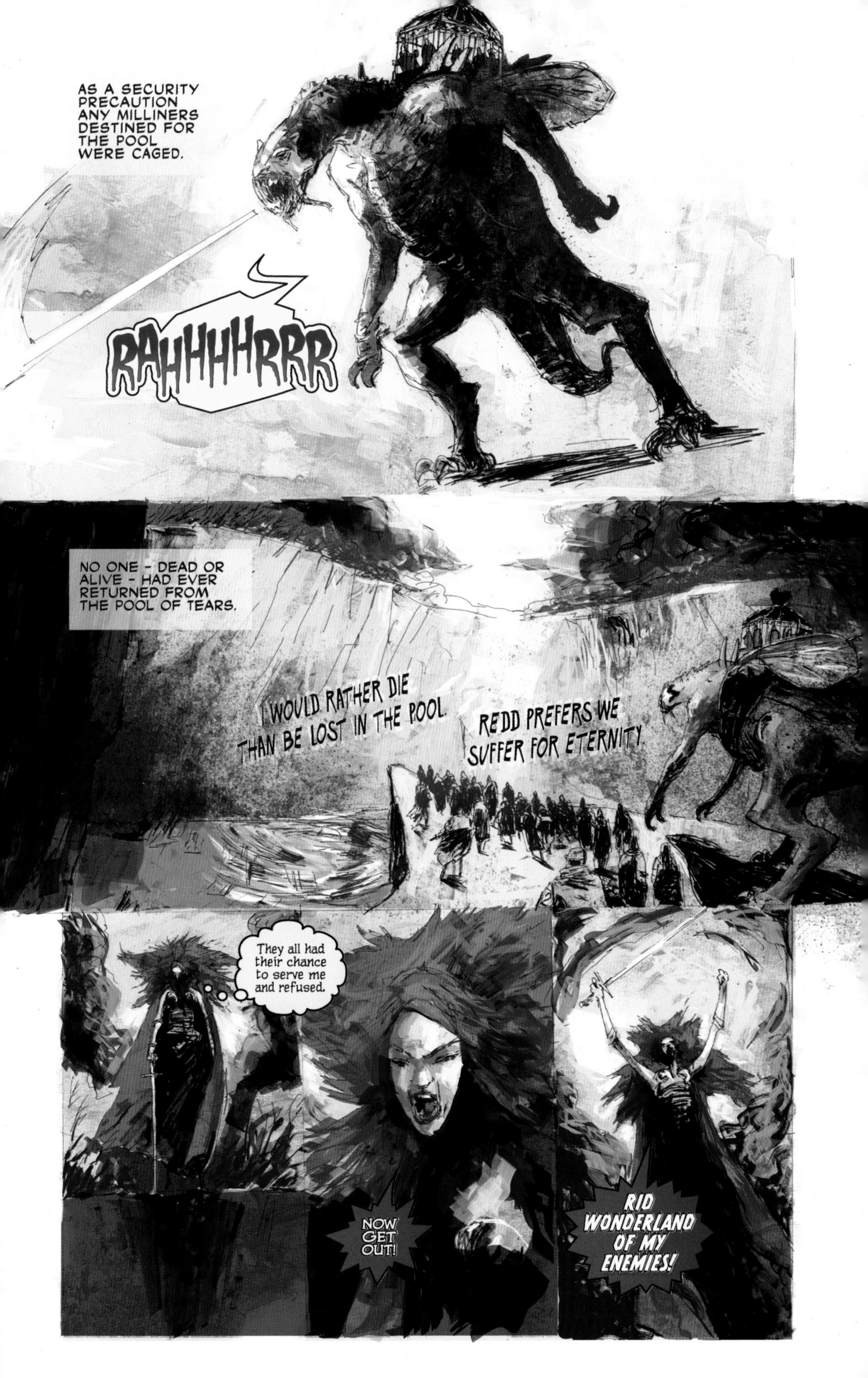
AS A SECURITY PRECAUTION ANY MILLINERS DESTINED FOR THE POOL WERE CAGED.
RAHHHHRRR
NO ONE - DEAD OR ALIVE - HAD EVER RETURNED FROM THE POOL OF TEARS.
I WOULD RATHER DIE THAN BE LOST IN THE POOL.
REDD PREFERS WE SUFFER FOR ETERNITY.
They all had their chance to serve me and refused.
NOW GET OUT!
RID WONDERLAND OF MY ENEMIES!

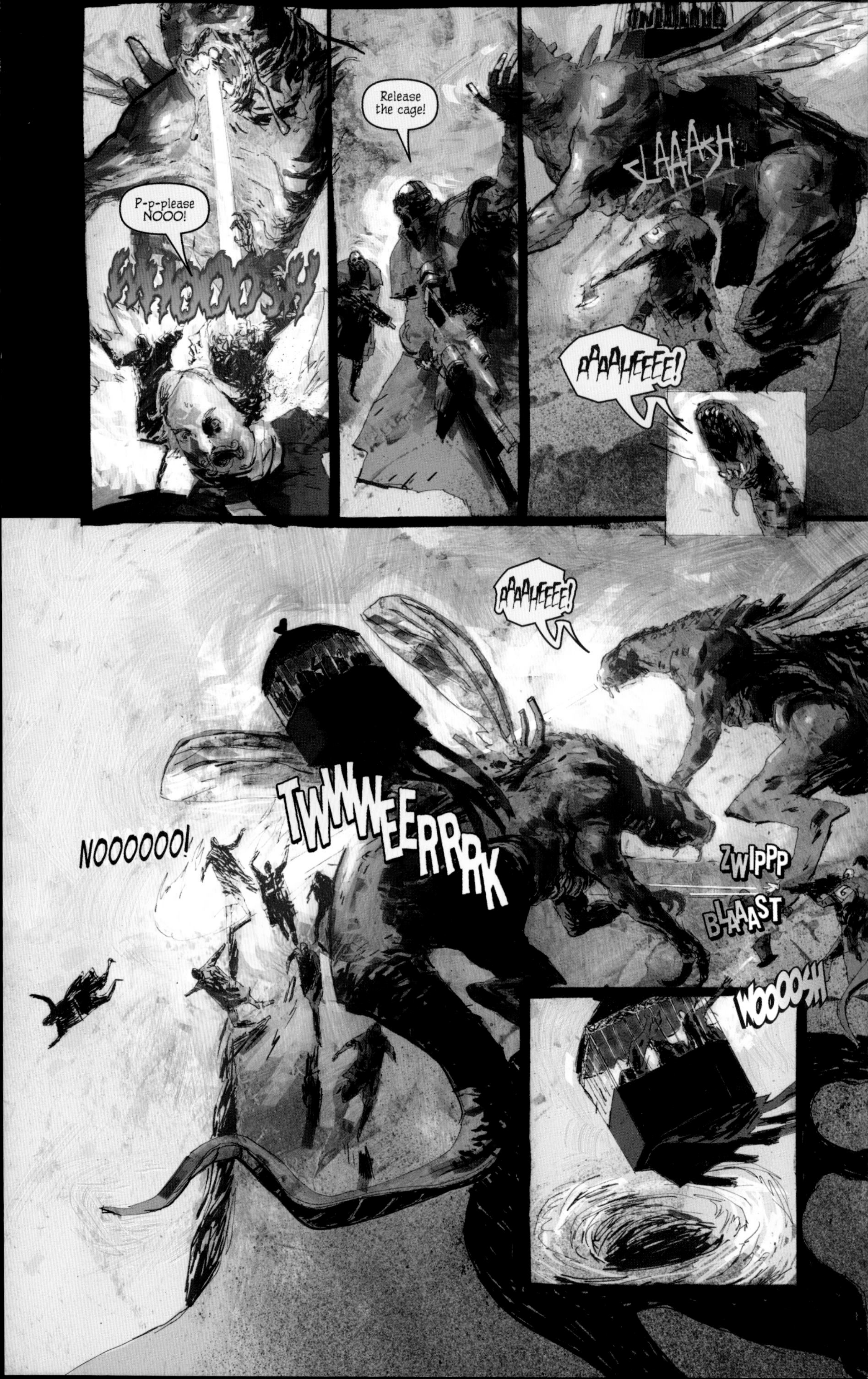
P-p-please NOOO!
WHOOOSH
Release the cage!
SLAAASH
AAAAHEEEE!
AAAAHEEEE!
TWWWEERRRRK
NOOOOOO!
ZWIPPP
BLAAAST
WOOOOSH

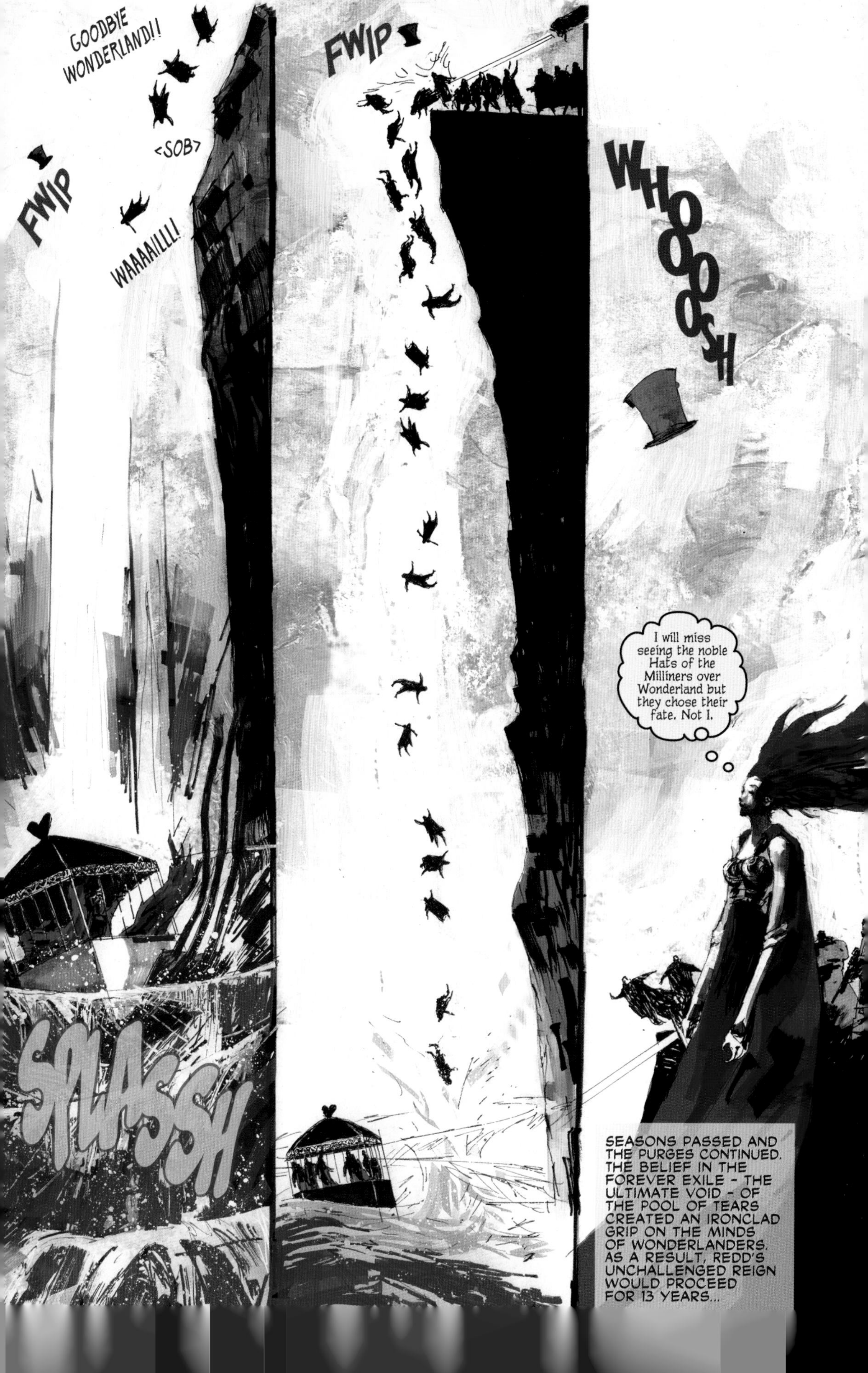

GOODBYE WONDERLAND!!
FWIP
<SOB>
WAAAAILLL!
SPLASH
FWIP
WHOOOOSH
I will miss seeing the noble Hats of the Milliners over Wonderland but they chose their fate. Not I.
SEASONS PASSED AND THE PURGES CONTINUED. THE BELIEF IN THE FOREVER EXILE - THE ULTIMATE VOID - OF THE POOL OF TEARS CREATED AN IRONCLAD GRIP ON THE MINDS OF WONDERLANDERS. AS A RESULT, REDD'S UNCHALLENGED REIGN WOULD PROCEED FOR 13 YEARS...

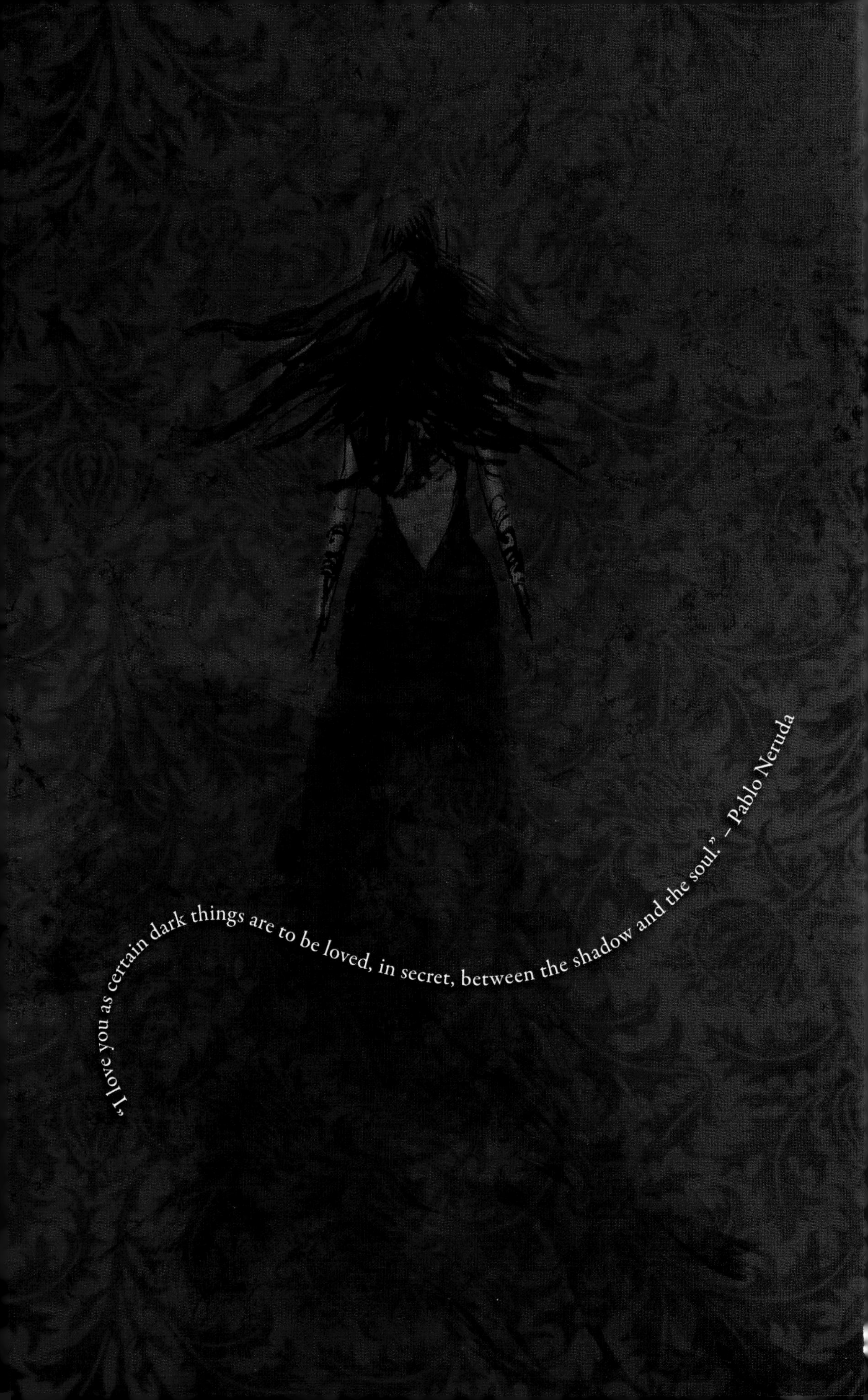
"I love you as certain dark things are to be loved, in secret, between the shadow and the soul." – Pablo Neruda

"The day the power of love overrules the love of power, the world will know peace." –Mahatma Gandhi

Part 1
The 13th year

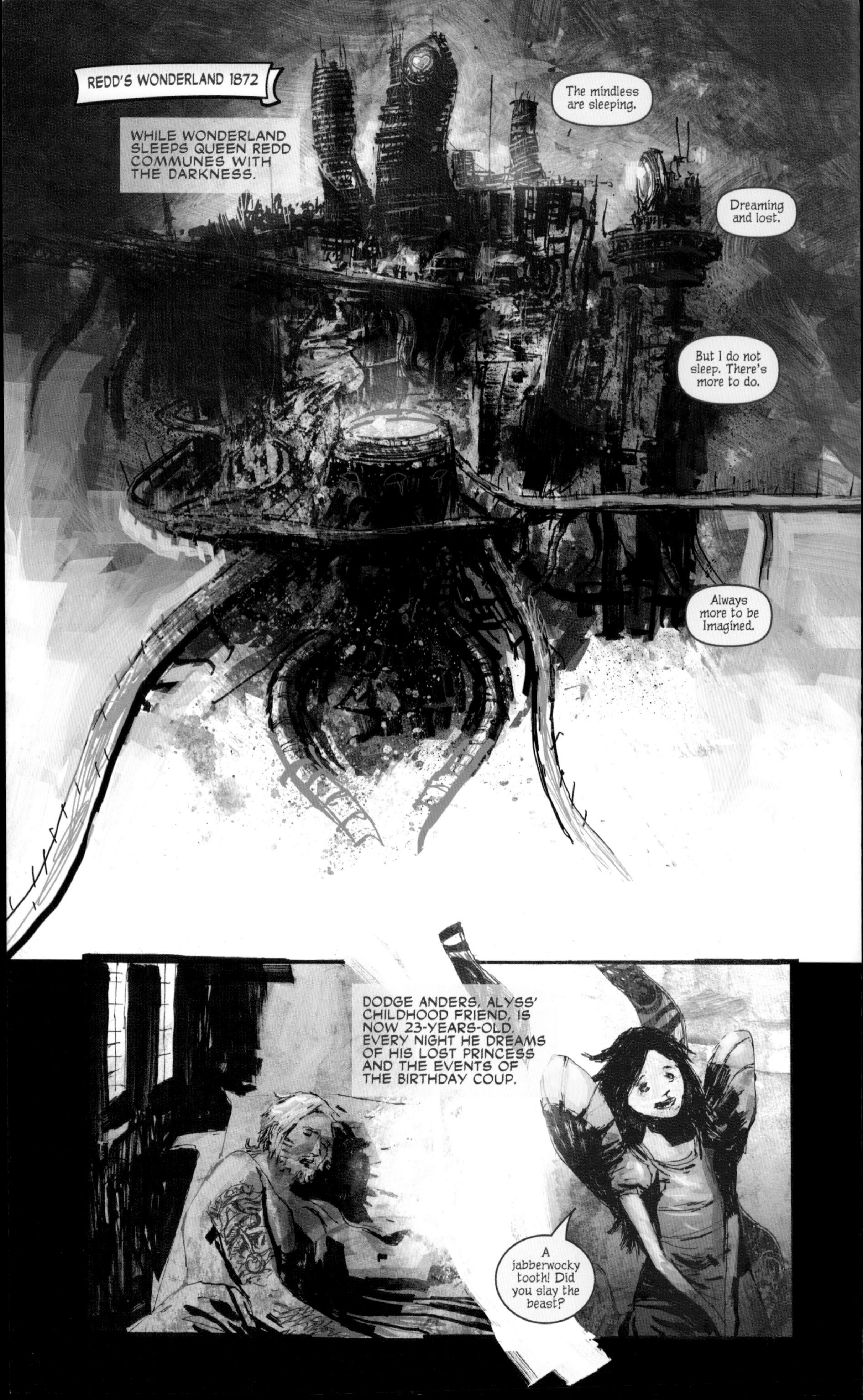
REDD'S WONDERLAND 1872
WHILE WONDERLAND SLEEPS QUEEN REDD COMMUNES WITH THE DARKNESS.
The mindless are sleeping.
Dreaming and lost.
But I do not sleep. There's more to do.
Always more to be Imagined.
DODGE ANDERS, ALYSS' CHILDHOOD FRIEND, IS NOW 23-YEARS-OLD. EVERY NIGHT HE DREAMS OF HIS LOST PRINCESS AND THE EVENTS OF THE BIRTHDAY COUP.
A jabberwocky tooth! Did you slay the beast?

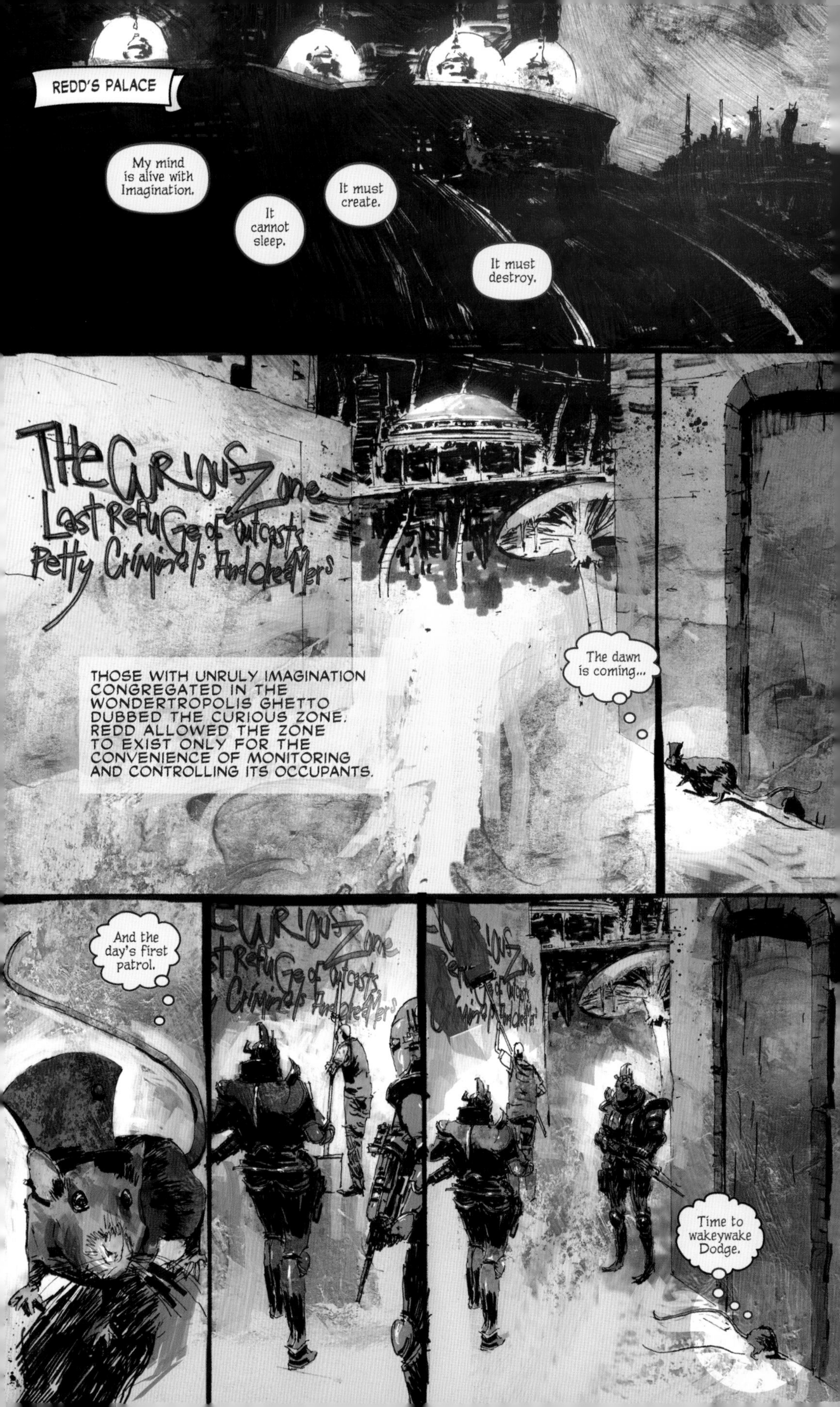
REDD'S PALACE
My mind is alive with Imagination.
It cannot sleep.
It must create.
It must destroy.
The Curious Zone
Last Refuge of Outcasts, Petty Criminals And Dreamers
THOSE WITH UNRULY IMAGINATION CONGREGATED IN THE WONDERTROPOLIS GHETTO DUBBED THE CURIOUS ZONE. REDD ALLOWED THE ZONE TO EXIST ONLY FOR THE CONVENIENCE OF MONITORING AND CONTROLLING ITS OCCUPANTS.
The dawn is coming...
And the day's first patrol.
Time to wakeywake Dodge.

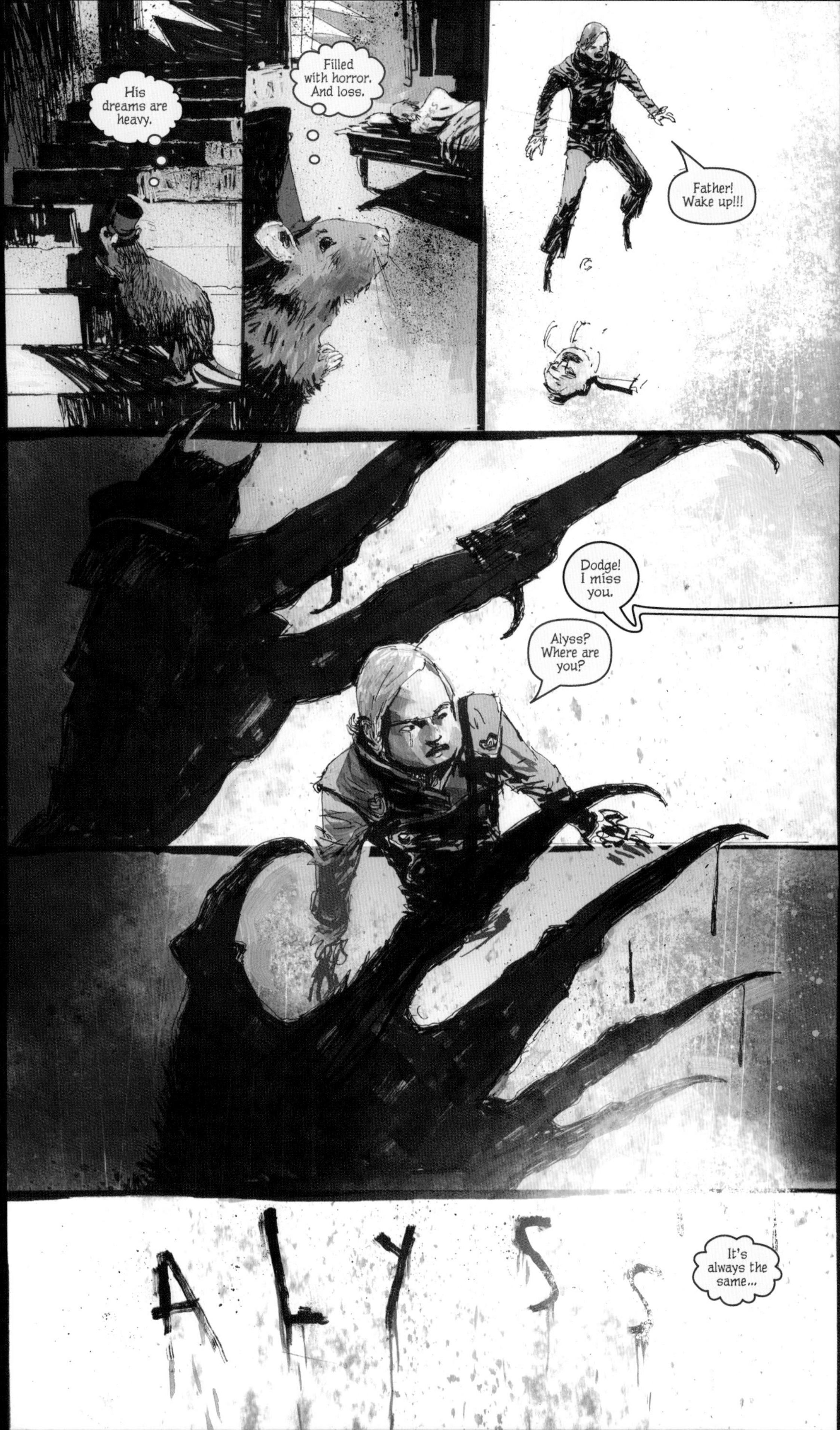
His dreams are heavy.
Filled with horror. And loss.
Father! Wake up!!!
Dodge! I miss you.
Alyss? Where are you?
ALYSS
It's always the same...

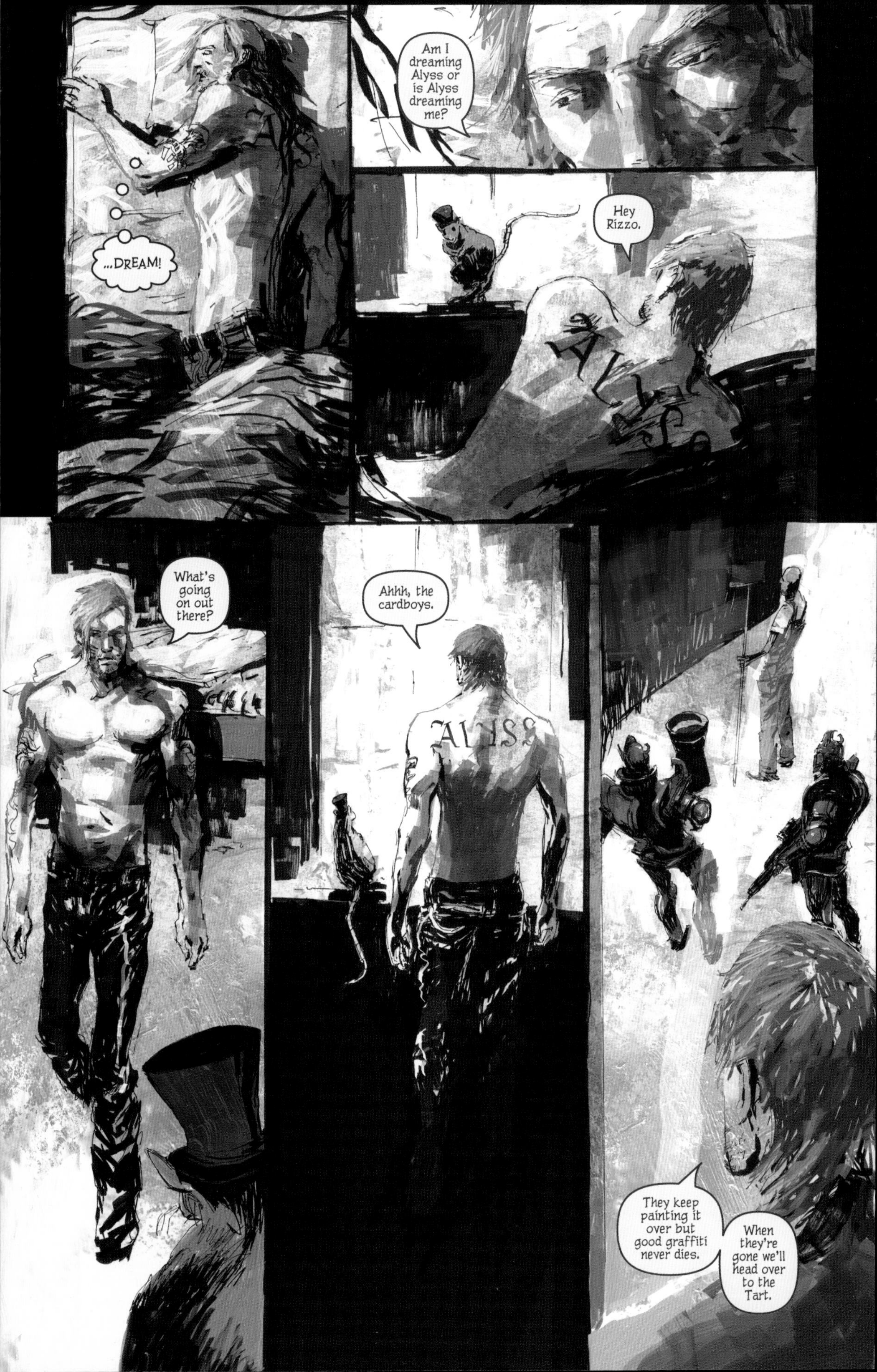
...DREAM!
Am I dreaming Alyss or is Alyss dreaming me?
Hey Rizzo.
What's going on out there?
Ahhh, the cardboys.
They keep painting it over but good graffiti never dies.
When they're gone we'll head over to the Tart.

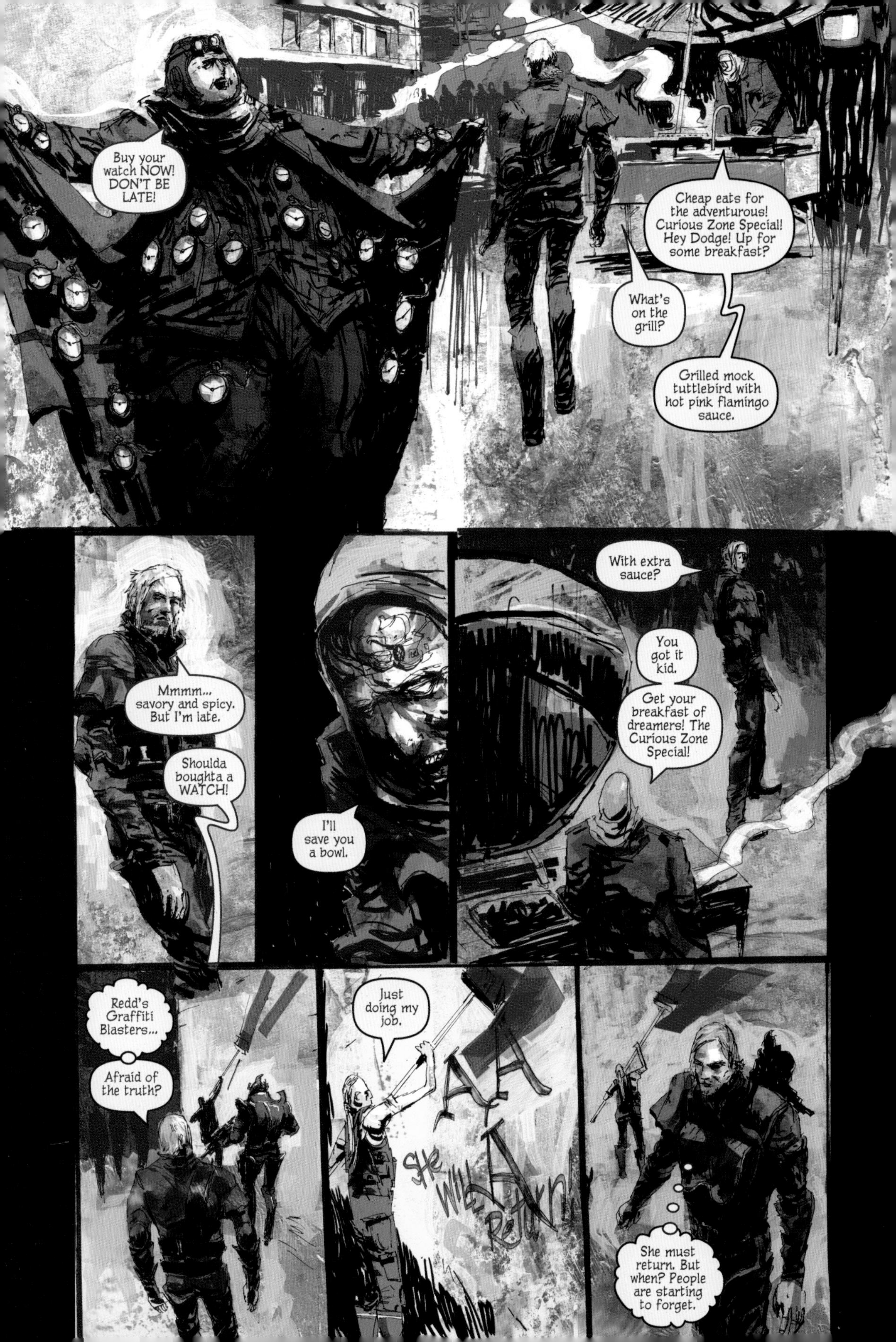
Buy your watch NOW! DON'T BE LATE!
Cheap eats for the adventurous! Curious Zone Special! Hey Dodge! Up for some breakfast?
What's on the grill?
Grilled mock tuttlebird with hot pink flamingo sauce.
Mmmm... savory and spicy. But I'm late.
Shoulda boughta a WATCH!
I'll save you a bowl.
With extra sauce?
You got it kid.
Get your breakfast of dreamers! The Curious Zone Special!
Redd's Graffiti Blasters...
Afraid of the truth?
Just doing my job.
SHE WILL RETURN!
She must return. But when? People are starting to forget.

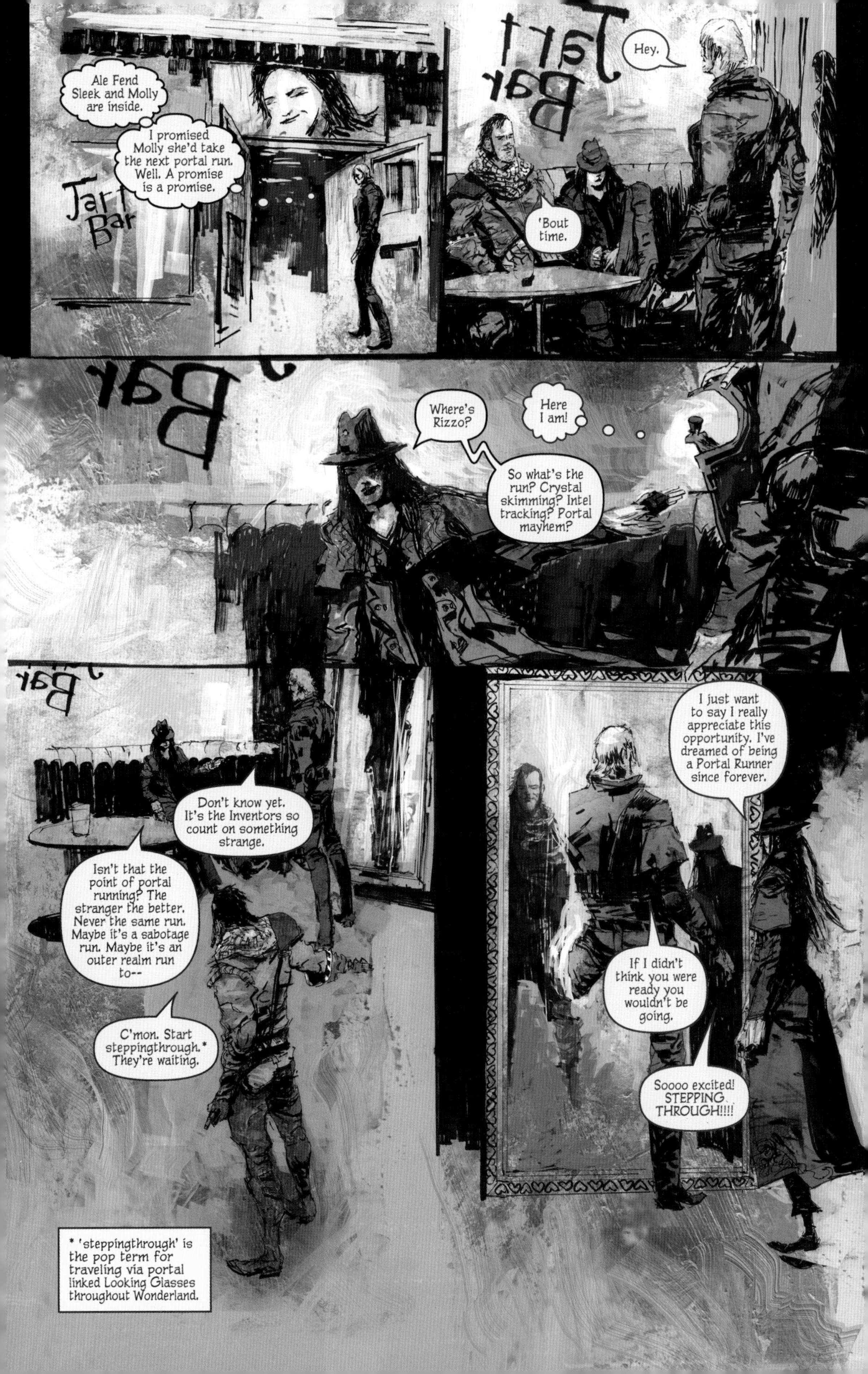
Ale Fend
Sleek and Molly are inside.
I promised Molly she'd take the next portal run. Well. A promise is a promise.
Jarf Bar
Jarf Bar
Hey.
'Bout time.
Where's Rizzo?
Here I am!
So what's the run? Crystal skimming? Intel tracking? Portal mayhem?
Don't know yet. It's the Inventors so count on something strange.
Isn't that the point of portal running? The stranger the better. Never the same run. Maybe it's a sabotage run. Maybe it's an outer realm run to--
C'mon. Start steppingthrough.* They're waiting.
I just want to say I really appreciate this opportunity. I've dreamed of being a Portal Runner since forever.
If I didn't think you were ready you wouldn't be going.
Soooo excited! STEPPING THROUGH!!!!
* 'steppingthrough' is the pop term for traveling via portal linked Looking Glasses throughout Wonderland.

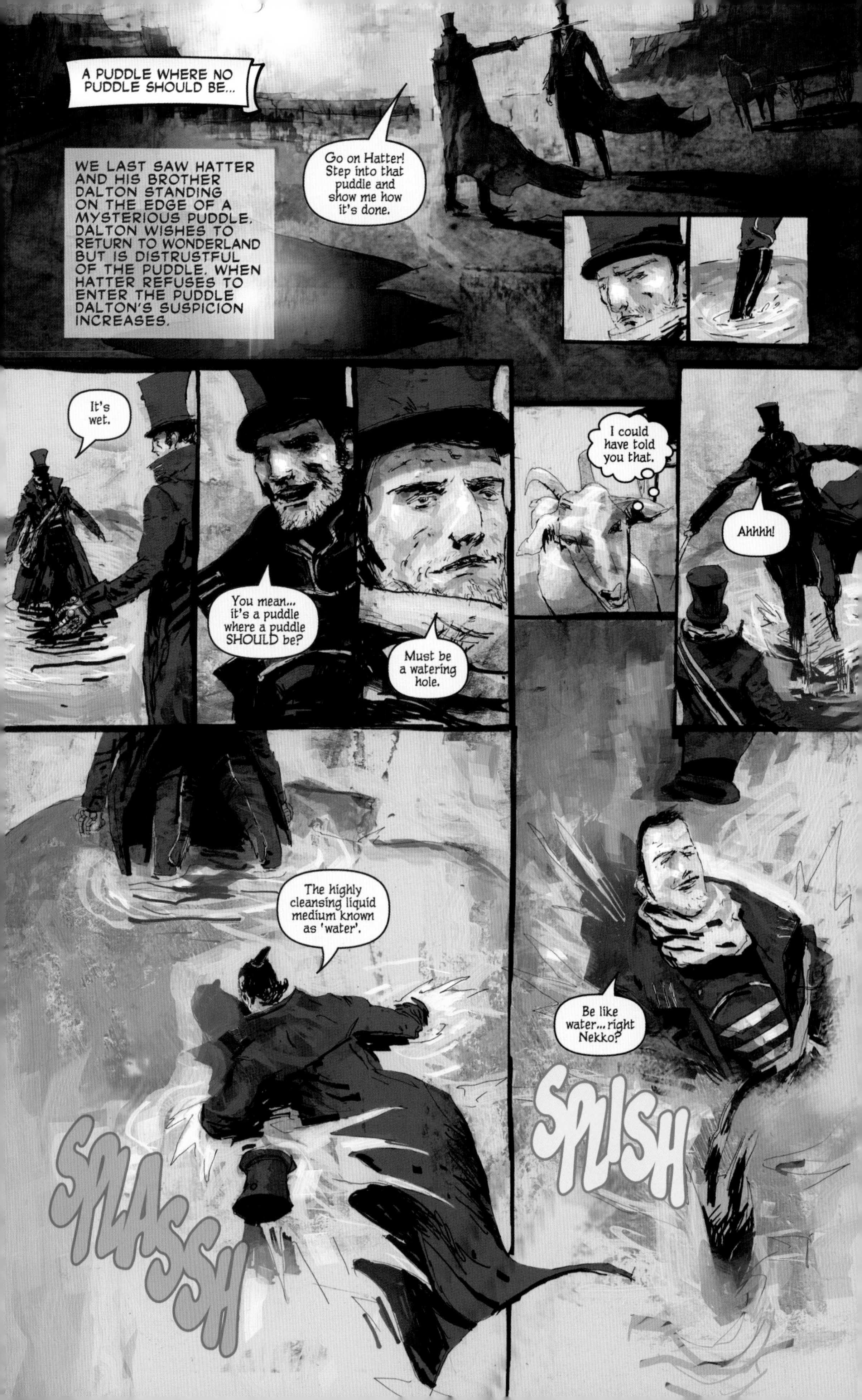
A PUDDLE WHERE NO PUDDLE SHOULD BE...
WE LAST SAW HATTER AND HIS BROTHER DALTON STANDING ON THE EDGE OF A MYSTERIOUS PUDDLE. DALTON WISHES TO RETURN TO WONDERLAND BUT IS DISTRUSTFUL OF THE PUDDLE. WHEN HATTER REFUSES TO ENTER THE PUDDLE DALTON'S SUSPICION INCREASES.
Go on Hatter! Step into that puddle and show me how it's done.
It's wet.
You mean... it's a puddle where a puddle SHOULD be?
Must be a watering hole.
I could have told you that.
Ahhhh!
The highly cleansing liquid medium known as 'water'.
SPLASSH
Be like water... right Nekko?
SPLISH

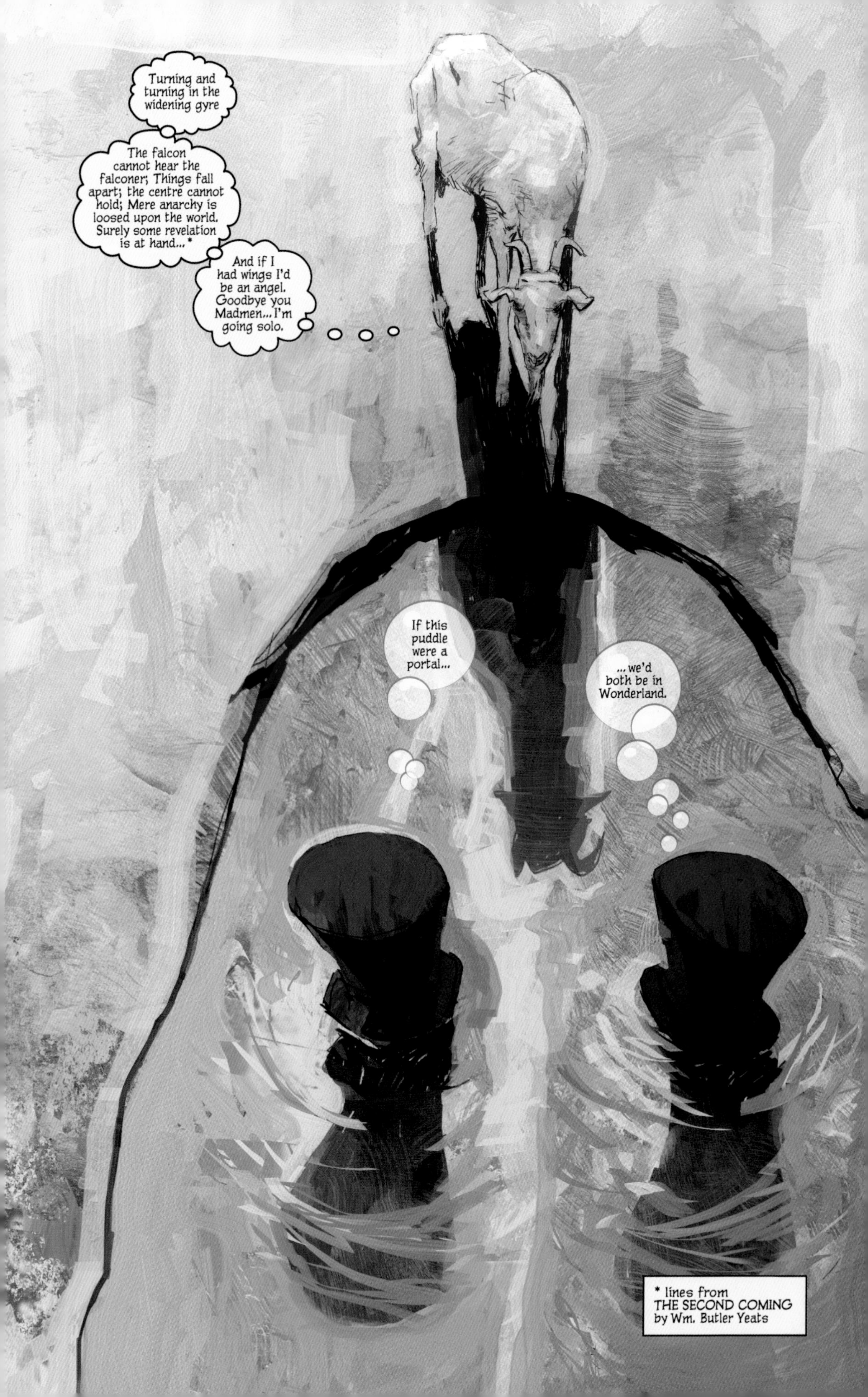
Turning and turning in the widening gyre
The falcon cannot hear the falconer; Things fall apart; the centre cannot hold; Mere anarchy is loosed upon the world. Surely some revelation is at hand...*
And if I had wings I'd be an angel. Goodbye you Madmen...I'm going solo.
If this puddle were a portal...
...we'd both be in Wonderland.
* lines from THE SECOND COMING by Wm. Butler Yeats

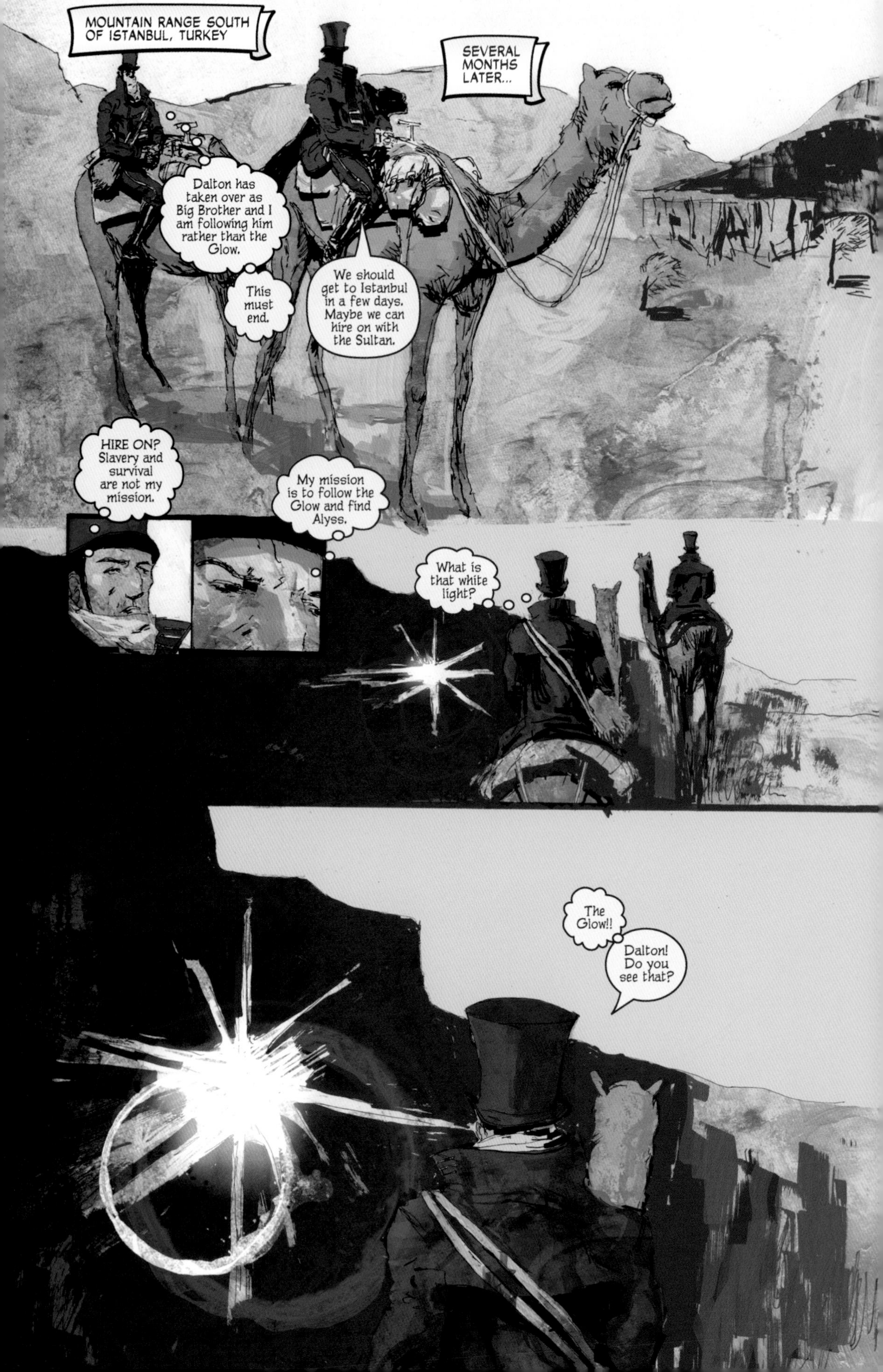
MOUNTAIN RANGE SOUTH OF ISTANBUL, TURKEY
SEVERAL MONTHS LATER...
Dalton has taken over as Big Brother and I am following him rather than the Glow.
This must end.
We should get to Istanbul in a few days. Maybe we can hire on with the Sultan.
HIRE ON? Slavery and survival are not my mission.
My mission is to follow the Glow and find Alyss.
What is that white light?
The Glow!!
Dalton! Do you see that?

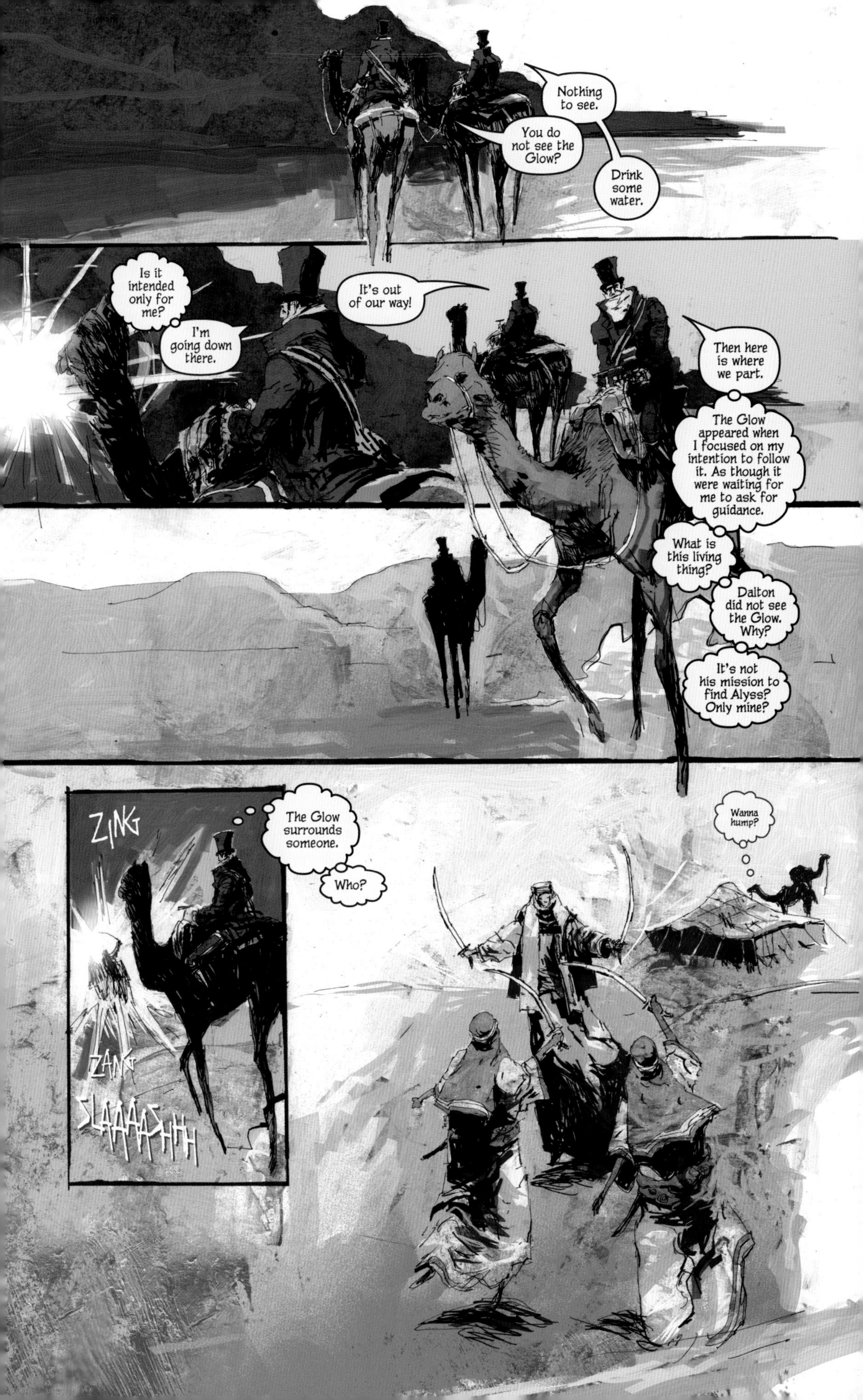
Nothing to see.
You do not see the Glow?
Drink some water.
Is it intended only for me?
I'm going down there.
It's out of our way!
Then here is where we part.
The Glow appeared when I focused on my intention to follow it. As though it were waiting for me to ask for guidance.
What is this living thing?
Dalton did not see the Glow. Why?
It's not his mission to find Alyss? Only mine?
ZING
ZANG
SLAAAASHHH
The Glow surrounds someone.
Who?
Wanna hump?

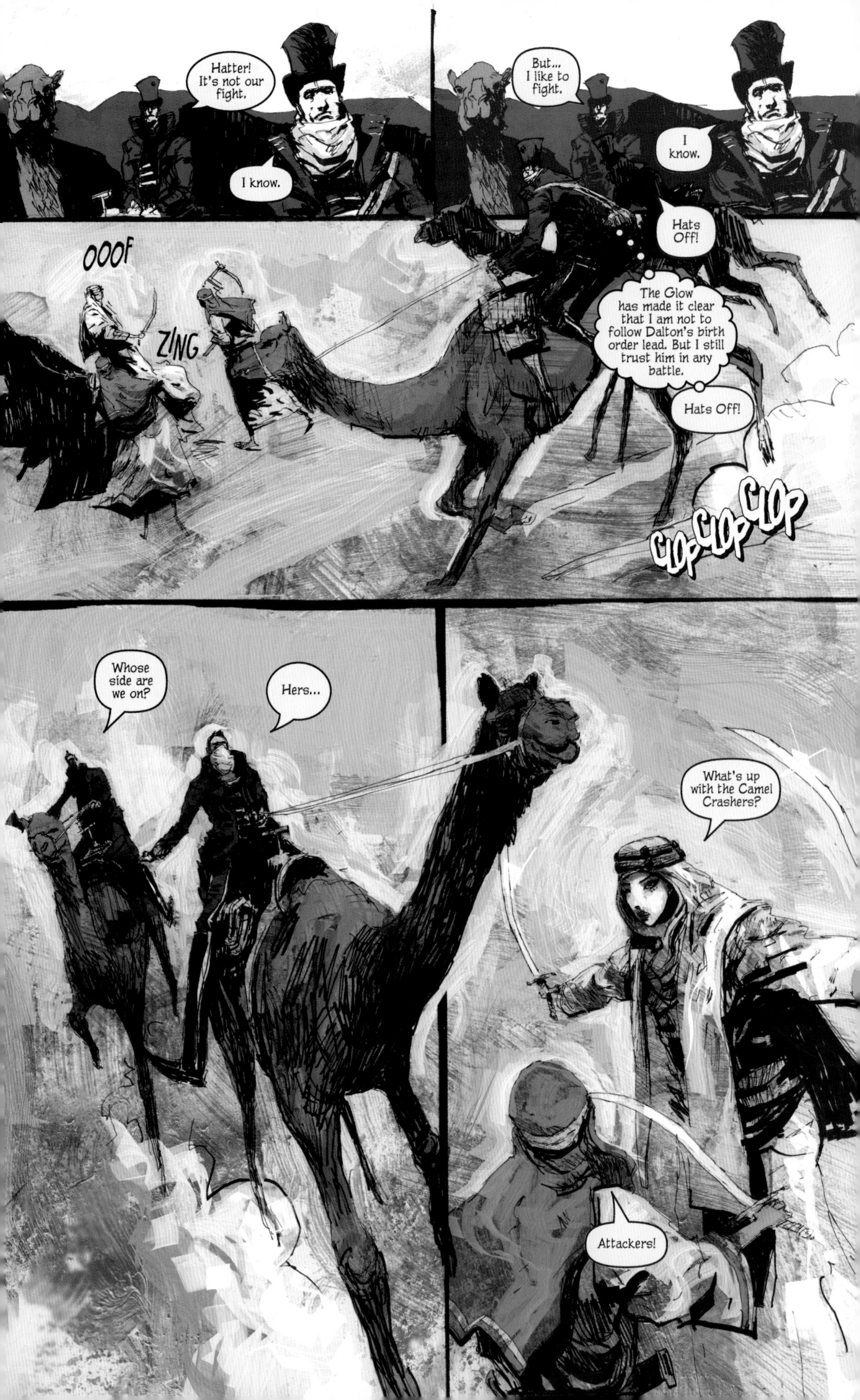
Hatter! It's not our fight.
I know.
But... I like to fight.
I know.
OOOF
ZING
Hats Off!
The Glow has made it clear that I am not to follow Dalton's birth order lead. But I still trust him in any battle.
Hats Off!
CLOP CLOP CLOP
Whose side are we on?
Hers...
What's up with the Camel Crashers?
Attackers!

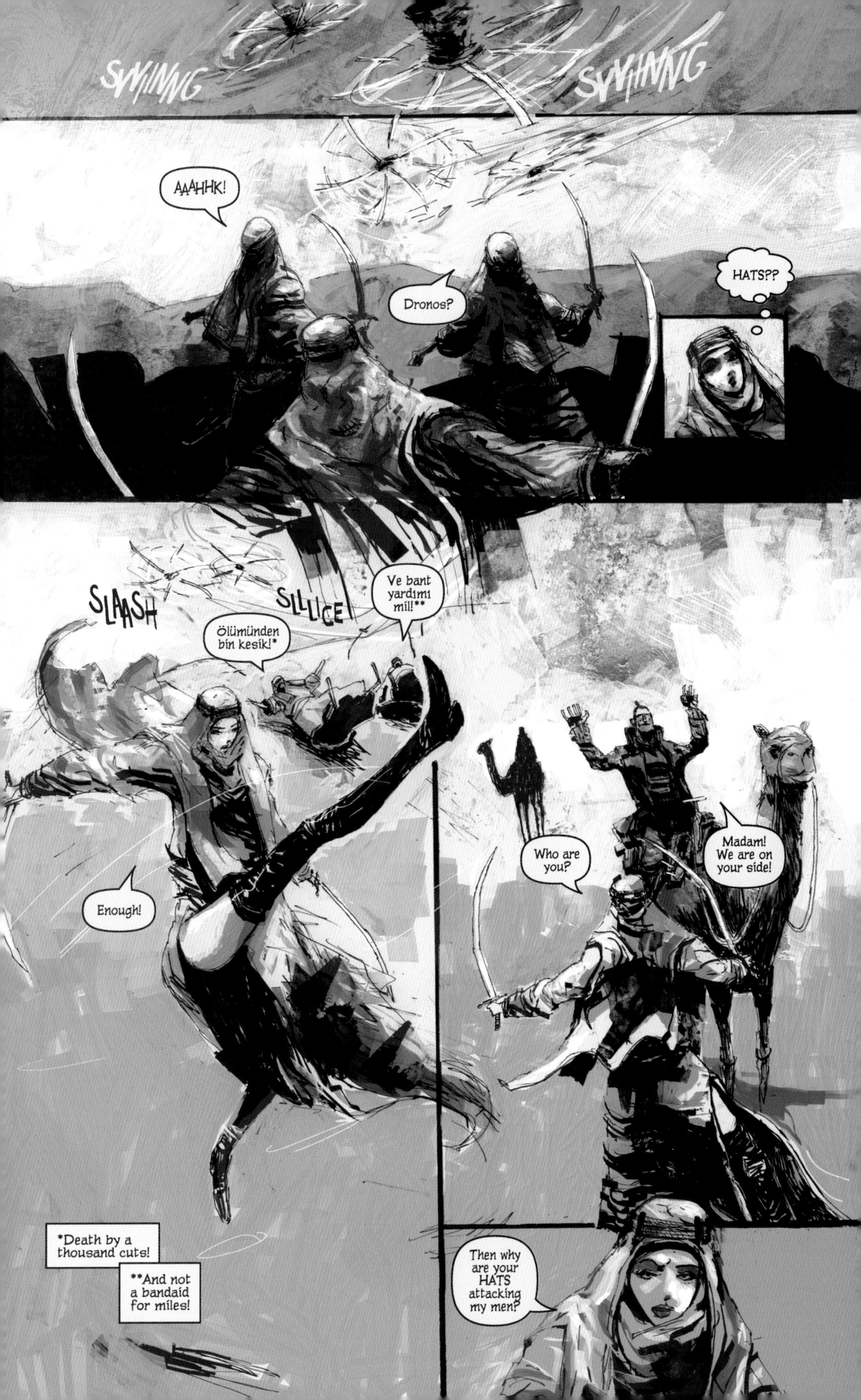
SWIIINNG
SWIIINNG
AAAHHK!
Dronos?
HATS??
SLAASH
SLLLICE
Ölümünden bin kesik!*
Ve bant yardımı mil!**
Enough!
Who are you?
Madam! We are on your side!
*Death by a thousand cuts!
**And not a bandaid for miles!
Then why are your HATS attacking my men?

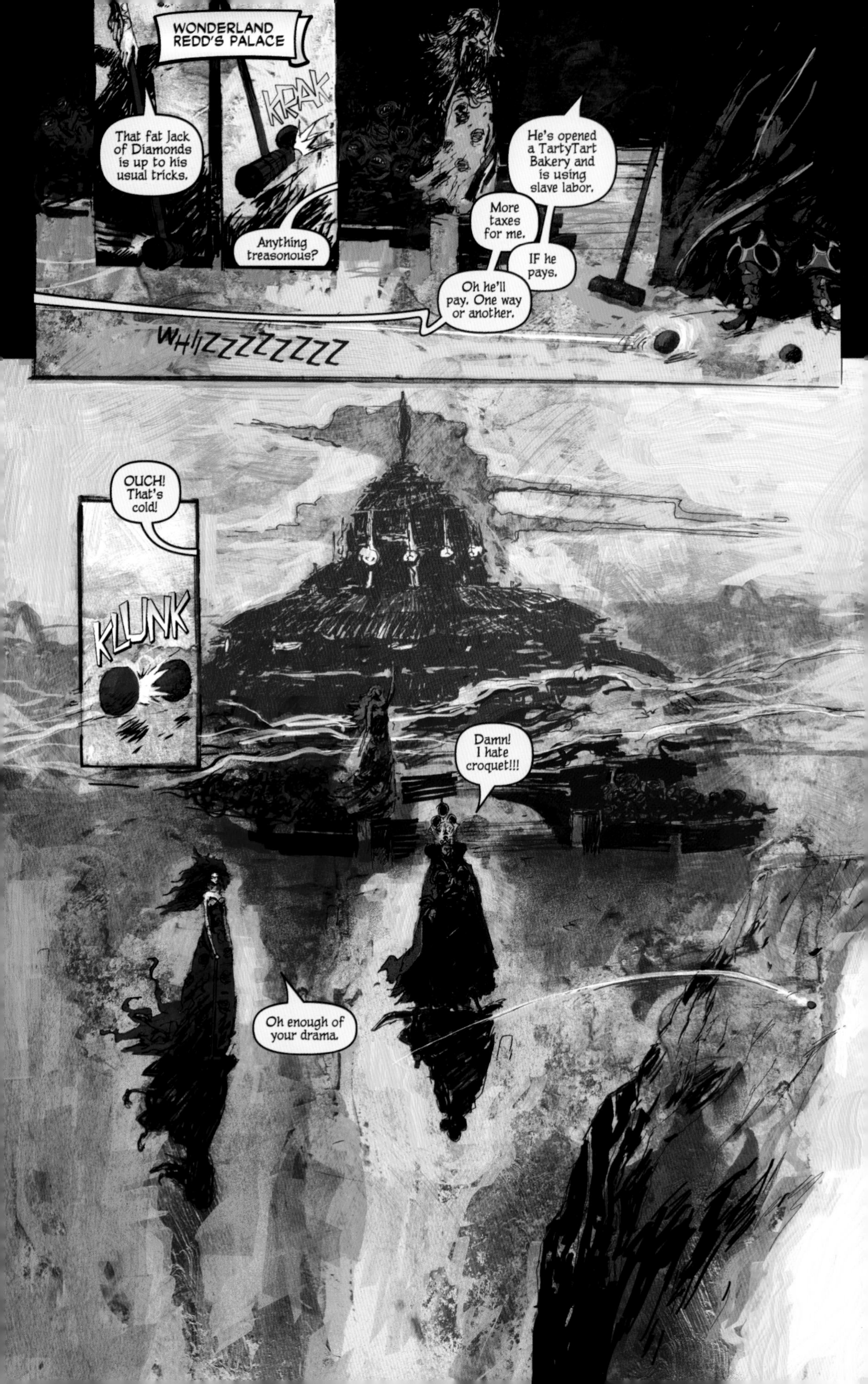
WONDERLAND REDD'S PALACE
That fat Jack of Diamonds is up to his usual tricks.
KRAK
Anything treasonous?
He's opened a TartyTart Bakery and is using slave labor.
More taxes for me.
IF he pays.
Oh he'll pay. One way or another.
WHIZZZZZZZZZ
OUCH! That's cold!
KLUNK
Damn! I hate croquet!!!
Oh enough of your drama.

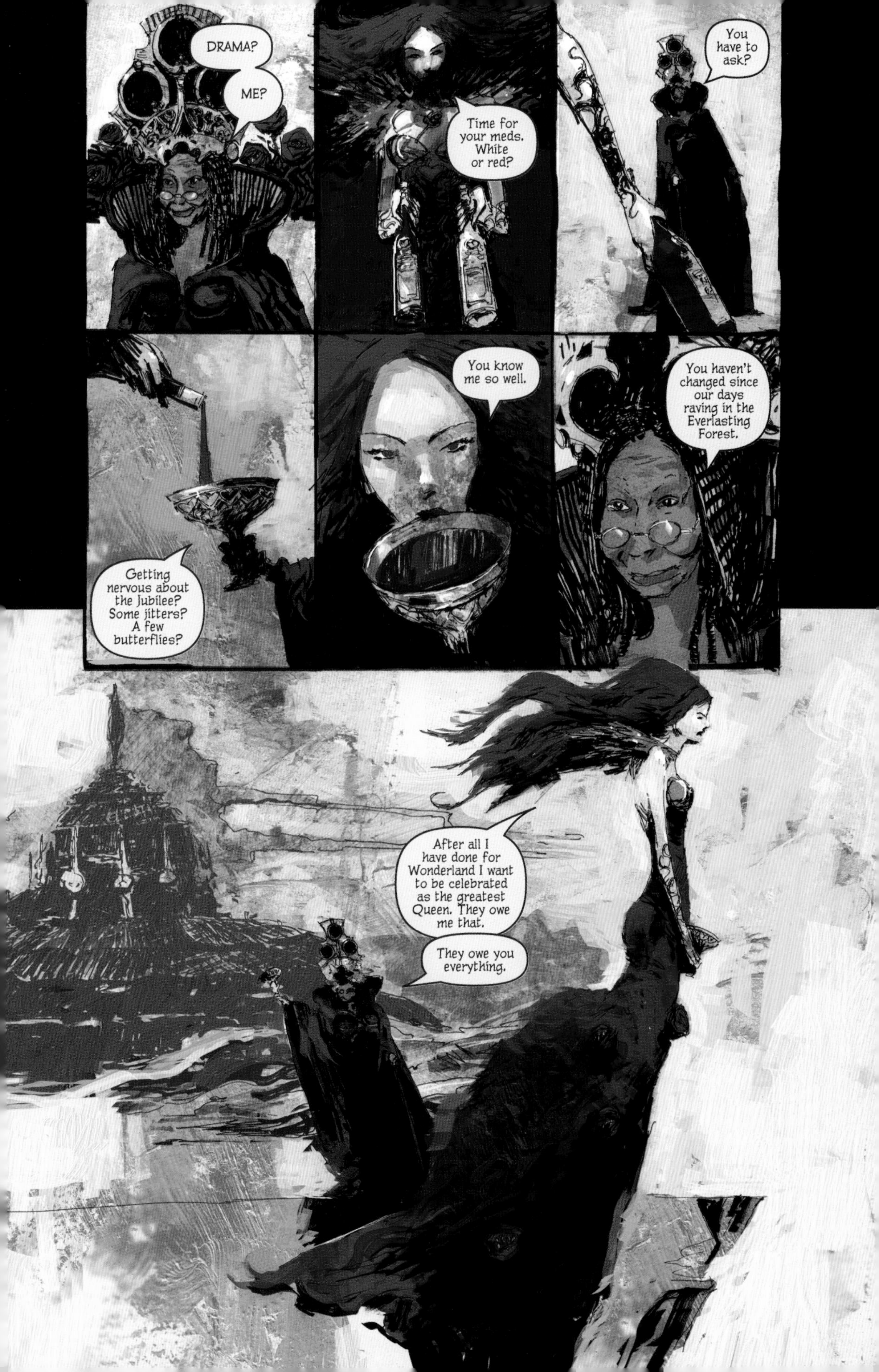
DRAMA?
ME?
Time for your meds. White or red?
You have to ask?
Getting nervous about the Jubilee? Some jitters? A few butterflies?
You know me so well.
You haven't changed since our days raving in the Everlasting Forest.
After all I have done for Wonderland I want to be celebrated as the greatest Queen. They owe me that.
They owe you everything.

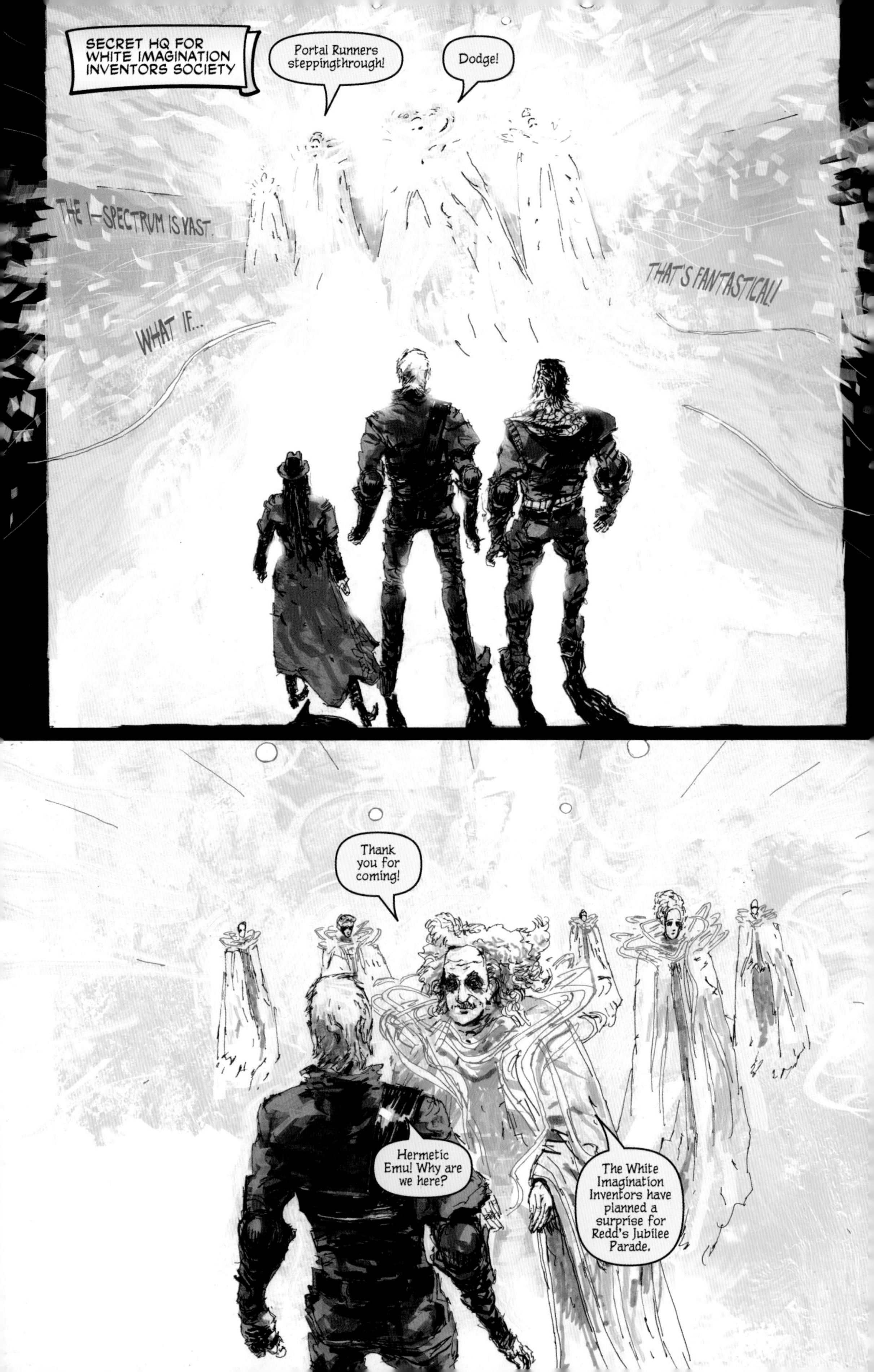
SECRET HQ FOR WHITE IMAGINATION INVENTORS SOCIETY
Portal Runners steppingthrough!
Dodge!
THE I-SPECTRUM IS VAST.
THAT'S FANTASTICAL!
WHAT IF...
Thank you for coming!
Hermetic Emu! Why are we here?
The White Imagination Inventors have planned a surprise for Redd's Jubilee Parade.

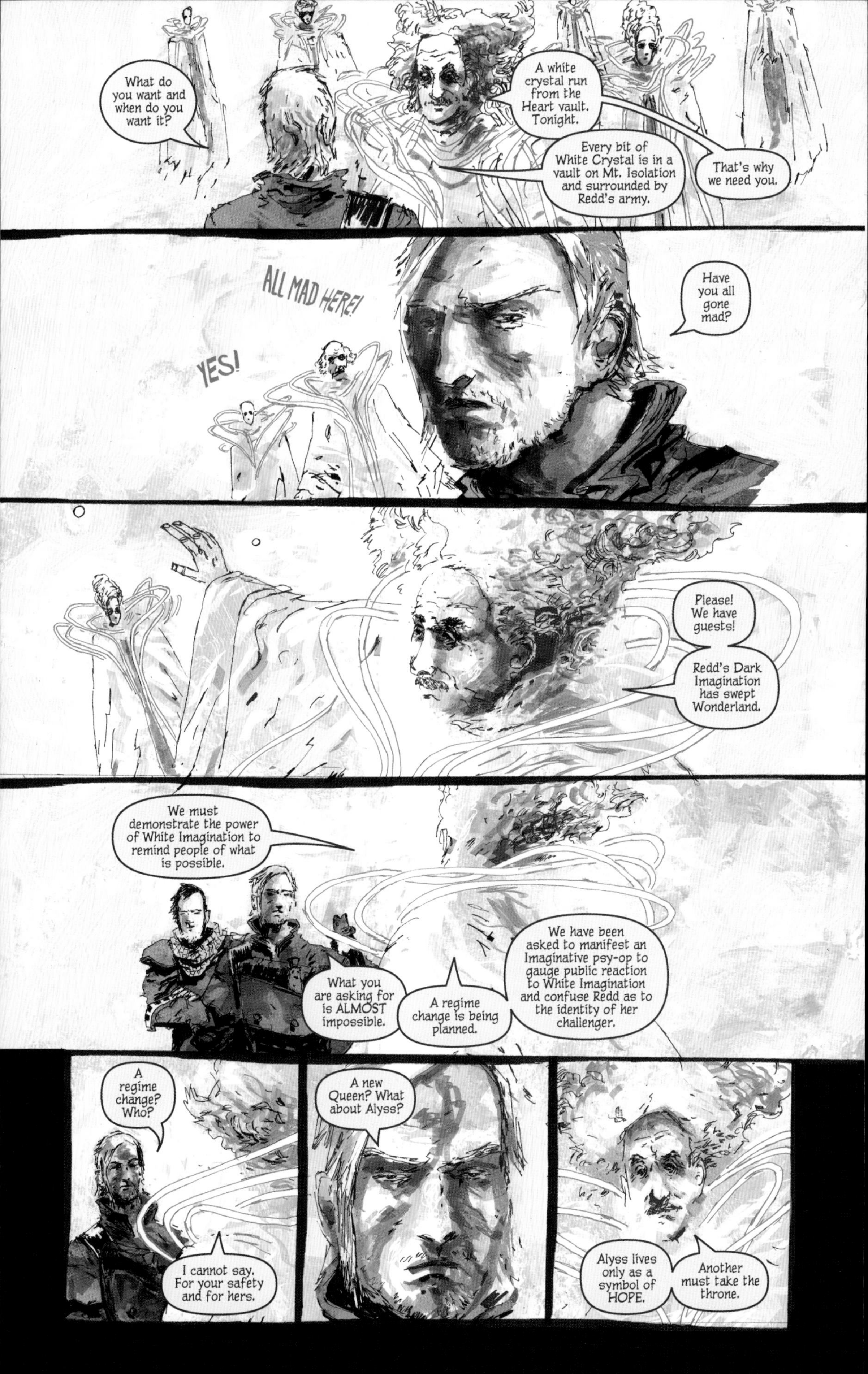
What do you want and when do you want it?
A white crystal run from the Heart vault. Tonight.
Every bit of White Crystal is in a vault on Mt. Isolation and surrounded by Redd's army.
That's why we need you.
Have you all gone mad?
ALL MAD HERE!
YES!
Please! We have guests!
Redd's Dark Imagination has swept Wonderland.
We must demonstrate the power of White Imagination to remind people of what is possible.
What you are asking for is ALMOST impossible.
A regime change is being planned.
We have been asked to manifest an Imaginative psy-op to gauge public reaction to White Imagination and confuse Redd as to the identity of her challenger.
A regime change? Who?
I cannot say. For your safety and for hers.
A new Queen? What about Alyss?
Alyss lives only as a symbol of HOPE.
Another must take the throne.

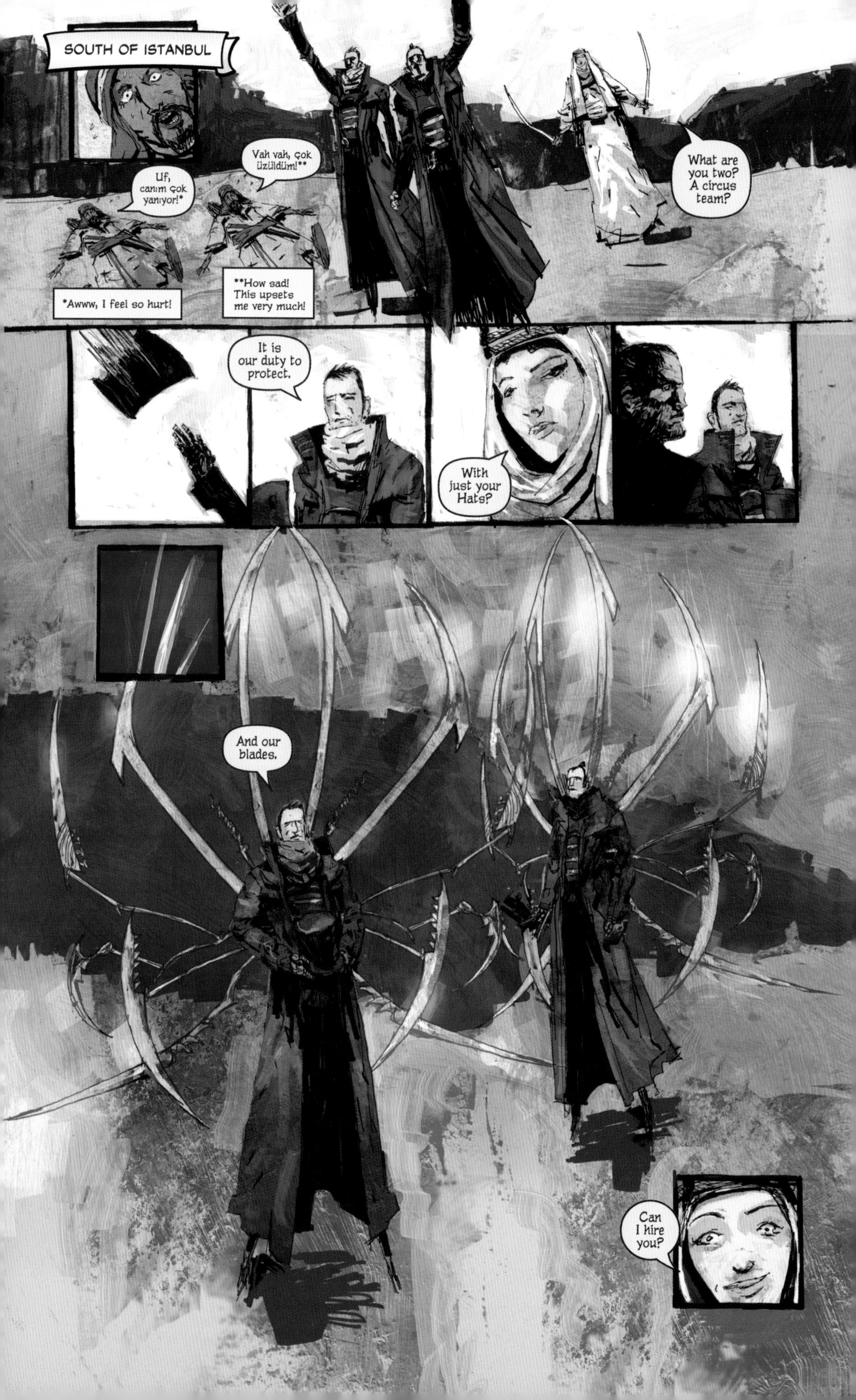
SOUTH OF ISTANBUL
Uf, canım çok yanıyor!*
Vah vah, çok üzüldüm!**
What are you two? A circus team?
*Awww, I feel so hurt!
**How sad! This upsets me very much!
It is our duty to protect.
With just your Hats?
And our blades.
Can I hire you?

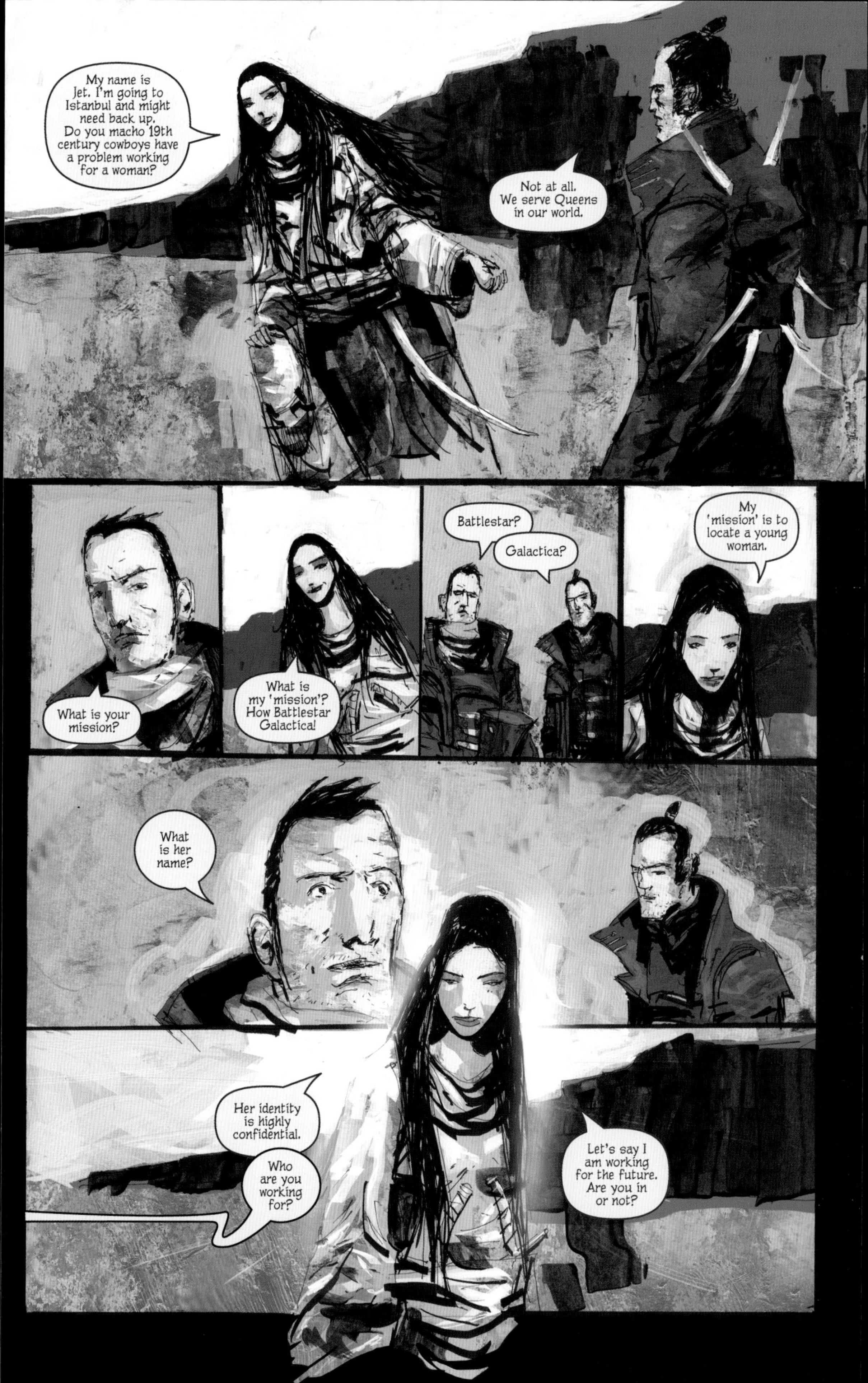
My name is Jet. I'm going to Istanbul and might need back up. Do you macho 19th century cowboys have a problem working for a woman?
Not at all. We serve Queens in our world.
What is your mission?
What is my 'mission'? How Battlestar Galactica!
Battlestar?
Galactica?
My 'mission' is to locate a young woman.
What is her name?
Her identity is highly confidential.
Who are you working for?
Let's say I am working for the future. Are you in or not?

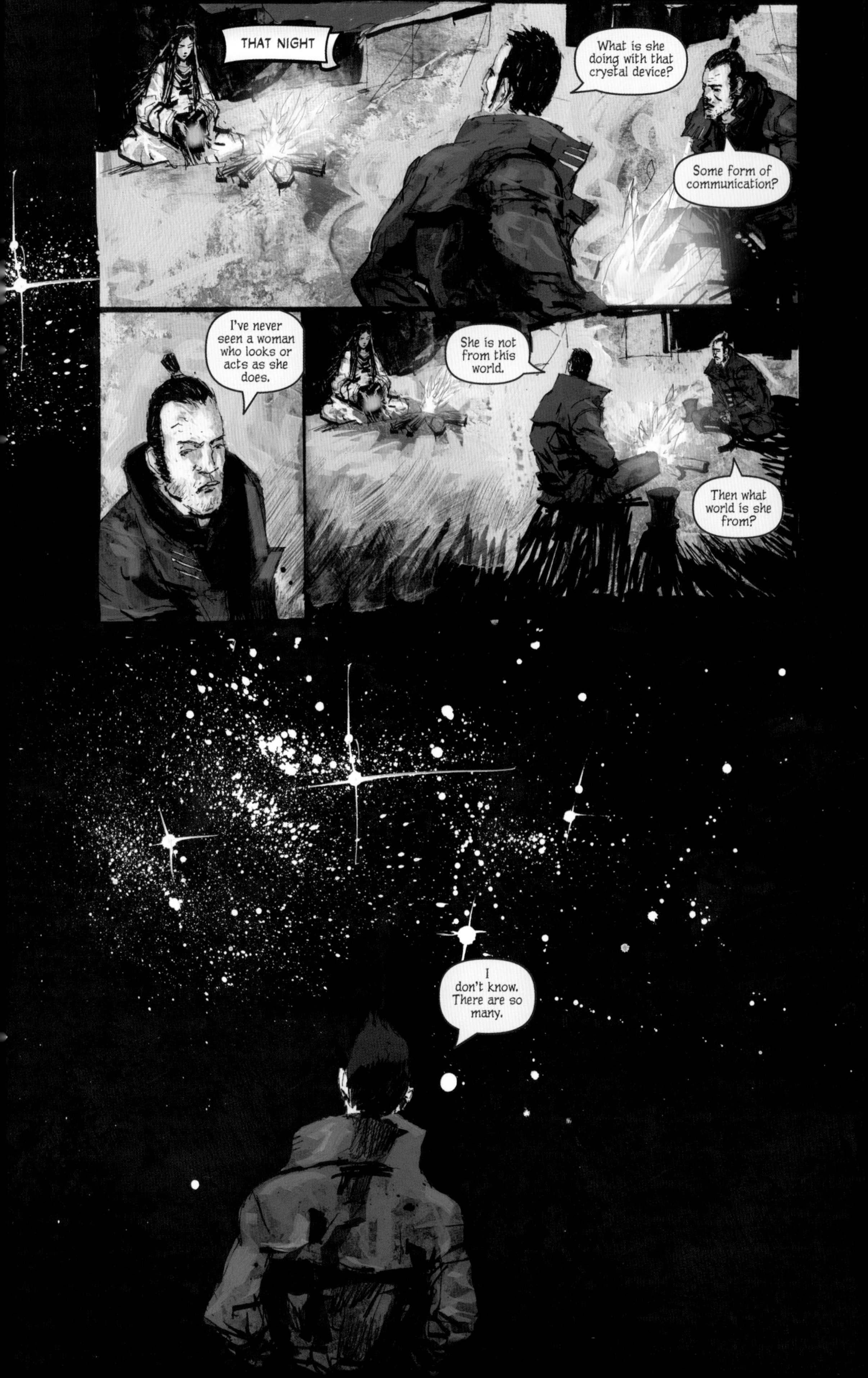
THAT NIGHT
What is she doing with that crystal device?
Some form of communication?
I've never seen a woman who looks or acts as she does.
She is not from this world.
Then what world is she from?
I don't know. There are so many.

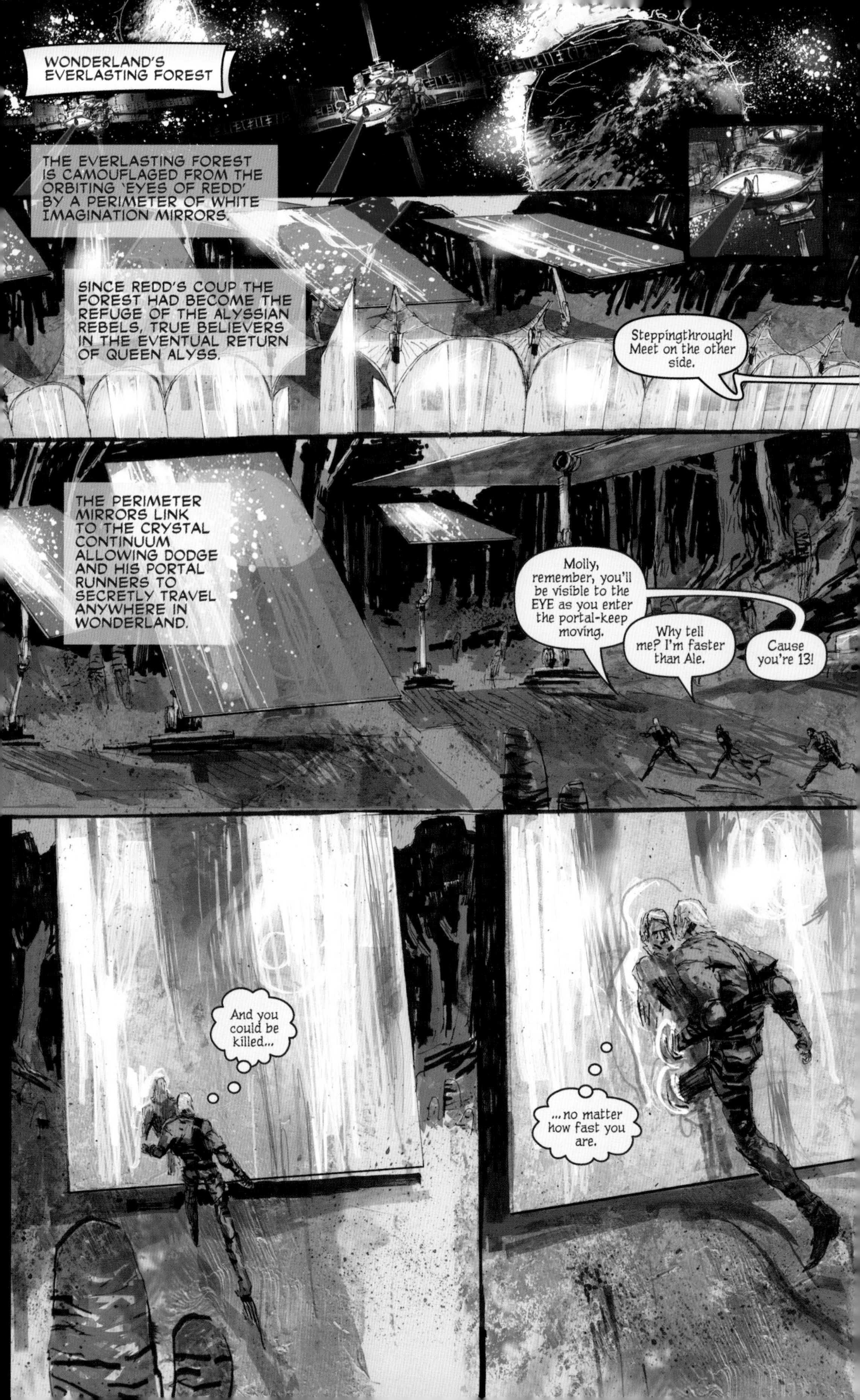
WONDERLAND'S EVERLASTING FOREST
THE EVERLASTING FOREST IS CAMOUFLAGED FROM THE ORBITING 'EYES OF REDD' BY A PERIMETER OF WHITE IMAGINATION MIRRORS.
SINCE REDD'S COUP THE FOREST HAD BECOME THE REFUGE OF THE ALYSSIAN REBELS, TRUE BELIEVERS IN THE EVENTUAL RETURN OF QUEEN ALYSS.
Steppingthrough! Meet on the other side.
THE PERIMETER MIRRORS LINK TO THE CRYSTAL CONTINUUM ALLOWING DODGE AND HIS PORTAL RUNNERS TO SECRETLY TRAVEL ANYWHERE IN WONDERLAND.
Molly, remember, you'll be visible to the EYE as you enter the portal-keep moving.
Why tell me? I'm faster than Ale.
Cause you're 13!
And you could be killed...
...no matter how fast you are.

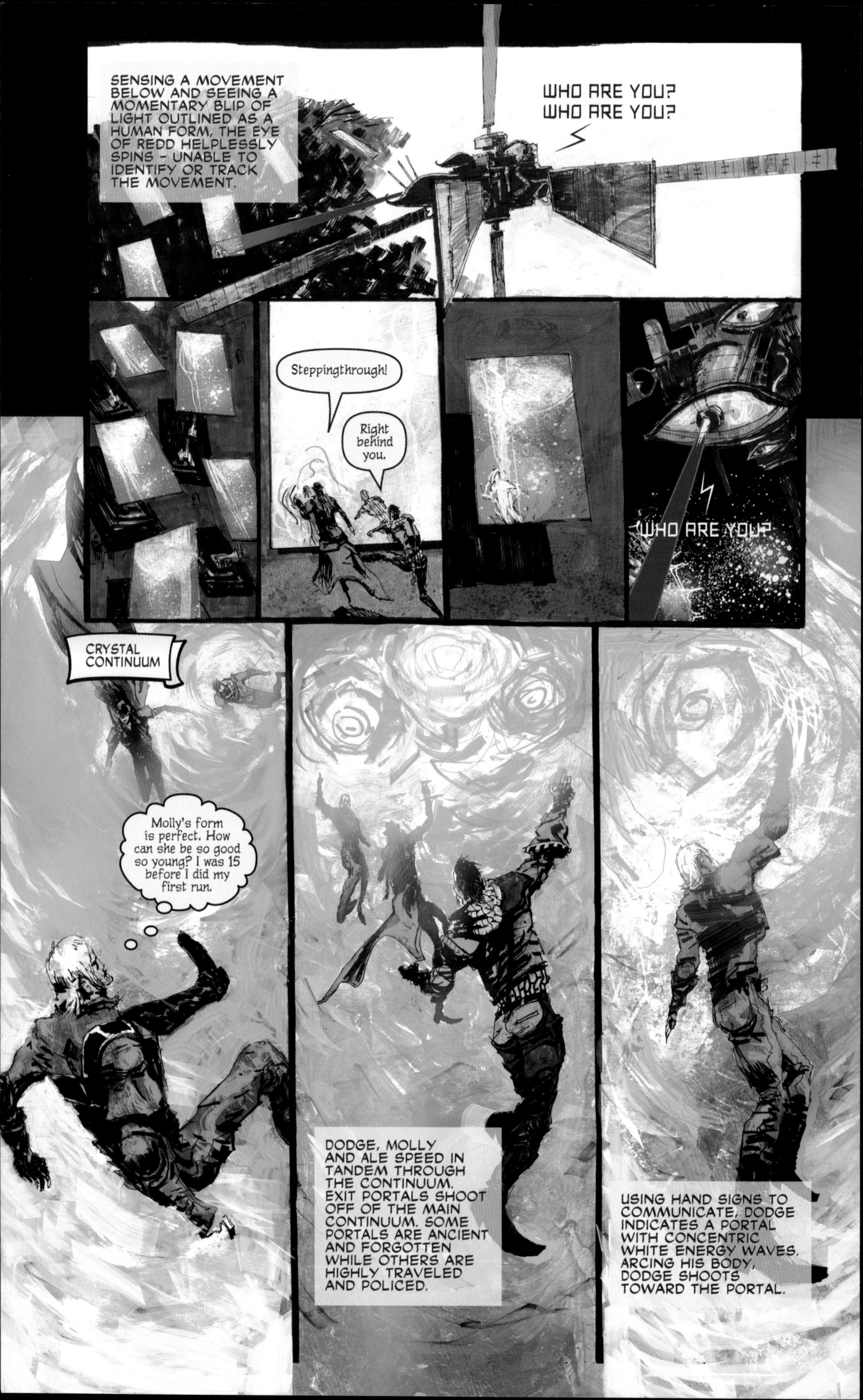
SENSING A MOVEMENT BELOW AND SEEING A MOMENTARY BLIP OF LIGHT OUTLINED AS A HUMAN FORM, THE EYE OF REDD HELPLESSLY SPINS - UNABLE TO IDENTIFY OR TRACK THE MOVEMENT.
WHO ARE YOU? WHO ARE YOU?
Steppingthrough!
Right behind you.
WHO ARE YOU?
CRYSTAL CONTINUUM
Molly's form is perfect. How can she be so good so young? I was 15 before I did my first run.
DODGE, MOLLY AND ALE SPEED IN TANDEM THROUGH THE CONTINUUM. EXIT PORTALS SHOOT OFF OF THE MAIN CONTINUUM. SOME PORTALS ARE ANCIENT AND FORGOTTEN WHILE OTHERS ARE HIGHLY TRAVELED AND POLICED.
USING HAND SIGNS TO COMMUNICATE, DODGE INDICATES A PORTAL WITH CONCENTRIC WHITE ENERGY WAVES. ARCING HIS BODY, DODGE SHOOTS TOWARD THE PORTAL.

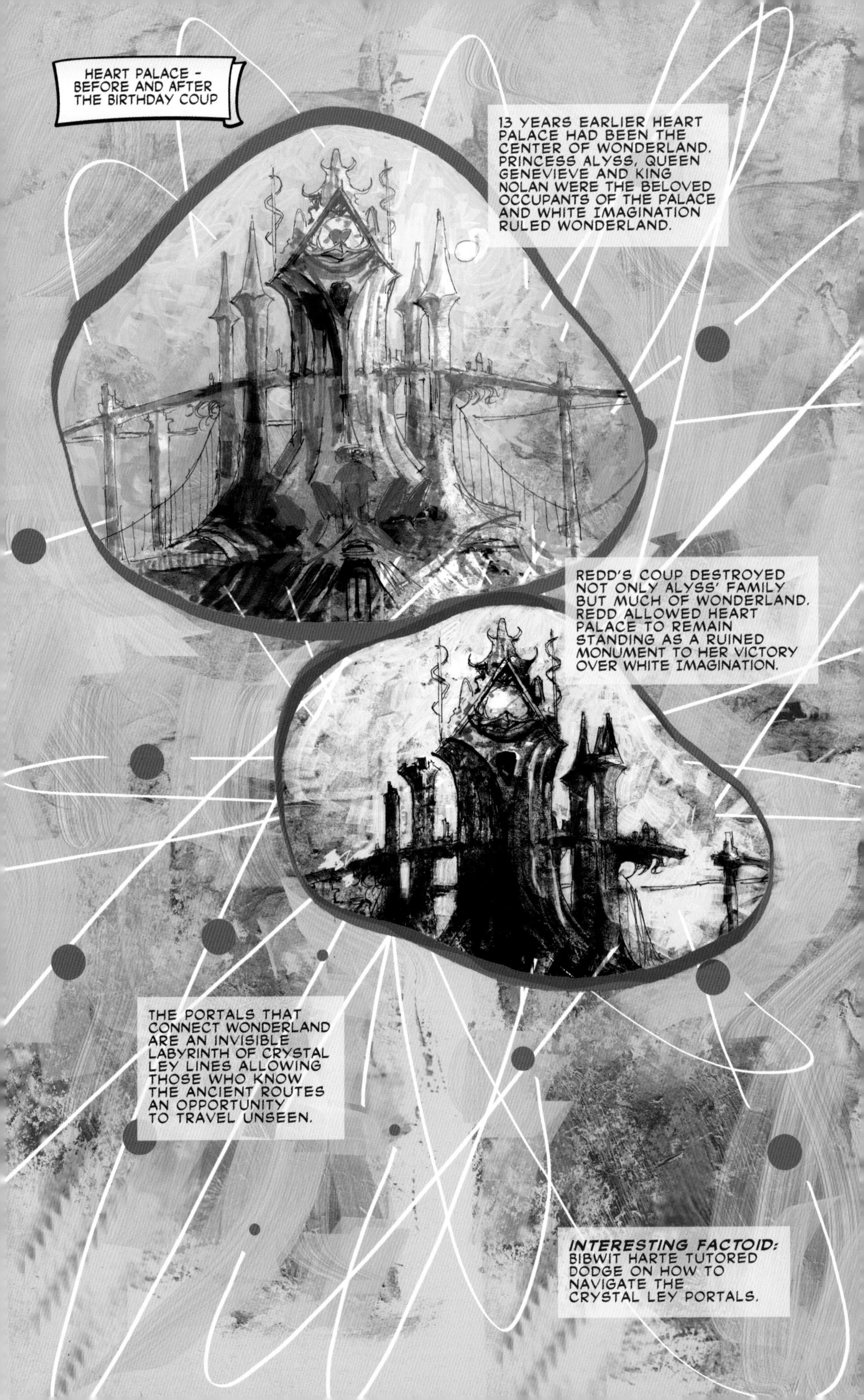
HEART PALACE - BEFORE AND AFTER THE BIRTHDAY COUP
13 YEARS EARLIER HEART PALACE HAD BEEN THE CENTER OF WONDERLAND. PRINCESS ALYSS, QUEEN GENEVIEVE AND KING NOLAN WERE THE BELOVED OCCUPANTS OF THE PALACE AND WHITE IMAGINATION RULED WONDERLAND.
REDD'S COUP DESTROYED NOT ONLY ALYSS' FAMILY BUT MUCH OF WONDERLAND. REDD ALLOWED HEART PALACE TO REMAIN STANDING AS A RUINED MONUMENT TO HER VICTORY OVER WHITE IMAGINATION.
THE PORTALS THAT CONNECT WONDERLAND ARE AN INVISIBLE LABYRINTH OF CRYSTAL LEY LINES ALLOWING THOSE WHO KNOW THE ANCIENT ROUTES AN OPPORTUNITY TO TRAVEL UNSEEN.
INTERESTING FACTOID: BIBWIT HARTE TUTORED DODGE ON HOW TO NAVIGATE THE CRYSTAL LEY PORTALS.

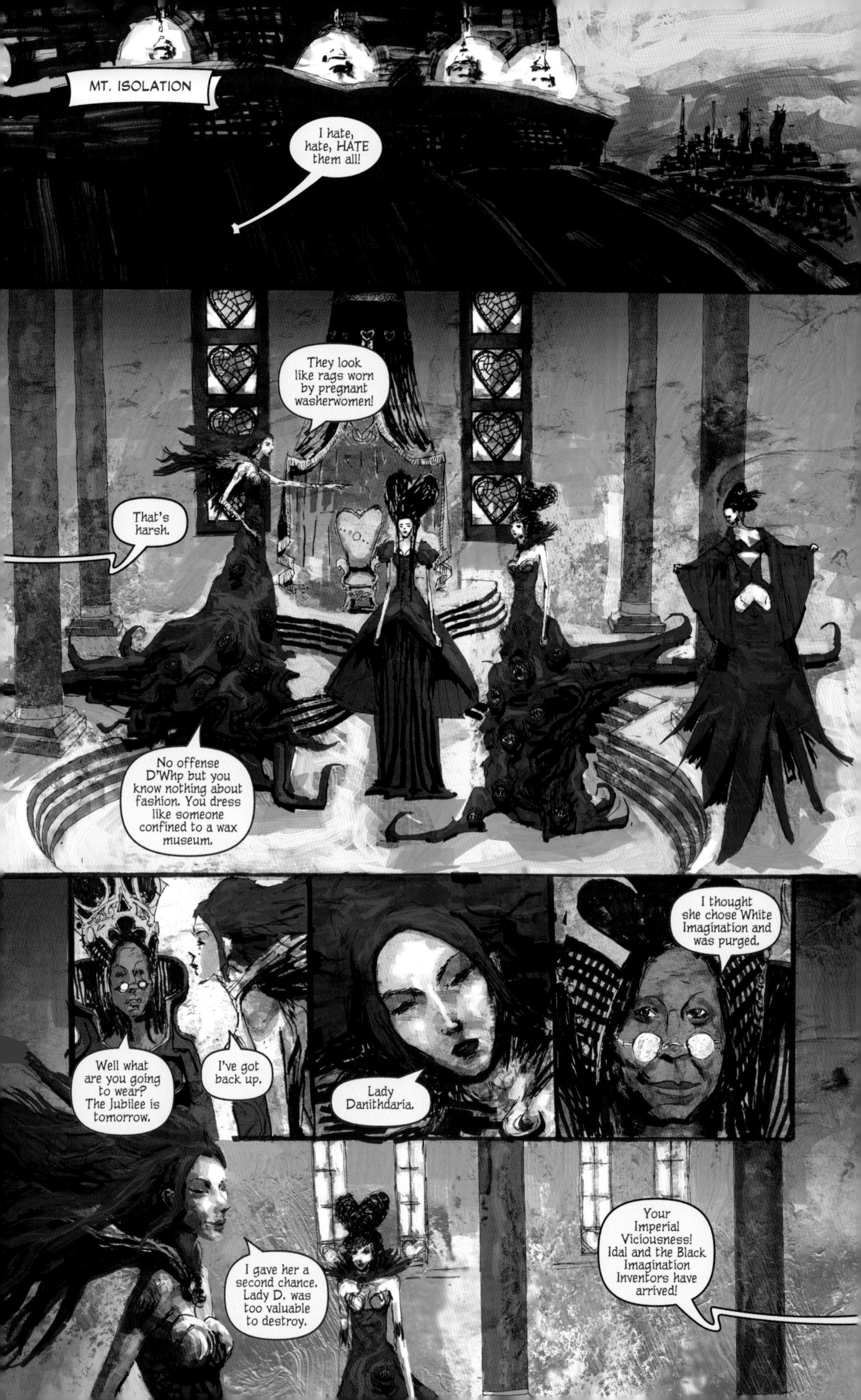
MT. ISOLATION
I hate, hate, HATE them all!
They look like rags worn by pregnant washerwomen!
That's harsh.
No offense D'Whp but you know nothing about fashion. You dress like someone confined to a wax museum.
Well what are you going to wear? The Jubilee is tomorrow.
I've got back up.
Lady Danithdaria.
I thought she chose White Imagination and was purged.
I gave her a second chance. Lady D. was too valuable to destroy.
Your Imperial Viciousness! Idal and the Black Imagination Inventors have arrived!

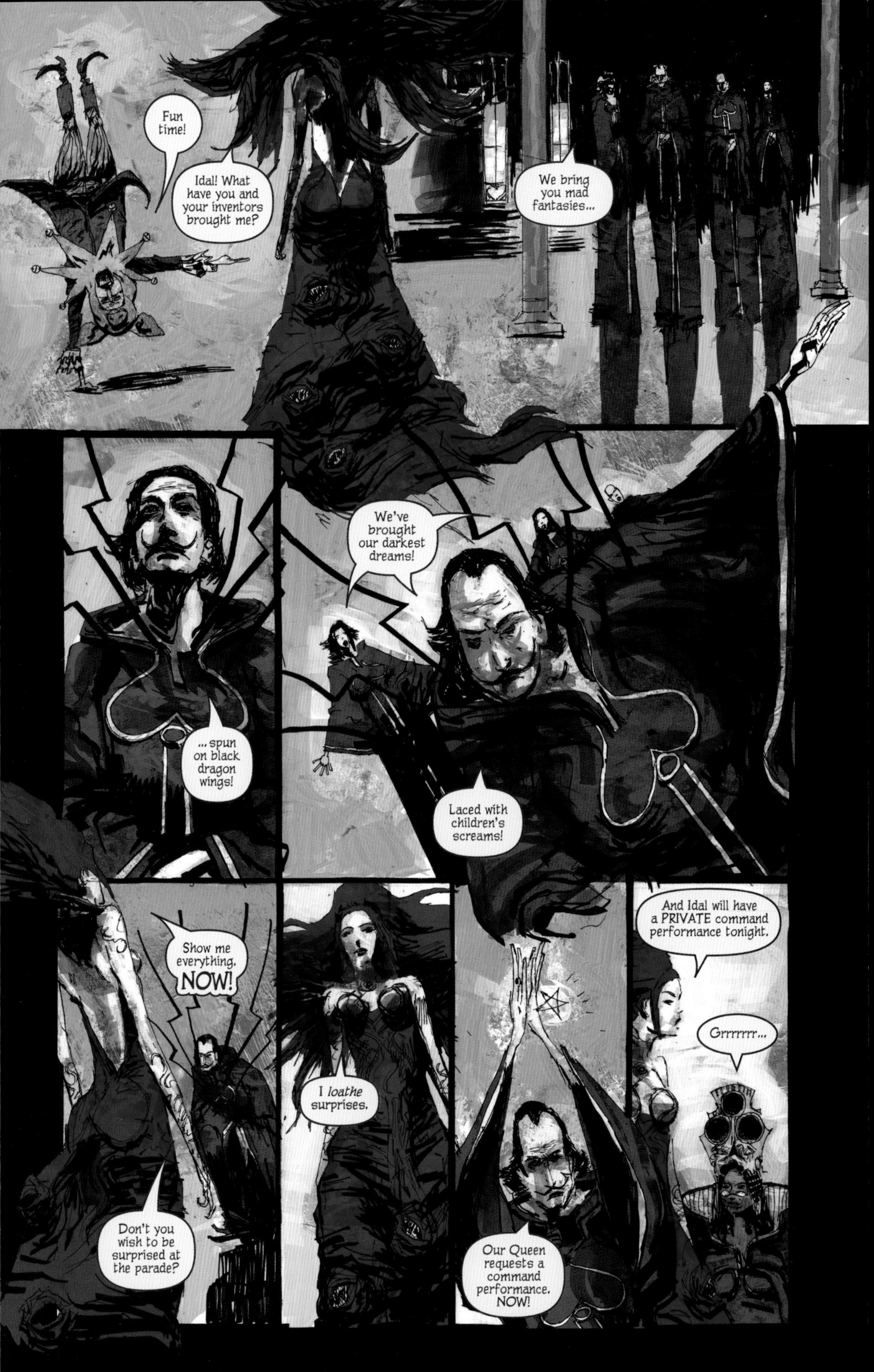
Fun time!
Idal! What have you and your inventors brought me?
We bring you mad fantasies...
...spun on black dragon wings!
We've brought our darkest dreams!
Laced with children's screams!
Show me everything. NOW!
Don't you wish to be surprised at the parade?
I loathe surprises.
Our Queen requests a command performance. NOW!
And Idal will have a PRIVATE command performance tonight.
Grrrrrrr...

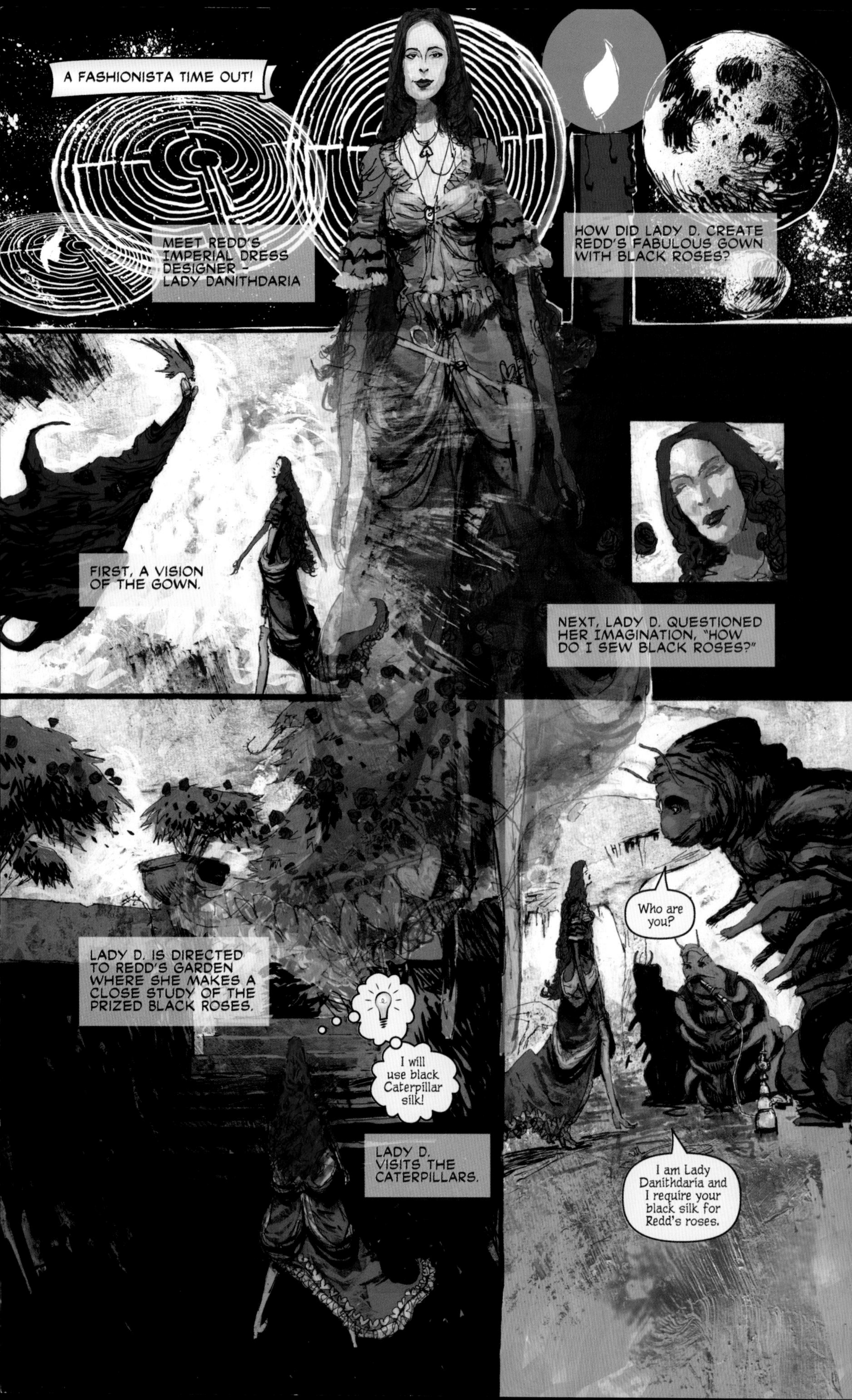
A FASHIONISTA TIME OUT!
MEET REDD'S IMPERIAL DRESS DESIGNER – LADY DANITHDARIA
HOW DID LADY D. CREATE REDD'S FABULOUS GOWN WITH BLACK ROSES?
FIRST, A VISION OF THE GOWN.
NEXT, LADY D. QUESTIONED HER IMAGINATION, "HOW DO I SEW BLACK ROSES?"
LADY D. IS DIRECTED TO REDD'S GARDEN WHERE SHE MAKES A CLOSE STUDY OF THE PRIZED BLACK ROSES.
I will use black Caterpillar silk!
LADY D. VISITS THE CATERPILLARS.
Who are you?
I am Lady Danithdaria and I require your black silk for Redd's roses.

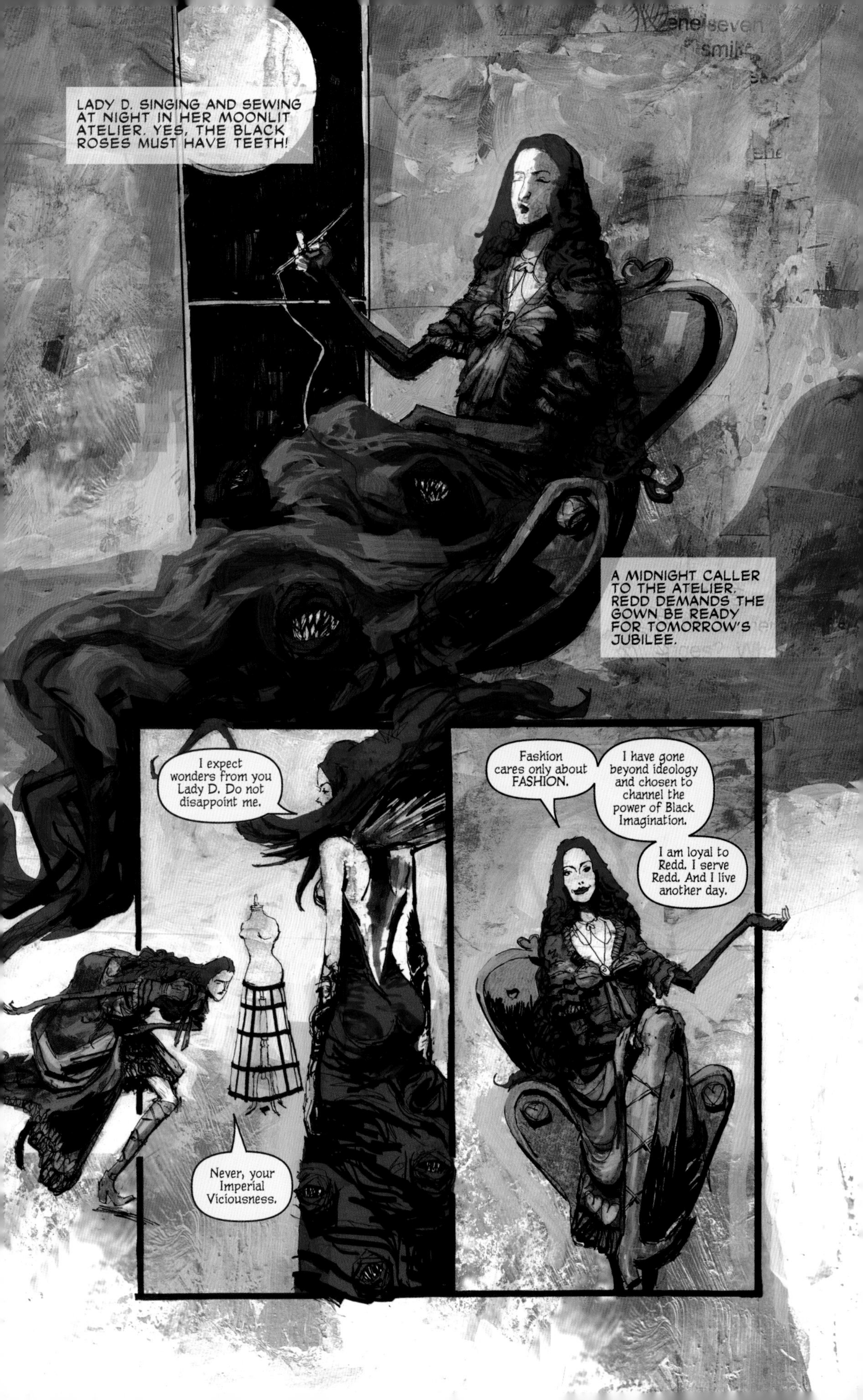
LADY D. SINGING AND SEWING AT NIGHT IN HER MOONLIT ATELIER. YES, THE BLACK ROSES MUST HAVE TEETH!
A MIDNIGHT CALLER TO THE ATELIER. REDD DEMANDS THE GOWN BE READY FOR TOMORROW'S JUBILEE.
I expect wonders from you Lady D. Do not disappoint me.
Never, your Imperial Viciousness.
Fashion cares only about FASHION.
I have gone beyond ideology and chosen to channel the power of Black Imagination.
I am loyal to Redd. I serve Redd. And I live another day.

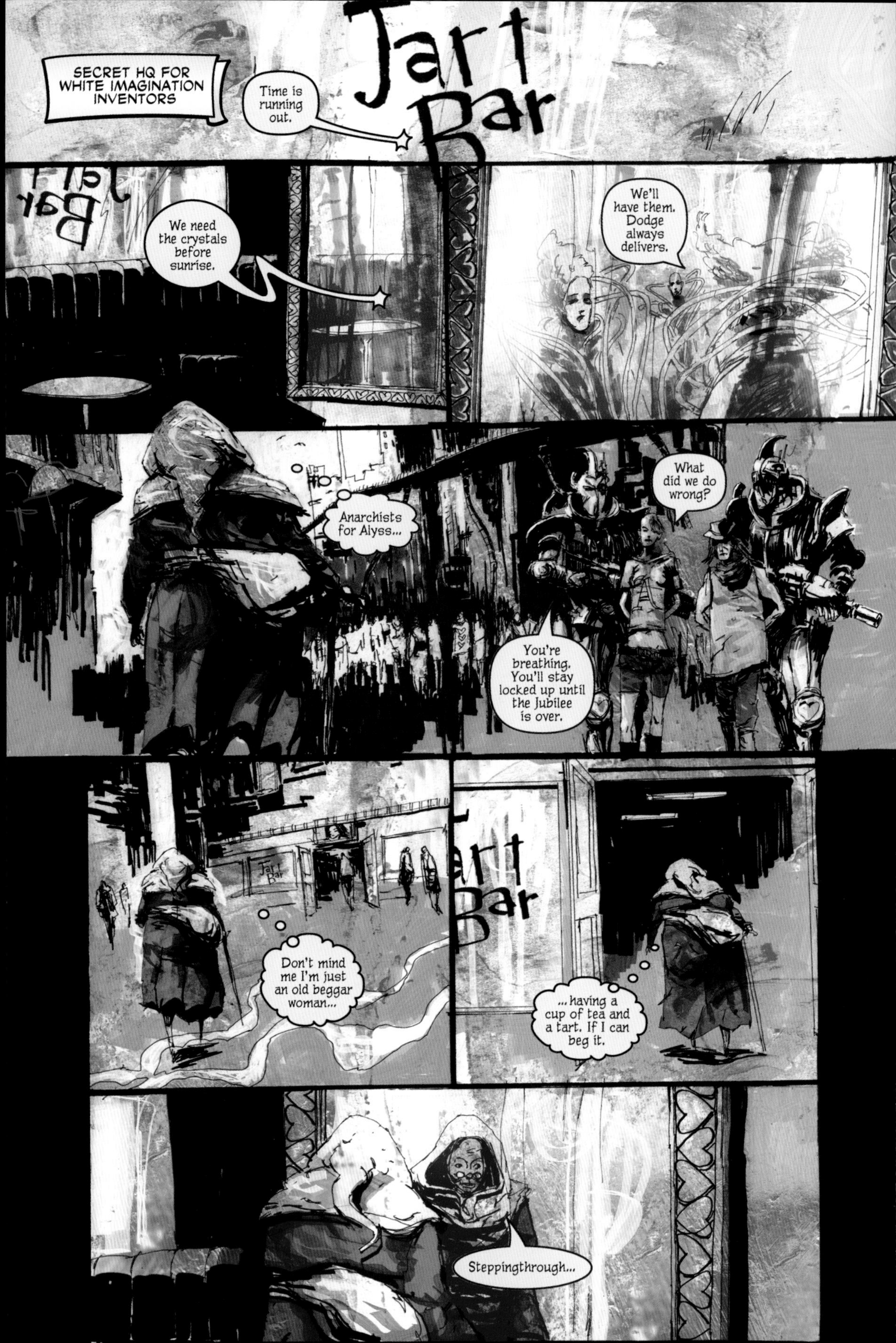
SECRET HQ FOR WHITE IMAGINATION INVENTORS
Jart Bar
Time is running out.
We need the crystals before sunrise.
We'll have them. Dodge always delivers.
Anarchists for Alyss...
What did we do wrong?
You're breathing. You'll stay locked up until the Jubilee is over.
Don't mind me I'm just an old beggar woman...
...having a cup of tea and a tart. If I can beg it.
Steppingthrough...

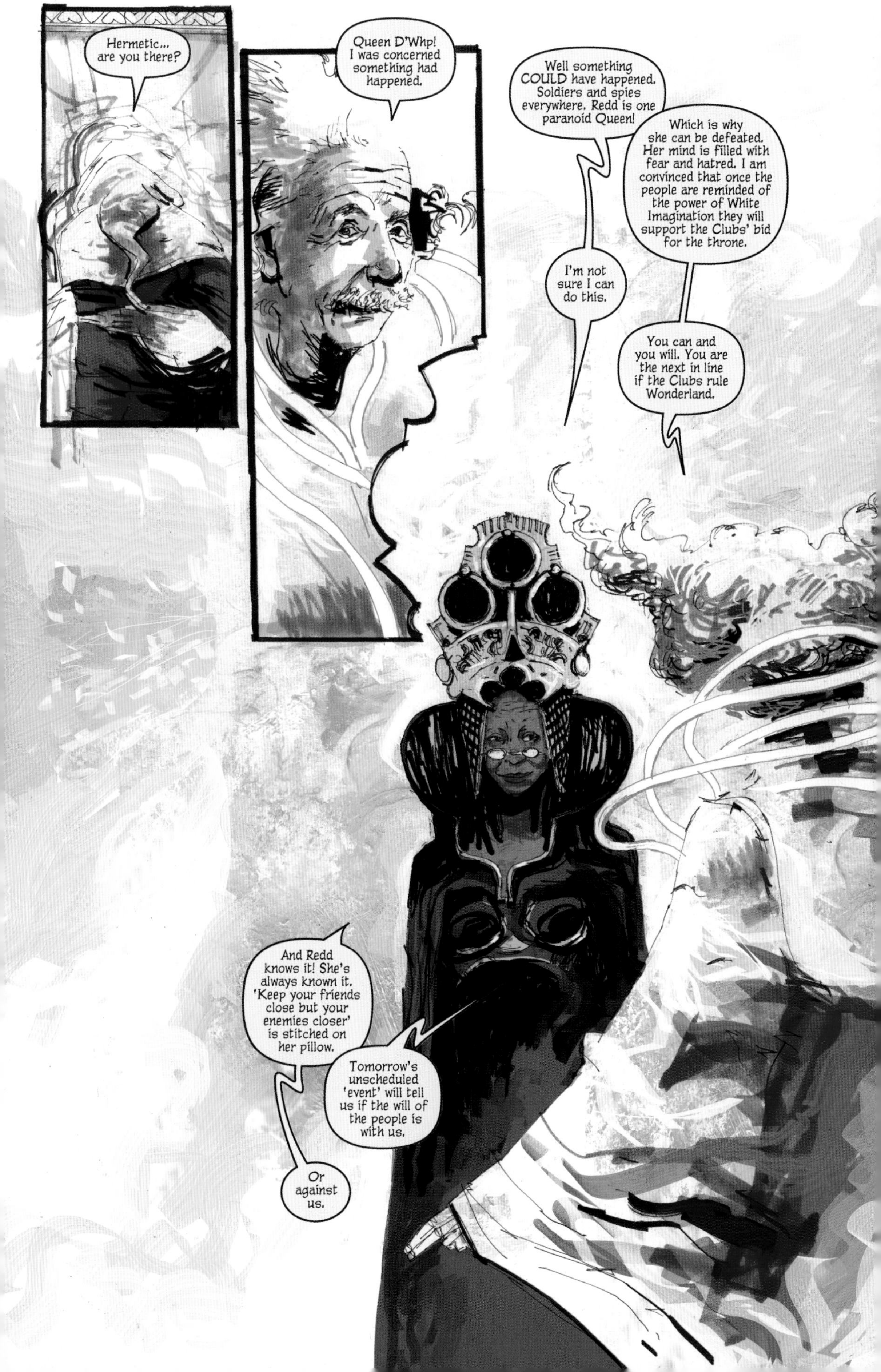
Hermetic... are you there?
Queen D'Whp! I was concerned something had happened.
Well something COULD have happened. Soldiers and spies everywhere. Redd is one paranoid Queen!
Which is why she can be defeated. Her mind is filled with fear and hatred. I am convinced that once the people are reminded of the power of White Imagination they will support the Clubs' bid for the throne.
I'm not sure I can do this.
You can and you will. You are the next in line if the Clubs rule Wonderland.
And Redd knows it! She's always known it. 'Keep your friends close but your enemies closer' is stitched on her pillow.
Tomorrow's unscheduled 'event' will tell us if the will of the people is with us.
Or against us.

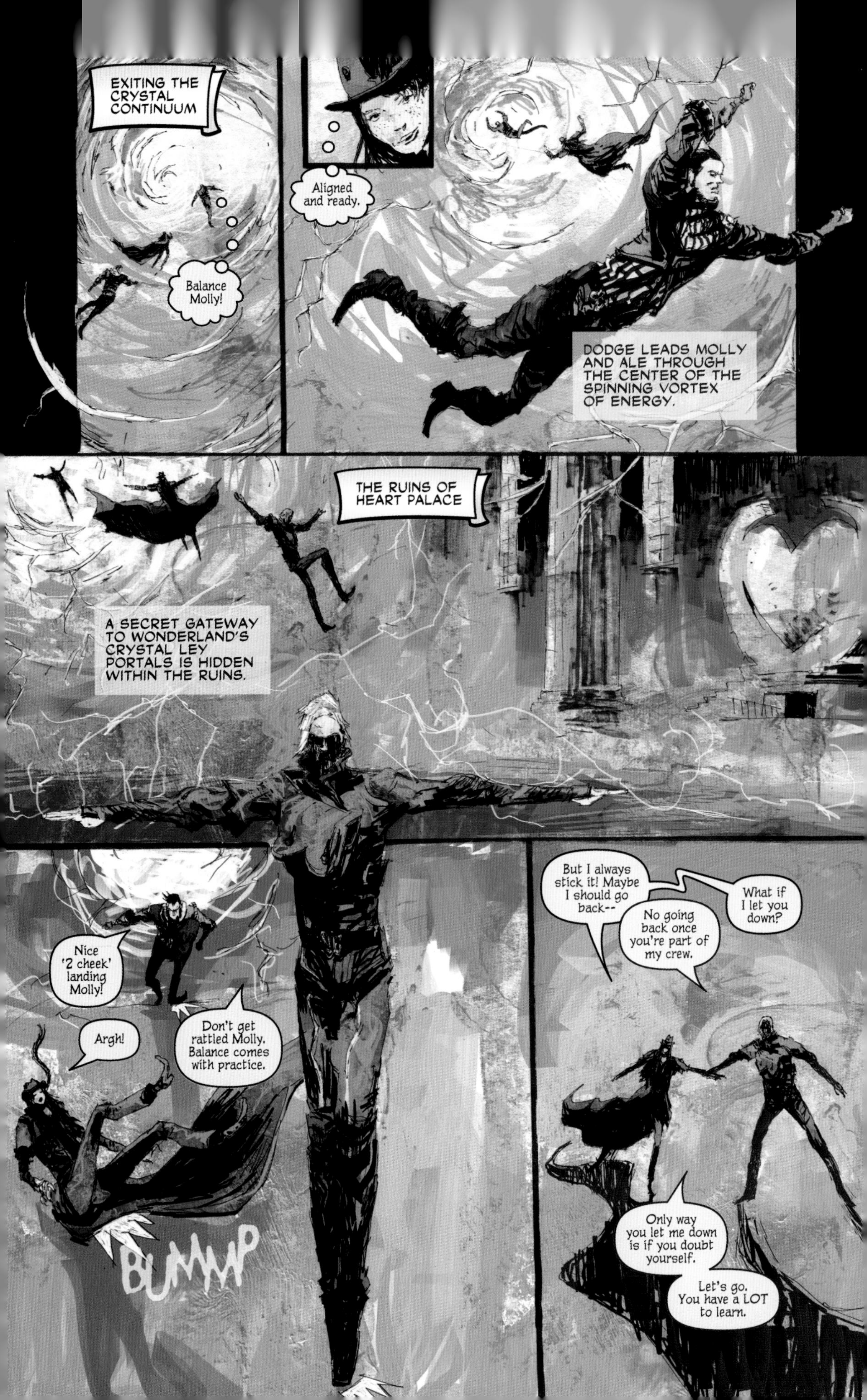
EXITING THE CRYSTAL CONTINUUM
Balance Molly!
Aligned and ready.
DODGE LEADS MOLLY AND ALE THROUGH THE CENTER OF THE SPINNING VORTEX OF ENERGY.
THE RUINS OF HEART PALACE
A SECRET GATEWAY TO WONDERLAND'S CRYSTAL LEY PORTALS IS HIDDEN WITHIN THE RUINS.
Nice '2 cheek' landing Molly!
Argh!
Don't get rattled Molly. Balance comes with practice.
BUMMP
But I always stick it! Maybe I should go back--
No going back once you're part of my crew.
What if I let you down?
Only way you let me down is if you doubt yourself.
Let's go. You have a LOT to learn.

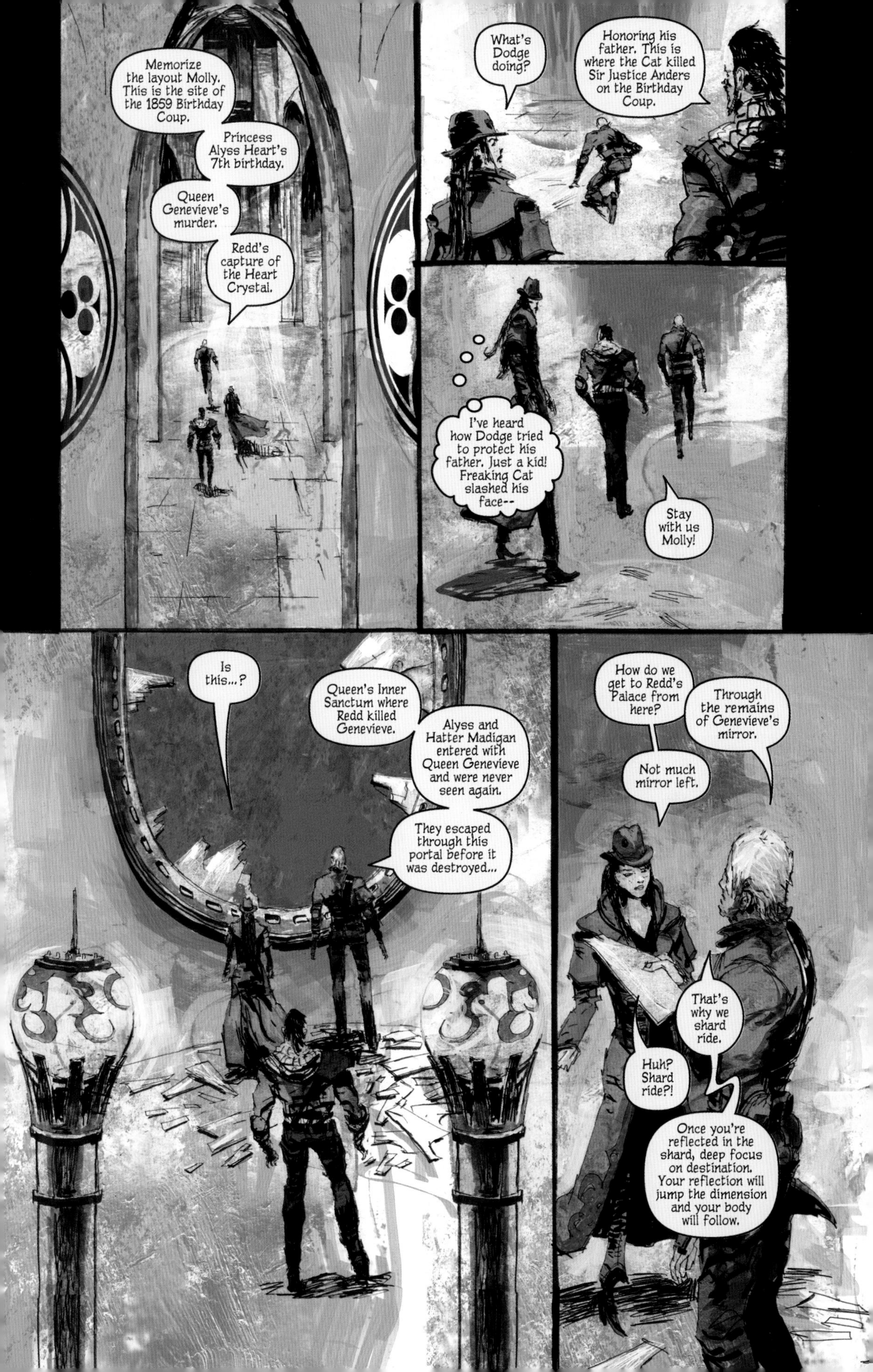
Memorize the layout Molly. This is the site of the 1859 Birthday Coup.
Princess Alyss Heart's 7th birthday.
Queen Genevieve's murder.
Redd's capture of the Heart Crystal.
What's Dodge doing?
Honoring his father. This is where the Cat killed Sir Justice Anders on the Birthday Coup.
I've heard how Dodge tried to protect his father. Just a kid! Freaking Cat slashed his face--
Stay with us Molly!
Is this...?
Queen's Inner Sanctum where Redd killed Genevieve.
Alyss and Hatter Madigan entered with Queen Genevieve and were never seen again.
They escaped through this portal before it was destroyed...
How do we get to Redd's Palace from here?
Through the remains of Genevieve's mirror.
Not much mirror left.
That's why we shard ride.
Huh? Shard ride?!
Once you're reflected in the shard, deep focus on destination. Your reflection will jump the dimension and your body will follow.

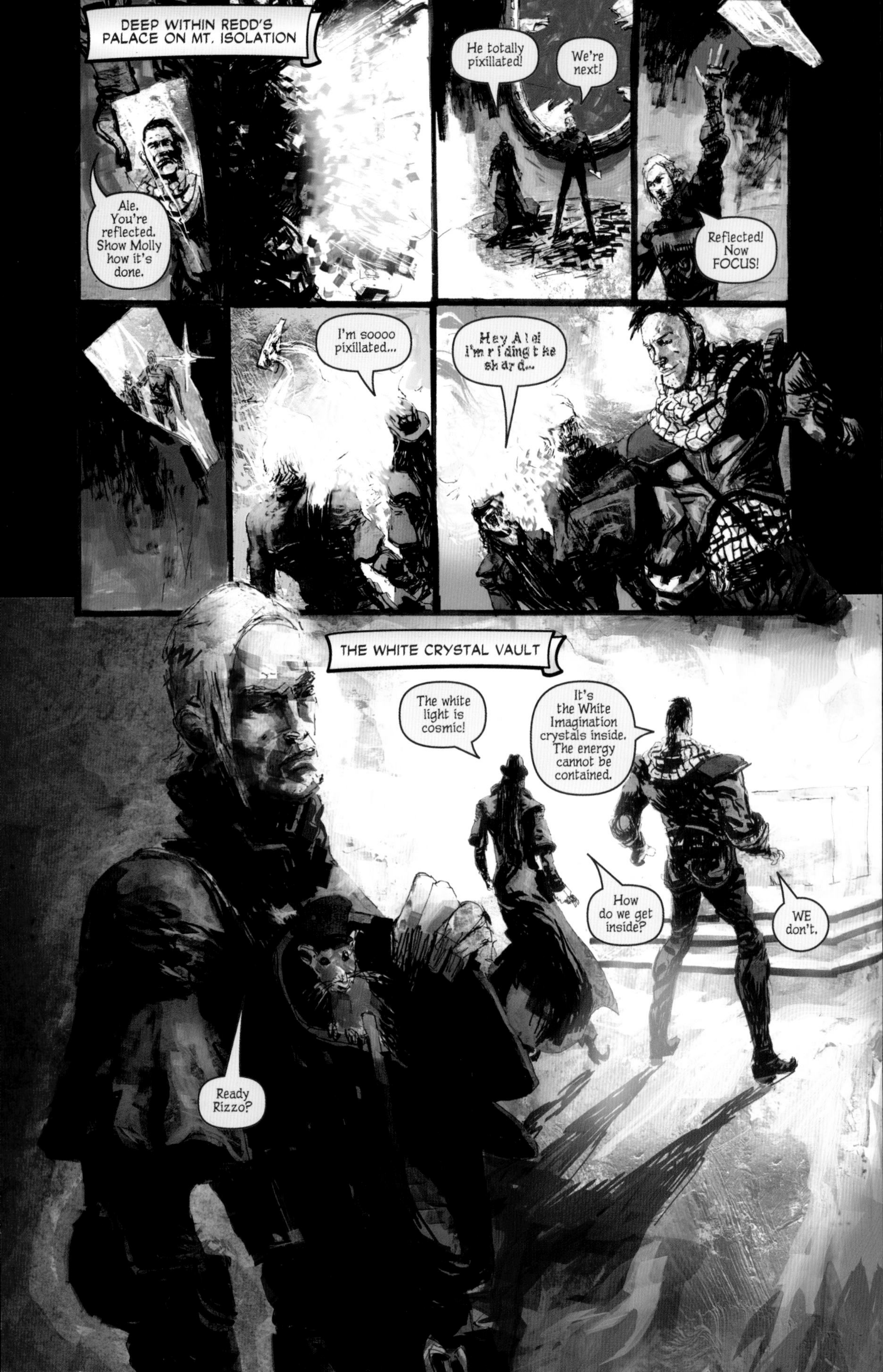
DEEP WITHIN REDD'S PALACE ON MT. ISOLATION
Ale. You're reflected. Show Molly how it's done.
He totally pixillated!
We're next!
Reflected! Now FOCUS!
I'm soooo pixillated...
Hey Ale! I'm riding the shard...
THE WHITE CRYSTAL VAULT
The white light is cosmic!
It's the White Imagination crystals inside. The energy cannot be contained.
How do we get inside?
WE don't.
Ready Rizzo?

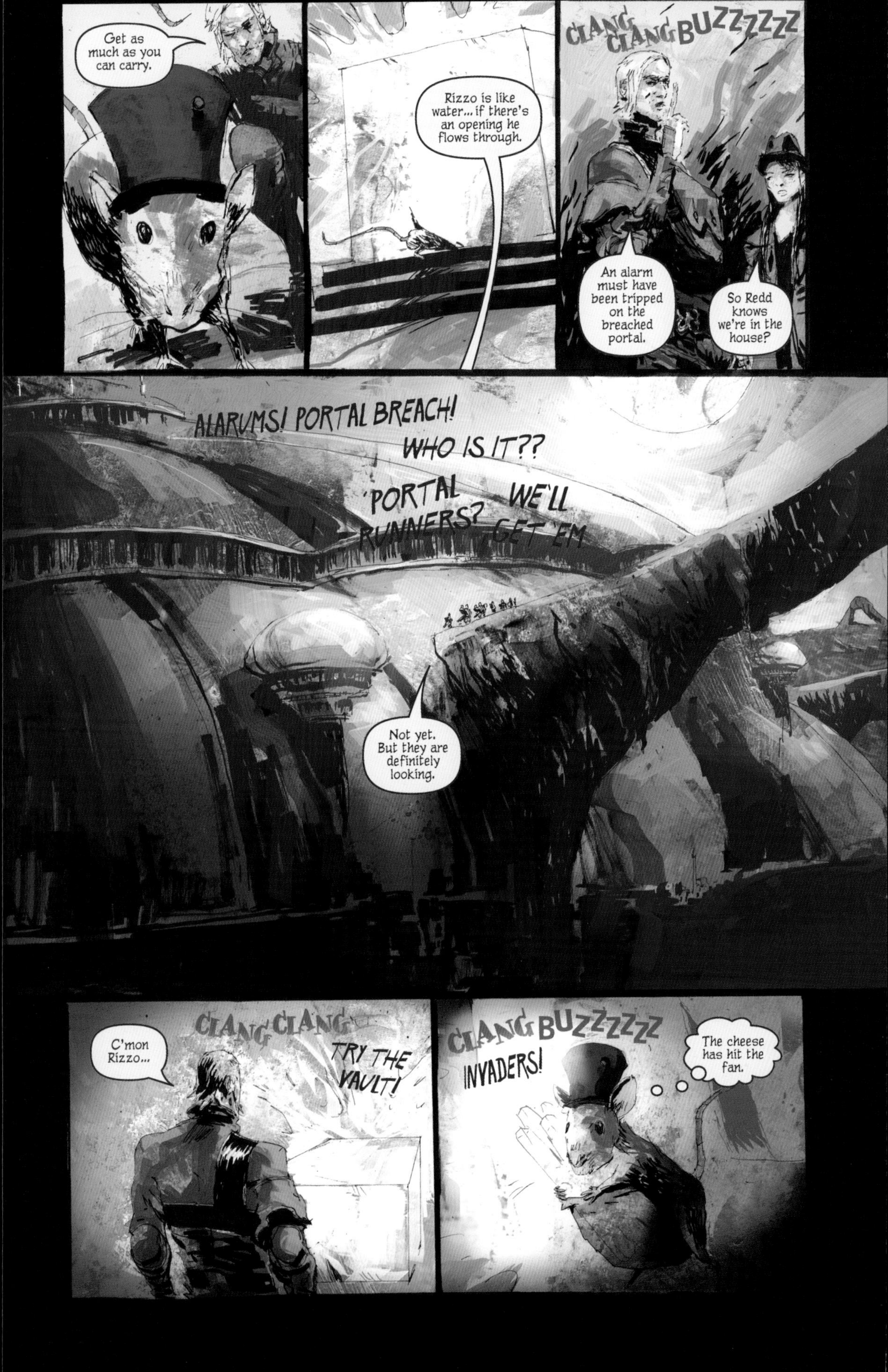
Get as much as you can carry.
Rizzo is like water... if there's an opening he flows through.
CLANG CLANG BUZZZZZZ
An alarm must have been tripped on the breached portal.
So Redd knows we're in the house?
ALARUMS! PORTAL BREACH!
WHO IS IT??
PORTAL RUNNERS?
WE'LL GET 'EM
Not yet. But they are definitely looking.
CLANG CLANG
C'mon Rizzo...
TRY THE VAULT!
CLANG BUZZZZZZ
INVADERS!
The cheese has hit the fan.

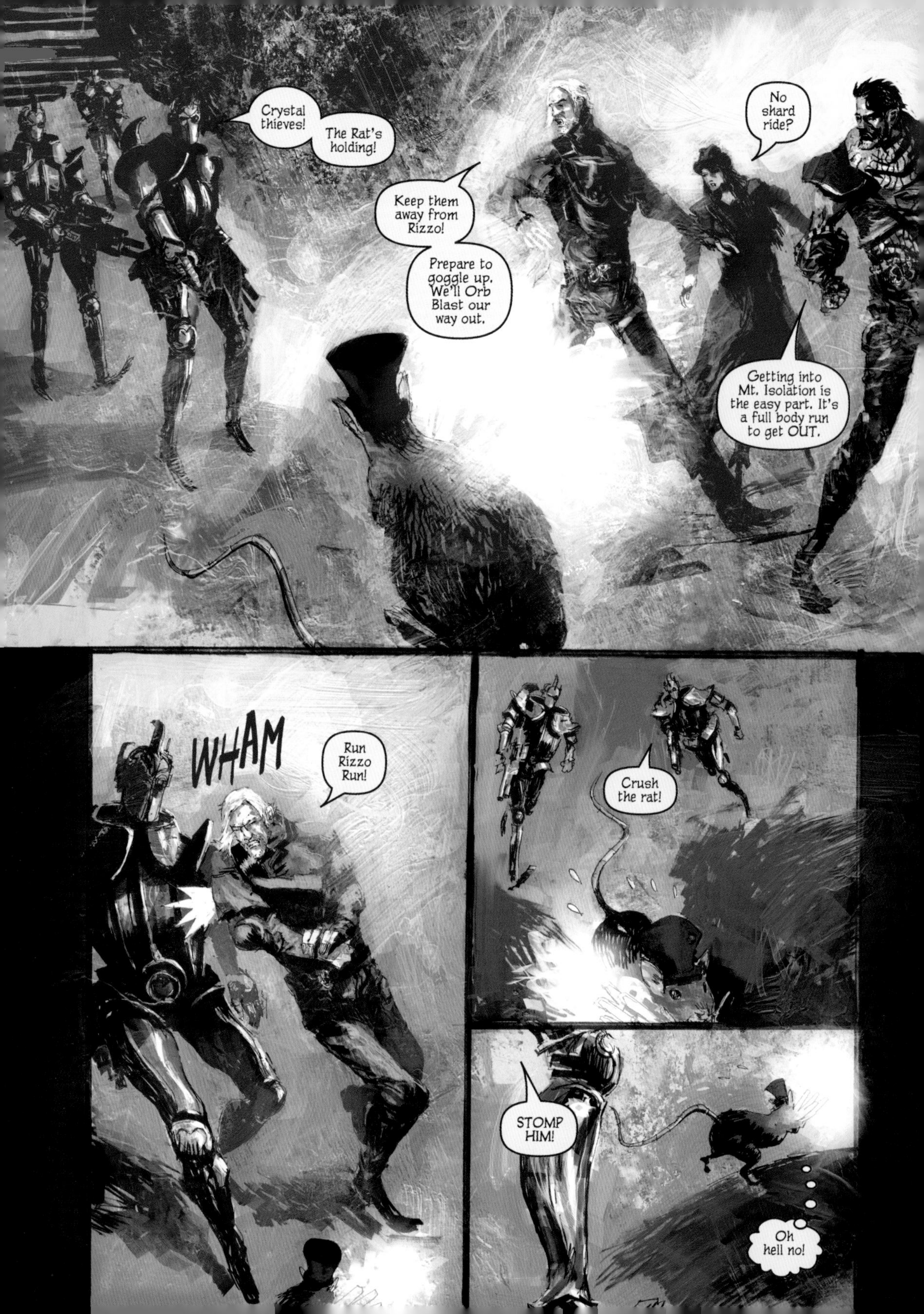
Crystal thieves!
The Rat's holding!
Keep them away from Rizzo!
Prepare to goggle up. We'll Orb Blast our way out.
No shard ride?
Getting into Mt. Isolation is the easy part. It's a full body run to get OUT.
WHAM
Run Rizzo Run!
Crush the rat!
STOMP HIM!
Oh hell no!

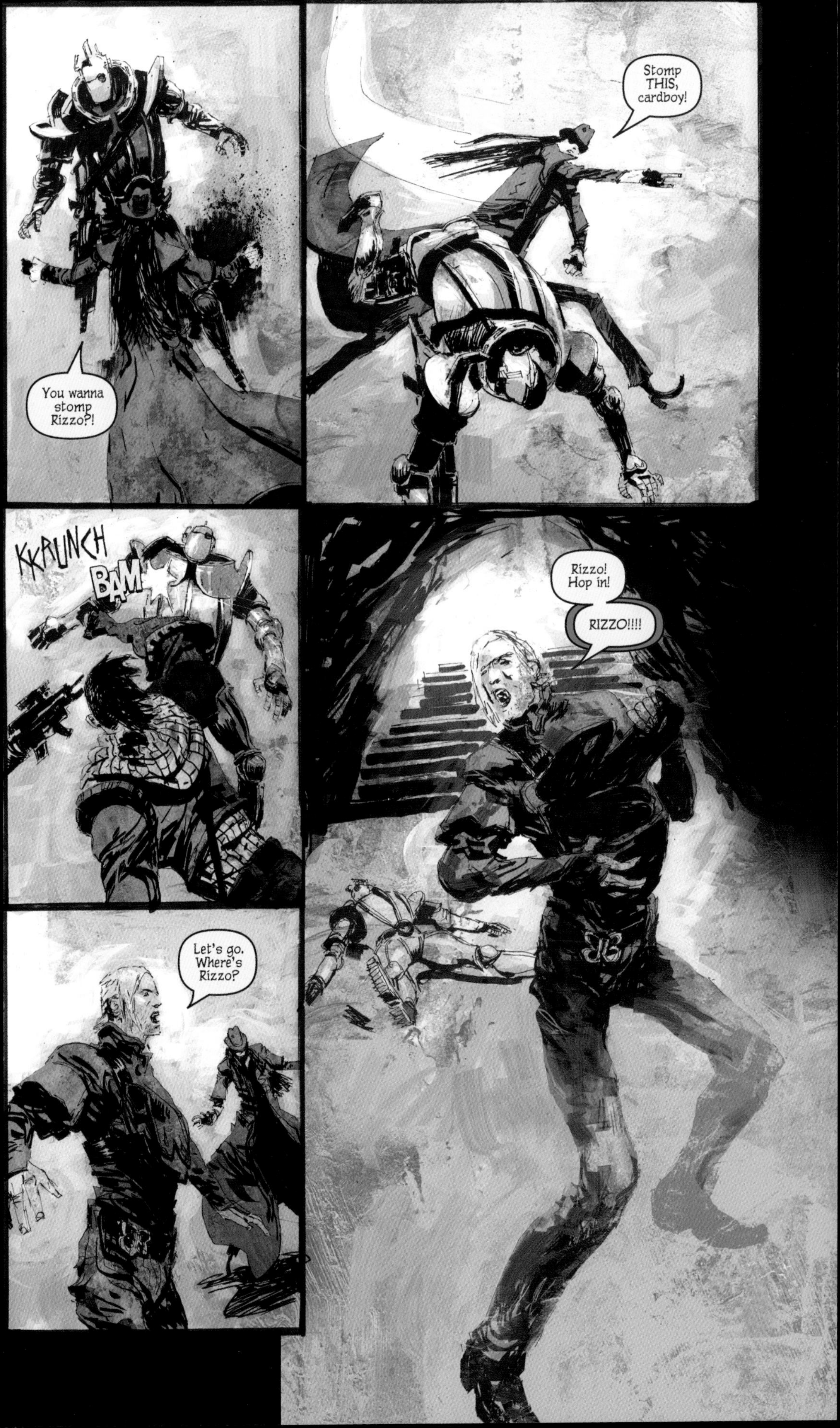
You wanna stomp Rizzo?!
Stomp THIS, cardboy!
KKRUNCH
BAM
Let's go. Where's Rizzo?
Rizzo! Hop in!
RIZZO!!!!

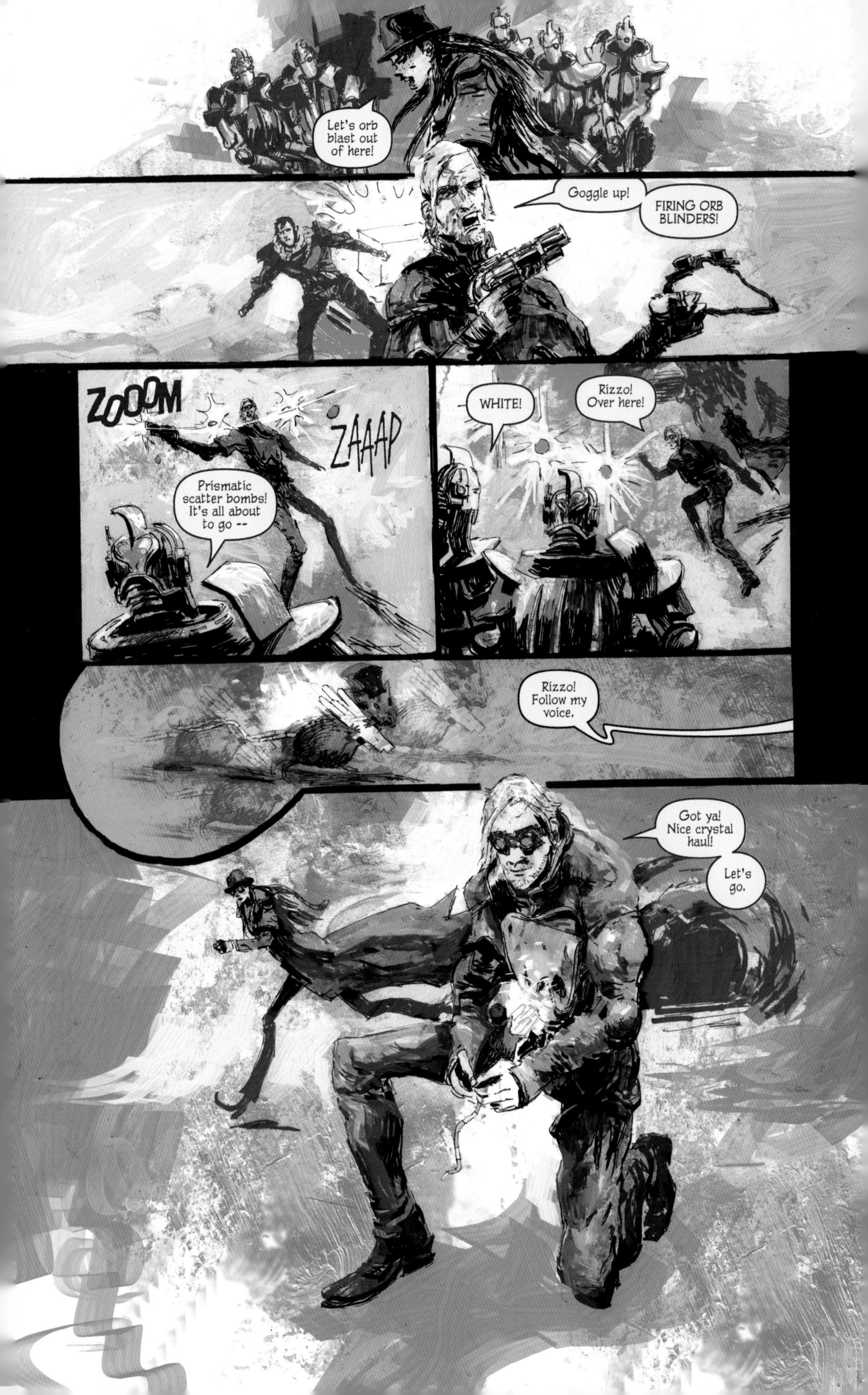
Let's orb blast out of here!
Goggle up!
FIRING ORB BLINDERS!
ZOOOM
ZAAAP
Prismatic scatter bombs! It's all about to go --
WHITE!
Rizzo! Over here!
Rizzo! Follow my voice.
Got ya! Nice crystal haul!
Let's go.

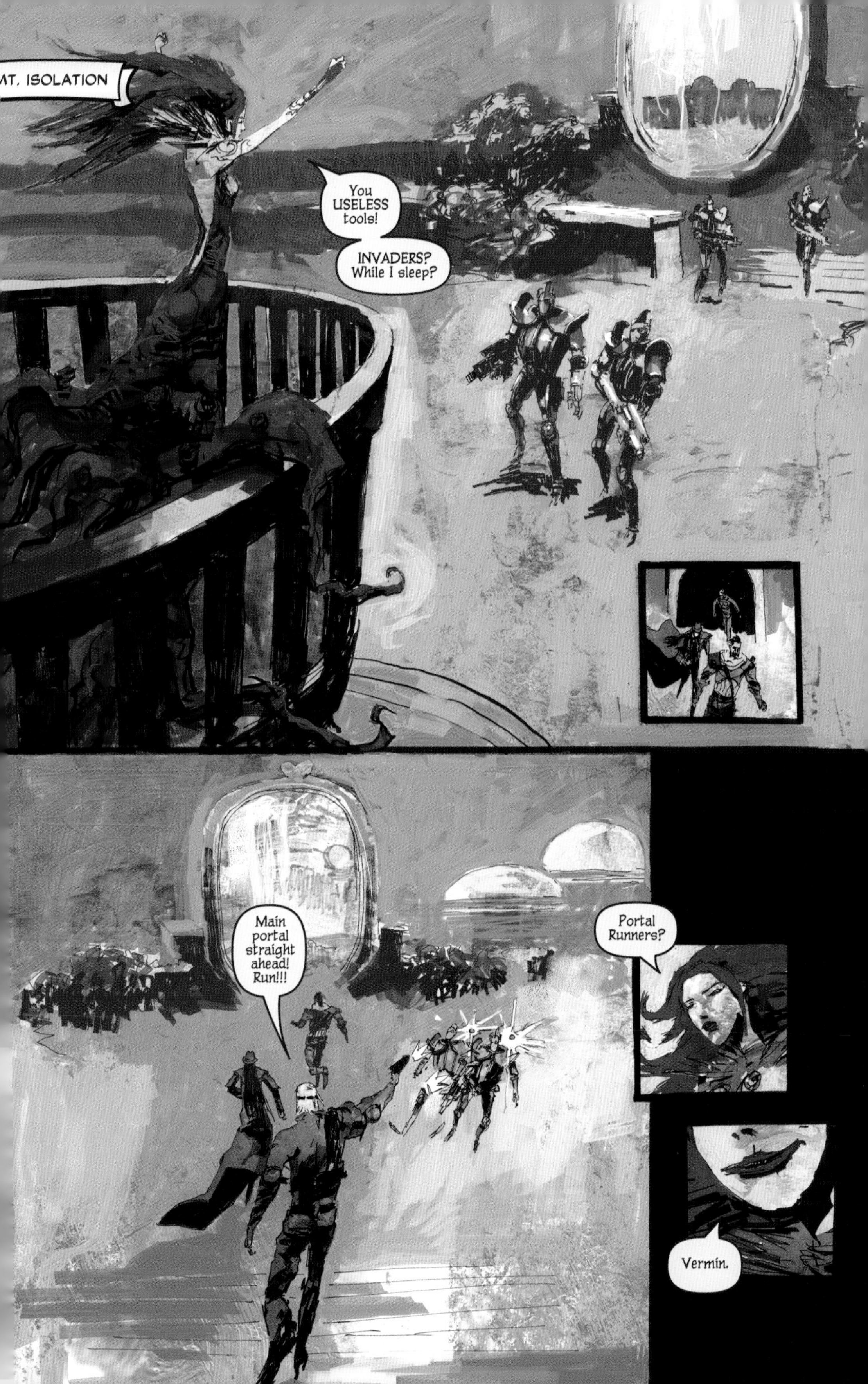
MT. ISOLATION
You USELESS tools!
INVADERS? While I sleep?
Main portal straight ahead! Run!!!
Portal Runners?
Vermin.

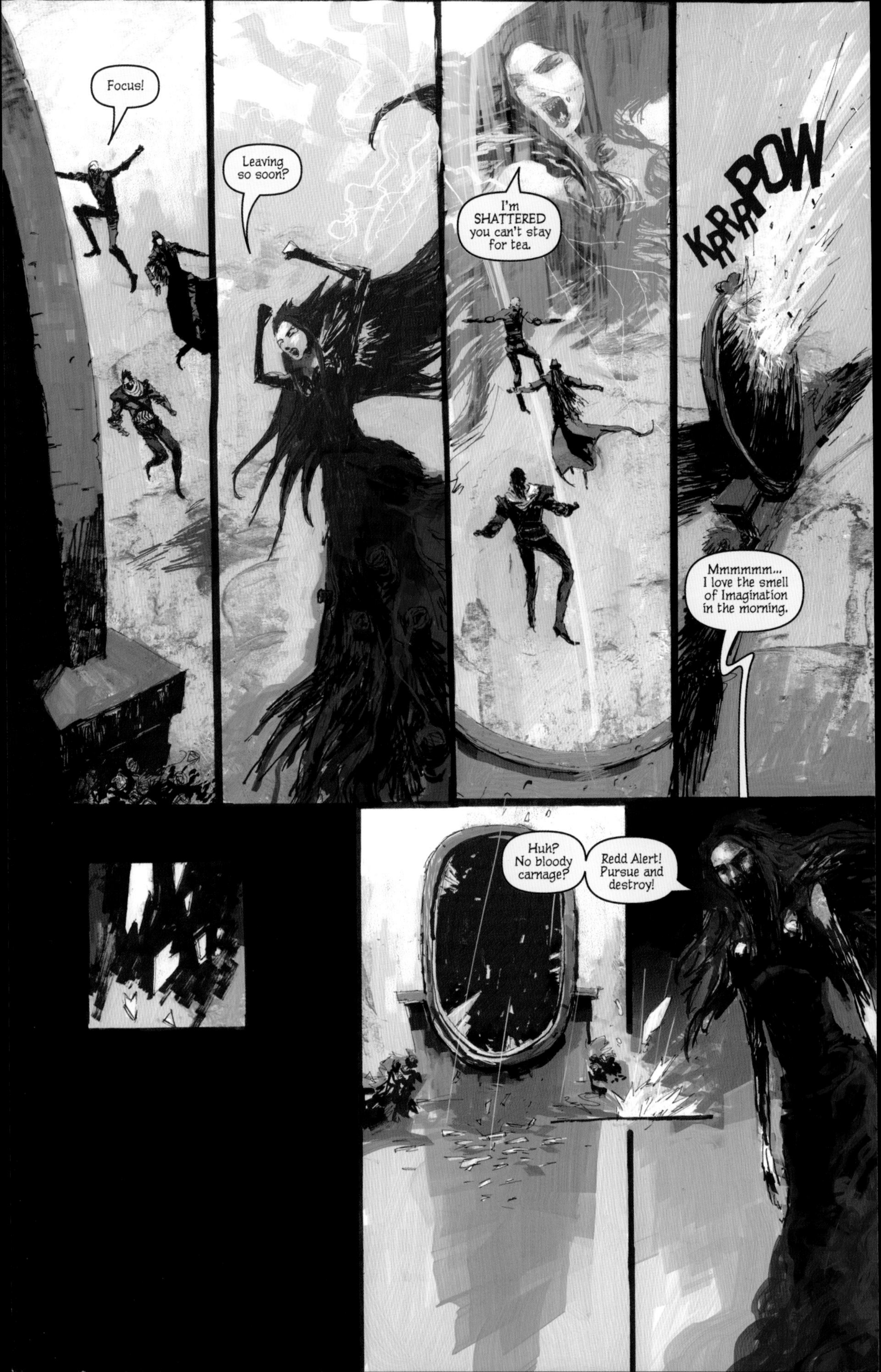
Focus!
Leaving so soon?
I'm SHATTERED you can't stay for tea.
KRRRRPOW
Mmmmmm... I love the smell of Imagination in the morning.
Huh? No bloody carnage?
Redd Alert! Pursue and destroy!

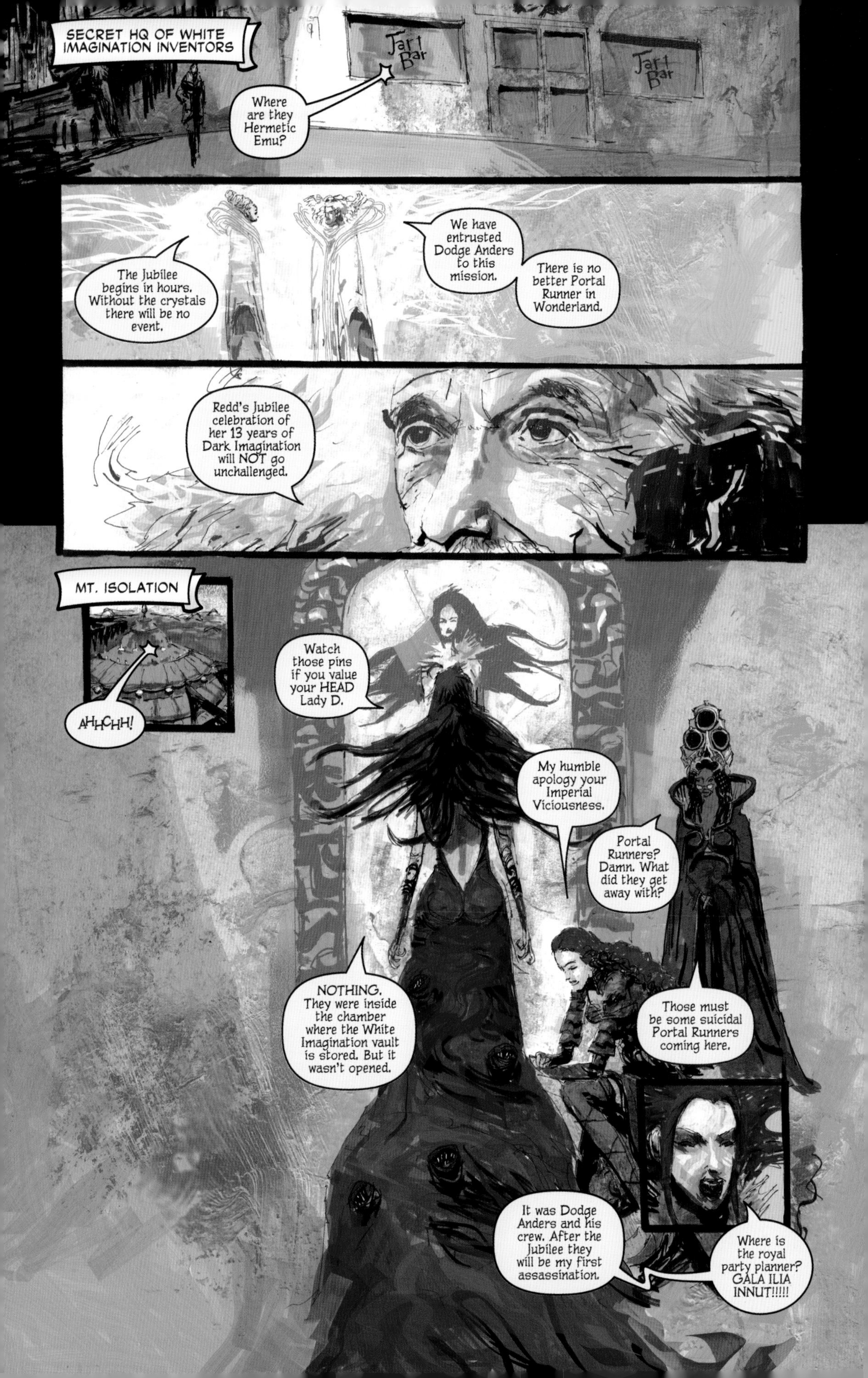
SECRET HQ OF WHITE IMAGINATION INVENTORS
Tart Bar
Tart Bar
Where are they Hermetic Emu?
The Jubilee begins in hours. Without the crystals there will be no event.
We have entrusted Dodge Anders to this mission.
There is no better Portal Runner in Wonderland.
Redd's Jubilee celebration of her 13 years of Dark Imagination will NOT go unchallenged.
MT. ISOLATION
AHHCHH!
Watch those pins if you value your HEAD Lady D.
My humble apology your Imperial Viciousness.
Portal Runners? Damn. What did they get away with?
NOTHING. They were inside the chamber where the White Imagination vault is stored. But it wasn't opened.
Those must be some suicidal Portal Runners coming here.
It was Dodge Anders and his crew. After the Jubilee they will be my first assassination.
Where is the royal party planner? GALA ILIA INNUT!!!!!

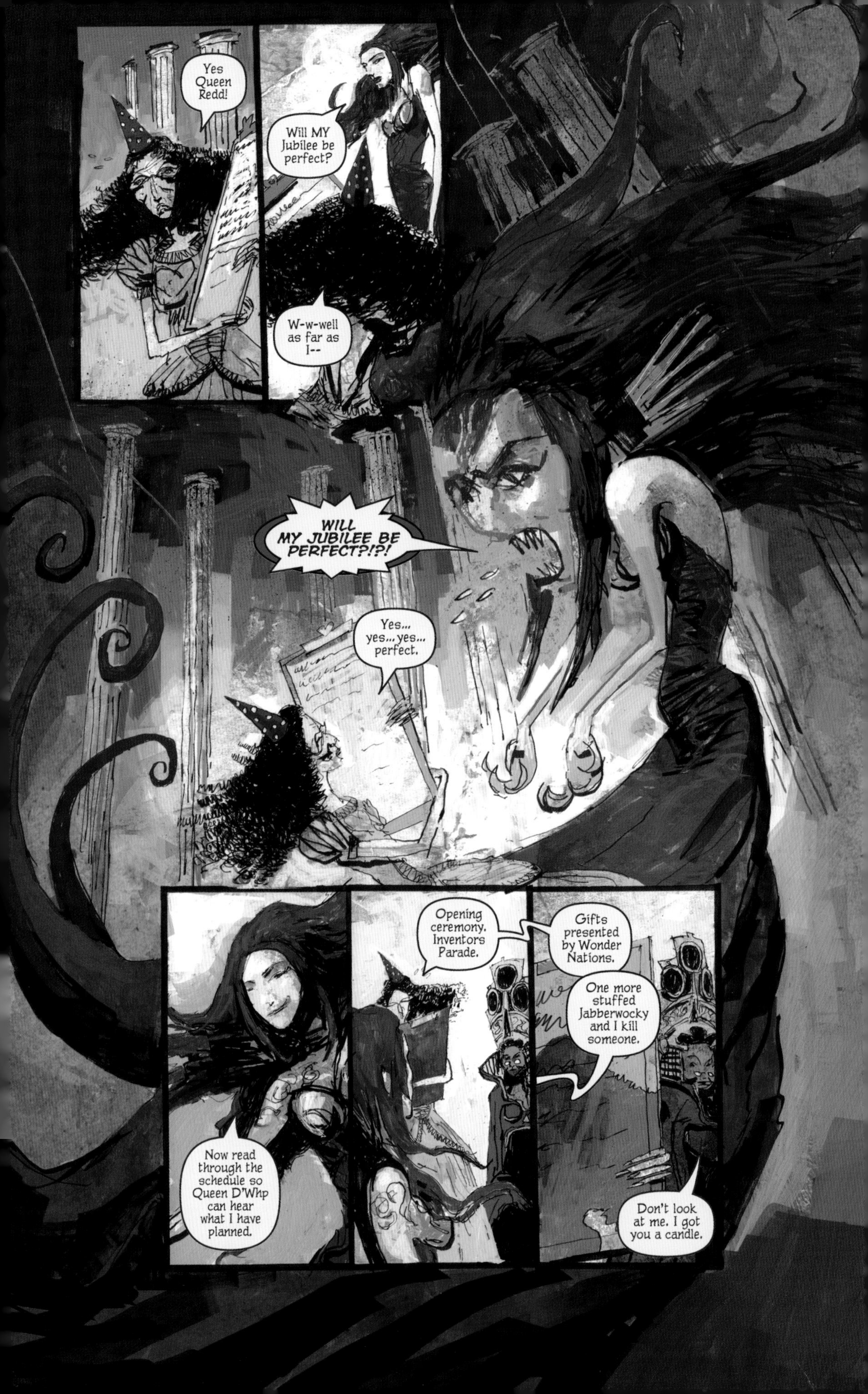
Yes Queen Redd!
Will MY Jubilee be perfect?
W-w-well as far as I--
WILL MY JUBILEE BE PERFECT?!?!
Yes... yes... yes... perfect.
Now read through the schedule so Queen D'Whp can hear what I have planned.
Opening ceremony. Inventors Parade.
Gifts presented by Wonder Nations.
One more stuffed Jabberwocky and I kill someone.
Don't look at me. I got you a candle.

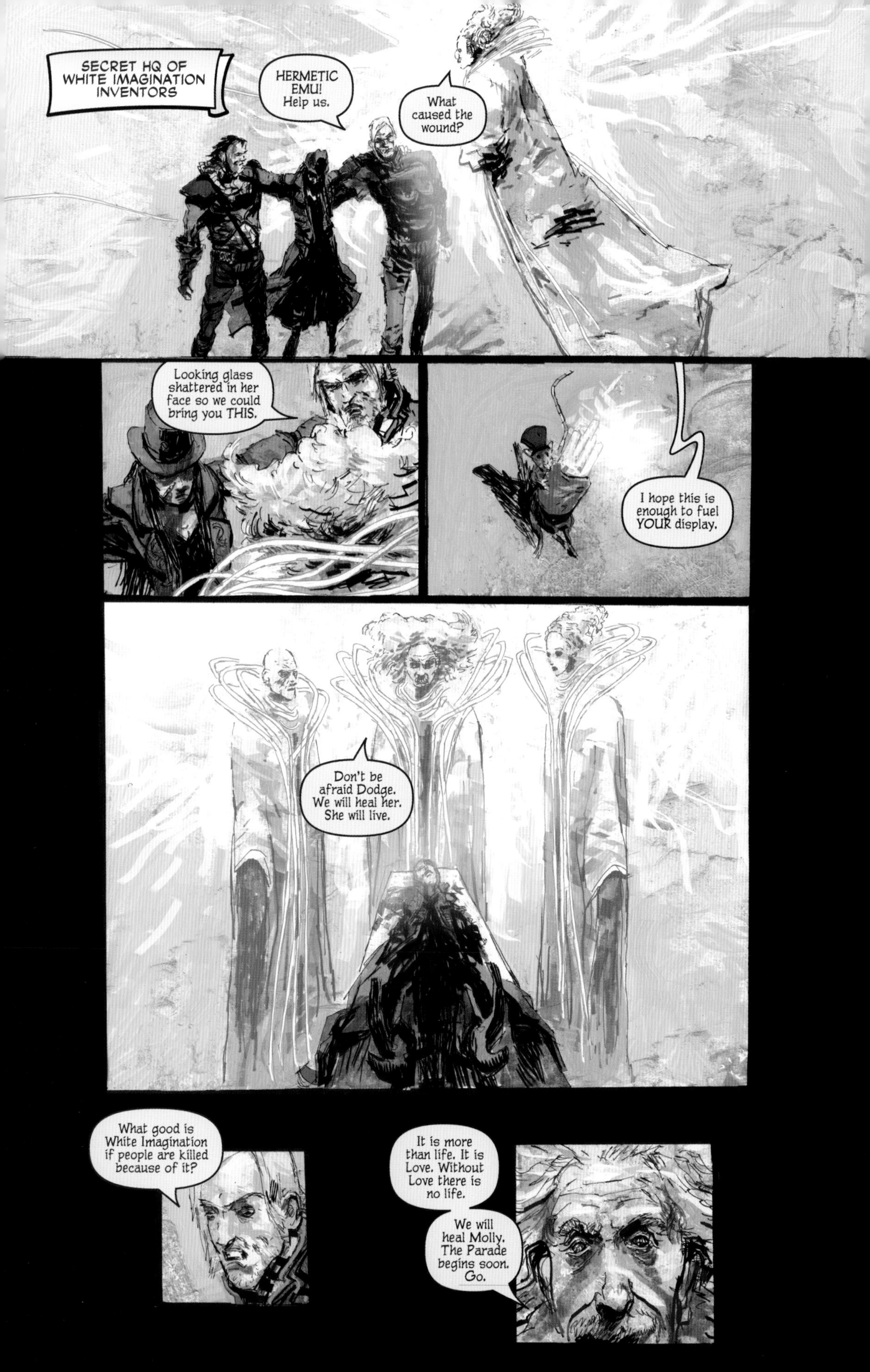
SECRET HQ OF WHITE IMAGINATION INVENTORS
HERMETIC EMU! Help us.
What caused the wound?
Looking glass shattered in her face so we could bring you THIS.
I hope this is enough to fuel YOUR display.
Don't be afraid Dodge. We will heal her. She will live.
What good is White Imagination if people are killed because of it?
It is more than life. It is Love. Without Love there is no life.
We will heal Molly. The Parade begins soon. Go.

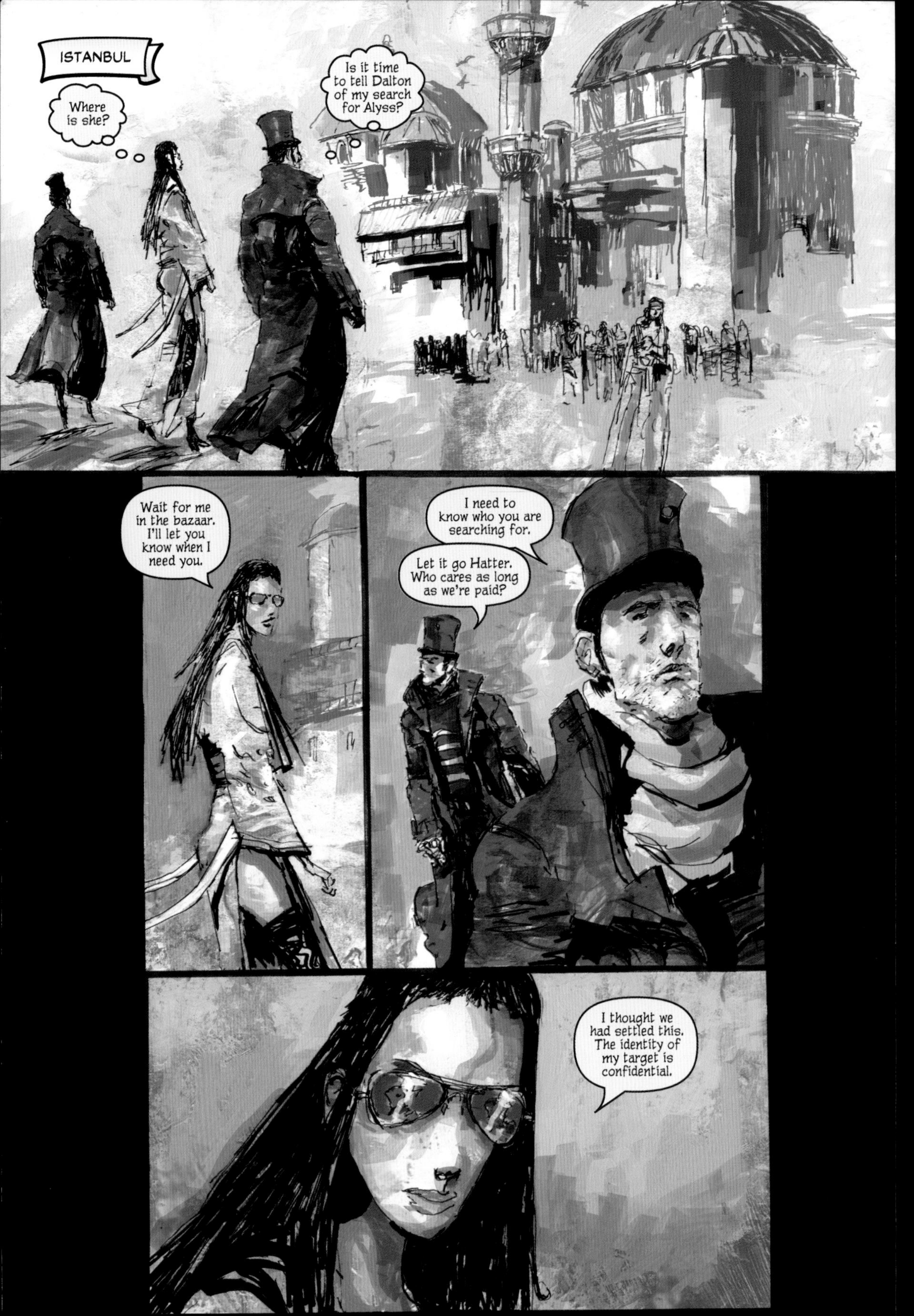
ISTANBUL
Where is she?
Is it time to tell Dalton of my search for Alyss?
Wait for me in the bazaar. I'll let you know when I need you.
I need to know who you are searching for.
Let it go Hatter. Who cares as long as we're paid?
I thought we had settled this. The identity of my target is confidential.

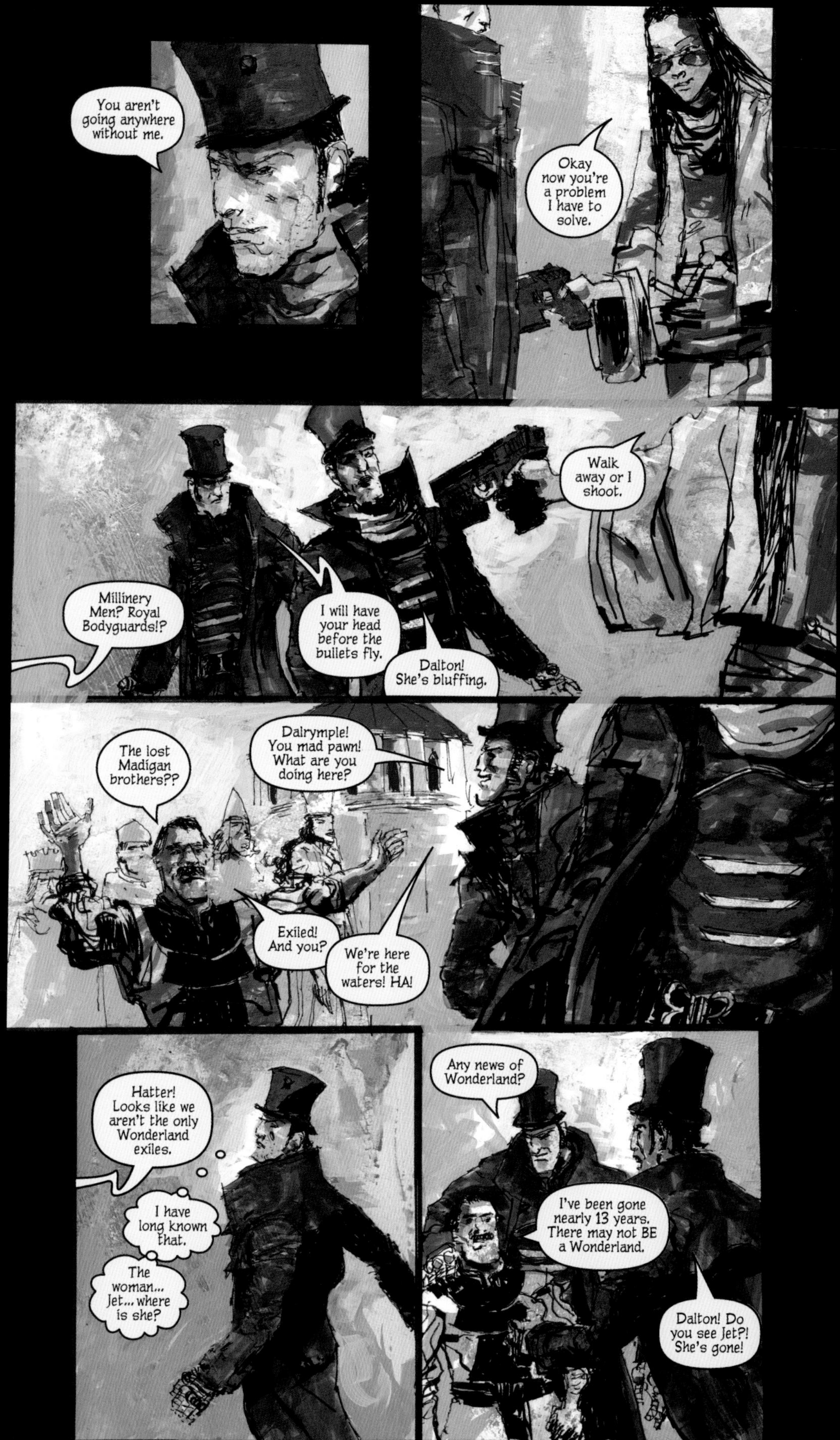
You aren't going anywhere without me.
Okay now you're a problem I have to solve.
Walk away or I shoot.
Millinery Men? Royal Bodyguards!?
I will have your head before the bullets fly.
Dalton! She's bluffing.
The lost Madigan brothers??
Dalrymple! You mad pawn! What are you doing here?
Exiled! And you?
We're here for the waters! HA!
Hatter! Looks like we aren't the only Wonderland exiles.
I have long known that.
The woman... Jet... where is she?
Any news of Wonderland?
I've been gone nearly 13 years. There may not BE a Wonderland.
Dalton! Do you see Jet?! She's gone!

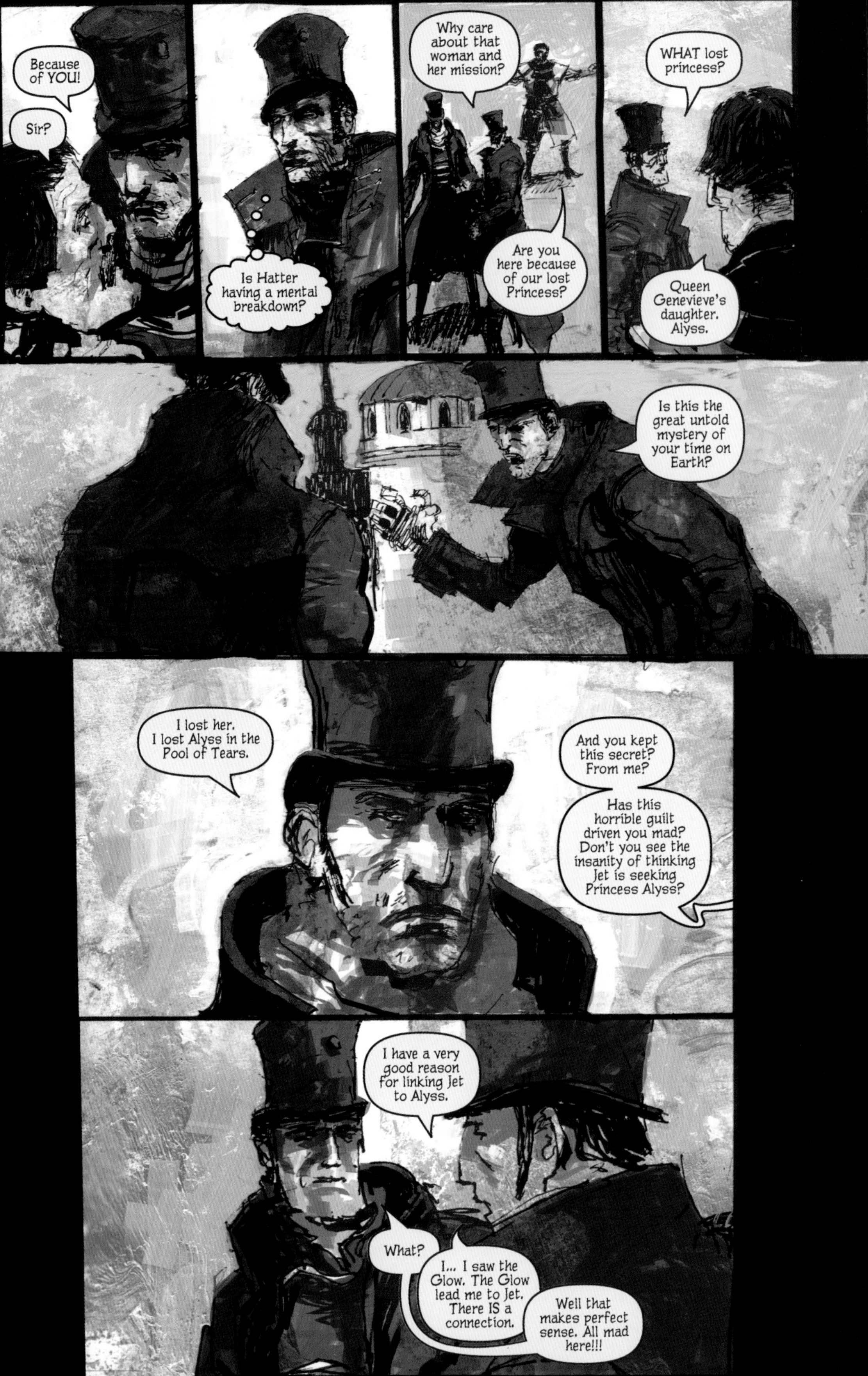
Because of YOU!
Sir?
Is Hatter having a mental breakdown?
Why care about that woman and her mission?
Are you here because of our lost Princess?
WHAT lost princess?
Queen Genevieve's daughter. Alyss.
Is this the great untold mystery of your time on Earth?
I lost her. I lost Alyss in the Pool of Tears.
And you kept this secret? From me?
Has this horrible guilt driven you mad? Don't you see the insanity of thinking Jet is seeking Princess Alyss?
I have a very good reason for linking Jet to Alyss.
What?
I... I saw the Glow. The Glow lead me to Jet. There IS a connection.
Well that makes perfect sense. All mad here!!!

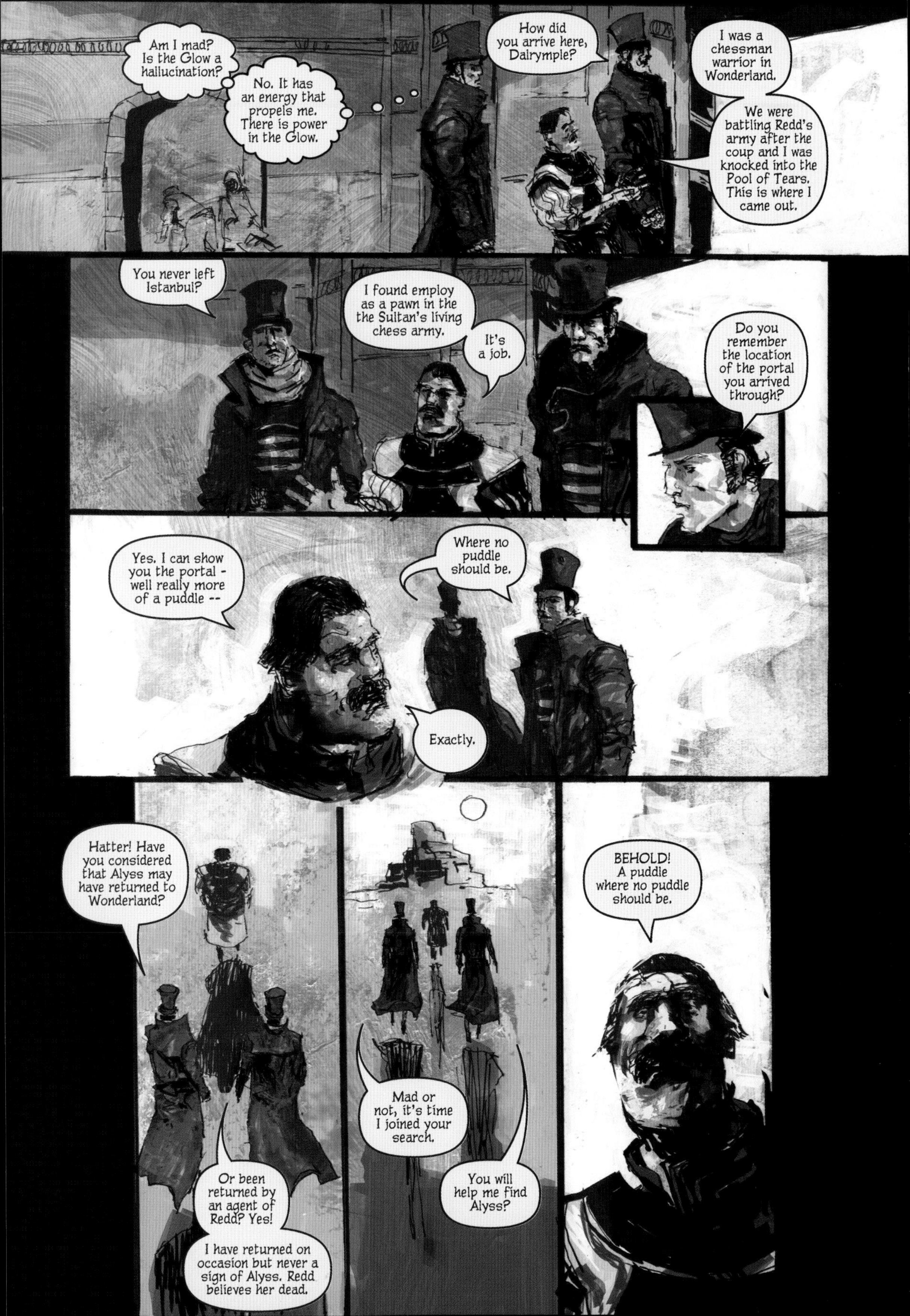

Am I mad? Is the Glow a hallucination?
No. It has an energy that propels me. There is power in the Glow.
How did you arrive here, Dalrymple?
I was a chessman warrior in Wonderland.
We were battling Redd's army after the coup and I was knocked into the Pool of Tears. This is where I came out.
You never left Istanbul?
I found employ as a pawn in the the Sultan's living chess army.
It's a job.
Do you remember the location of the portal you arrived through?
Yes. I can show you the portal - well really more of a puddle --
Where no puddle should be.
Exactly.
Hatter! Have you considered that Alyss may have returned to Wonderland?
Or been returned by an agent of Redd? Yes!
I have returned on occasion but never a sign of Alyss. Redd believes her dead.
Mad or not, it's time I joined your search.
You will help me find Alyss?
BEHOLD! A puddle where no puddle should be.

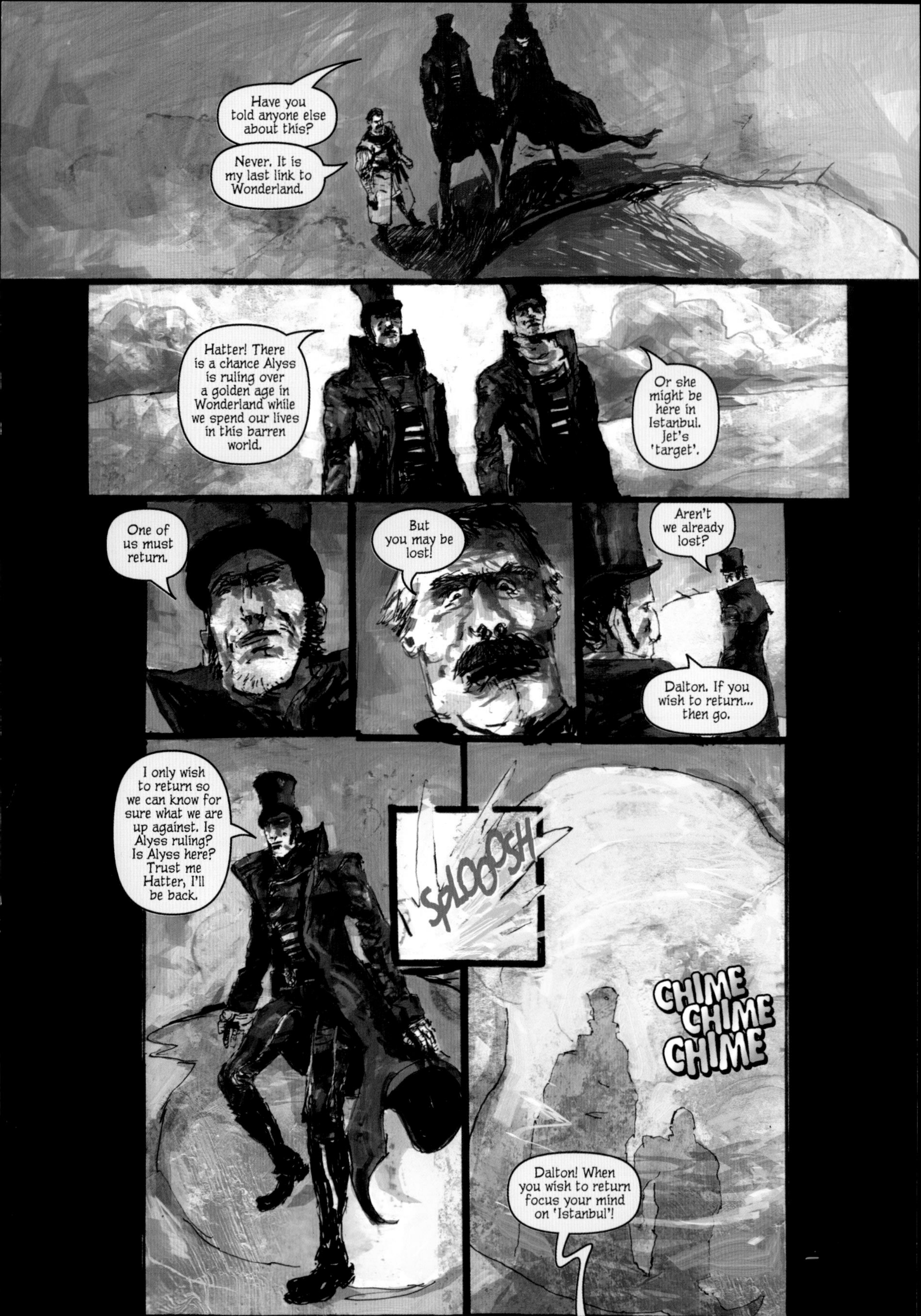
Have you told anyone else about this?
Never. It is my last link to Wonderland.
Hatter! There is a chance Alyss is ruling over a golden age in Wonderland while we spend our lives in this barren world.
Or she might be here in Istanbul. Jet's 'target'.
One of us must return.
But you may be lost!
Aren't we already lost?
Dalton. If you wish to return... then go.
I only wish to return so we can know for sure what we are up against. Is Alyss ruling? Is Alyss here? Trust me Hatter, I'll be back.
SPLOOOSH
CHIME CHIME CHIME
Dalton! When you wish to return focus your mind on 'Istanbul'!

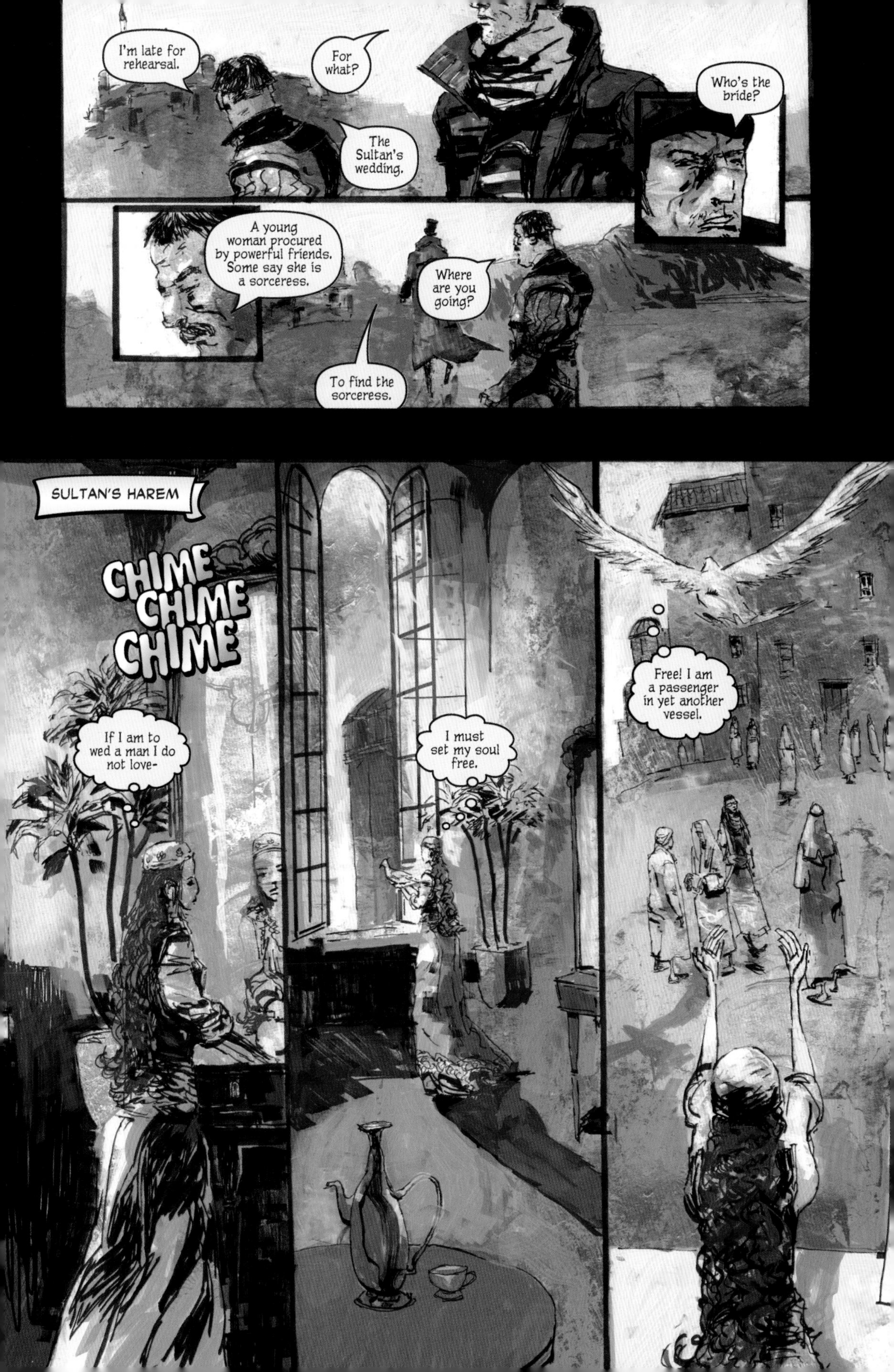
I'm late for rehearsal.
For what?
The Sultan's wedding.
Who's the bride?
A young woman procured by powerful friends. Some say she is a sorceress.
Where are you going?
To find the sorceress.
SULTAN'S HAREM
CHIME CHIME CHIME
If I am to wed a man I do not love-
I must set my soul free.
Free! I am a passenger in yet another vessel.

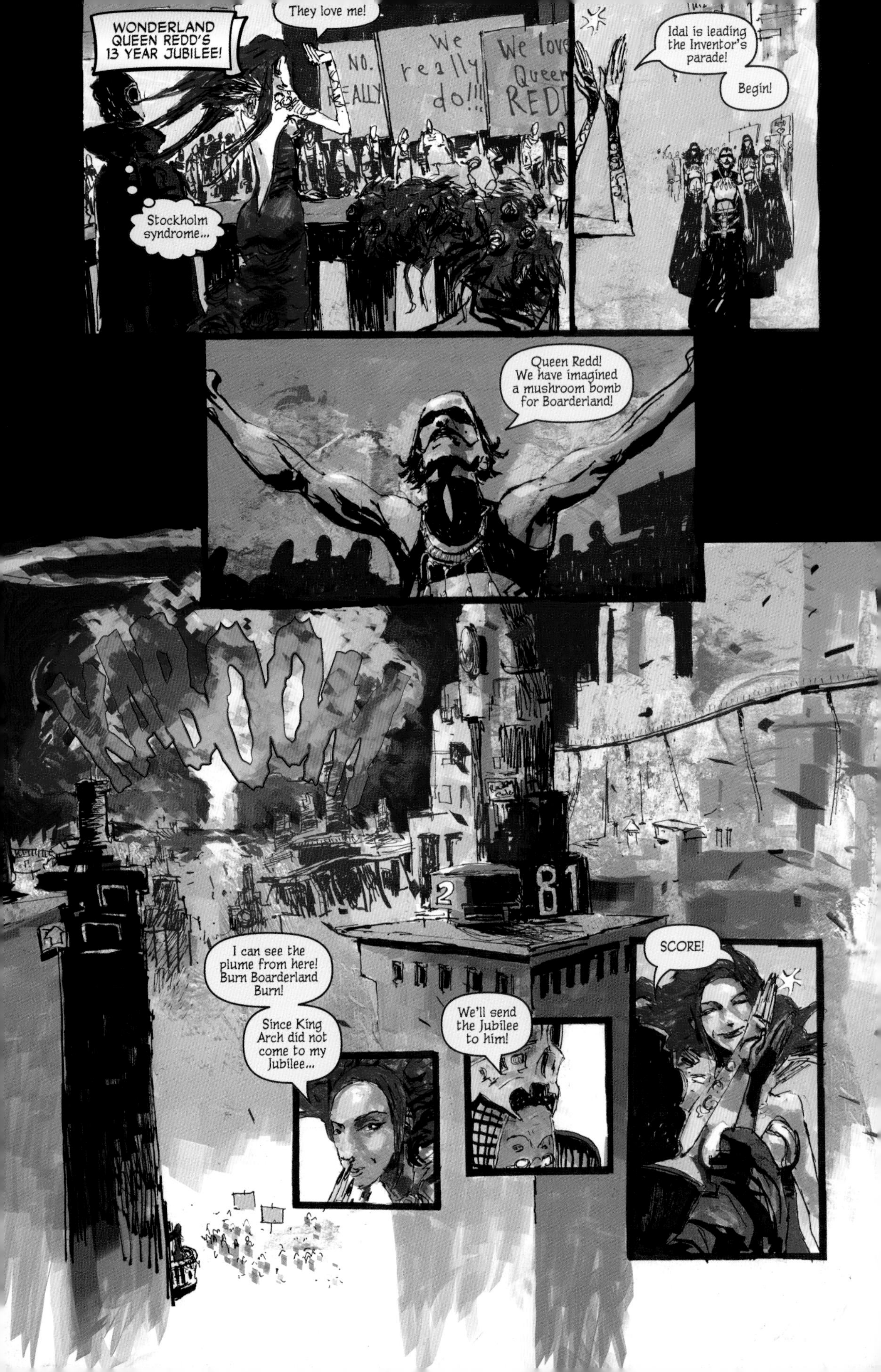
WONDERLAND QUEEN REDD'S 13 YEAR JUBILEE!
They love me!
NO. REALLY
We really do!!!
We love Queen REDD
Stockholm syndrome...
Idal is leading the Inventor's parade!
Begin!
Queen Redd! We have imagined a mushroom bomb for Boarderland!
2
81
I can see the plume from here! Burn Boarderland Burn!
Since King Arch did not come to my Jubilee...
We'll send the Jubilee to him!
SCORE!

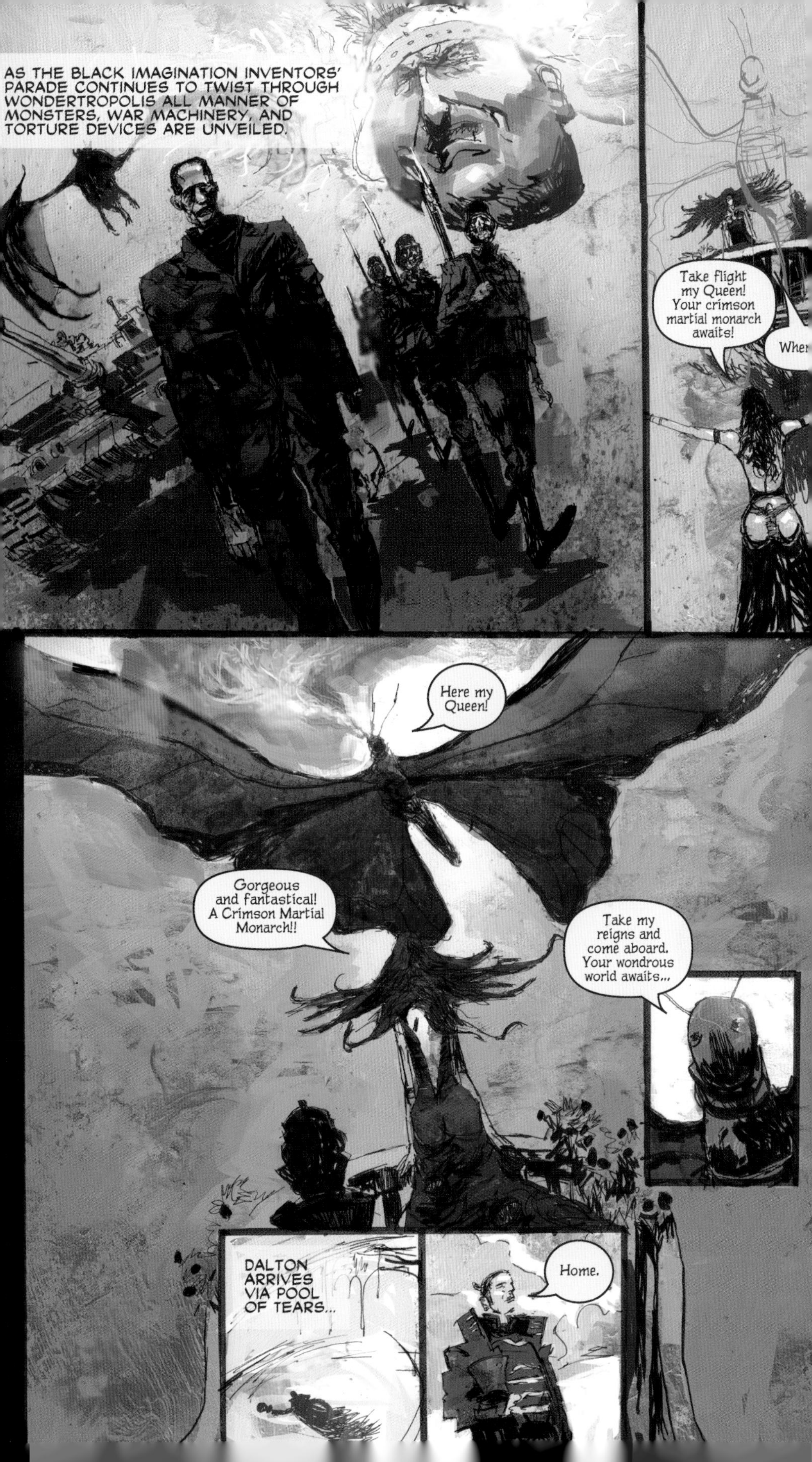
AS THE BLACK IMAGINATION INVENTORS' PARADE CONTINUES TO TWIST THROUGH WONDERTROPOLIS ALL MANNER OF MONSTERS, WAR MACHINERY, AND TORTURE DEVICES ARE UNVEILED.
Take flight my Queen! Your crimson martial monarch awaits!
Here my Queen!
Gorgeous and fantastical! A Crimson Martial Monarch!!
Take my reigns and come aboard. Your wondrous world awaits...
DALTON ARRIVES VIA POOL OF TEARS...
Home.

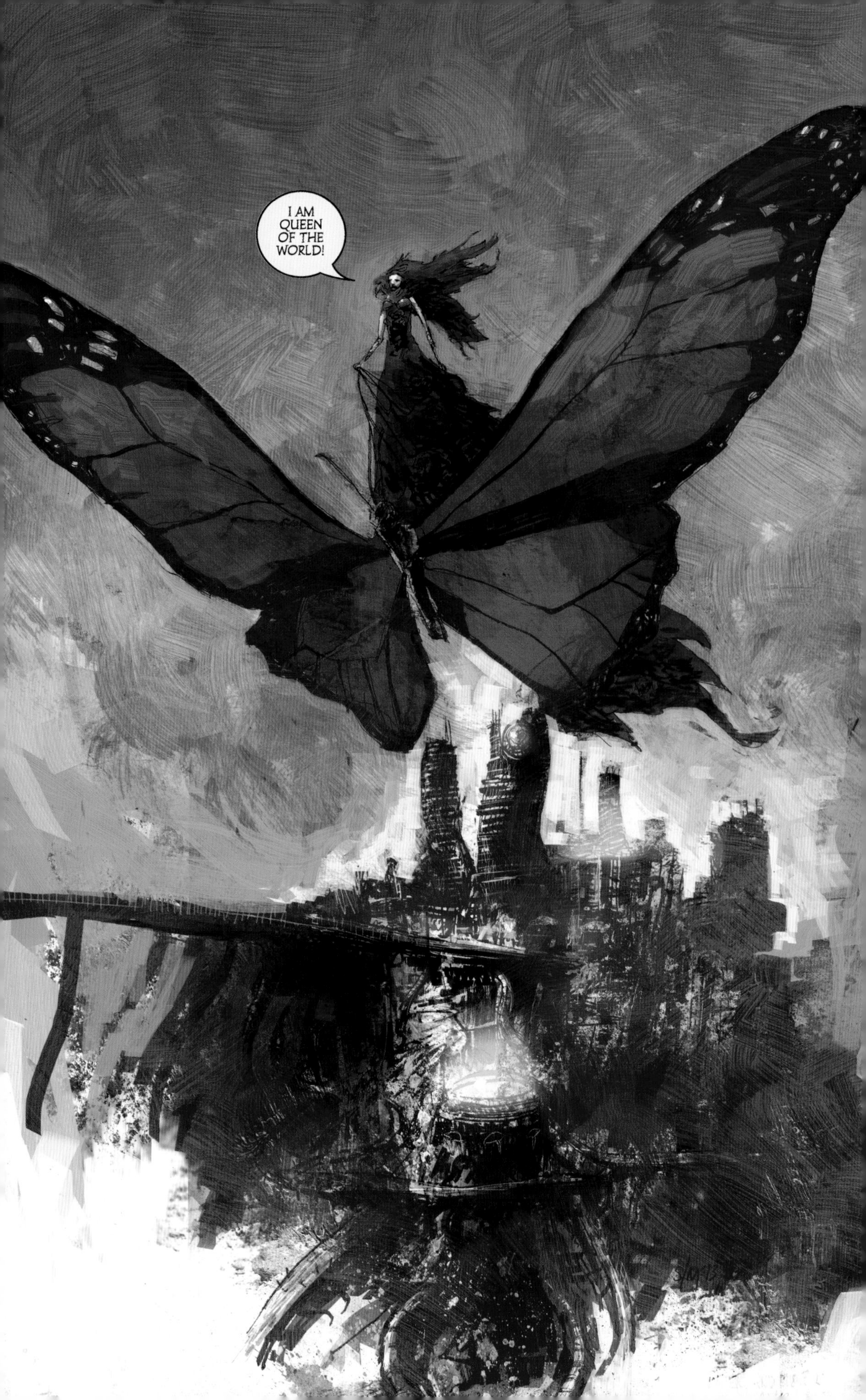
I AM QUEEN OF THE WORLD!

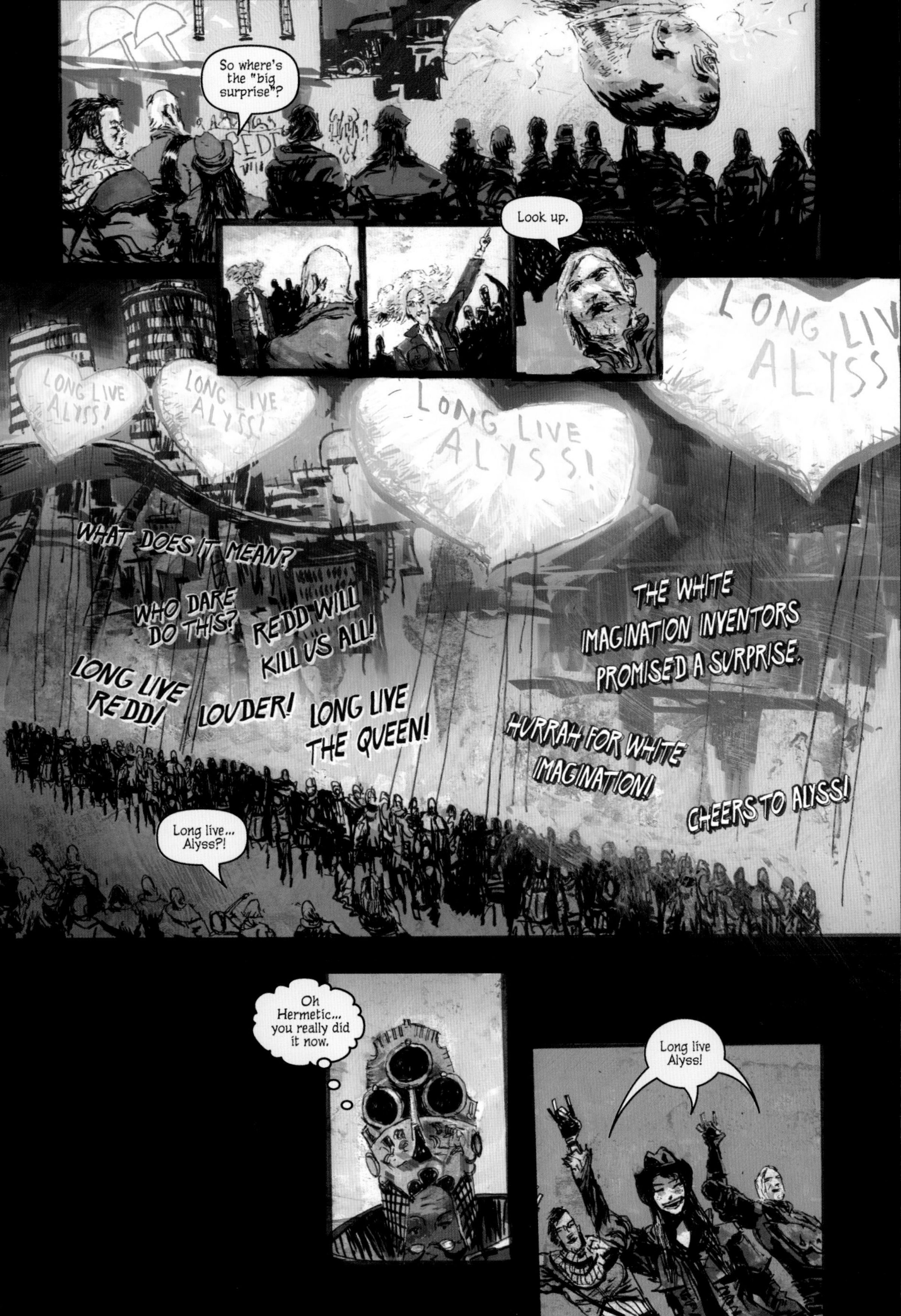

So where's the "big surprise"?
Look up.
LONG LIVE ALYSS!
LONG LIVE ALYSS!
LONG LIVE ALYSS!
LONG LIVE ALYSS
WHAT DOES IT MEAN?
WHO DARE DO THIS?
REDD WILL KILL US ALL!
LONG LIVE REDD!
LOUDER!
LONG LIVE THE QUEEN!
THE WHITE IMAGINATION INVENTORS PROMISED A SURPRISE.
HURRAH FOR WHITE IMAGINATION!
CHEERS TO ALYSS!
Long live... Alyss?!
Oh Hermetic... you really did it now.
Long live Alyss!

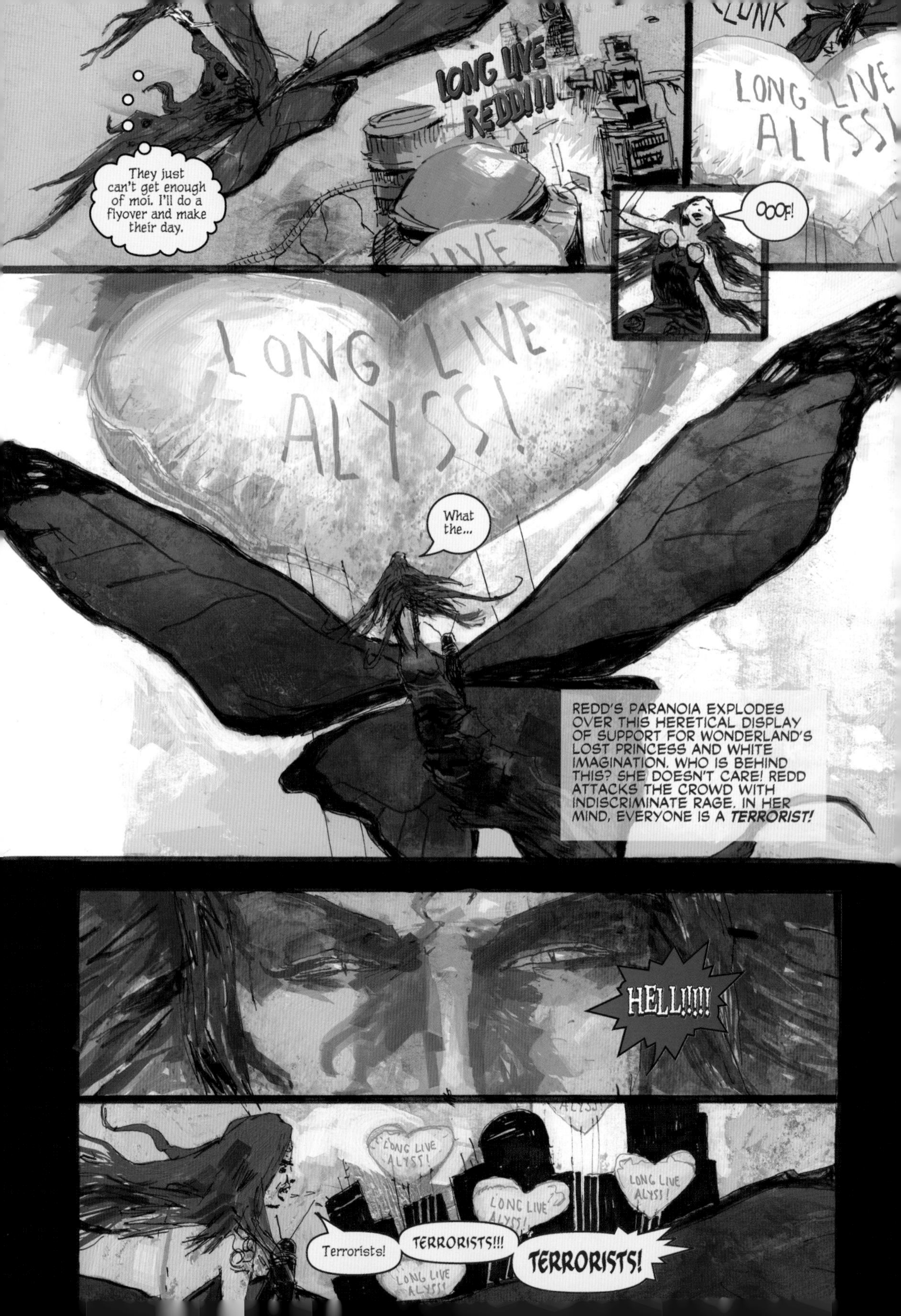

They just can't get enough of moi. I'll do a flyover and make their day.
LONG LIVE REDD!!!
CLUNK
LONG LIVE ALYSS!
OOOF!
LONG LIVE ALYSS!
What the...
REDD'S PARANOIA EXPLODES OVER THIS HERETICAL DISPLAY OF SUPPORT FOR WONDERLAND'S LOST PRINCESS AND WHITE IMAGINATION. WHO IS BEHIND THIS? SHE DOESN'T CARE! REDD ATTACKS THE CROWD WITH INDISCRIMINATE RAGE. IN HER MIND, EVERYONE IS A *TERRORIST!*
HELL!!!!!
LONG LIVE ALYSS!
LONG LIVE ALYSS!
LONG LIVE ALYSS!
Terrorists!
TERRORISTS!!!
TERRORISTS!
LONG LIVE ALYSS!

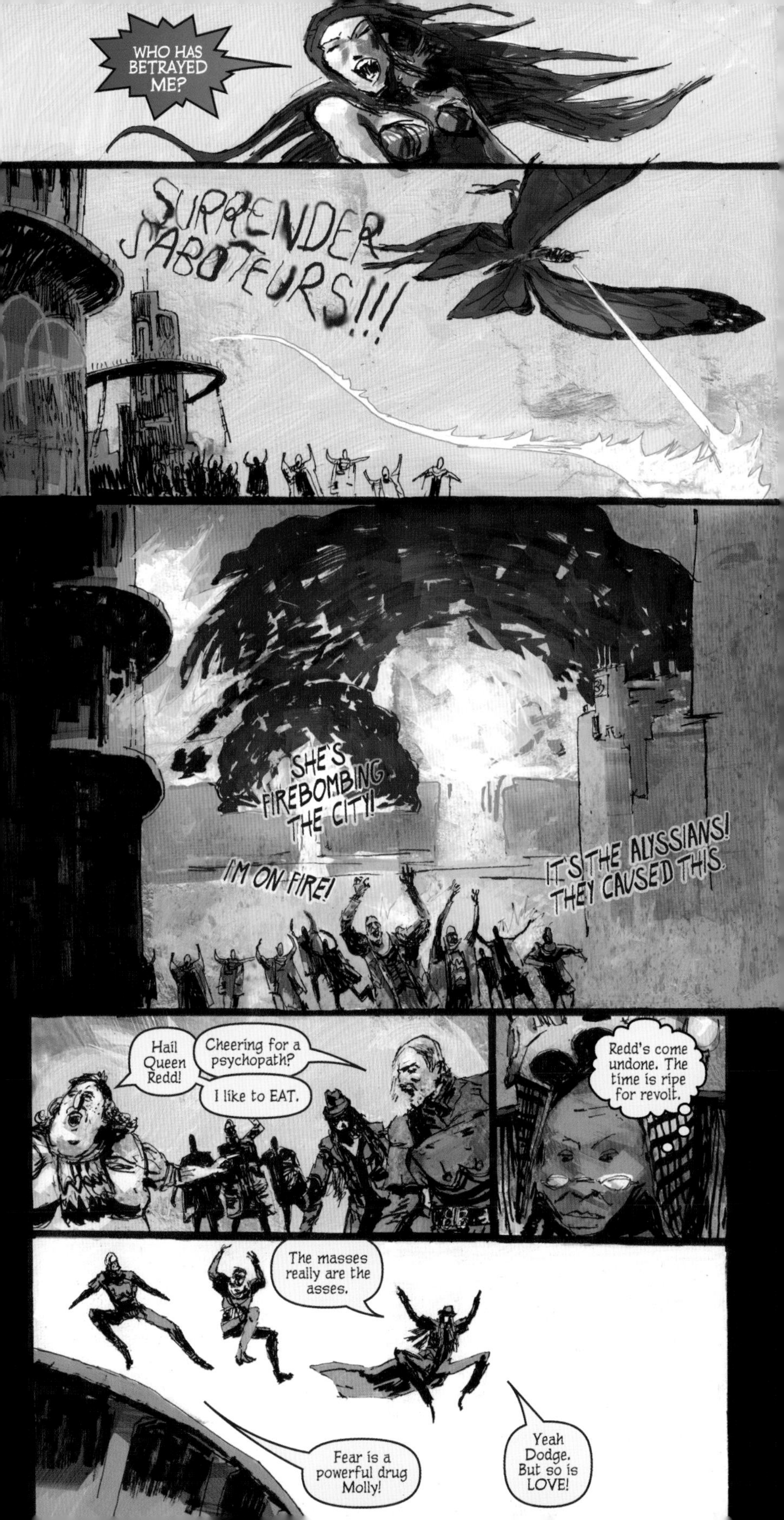

WHO HAS BETRAYED ME?
SURRENDER SABOTEURS!!!
SHE'S FIREBOMBING THE CITY!
I'M ON FIRE!
IT'S THE ALYSSIANS! THEY CAUSED THIS.
Hail Queen Redd!
Cheering for a psychopath?
I like to EAT.
Redd's come undone. The time is ripe for revolt.
The masses really are the asses.
Fear is a powerful drug Molly!
Yeah Dodge. But so is LOVE!

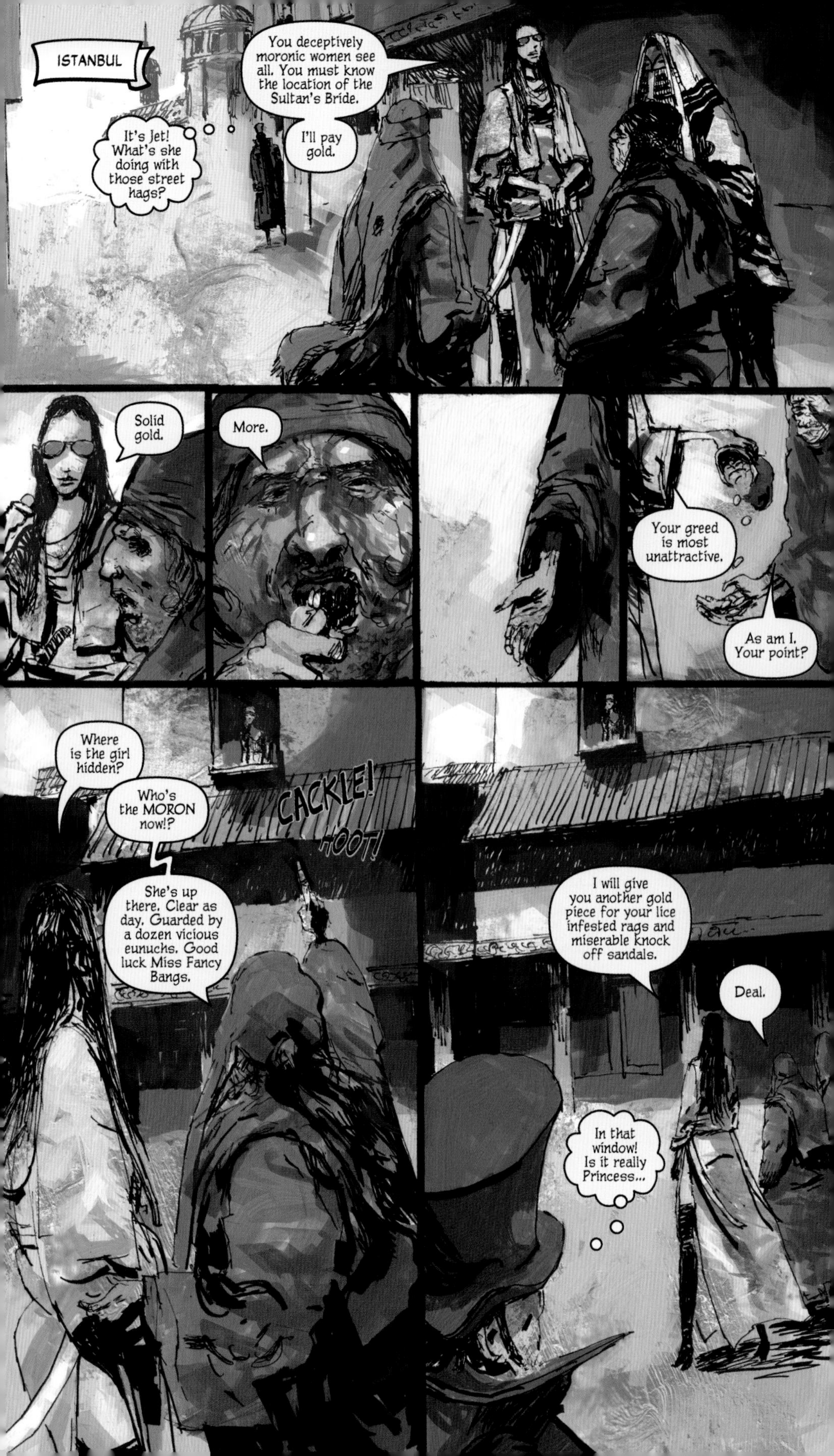
ISTANBUL
It's Jet! What's she doing with those street hags?
You deceptively moronic women see all. You must know the location of the Sultan's Bride.
I'll pay gold.
Solid gold.
More.
Your greed is most unattractive.
As am I. Your point?
Where is the girl hidden?
Who's the MORON now!?
CACKLE!
HOOT!
She's up there. Clear as day. Guarded by a dozen vicious eunuchs. Good luck Miss Fancy Bangs.
I will give you another gold piece for your lice infested rags and miserable knock off sandals.
Deal.
In that window! Is it really Princess...

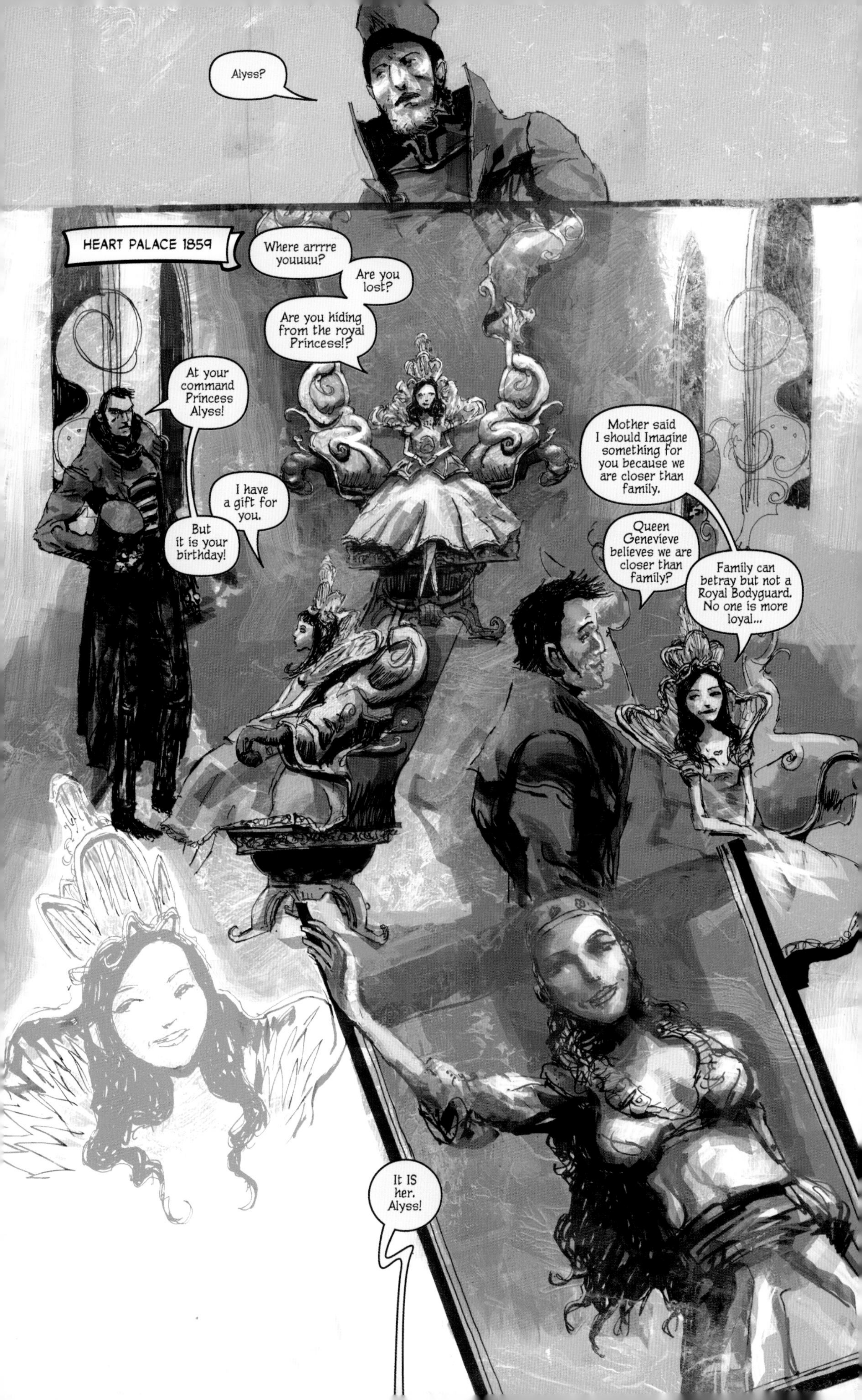
Alyss?
HEART PALACE 1859
Where arrrre youuuu?
Are you lost?
Are you hiding from the royal Princess!?
At your command Princess Alyss!
I have a gift for you.
But it is your birthday!
Mother said I should Imagine something for you because we are closer than family.
Queen Genevieve believes we are closer than family?
Family can betray but not a Royal Bodyguard. No one is more loyal...
It IS her. Alyss!

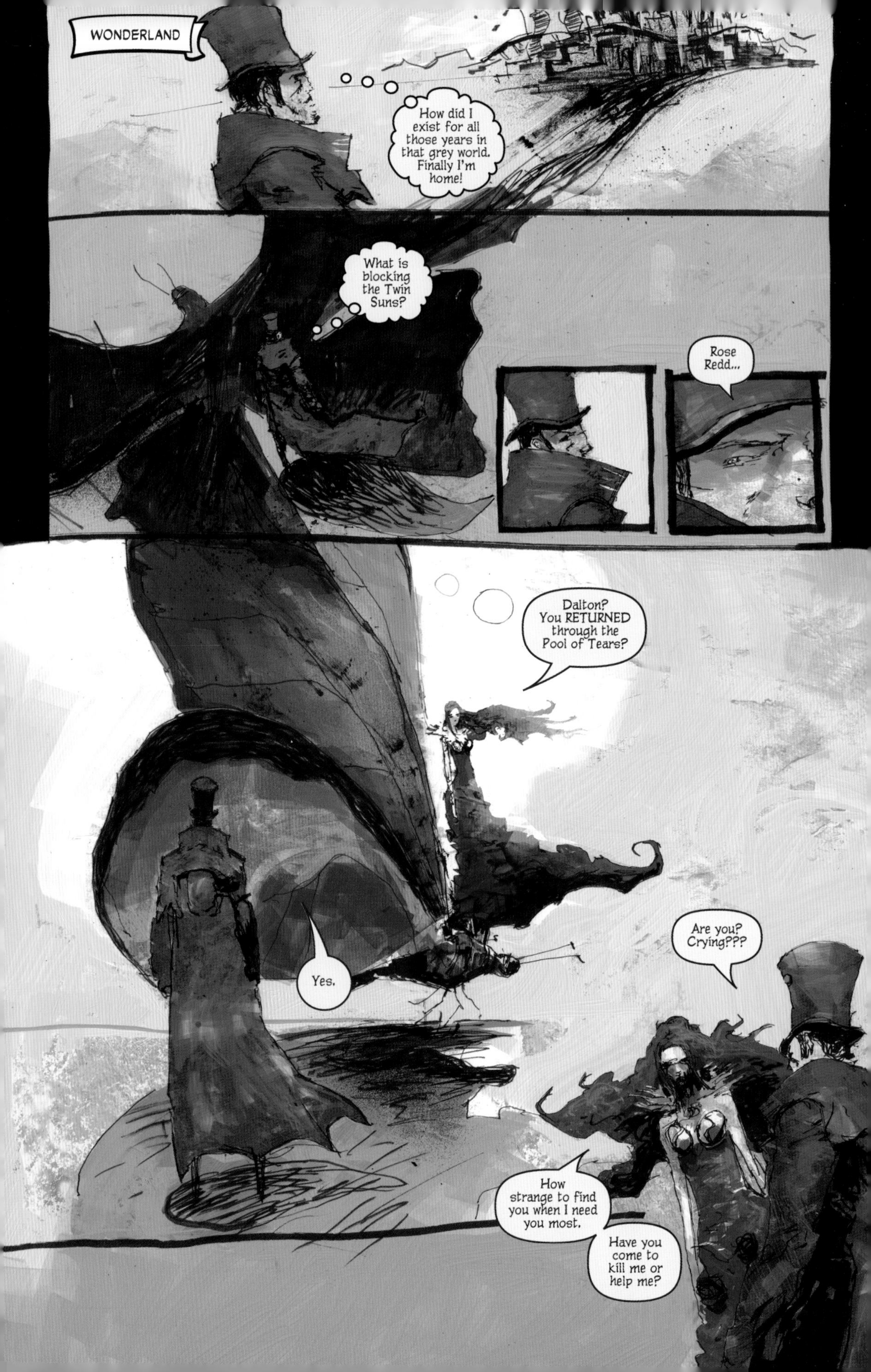
WONDERLAND
How did I exist for all those years in that grey world. Finally I'm home!
What is blocking the Twin Suns?
Rose Redd...
Dalton? You RETURNED through the Pool of Tears?
Yes.
Are you? Crying???
How strange to find you when I need you most.
Have you come to kill me or help me?

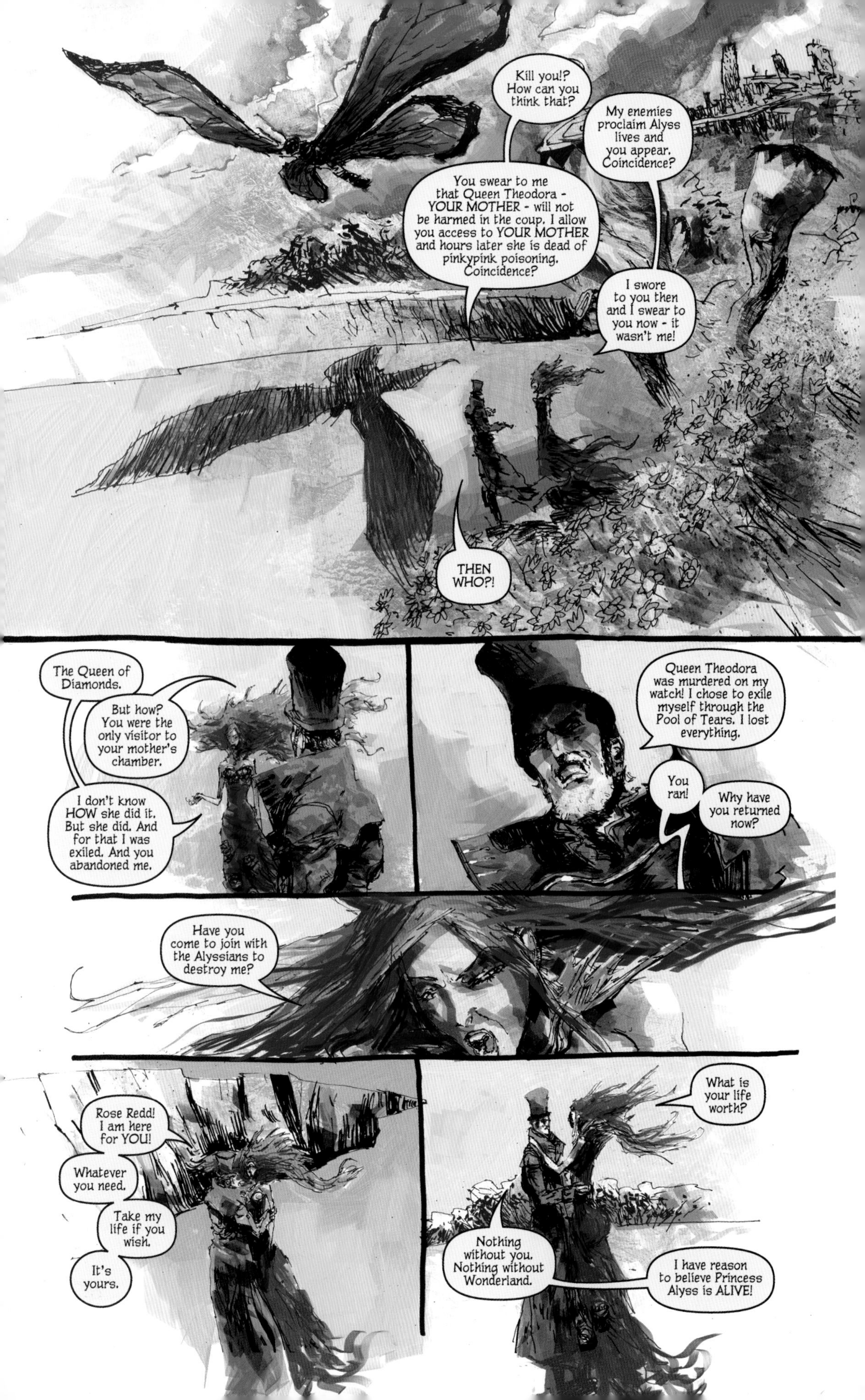
Kill you!? How can you think that?
My enemies proclaim Alyss lives and you appear. Coincidence?
You swear to me that Queen Theodora - YOUR MOTHER - will not be harmed in the coup. I allow you access to YOUR MOTHER and hours later she is dead of pinkypink poisoning. Coincidence?
I swore to you then and I swear to you now - it wasn't me!
THEN WHO?!
The Queen of Diamonds.
But how? You were the only visitor to your mother's chamber.
I don't know HOW she did it. But she did. And for that I was exiled. And you abandoned me.
Queen Theodora was murdered on my watch! I chose to exile myself through the Pool of Tears. I lost everything.
You ran!
Why have you returned now?
Have you come to join with the Alyssians to destroy me?
Rose Redd! I am here for YOU!
Whatever you need.
Take my life if you wish.
It's yours.
What is your life worth?
Nothing without you. Nothing without Wonderland.
I have reason to believe Princess Alyss is ALIVE!

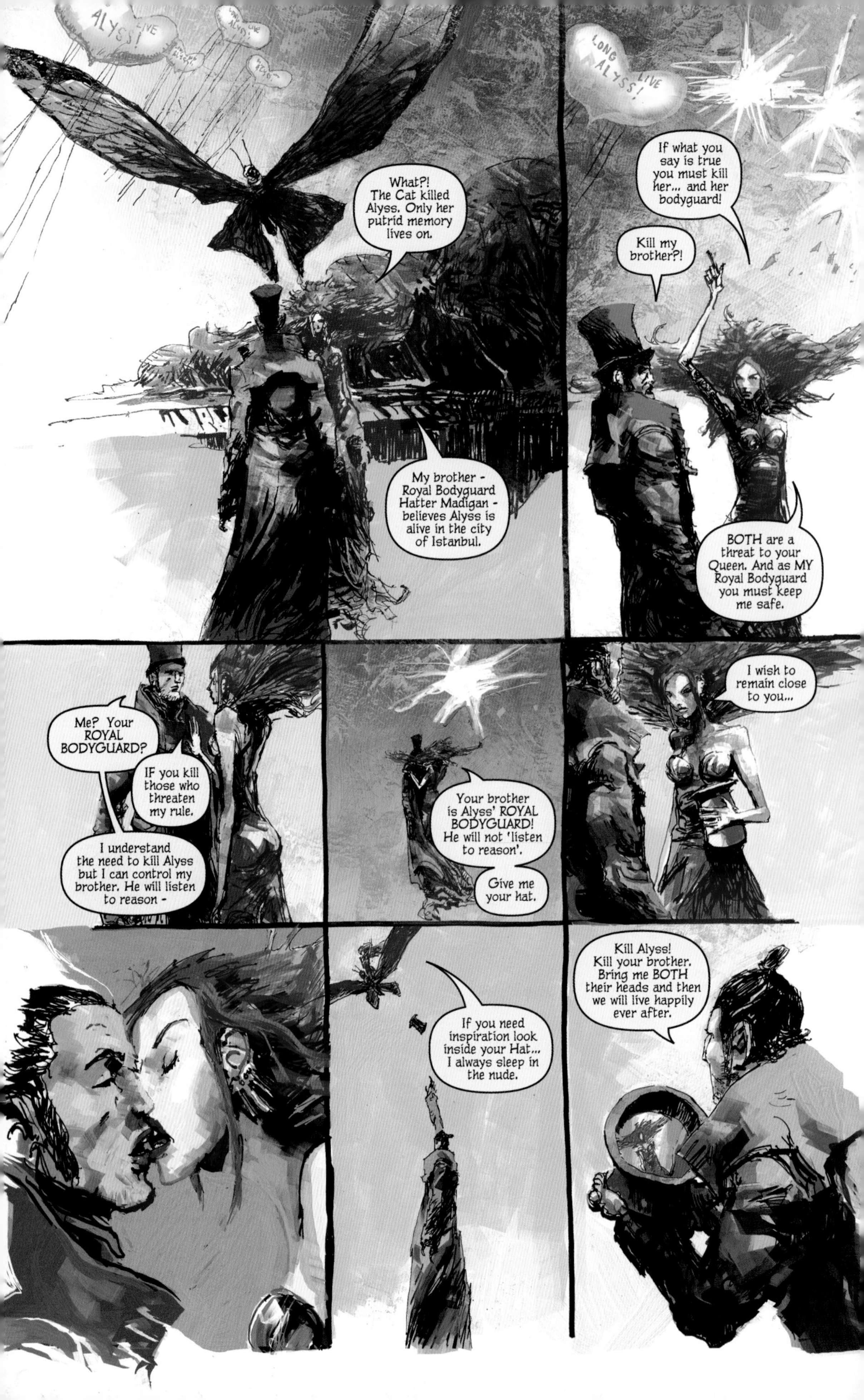

LONG LIVE ALYSS!
What?! The Cat killed Alyss. Only her putrid memory lives on.
My brother - Royal Bodyguard Hatter Madigan - believes Alyss is alive in the city of Istanbul.
LONG LIVE ALYSS!
If what you say is true you must kill her... and her bodyguard!
Kill my brother?!
BOTH are a threat to your Queen. And as MY Royal Bodyguard you must keep me safe.
Me? Your ROYAL BODYGUARD?
IF you kill those who threaten my rule.
I understand the need to kill Alyss but I can control my brother. He will listen to reason -
Your brother is Alyss' ROYAL BODYGUARD! He will not 'listen to reason'.
Give me your hat.
I wish to remain close to you...
If you need inspiration look inside your Hat... I always sleep in the nude.
Kill Alyss! Kill your brother. Bring me BOTH their heads and then we will live happily ever after.

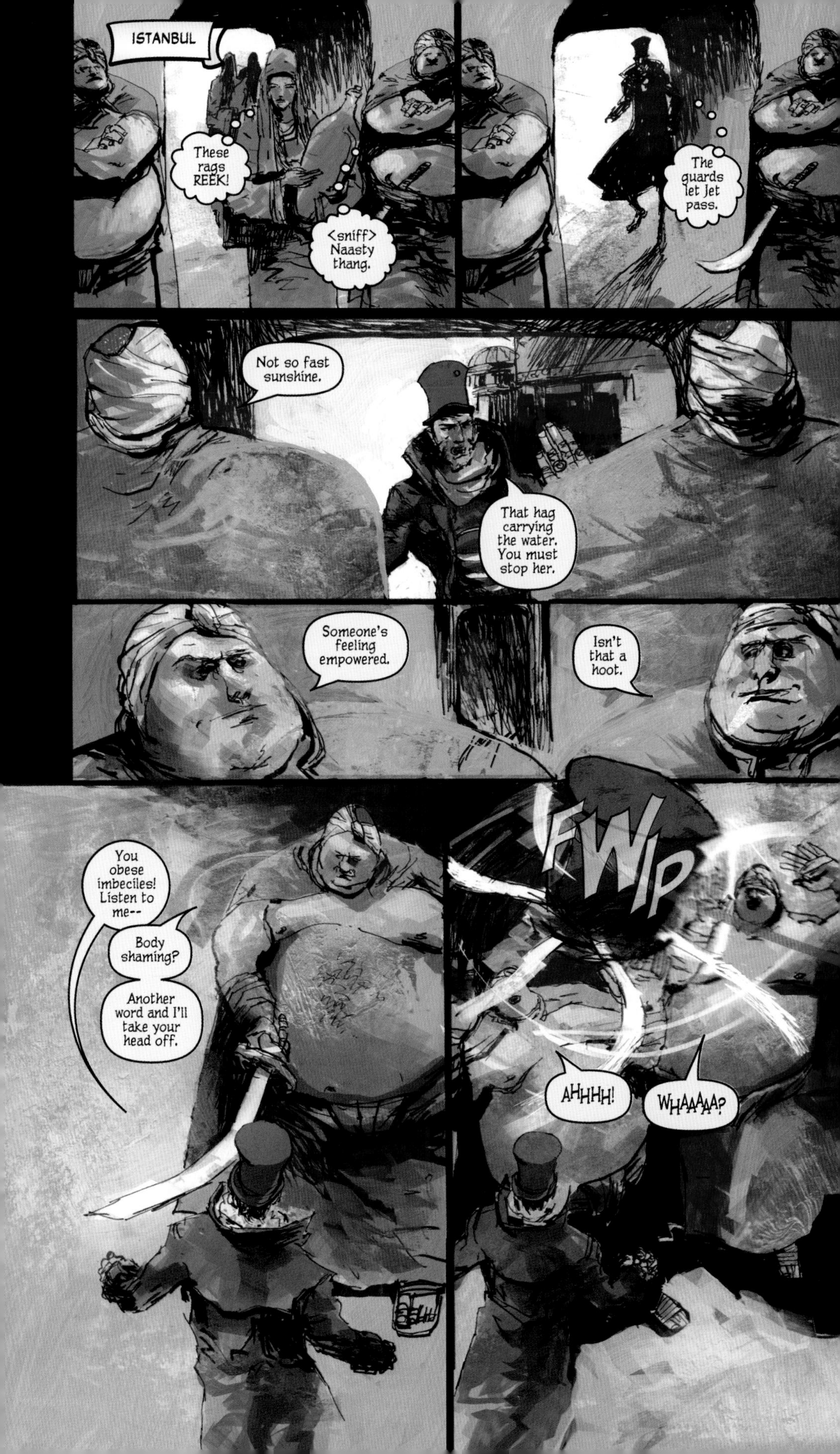
ISTANBUL
These rags REEK!
<sniff> Naasty thang.
The guards let Jet pass.
Not so fast sunshine.
That hag carrying the water. You must stop her.
Someone's feeling empowered.
Isn't that a hoot.
You obese imbeciles! Listen to me--
Body shaming?
Another word and I'll take your head off.
FWIP
AHHHH!
WHAAAAA?

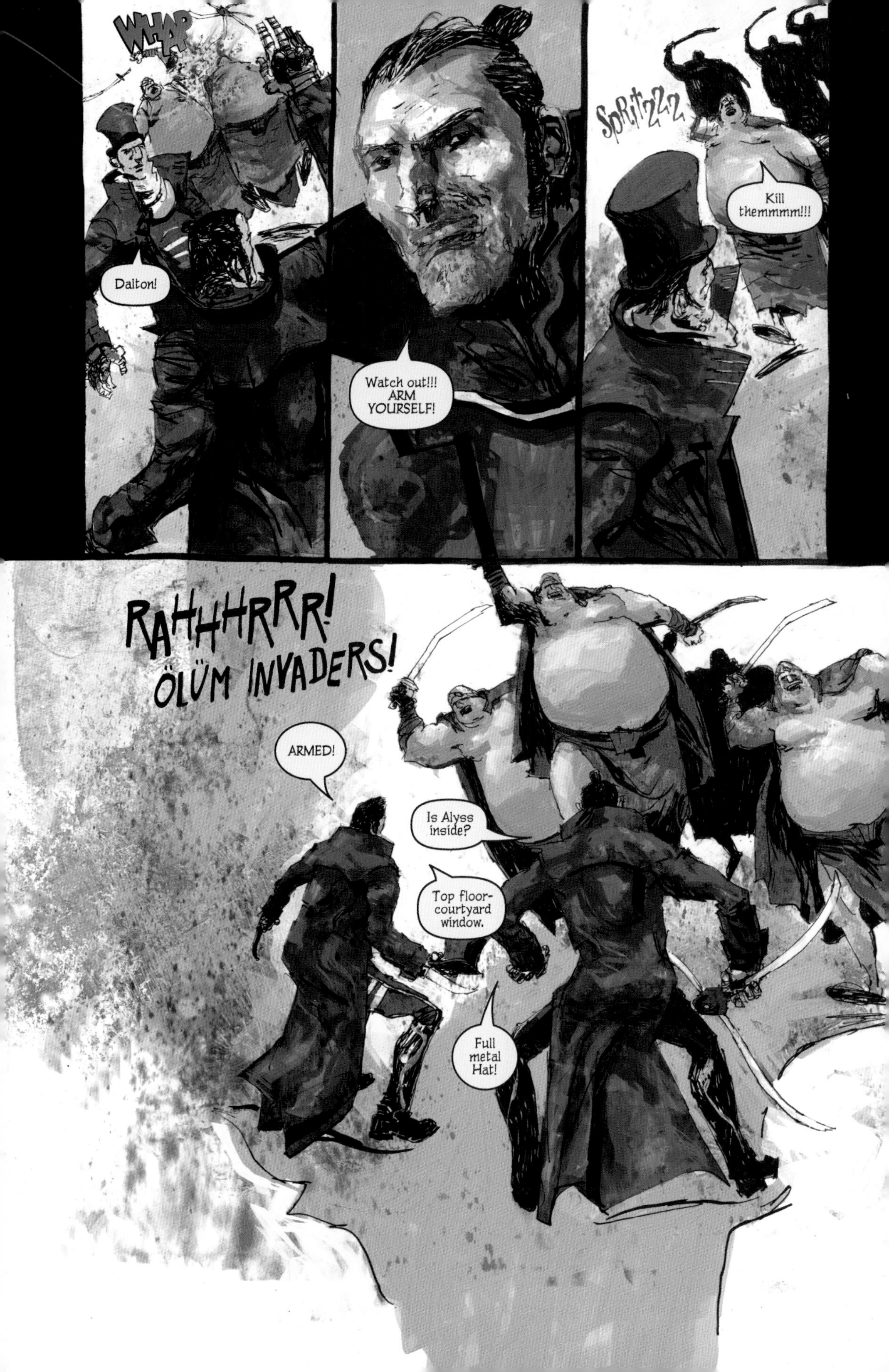
WHAP
Dalton!
Watch out!!! ARM YOURSELF!
SPRITZZZ
Kill themmmm!!!
RAHHHRRR! ÖLÜM INVADERS!
ARMED!
Is Alyss inside?
Top floor-courtyard window.
Full metal Hat!

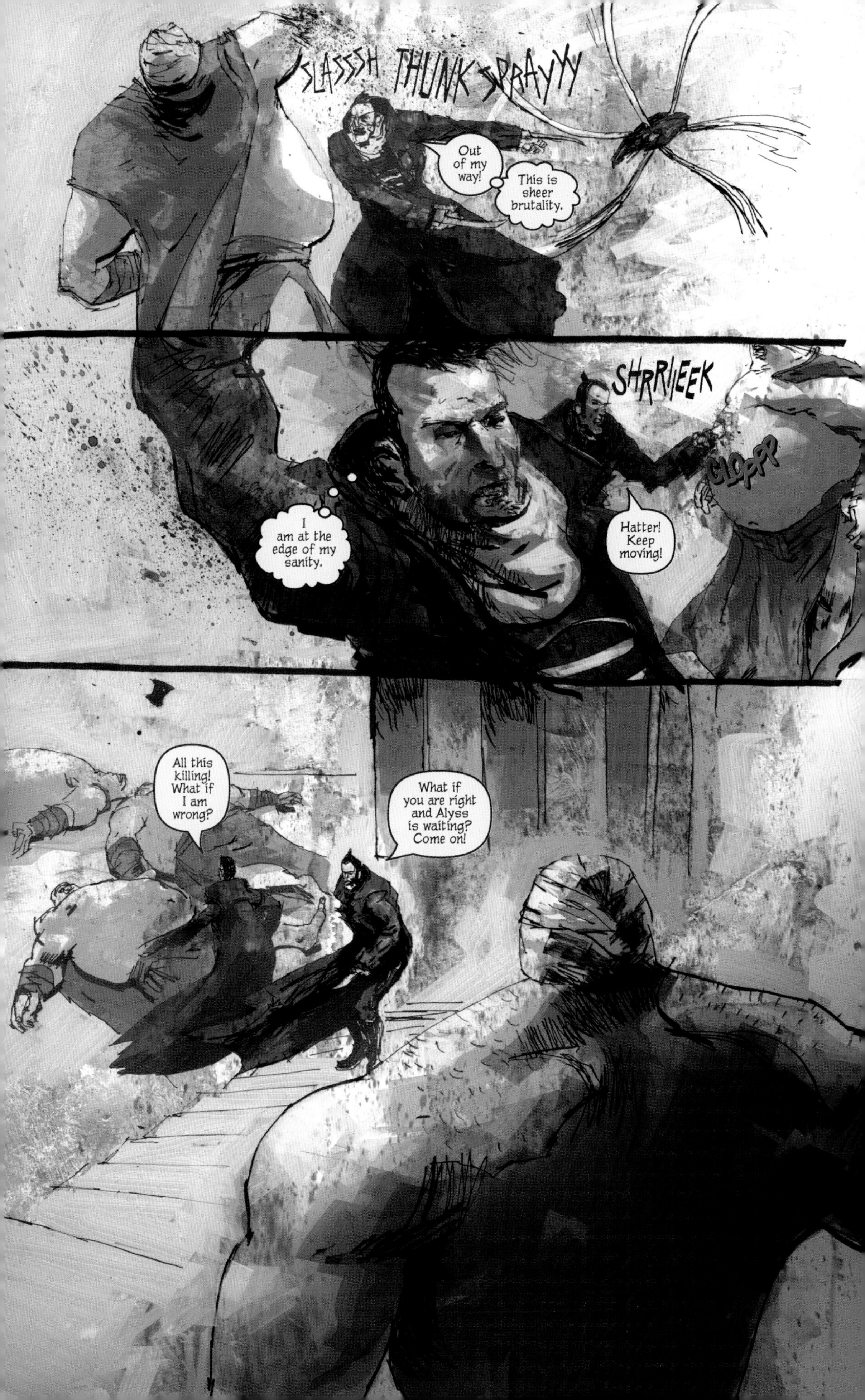
SLASSSH
THUNK
SPRAYYY
Out of my way!
This is sheer brutality.
SHRRIIEEK
GLOPPP
I am at the edge of my sanity.
Hatter! Keep moving!
All this killing! What if I am wrong?
What if you are right and Alyss is waiting? Come on!

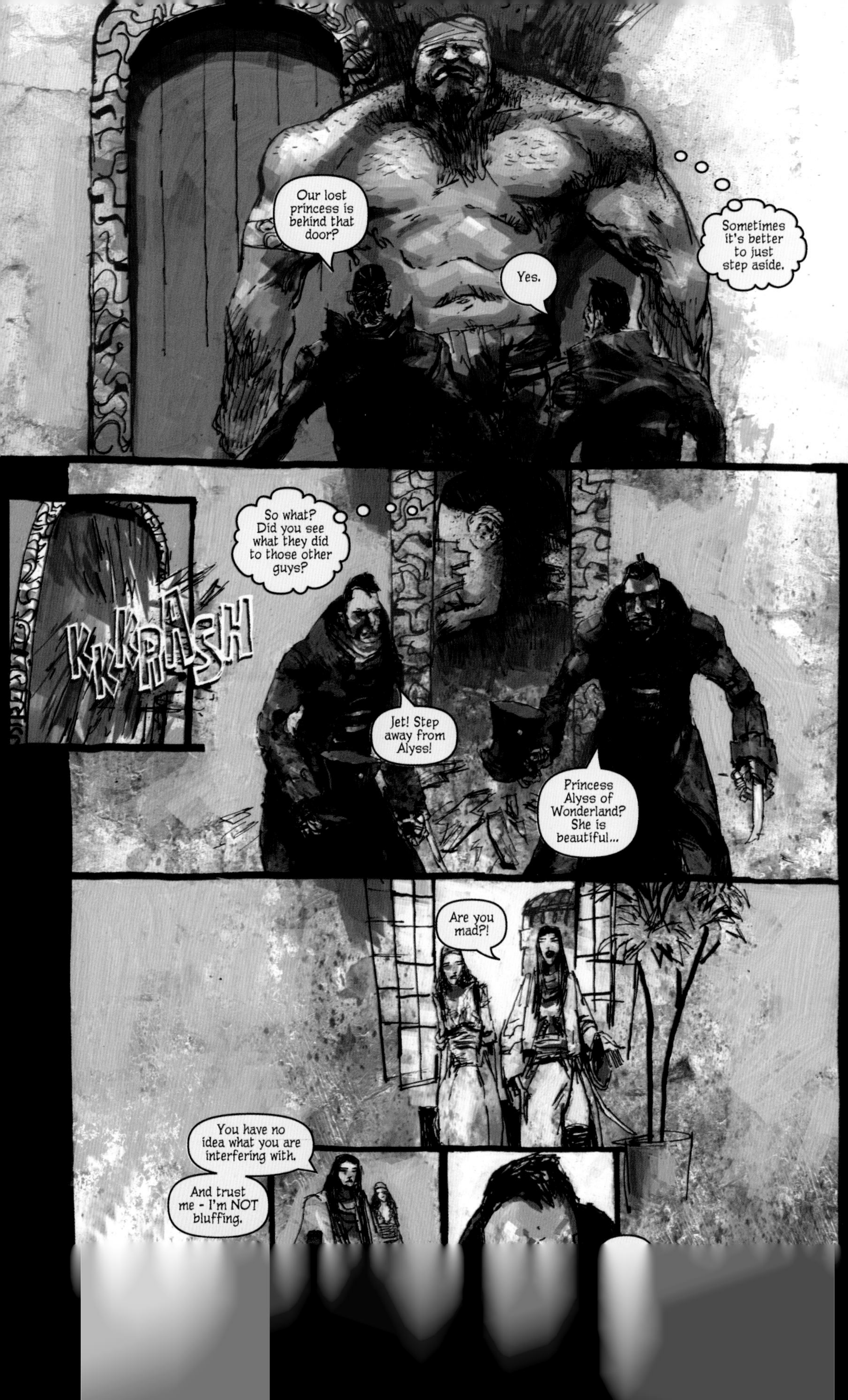
Our lost princess is behind that door?
Yes.
Sometimes it's better to just step aside.
So what? Did you see what they did to those other guys?
KKRASH
Jet! Step away from Alyss!
Princess Alyss of Wonderland? She is beautiful...
Are you mad?!
You have no idea what you are interfering with.
And trust me - I'm NOT bluffing.

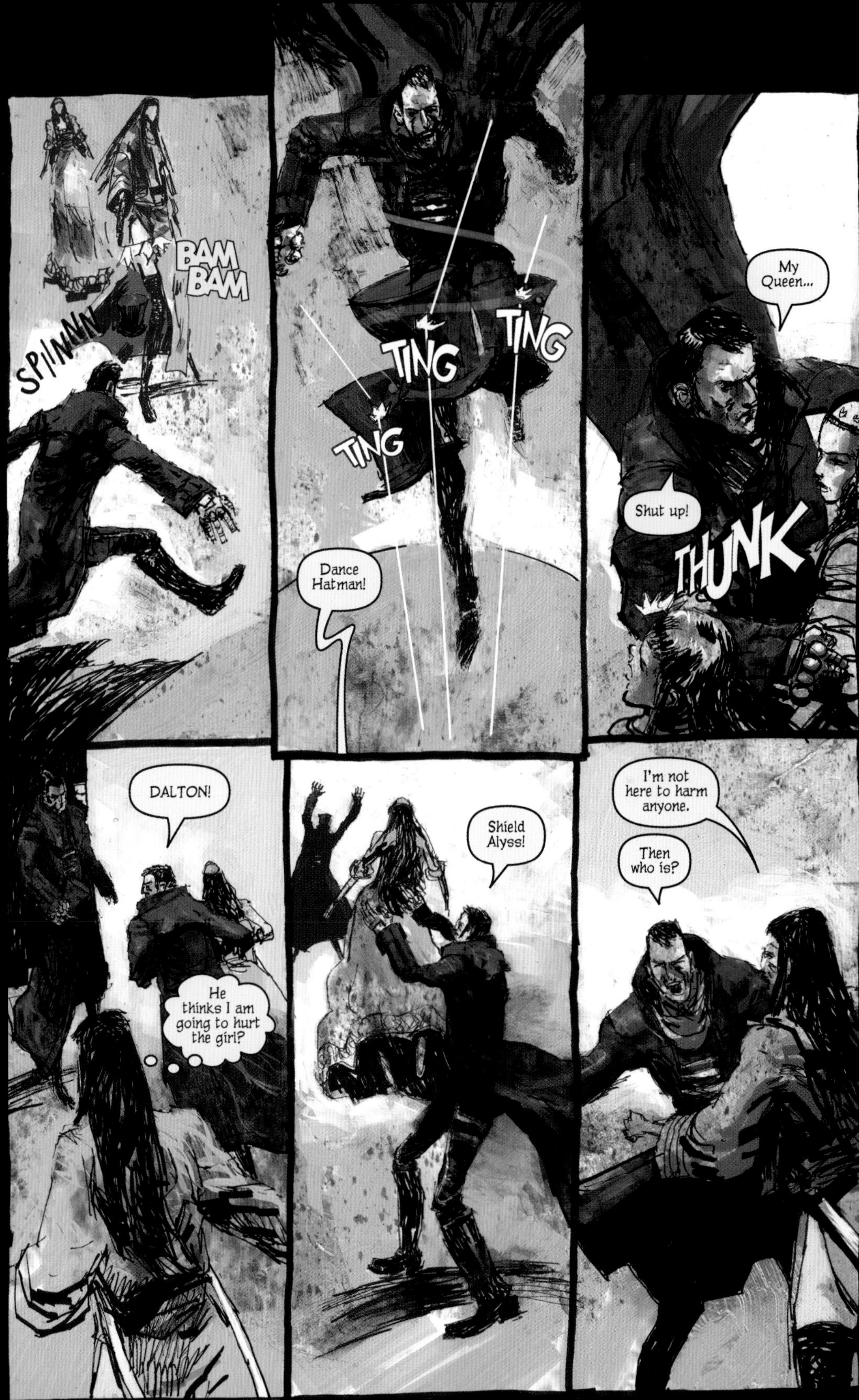
BAM BAM
SPINNN
TING
TING
TING
Dance Hatman!
My Queen...
Shut up!
THUNK
DALTON!
He thinks I am going to hurt the girl?
Shield Alyss!
I'm not here to harm anyone.
Then who is?

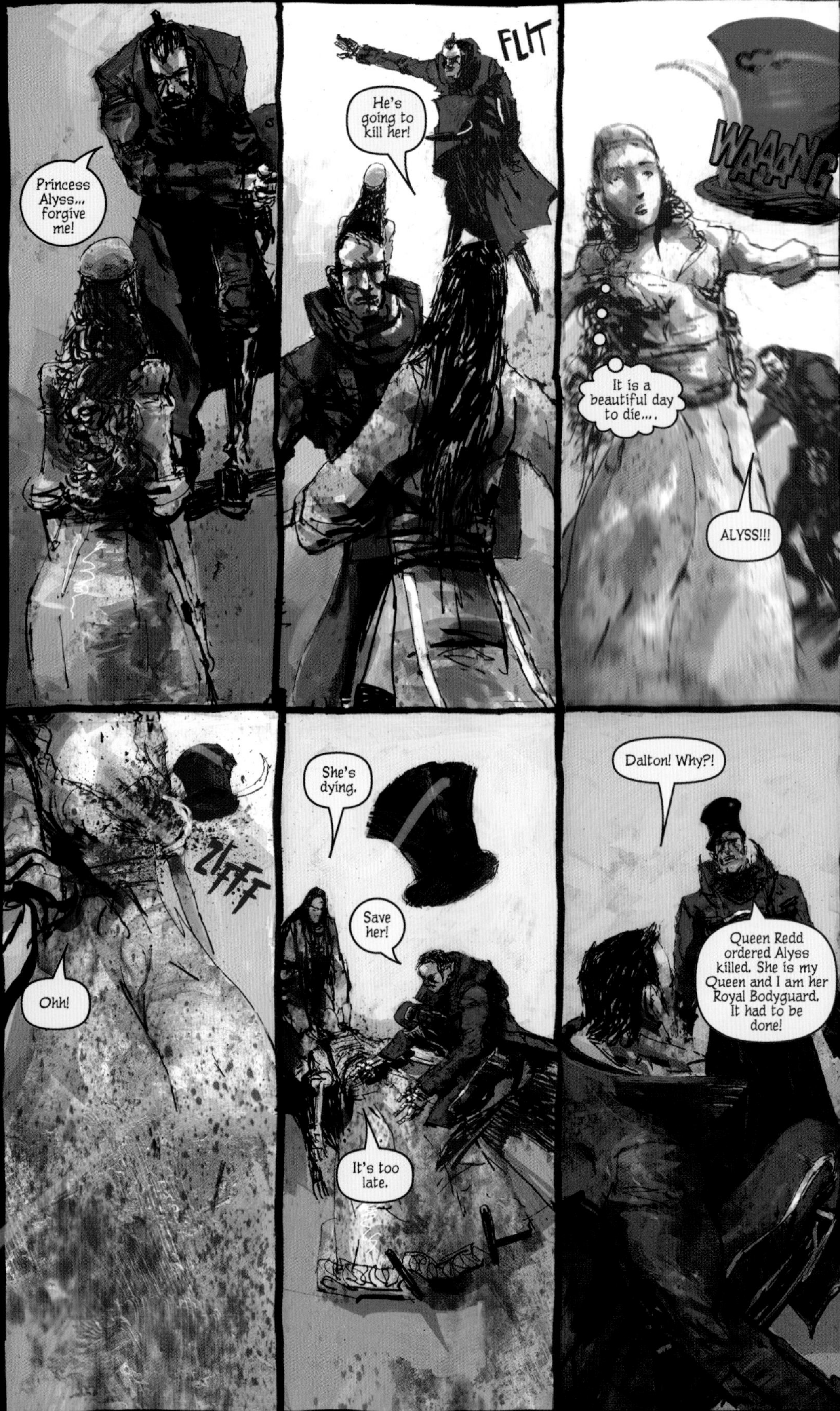
Princess Alyss... forgive me!
FLIT
He's going to kill her!
WAAANG
It is a beautiful day to die....
ALYSS!!!
ZIFFF
Ohh!
She's dying.
Save her!
It's too late.
Dalton! Why?!
Queen Redd ordered Alyss killed. She is my Queen and I am her Royal Bodyguard. It had to be done!

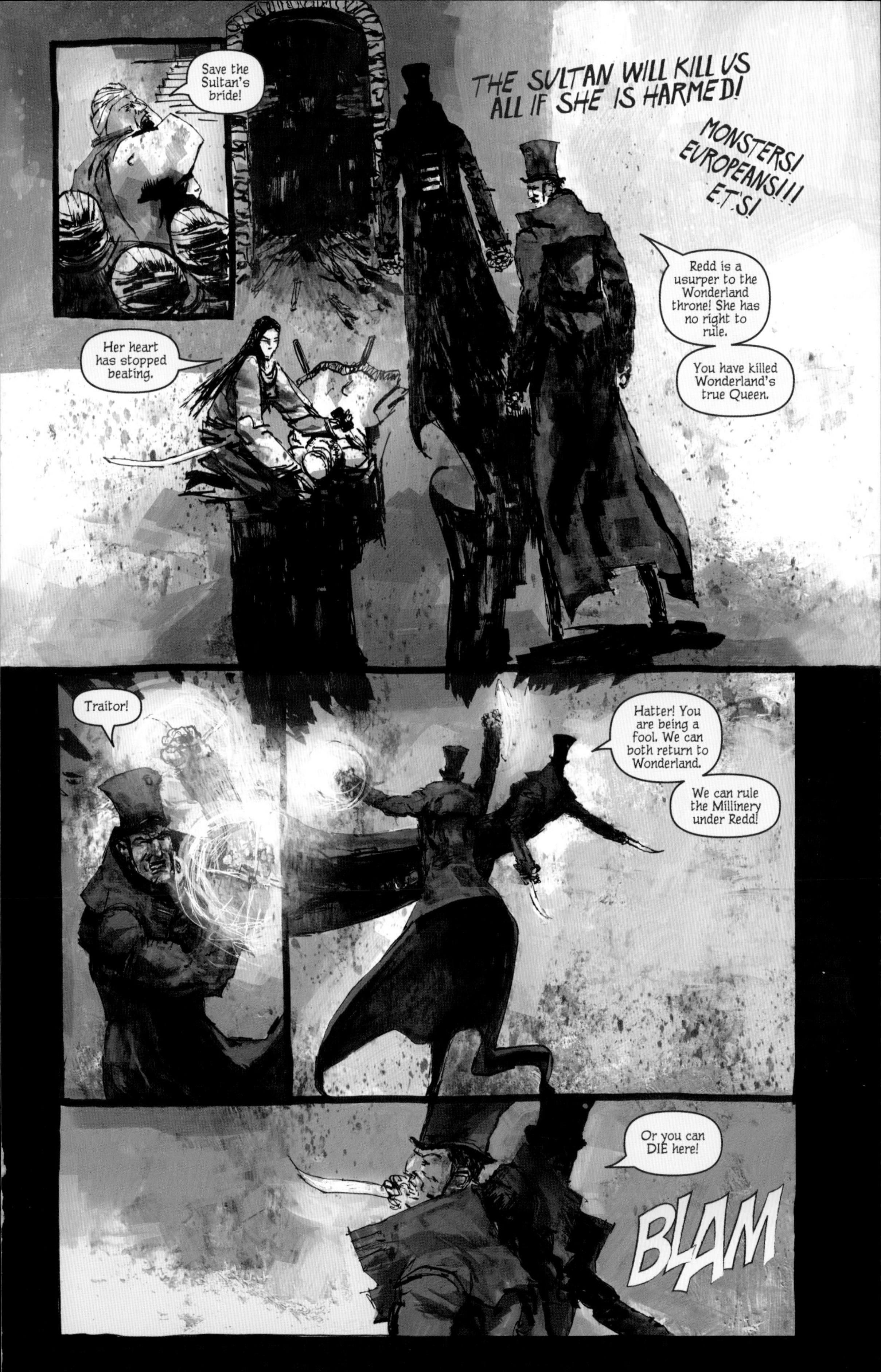
Save the Sultan's bride!
THE SULTAN WILL KILL US ALL IF SHE IS HARMED!
MONSTERS! EUROPEANS!!! E.T.'S!
Redd is a usurper to the Wonderland throne! She has no right to rule.
You have killed Wonderland's true Queen.
Her heart has stopped beating.
Traitor!
Hatter! You are being a fool. We can both return to Wonderland.
We can rule the Millinery under Redd!
Or you can DIE here!
BLAM

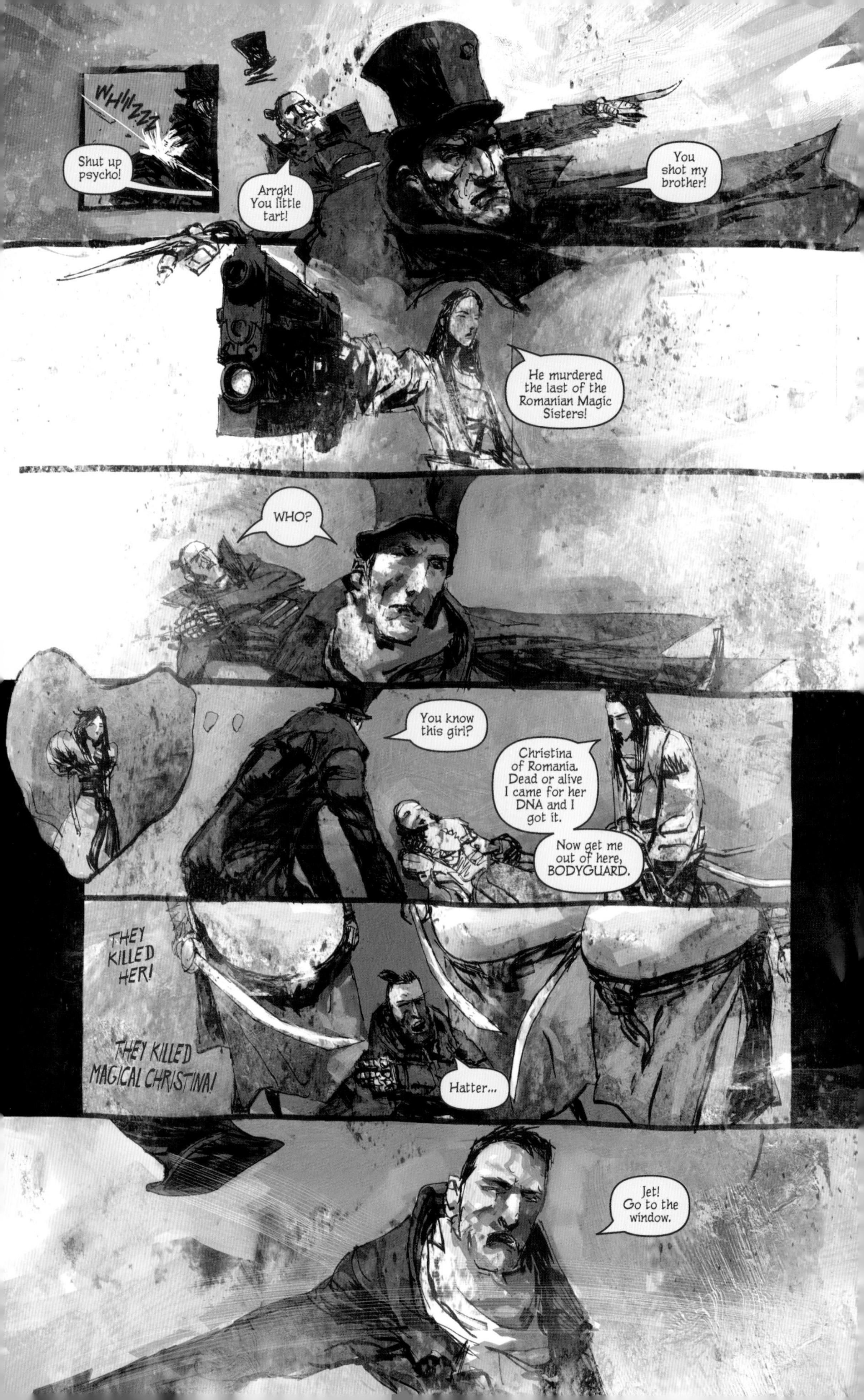
WHIIIZZZ
Shut up psycho!
Arrgh! You little tart!
You shot my brother!
He murdered the last of the Romanian Magic Sisters!
WHO?
You know this girl?
Christina of Romania. Dead or alive I came for her DNA and I got it.
Now get me out of here, BODYGUARD.
THEY KILLED HER!
THEY KILLED MAGICAL CHRISTINA!
Hatter...
Jet! Go to the window.

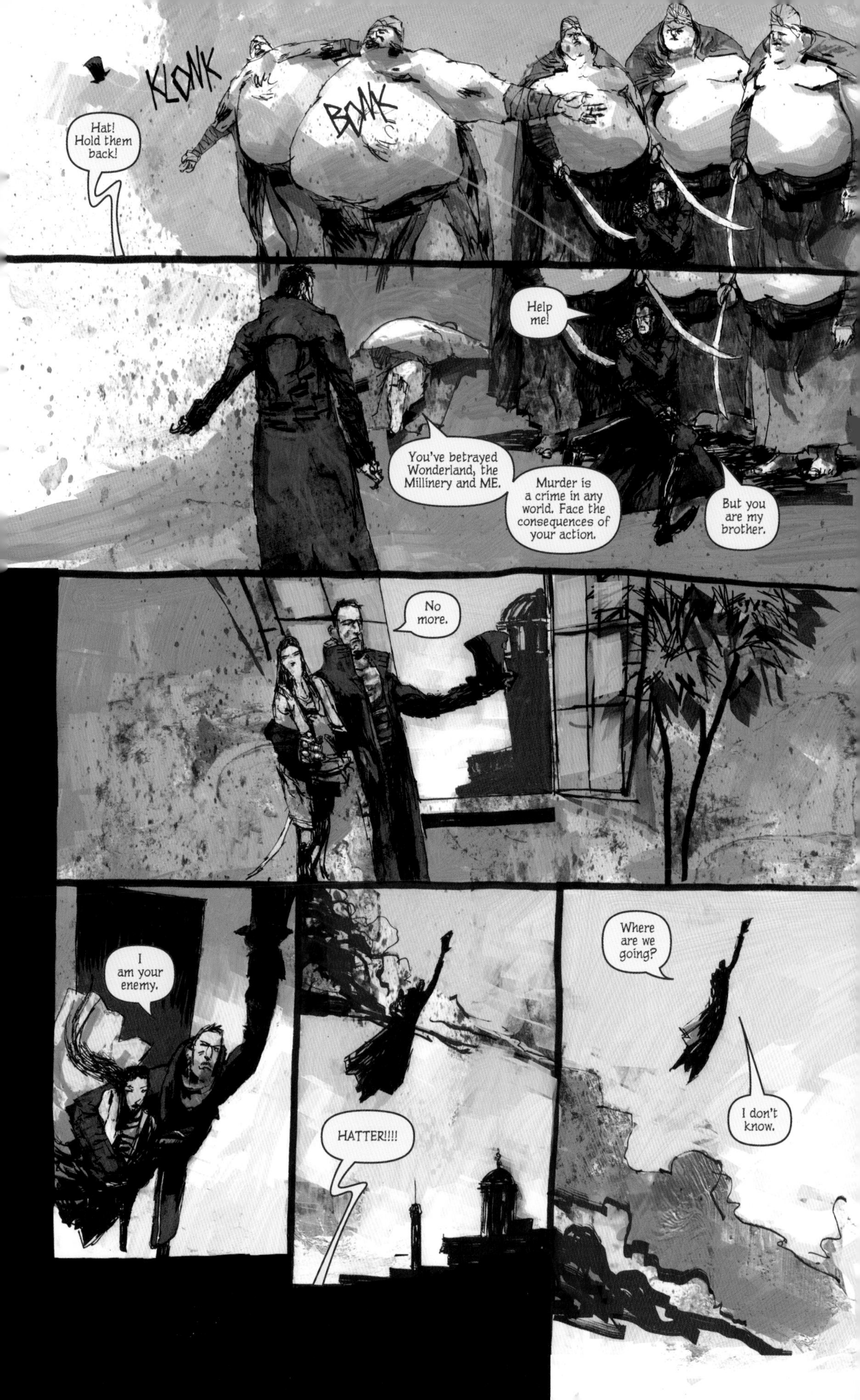
KLONK
BONK
Hat! Hold them back!
Help me!
You've betrayed Wonderland, the Millinery and ME.
Murder is a crime in any world. Face the consequences of your action.
But you are my brother.
No more.
I am your enemy.
HATTER!!!!
Where are we going?
I don't know.

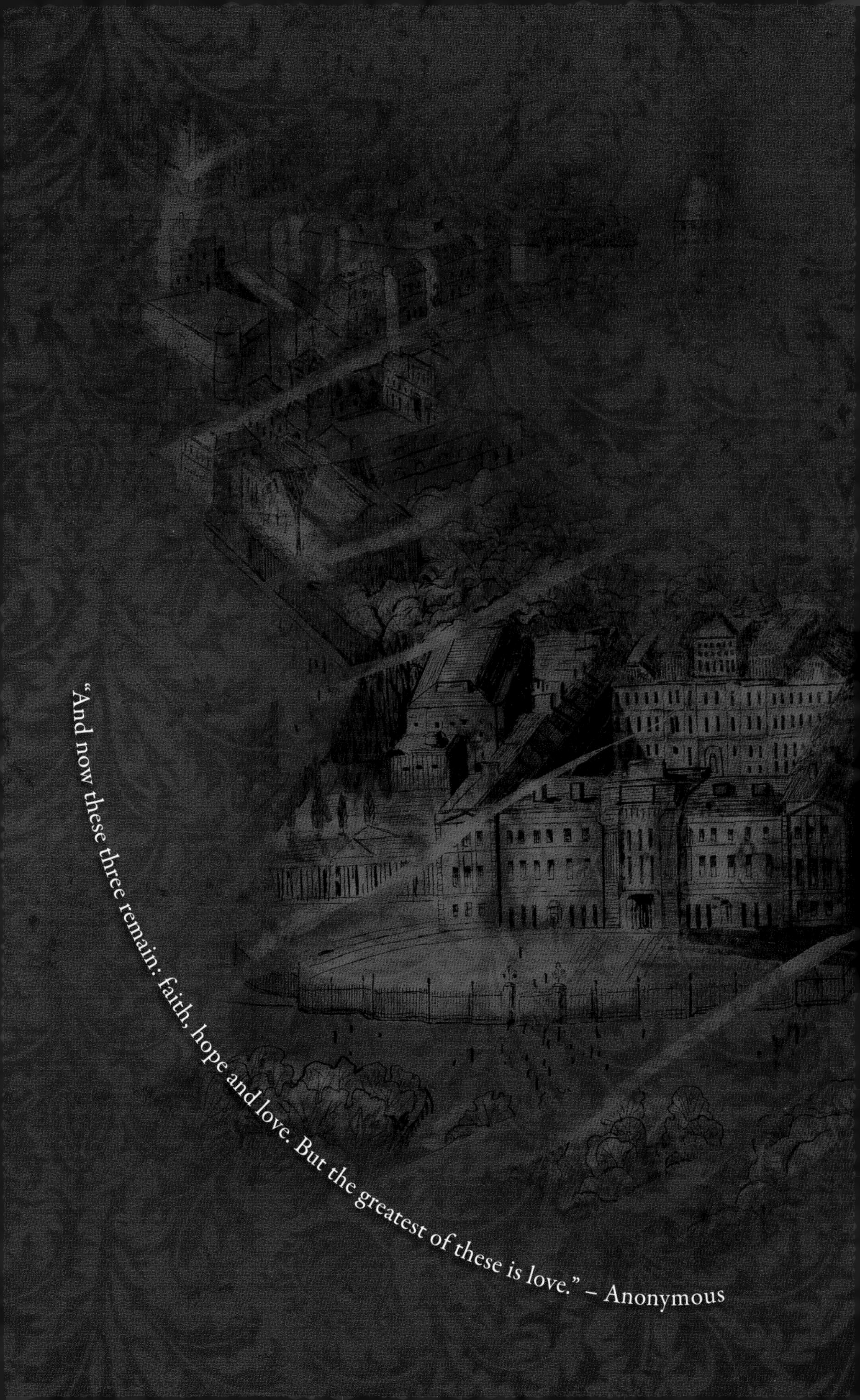

"And now these three remain: faith, hope and love. But the greatest of these is love." – Anonymous

"Nobody has ever measured, not even poets, how much the heart can hold." – Zelda Fitzgerald

Part 2
The 11th Hour

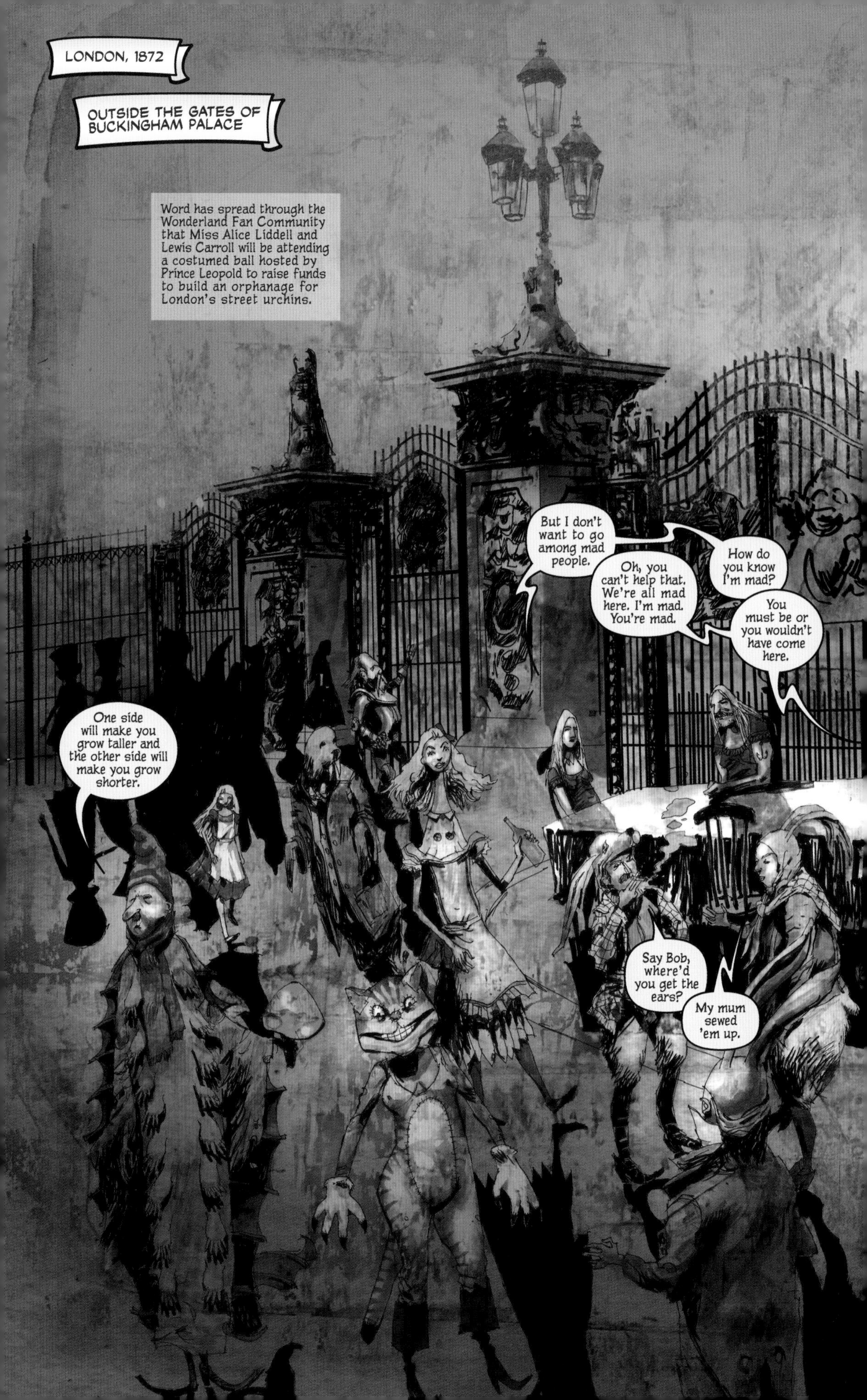
LONDON, 1872
OUTSIDE THE GATES OF BUCKINGHAM PALACE
Word has spread through the Wonderland Fan Community that Miss Alice Liddell and Lewis Carroll will be attending a costumed ball hosted by Prince Leopold to raise funds to build an orphanage for London's street urchins.
But I don't want to go among mad people.
Oh, you can't help that. We're all mad here. I'm mad. You're mad.
How do you know I'm mad?
You must be or you wouldn't have come here.
One side will make you grow taller and the other side will make you grow shorter.
Say Bob, where'd you get the ears?
My mum sewed 'em up.

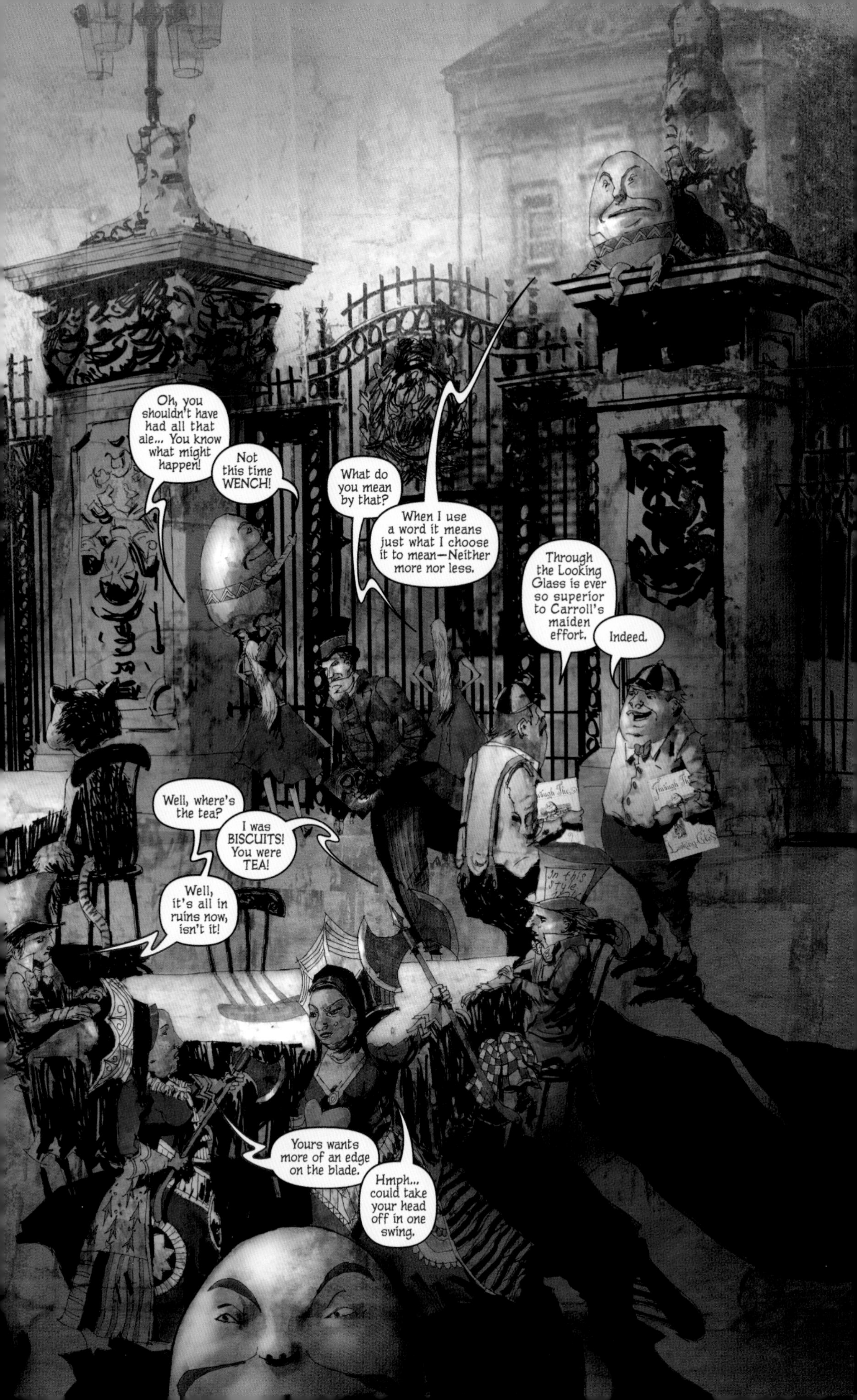
Oh, you shouldn't have had all that ale... You know what might happen!
Not this time WENCH!
What do you mean by that?
When I use a word it means just what I choose it to mean—Neither more nor less.
Through the Looking Glass is ever so superior to Carroll's maiden effort.
Indeed.
Well, where's the tea?
I was BISCUITS! You were TEA!
Well, it's all in ruins now, isn't it!
Yours wants more of an edge on the blade.
Hmph... could take your head off in one swing.

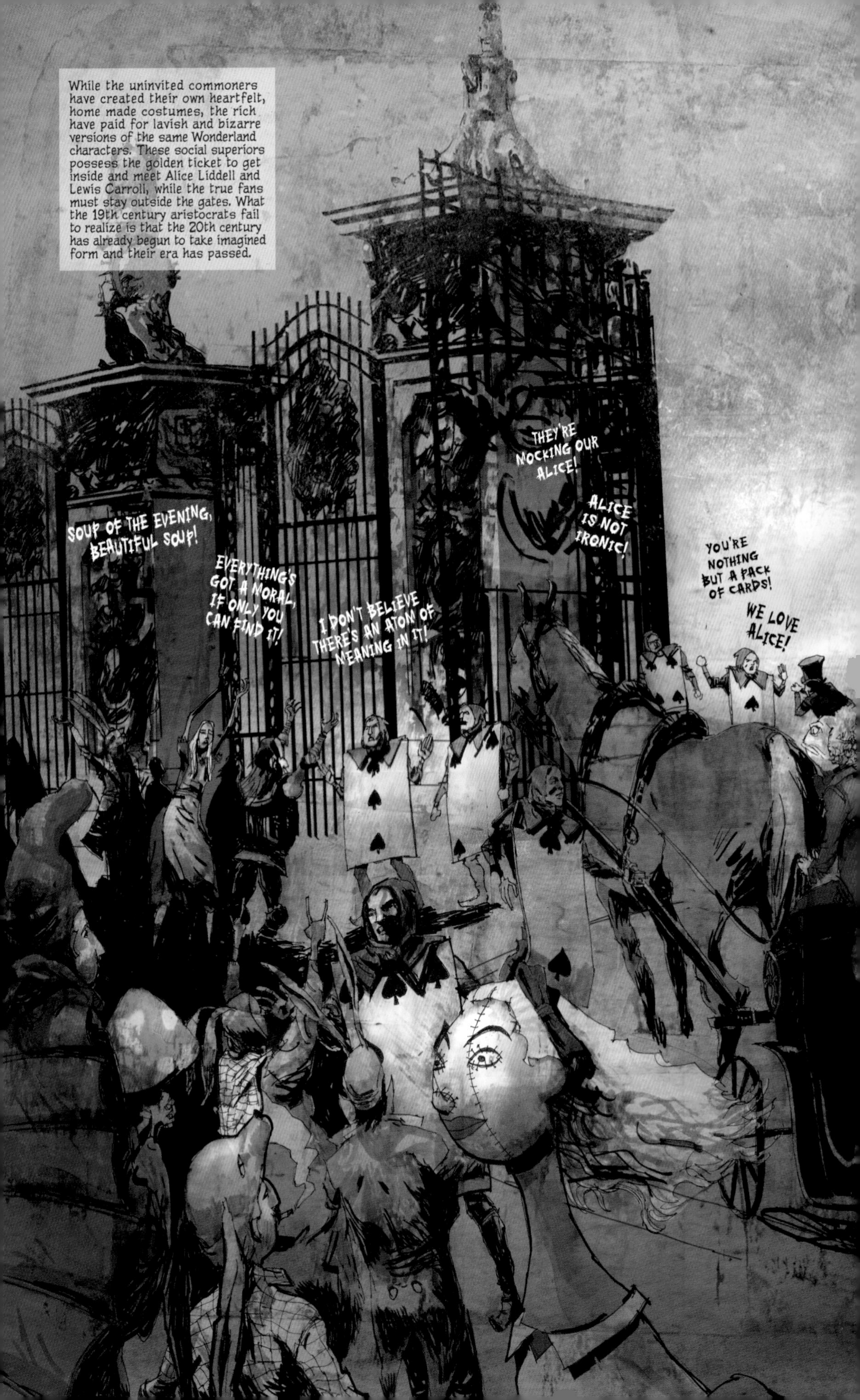
While the uninvited commoners have created their own heartfelt, home made costumes, the rich have paid for lavish and bizarre versions of the same Wonderland characters. These social superiors possess the golden ticket to get inside and meet Alice Liddell and Lewis Carroll, while the true fans must stay outside the gates. What the 19th century aristocrats fail to realize is that the 20th century has already begun to take imagined form and their era has passed.
SOUP OF THE EVENING, BEAUTIFUL SOUP!
EVERYTHING'S GOT A MORAL, IF ONLY YOU CAN FIND IT!
I DON'T BELIEVE THERE'S AN ATOM OF MEANING IN IT!
THEY'RE MOCKING OUR ALICE!
ALICE IS NOT IRONIC!
YOU'RE NOTHING BUT A PACK OF CARDS!
WE LOVE ALICE!

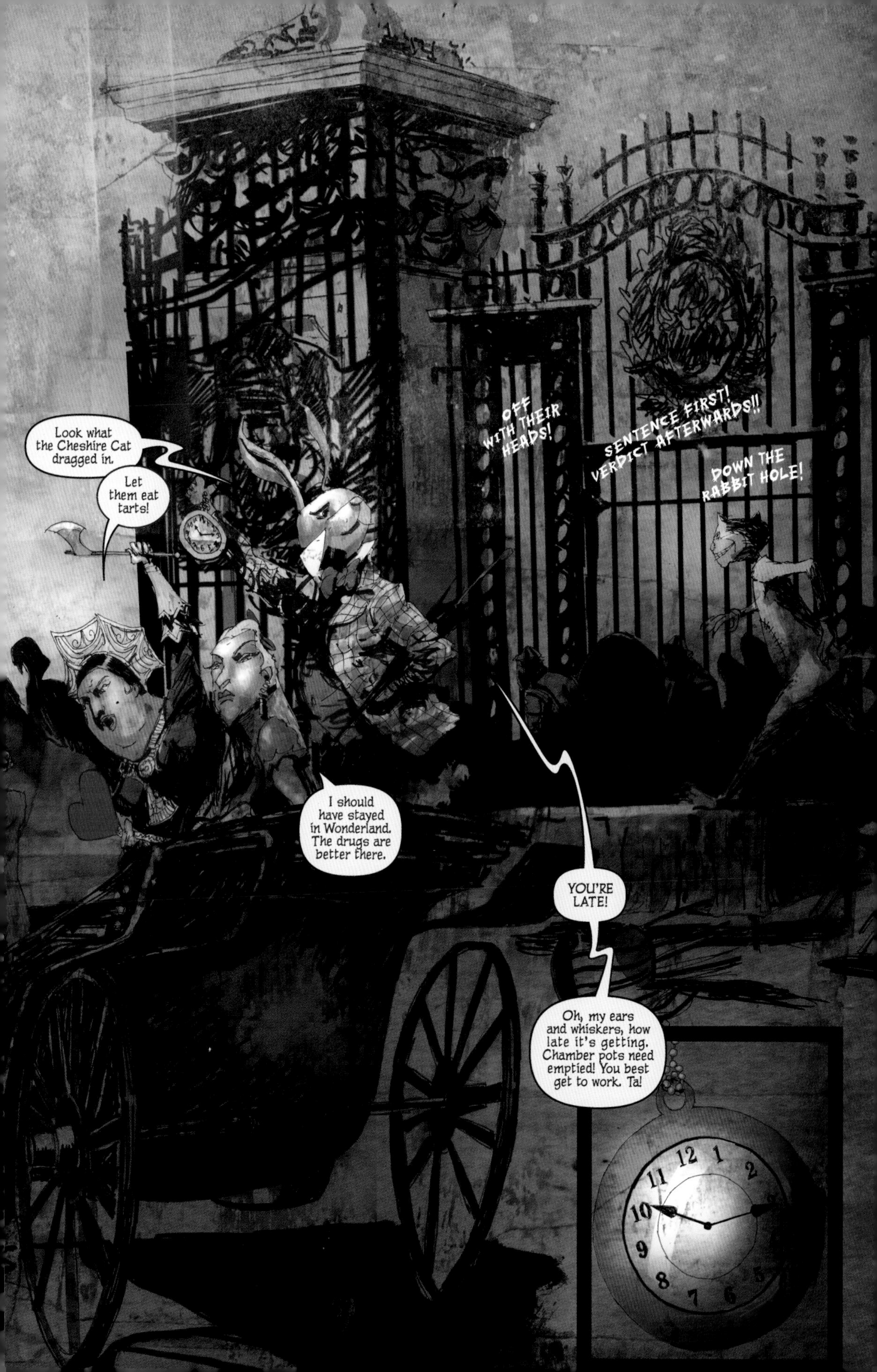
Look what the Cheshire Cat dragged in.
Let them eat tarts!
OFF WITH THEIR HEADS!
SENTENCE FIRST! VERDICT AFTERWARDS!!
DOWN THE RABBIT HOLE!
I should have stayed in Wonderland. The drugs are better there.
YOU'RE LATE!
Oh, my ears and whiskers, how late it's getting. Chamber pots need emptied! You best get to work. Ta!

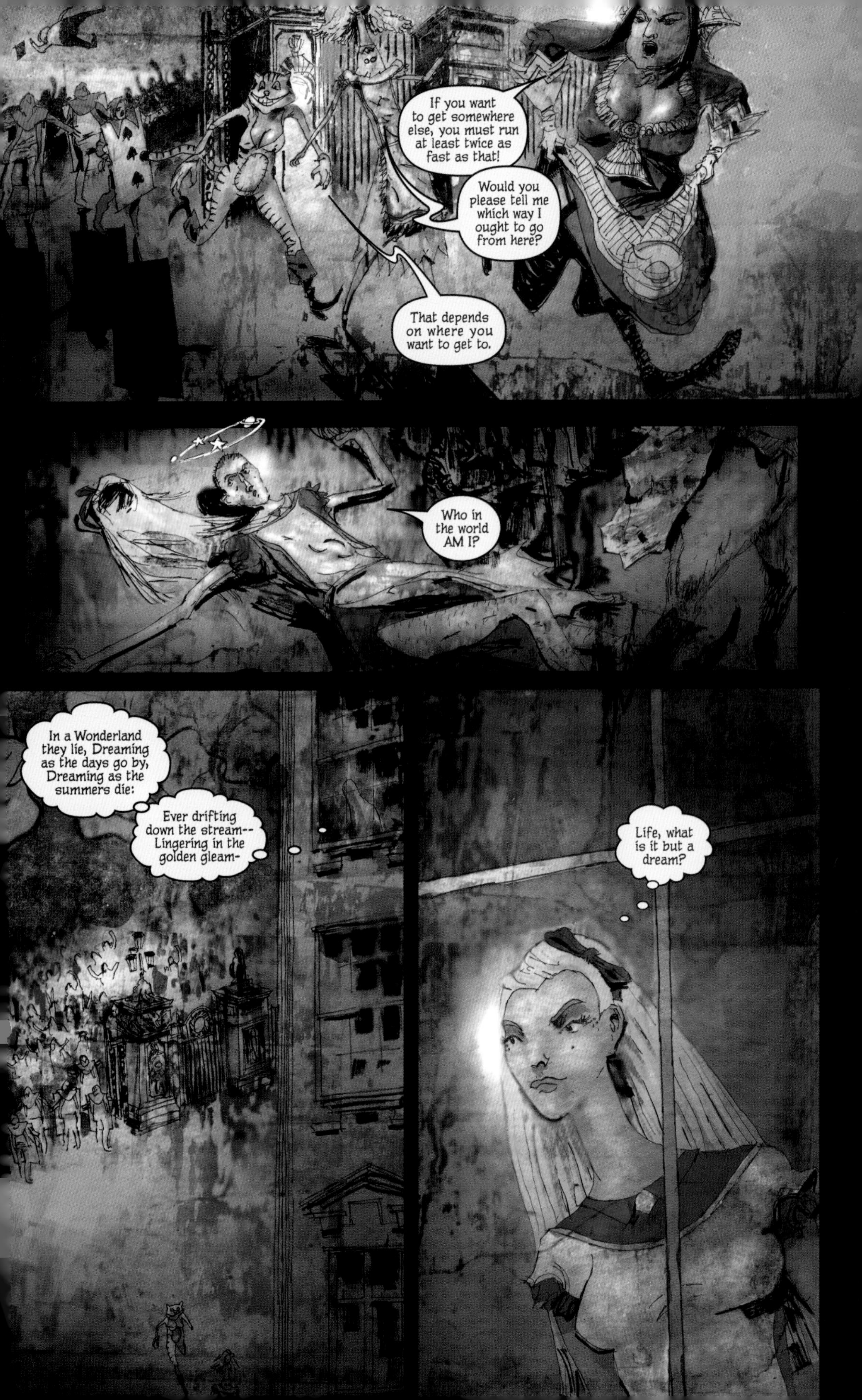
If you want to get somewhere else, you must run at least twice as fast as that!
Would you please tell me which way I ought to go from here?
That depends on where you want to get to.
Who in the world AM I?
In a Wonderland they lie, Dreaming as the days go by, Dreaming as the summers die:
Ever drifting down the stream--Lingering in the golden gleam-
Life, what is it but a dream?

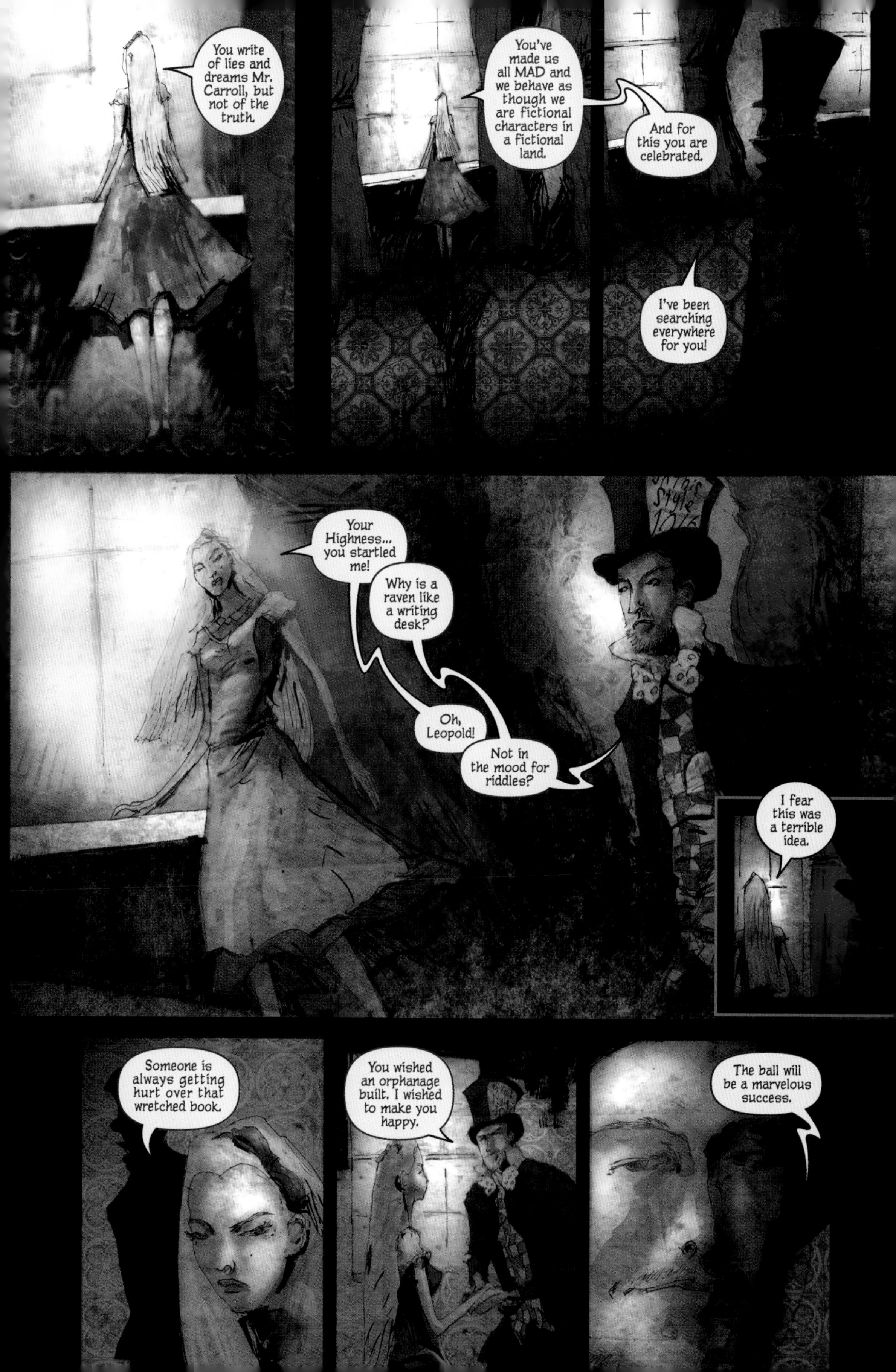
You write of lies and dreams Mr. Carroll, but not of the truth.
You've made us all MAD and we behave as though we are fictional characters in a fictional land.
And for this you are celebrated.
I've been searching everywhere for you!
Your Highness... you startled me!
Why is a raven like a writing desk?
Oh, Leopold!
Not in the mood for riddles?
I fear this was a terrible idea.
Someone is always getting hurt over that wretched book.
You wished an orphanage built. I wished to make you happy.
The ball will be a marvelous success.

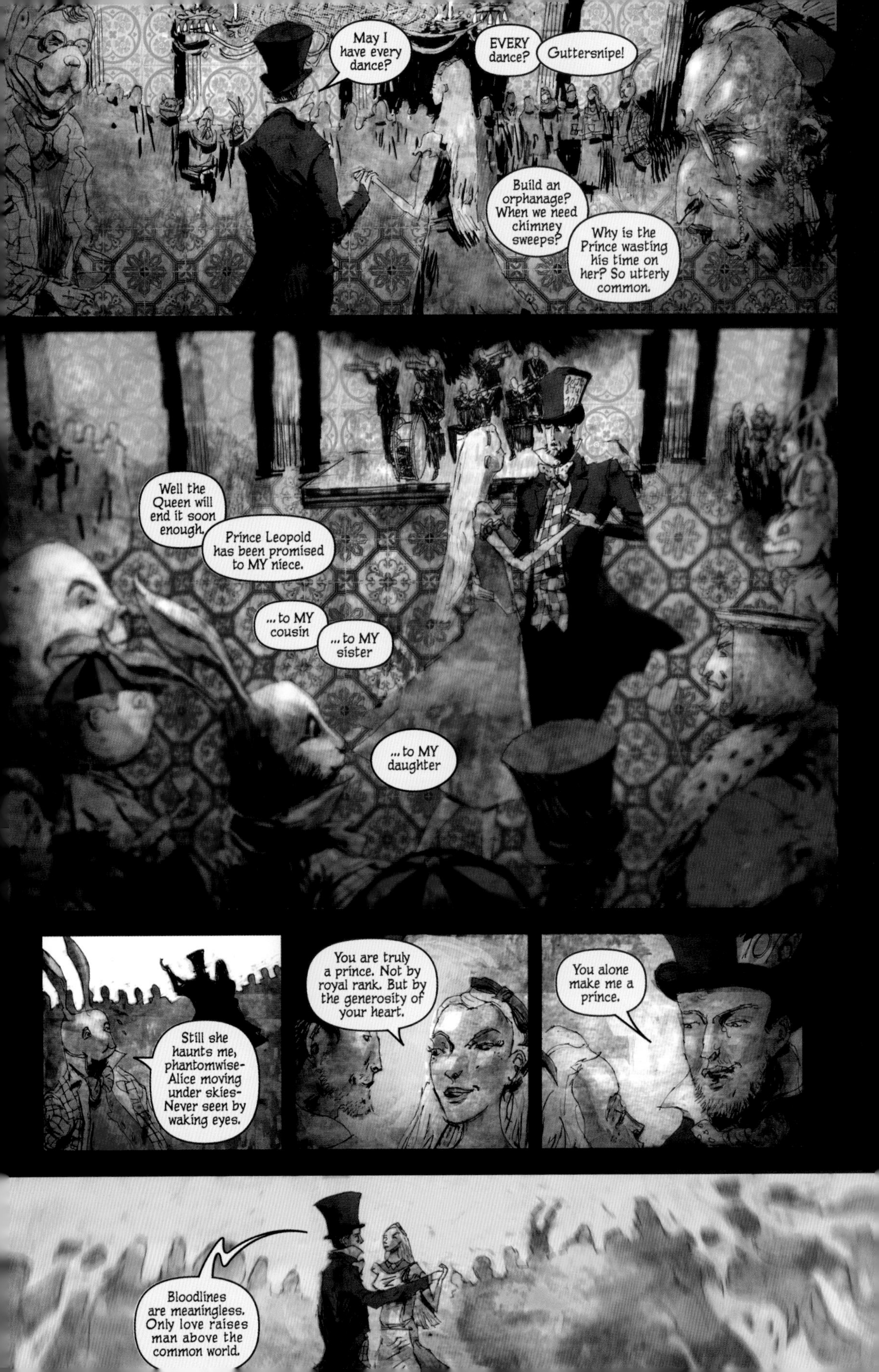

May I have every dance?
EVERY dance?
Guttersnipe!
Build an orphanage? When we need chimney sweeps?
Why is the Prince wasting his time on her? So utterly common.
Well the Queen will end it soon enough.
Prince Leopold has been promised to MY niece.
...to MY cousin
...to MY sister
...to MY daughter
Still she haunts me, phantomwise- Alice moving under skies- Never seen by waking eyes.
You are truly a prince. Not by royal rank. But by the generosity of your heart.
You alone make me a prince.
Bloodlines are meaningless. Only love raises man above the common world.

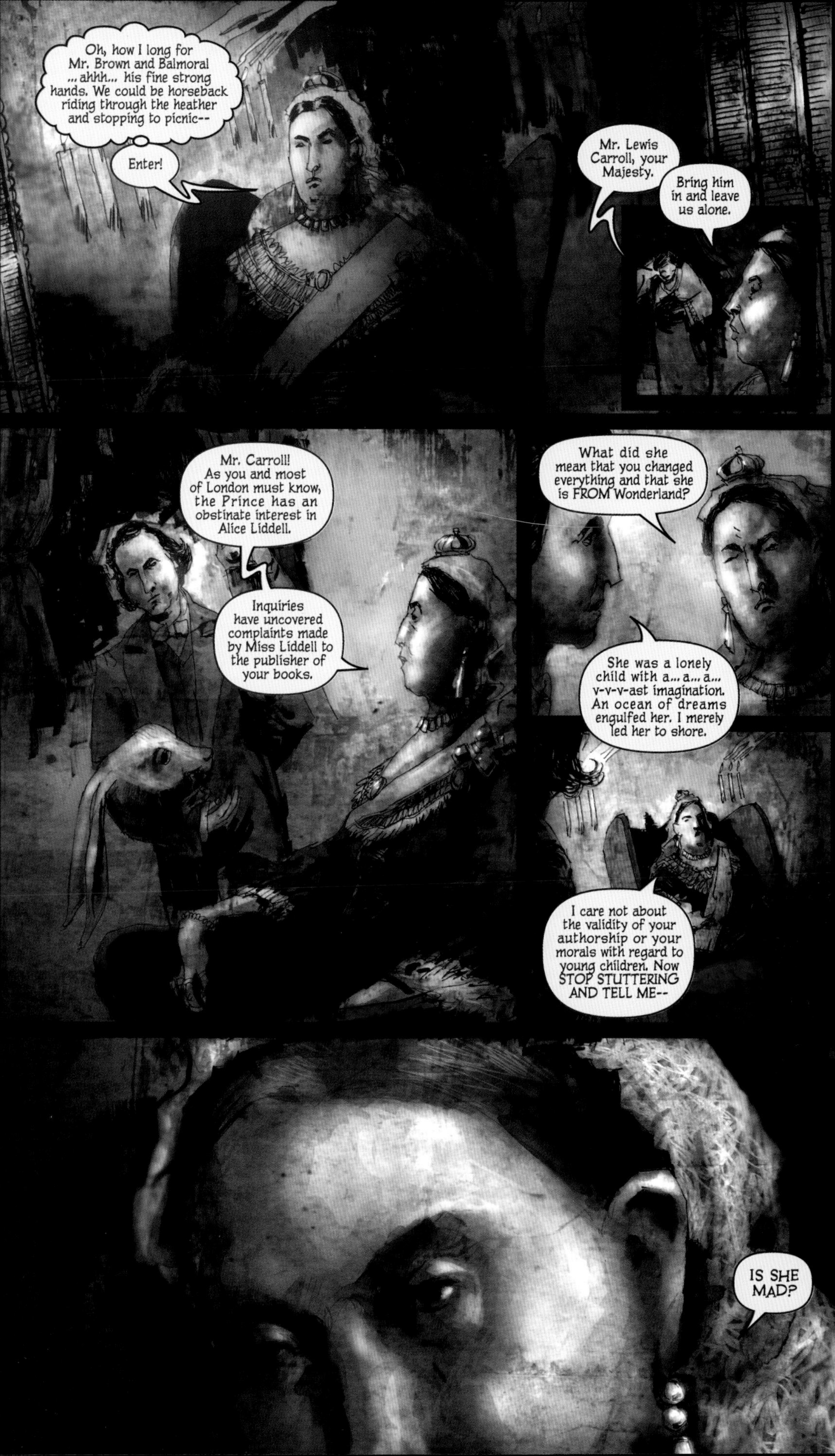
Oh, how I long for Mr. Brown and Balmoral ...ahhh... his fine strong hands. We could be horseback riding through the heather and stopping to picnic--
Enter!
Mr. Lewis Carroll, your Majesty.
Bring him in and leave us alone.
Mr. Carroll! As you and most of London must know, the Prince has an obstinate interest in Alice Liddell.
Inquiries have uncovered complaints made by Miss Liddell to the publisher of your books.
What did she mean that you changed everything and that she is FROM Wonderland?
She was a lonely child with a... a... a... v-v-v-ast imagination. An ocean of dreams engulfed her. I merely led her to shore.
I care not about the validity of your authorship or your morals with regard to young children. Now STOP STUTTERING AND TELL ME--
IS SHE MAD?

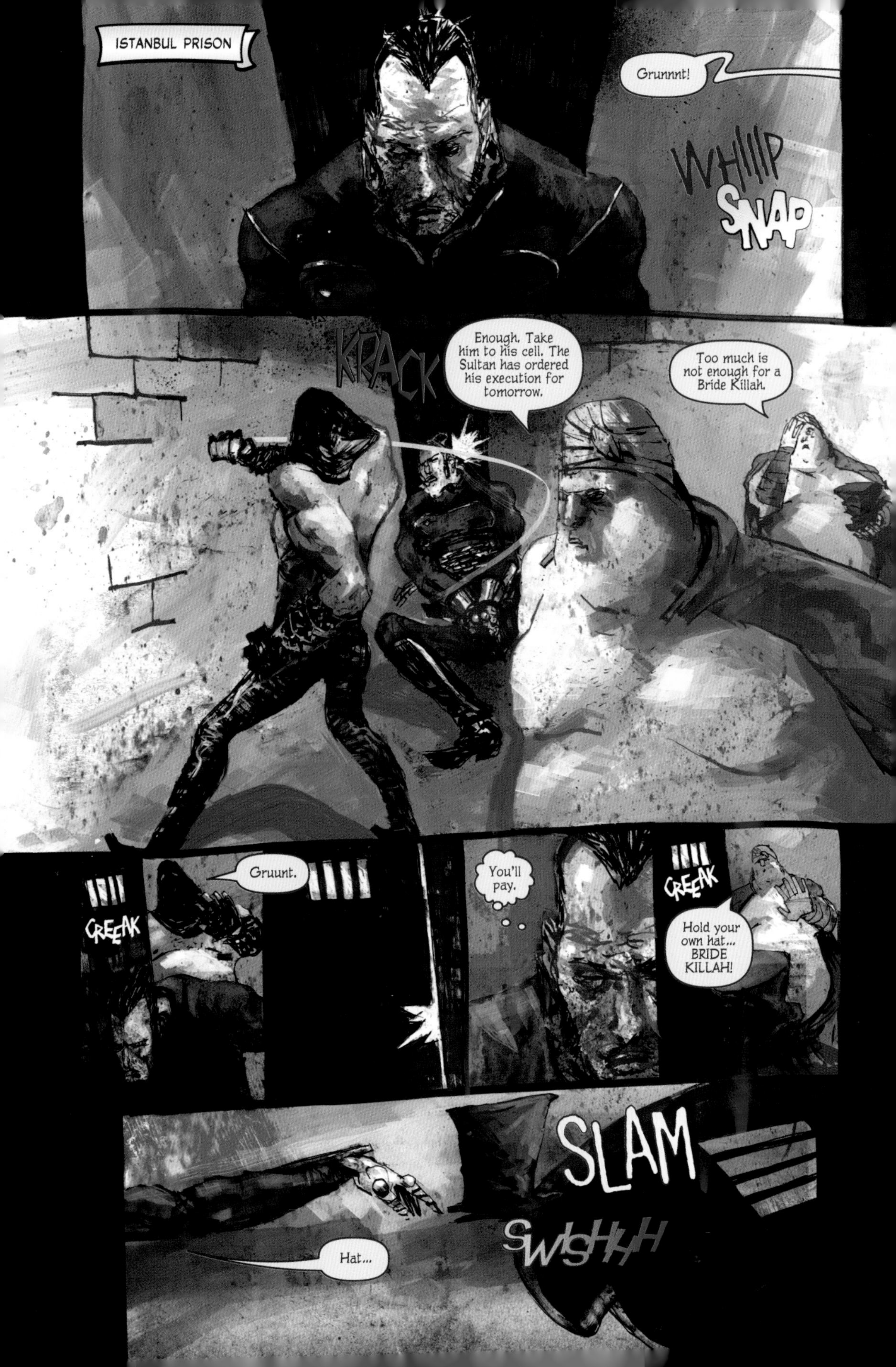
ISTANBUL PRISON
Grunnnt!
WHIIIP
SNAP
KRACK
Enough. Take him to his cell. The Sultan has ordered his execution for tomorrow.
Too much is not enough for a Bride Killah.
Gruunt.
CREEAK
You'll pay.
CREEAK
Hold your own hat... BRIDE KILLAH!
SLAM
SWISHHH
Hat...

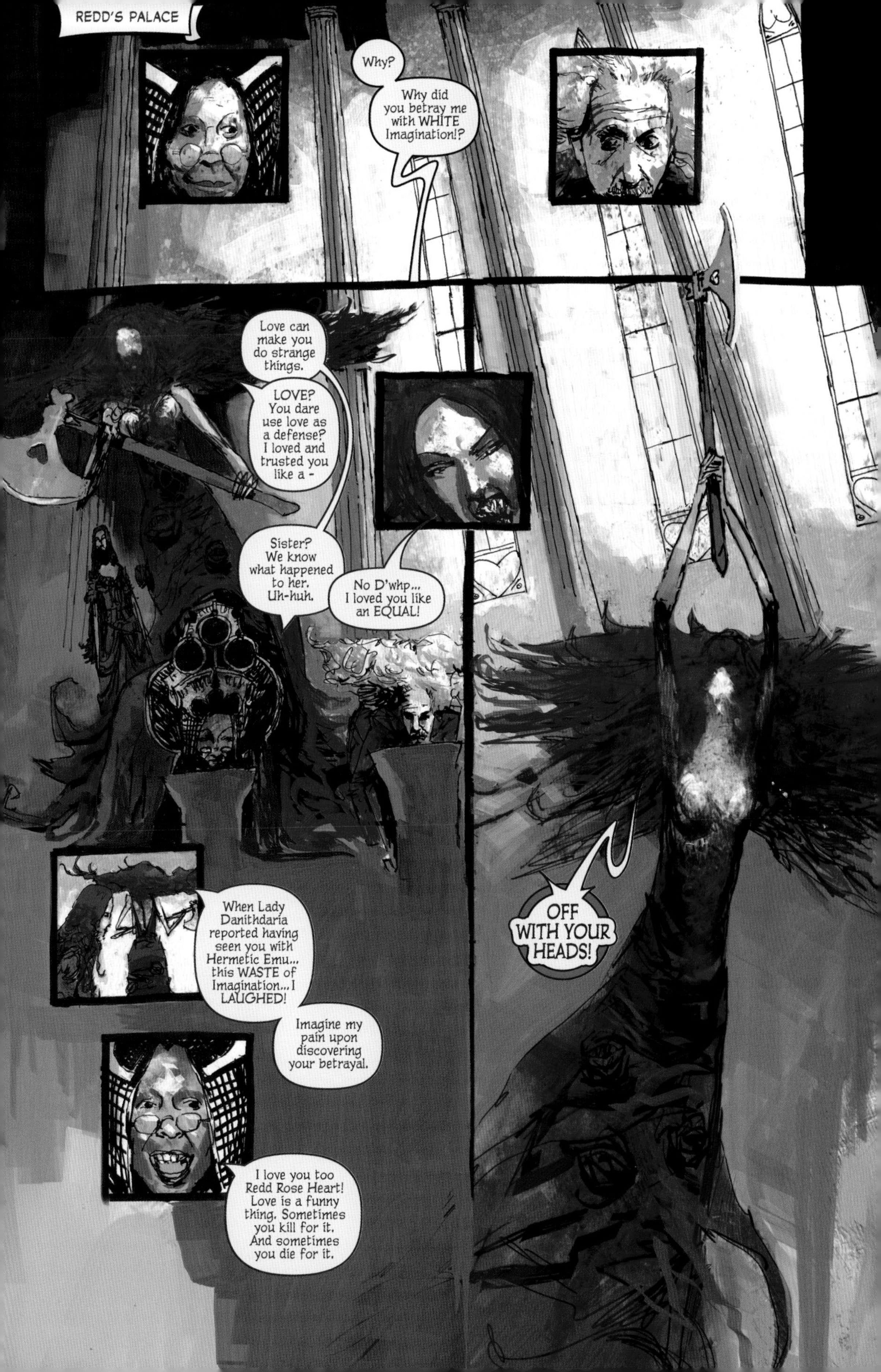
REDD'S PALACE
Why?
Why did you betray me with WHITE Imagination!?
Love can make you do strange things.
LOVE? You dare use love as a defense? I loved and trusted you like a -
Sister? We know what happened to her. Uh-huh.
No D'whp... I loved you like an EQUAL!
When Lady Danithdaria reported having seen you with Hermetic Emu... this WASTE of Imagination... I LAUGHED!
Imagine my pain upon discovering your betrayal.
I love you too Redd Rose Heart! Love is a funny thing. Sometimes you kill for it. And sometimes you die for it.
OFF WITH YOUR HEADS!

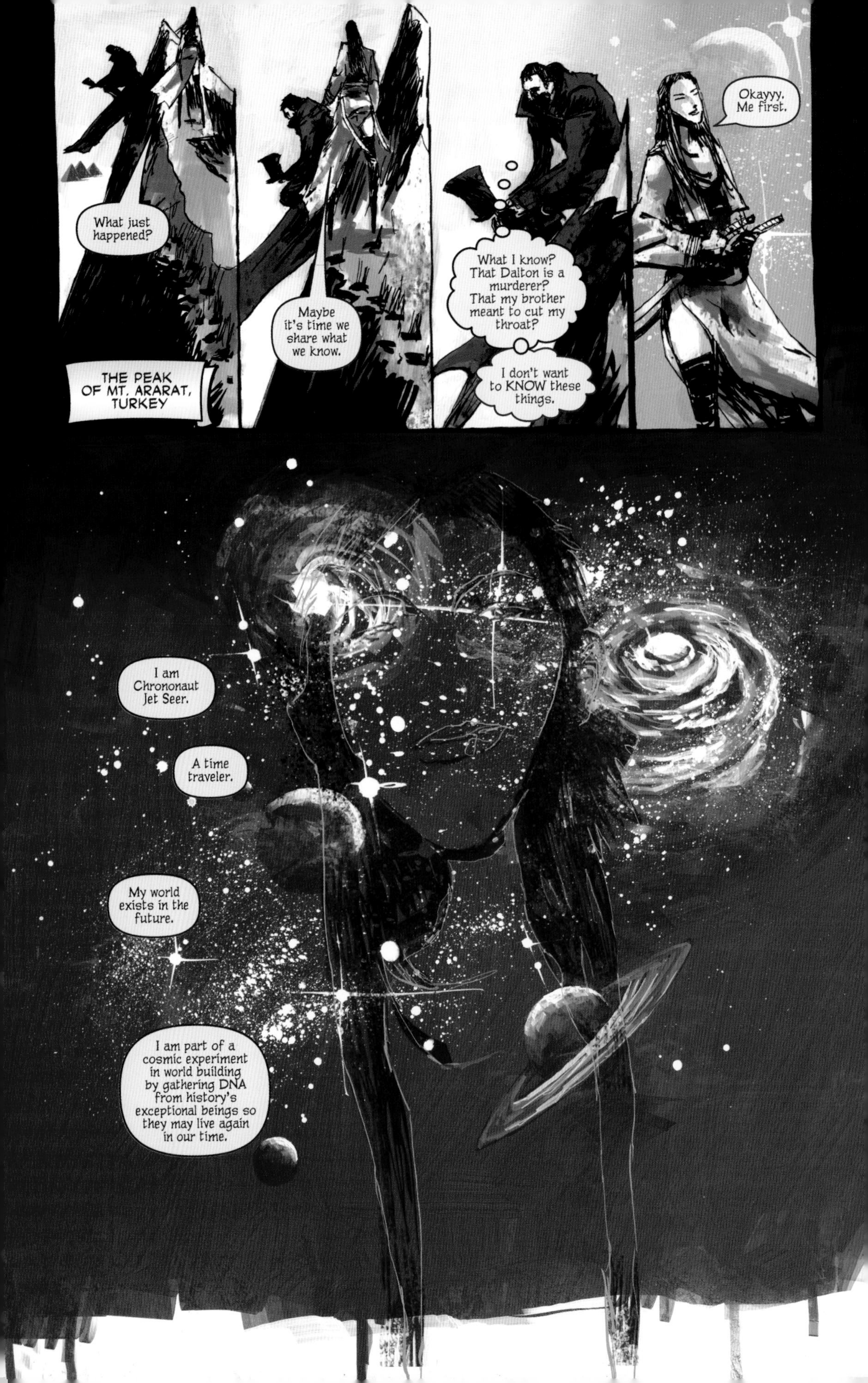
THE PEAK OF MT. ARARAT, TURKEY
What just happened?
Maybe it's time we share what we know.
What I know? That Dalton is a murderer? That my brother meant to cut my throat?
I don't want to KNOW these things.
Okayyy. Me first.
I am Chrononaut Jet Seer.
A time traveler.
My world exists in the future.
I am part of a cosmic experiment in world building by gathering DNA from history's exceptional beings so they may live again in our time.

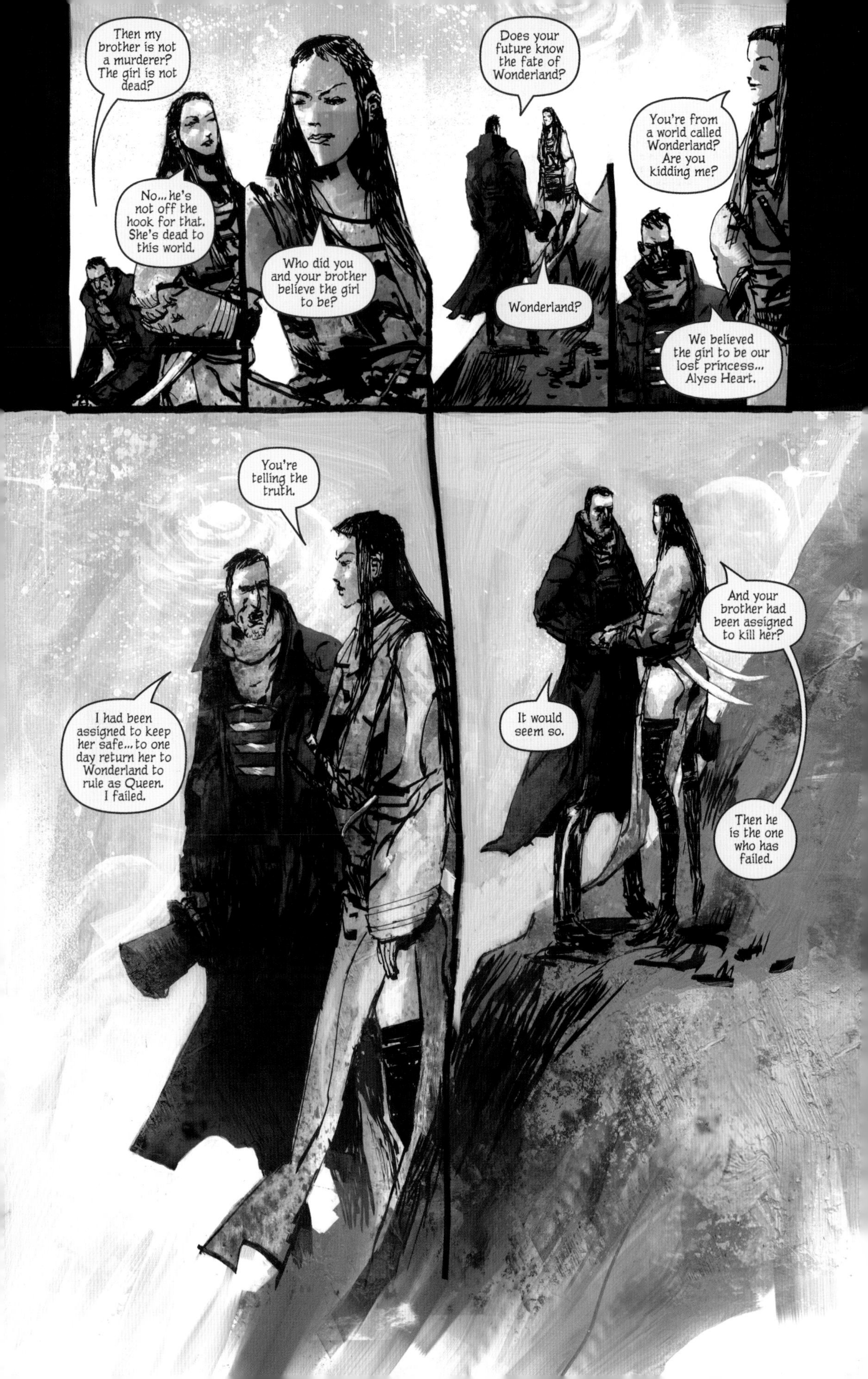
Then my brother is not a murderer? The girl is not dead?
No... he's not off the hook for that. She's dead to this world.
Who did you and your brother believe the girl to be?
Does your future know the fate of Wonderland?
Wonderland?
You're from a world called Wonderland? Are you kidding me?
We believed the girl to be our lost princess... Alyss Heart.
You're telling the truth.
I had been assigned to keep her safe... to one day return her to Wonderland to rule as Queen. I failed.
And your brother had been assigned to kill her?
It would seem so.
Then he is the one who has failed.

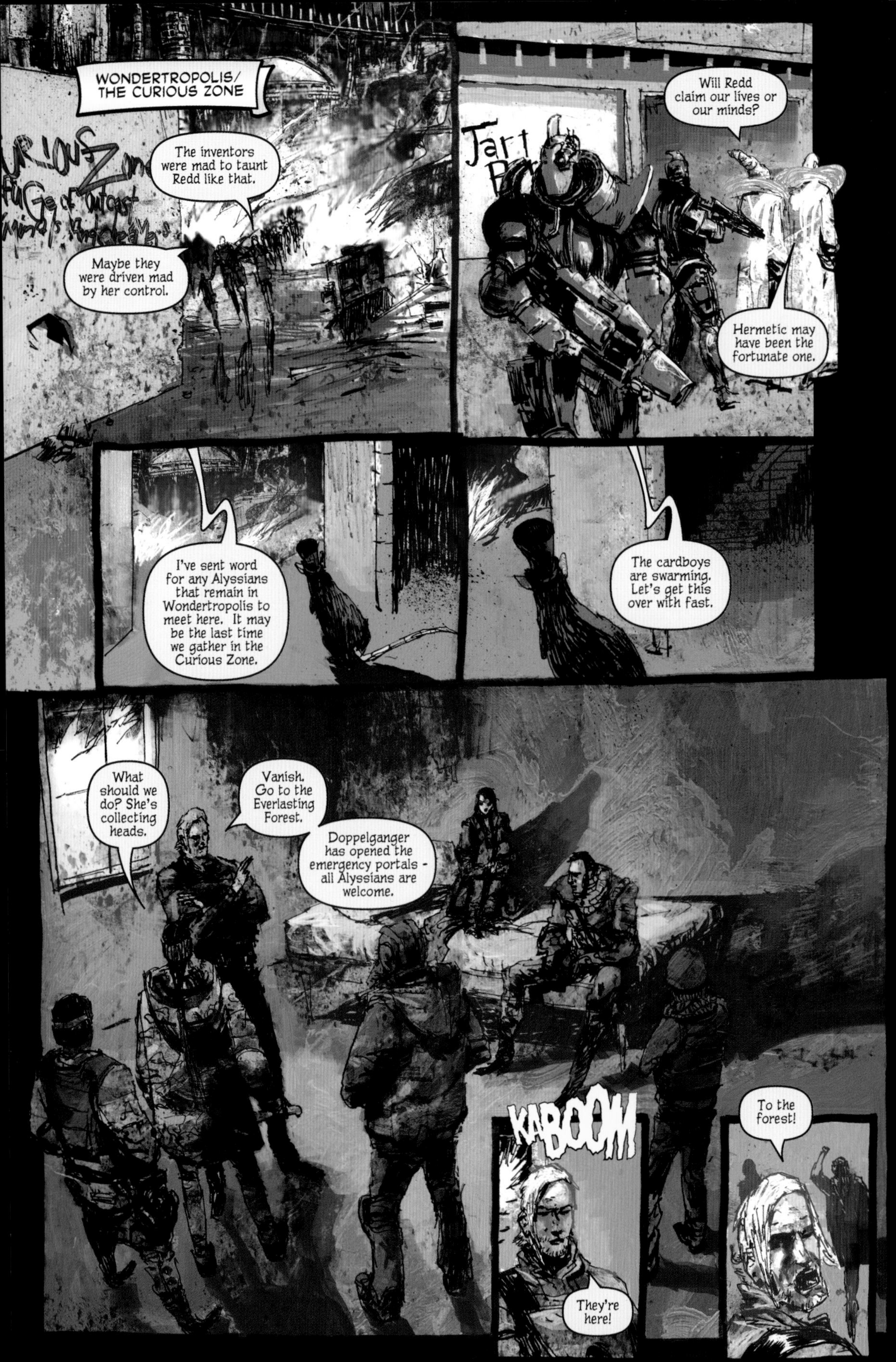
WONDERTROPOLIS/ THE CURIOUS ZONE
The inventors were mad to taunt Redd like that.
Maybe they were driven mad by her control.
Will Redd claim our lives or our minds?
Hermetic may have been the fortunate one.
I've sent word for any Alyssians that remain in Wondertropolis to meet here. It may be the last time we gather in the Curious Zone.
The cardboys are swarming. Let's get this over with fast.
What should we do? She's collecting heads.
Vanish. Go to the Everlasting Forest.
Doppelganger has opened the emergency portals - all Alyssians are welcome.
KABOOM
They're here!
To the forest!

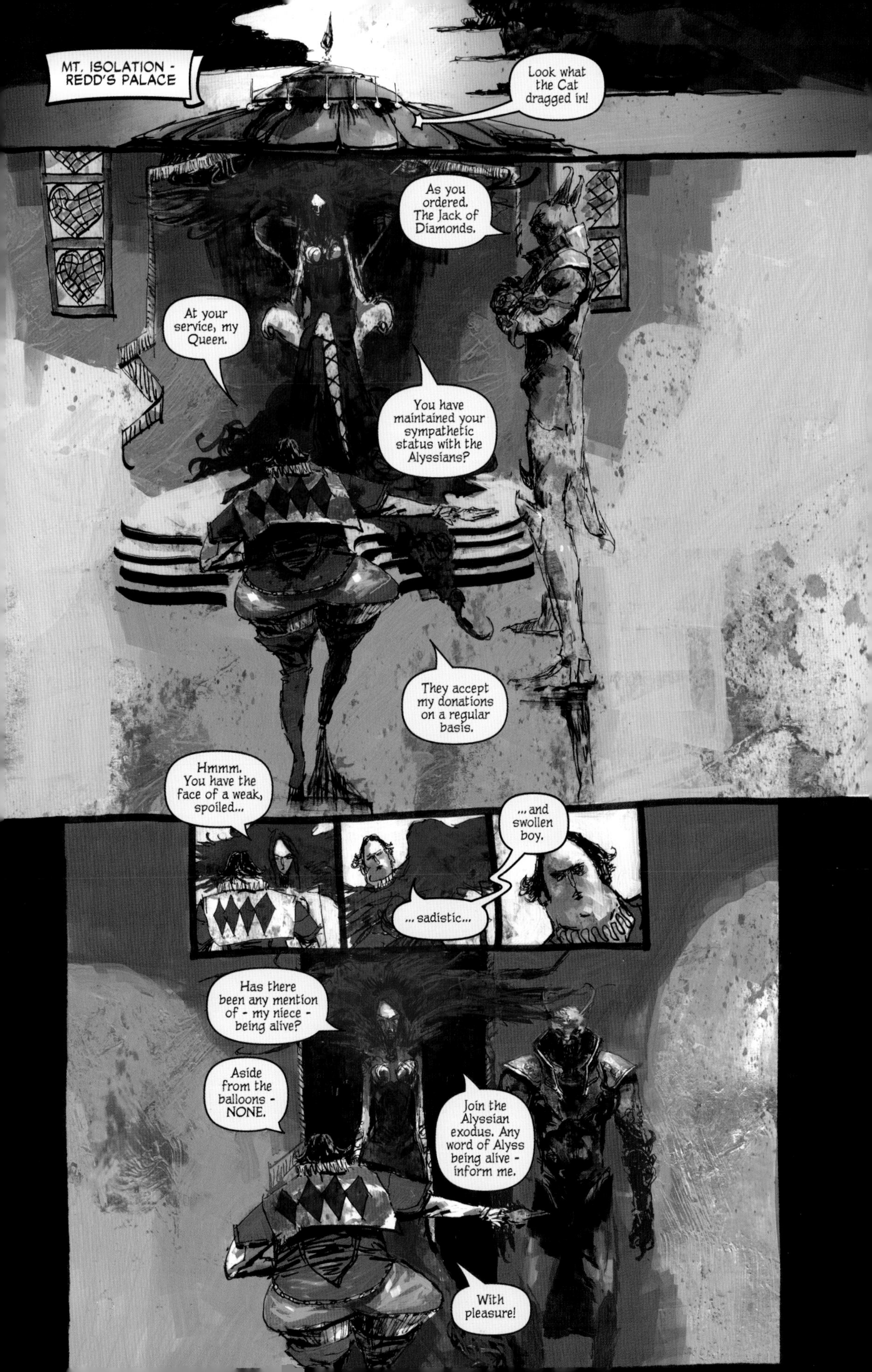
MT. ISOLATION - REDD'S PALACE
Look what the Cat dragged in!
As you ordered. The Jack of Diamonds.
At your service, my Queen.
You have maintained your sympathetic status with the Alyssians?
They accept my donations on a regular basis.
Hmmm. You have the face of a weak, spoiled...
...sadistic...
...and swollen boy.
Has there been any mention of - my niece - being alive?
Aside from the balloons - NONE.
Join the Alyssian exodus. Any word of Alyss being alive - inform me.
With pleasure!

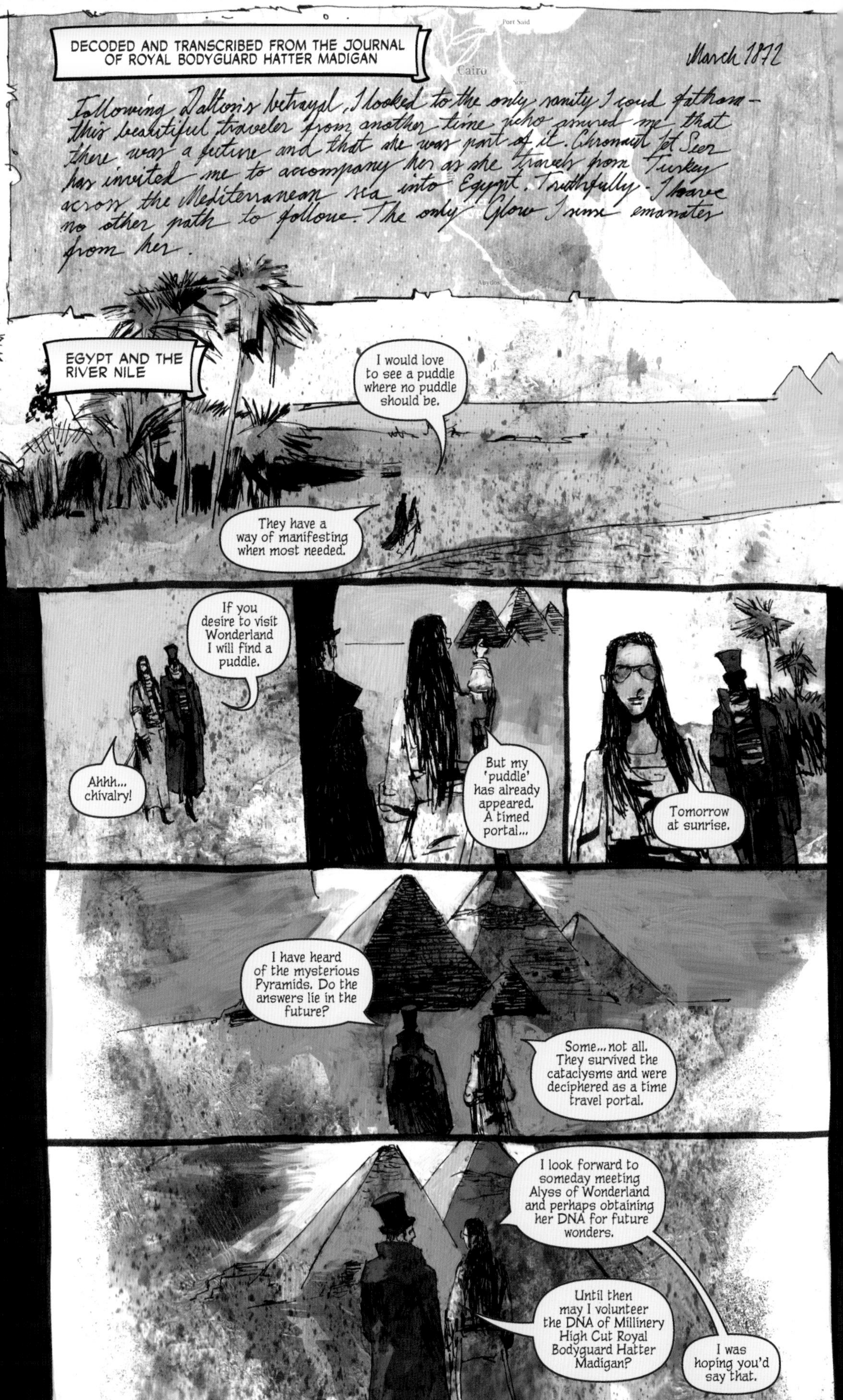

DECODED AND TRANSCRIBED FROM THE JOURNAL OF ROYAL BODYGUARD HATTER MADIGAN
March 1872
Port Said
Cairo
Following Dalton's betrayal, I looked to the only sanity I could fathom – this beautiful traveler from another time who assured me that there was a future and that she was part of it. Chronaut Jet Seer has invited me to accompany her as she travels from Turkey across the Mediterranean sea into Egypt. Truthfully – I have no other path to follow. The only Glow I sense emanates from her.
Abydos
EGYPT AND THE RIVER NILE
I would love to see a puddle where no puddle should be.
They have a way of manifesting when most needed.
If you desire to visit Wonderland I will find a puddle.
Ahhh... chivalry!
But my 'puddle' has already appeared. A timed portal...
Tomorrow at sunrise.
I have heard of the mysterious Pyramids. Do the answers lie in the future?
Some... not all. They survived the cataclysms and were deciphered as a time travel portal.
I look forward to someday meeting Alyss of Wonderland and perhaps obtaining her DNA for future wonders.
Until then may I volunteer the DNA of Millinery High Cut Royal Bodyguard Hatter Madigan?
I was hoping you'd say that.

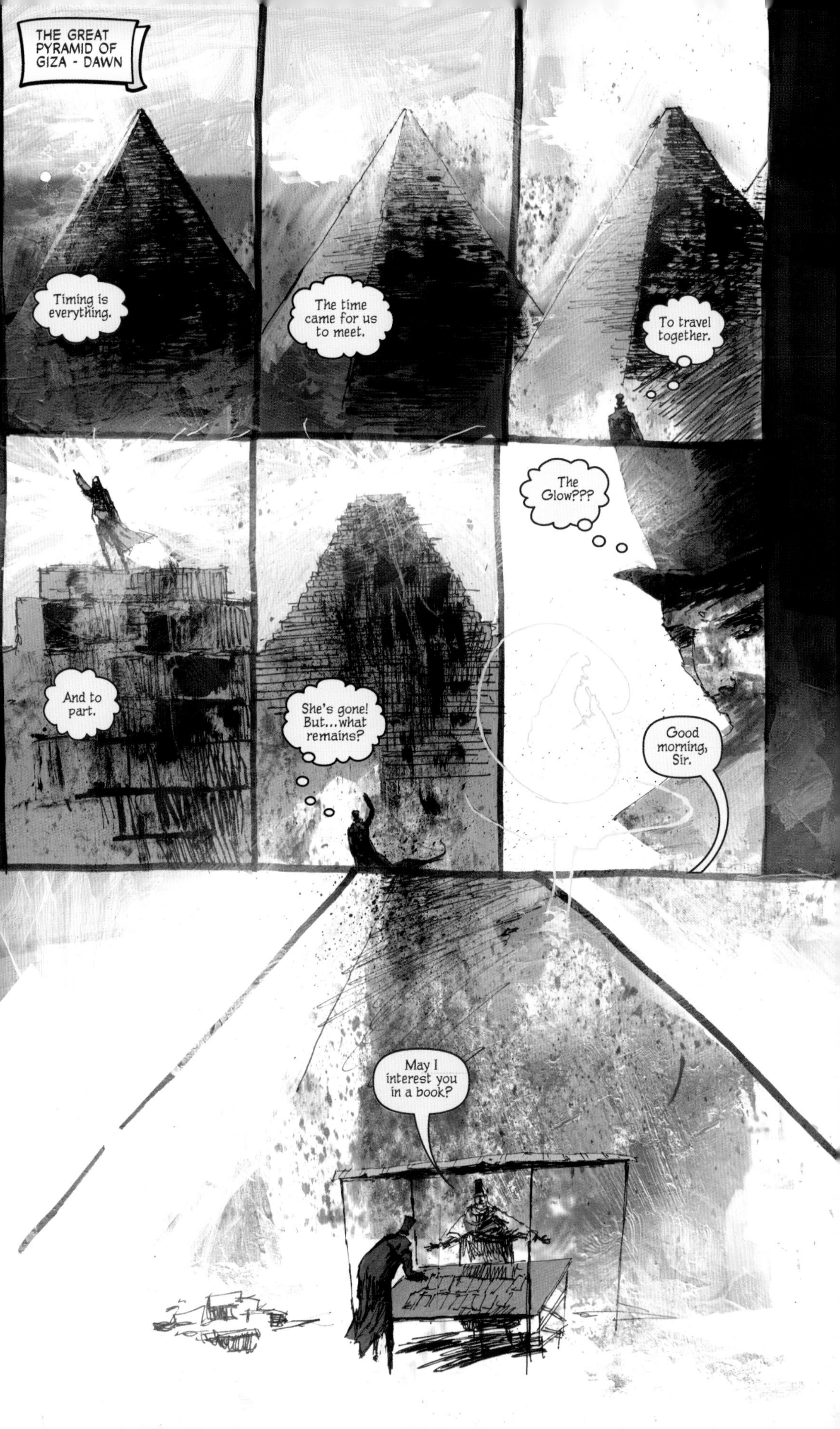
THE GREAT PYRAMID OF GIZA - DAWN
Timing is everything.
The time came for us to meet.
To travel together.
And to part.
She's gone! But...what remains?
The Glow???
Good morning, Sir.
May I interest you in a book?

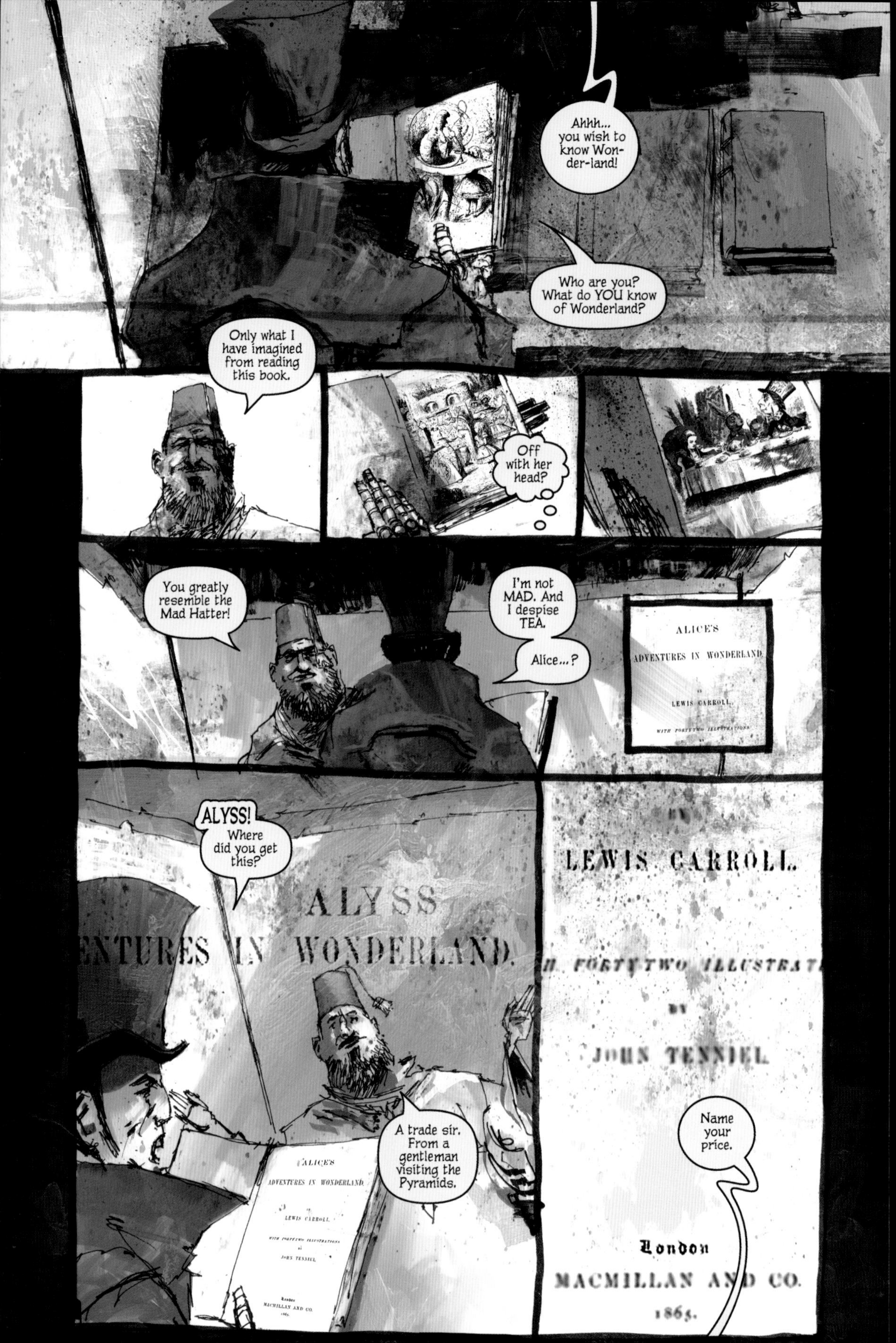

Ahhh... you wish to know Won-der-land!
Who are you? What do YOU know of Wonderland?
Only what I have imagined from reading this book.
Off with her head?
You greatly resemble the Mad Hatter!
I'm not MAD. And I despise TEA.
Alice...?
ALICE'S
ADVENTURES IN WONDERLAND.
LEWIS CARROLL.
ALYSS! Where did you get this?
ALYSS
WONDERLAND.
LEWIS CARROLL.
JOHN TENNIEL
A trade sir. From a gentleman visiting the Pyramids.
Name your price.
London
MACMILLAN AND CO.
1865.

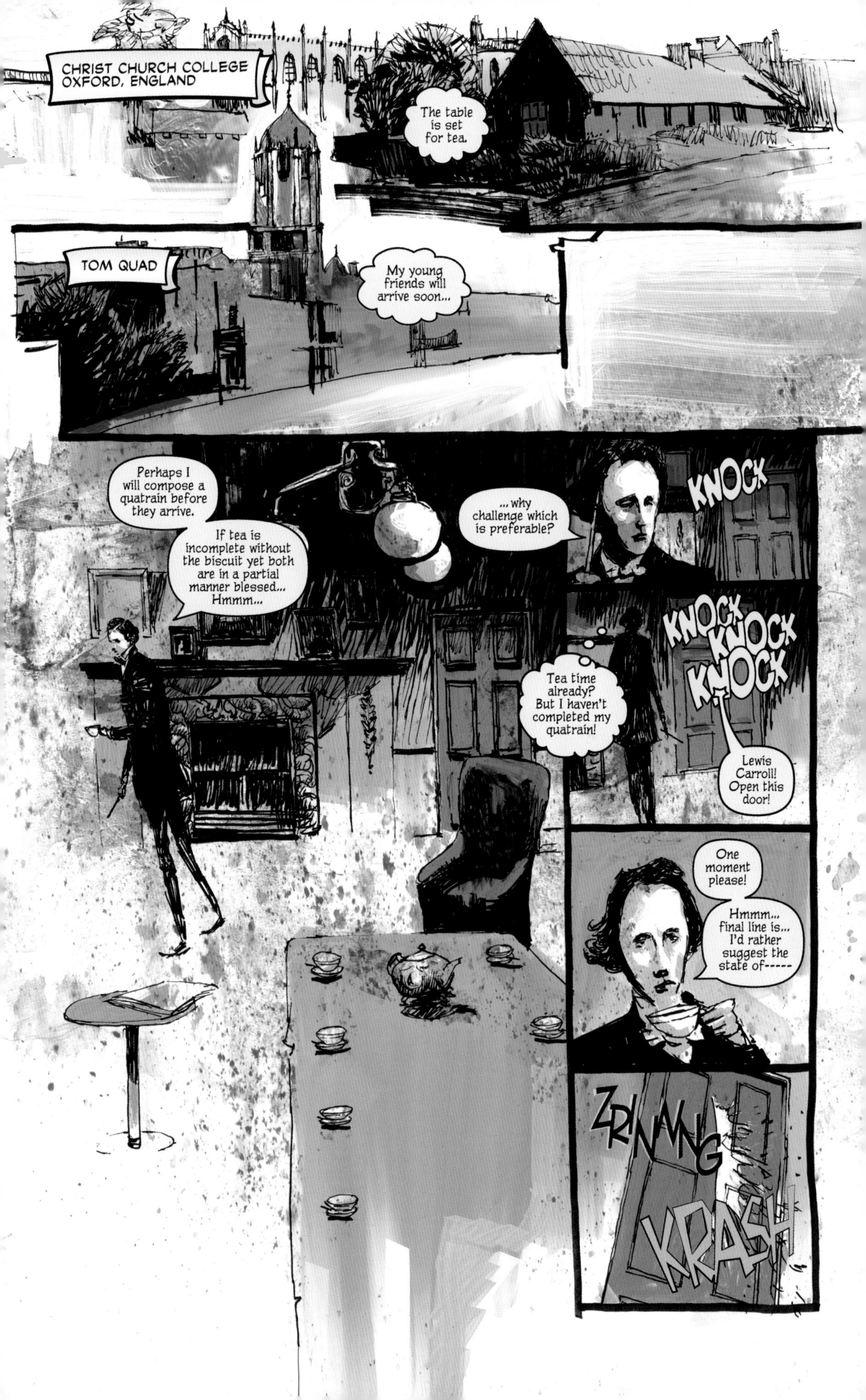

CHRIST CHURCH COLLEGE
OXFORD, ENGLAND
The table is set for tea.
TOM QUAD
My young friends will arrive soon...
Perhaps I will compose a quatrain before they arrive.
If tea is incomplete without the biscuit yet both are in a partial manner blessed... Hmmm...
...why challenge which is preferable?
KNOCK
KNOCK KNOCK KNOCK
Tea time already? But I haven't completed my quatrain!
Lewis Carroll! Open this door!
One moment please!
Hmmm... final line is... I'd rather suggest the state of-----
ZRINNNG
KRASH

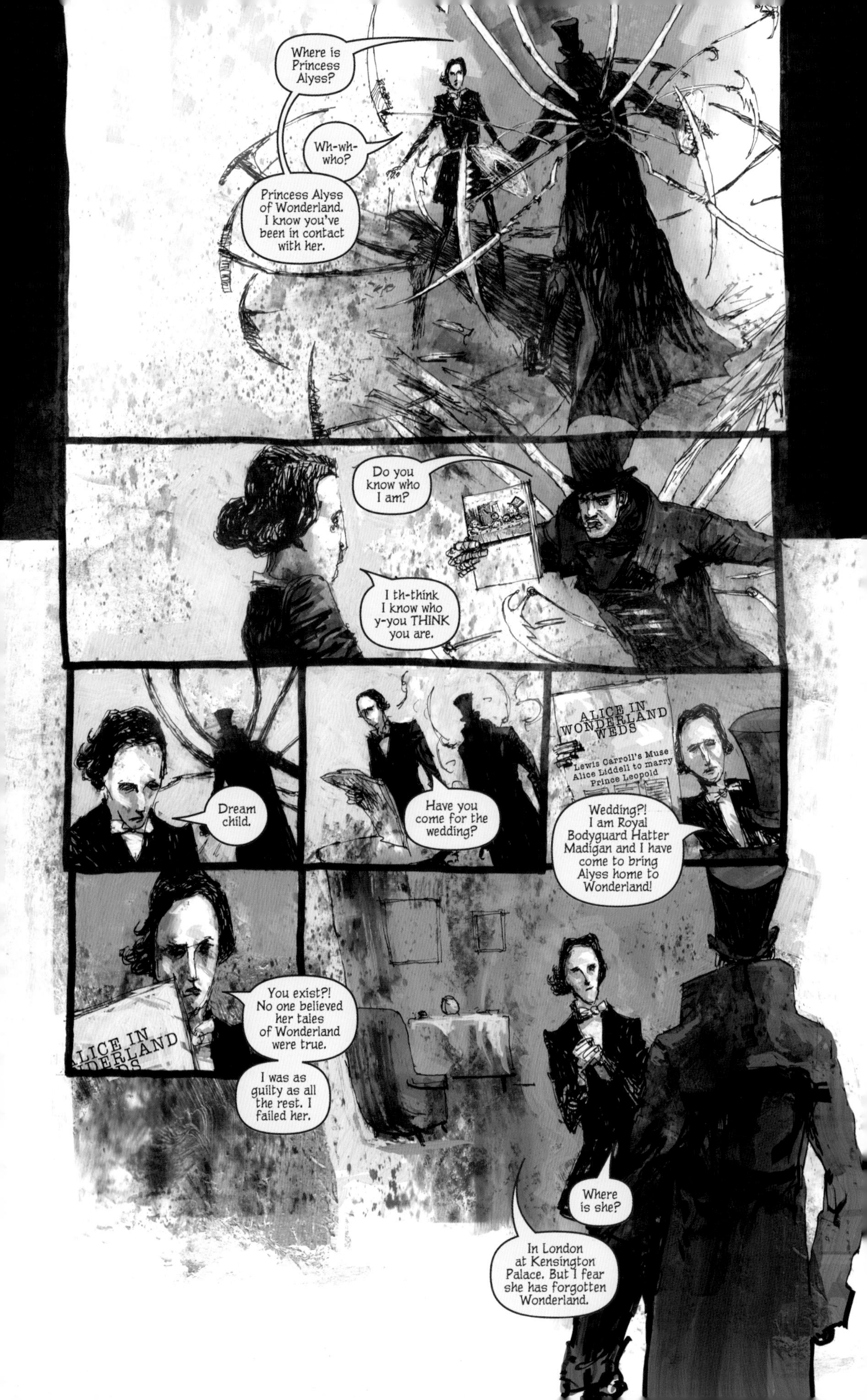
Where is Princess Alyss?
Wh-wh-who?
Princess Alyss of Wonderland. I know you've been in contact with her.
Do you know who I am?
I th-think I know who y-you THINK you are.
Dream child.
Have you come for the wedding?
ALICE IN WONDERLAND WEDS
Lewis Carroll's Muse Alice Liddell to marry Prince Leopold
Wedding?! I am Royal Bodyguard Hatter Madigan and I have come to bring Alyss home to Wonderland!
You exist?! No one believed her tales of Wonderland were true.
I was as guilty as all the rest. I failed her.
Where is she?
In London at Kensington Palace. But I fear she has forgotten Wonderland.

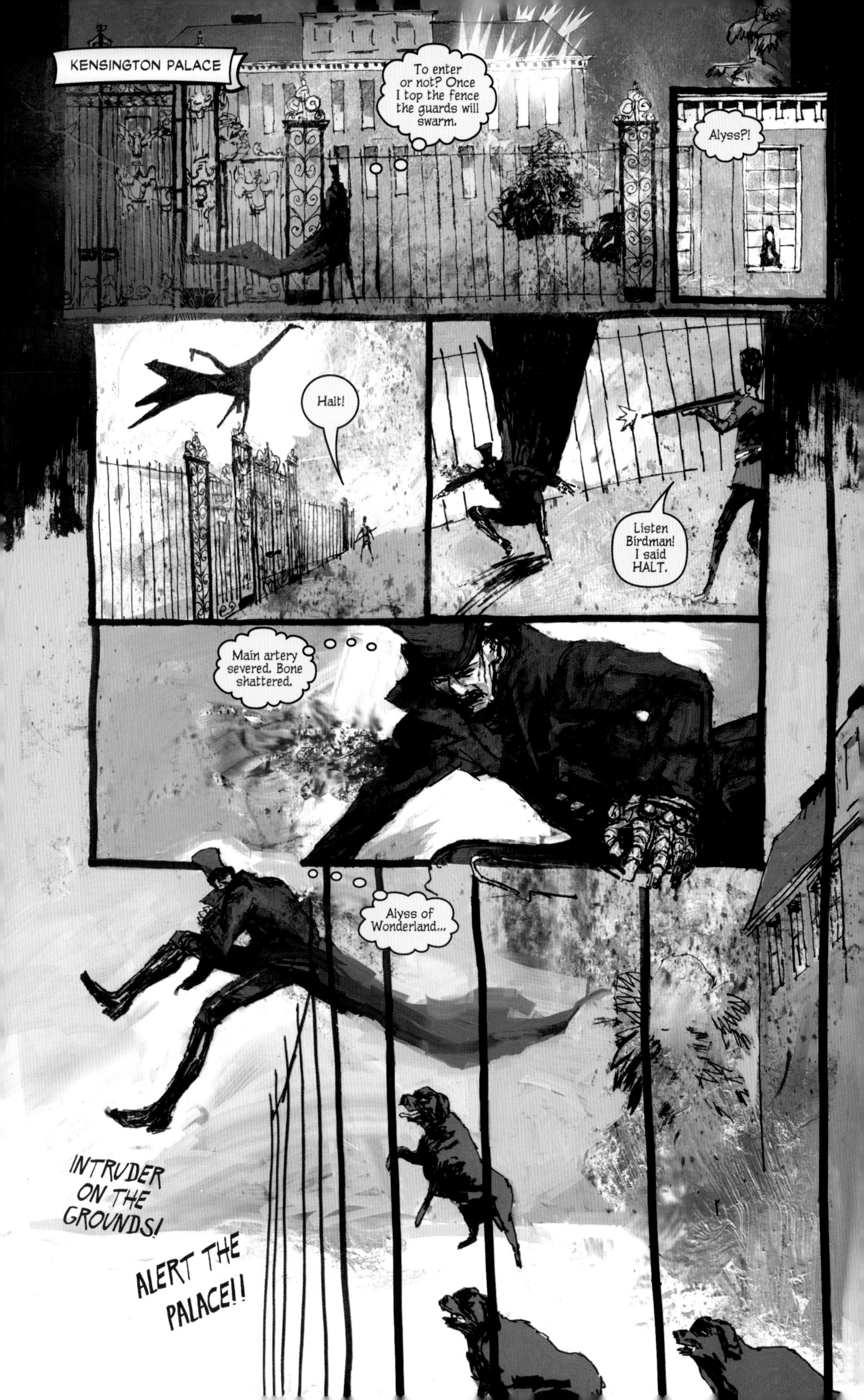
KENSINGTON PALACE
To enter or not? Once I top the fence the guards will swarm.
Alyss?!
Halt!
Listen Birdman! I said HALT.
Main artery severed. Bone shattered.
Alyss of Wonderland...
INTRUDER ON THE GROUNDS!
ALERT THE PALACE!!

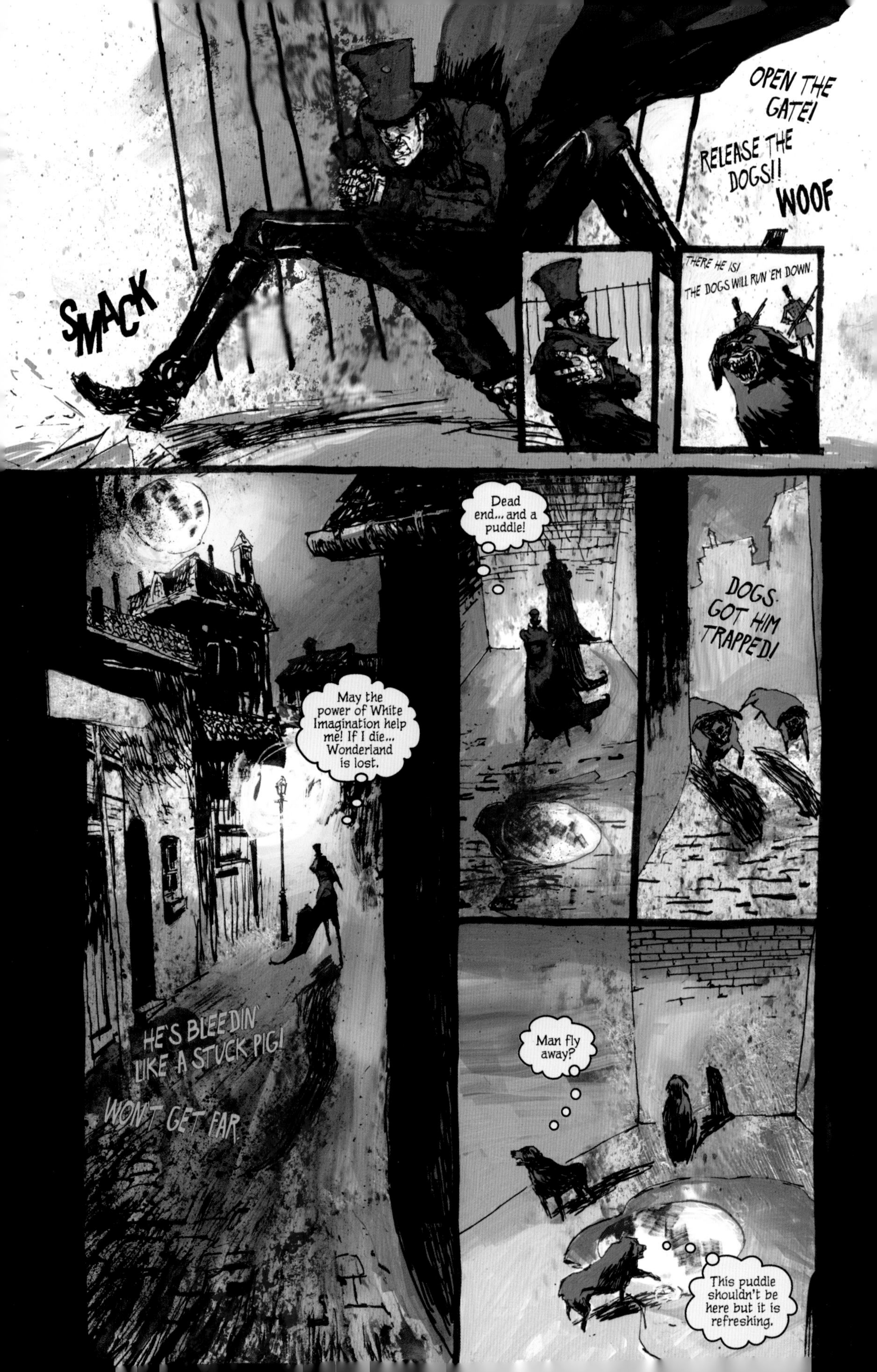
SMACK
OPEN THE GATE!
RELEASE THE DOGS!!
WOOF
THERE HE IS!
THE DOGS WILL RUN 'EM DOWN.
May the power of White Imagination help me! If I die... Wonderland is lost.
HE'S BLEEDIN' LIKE A STUCK PIG!
WON'T GET FAR
Dead end... and a puddle!
DOGS GOT HIM TRAPPED!
Man fly away?
This puddle shouldn't be here but it is refreshing.

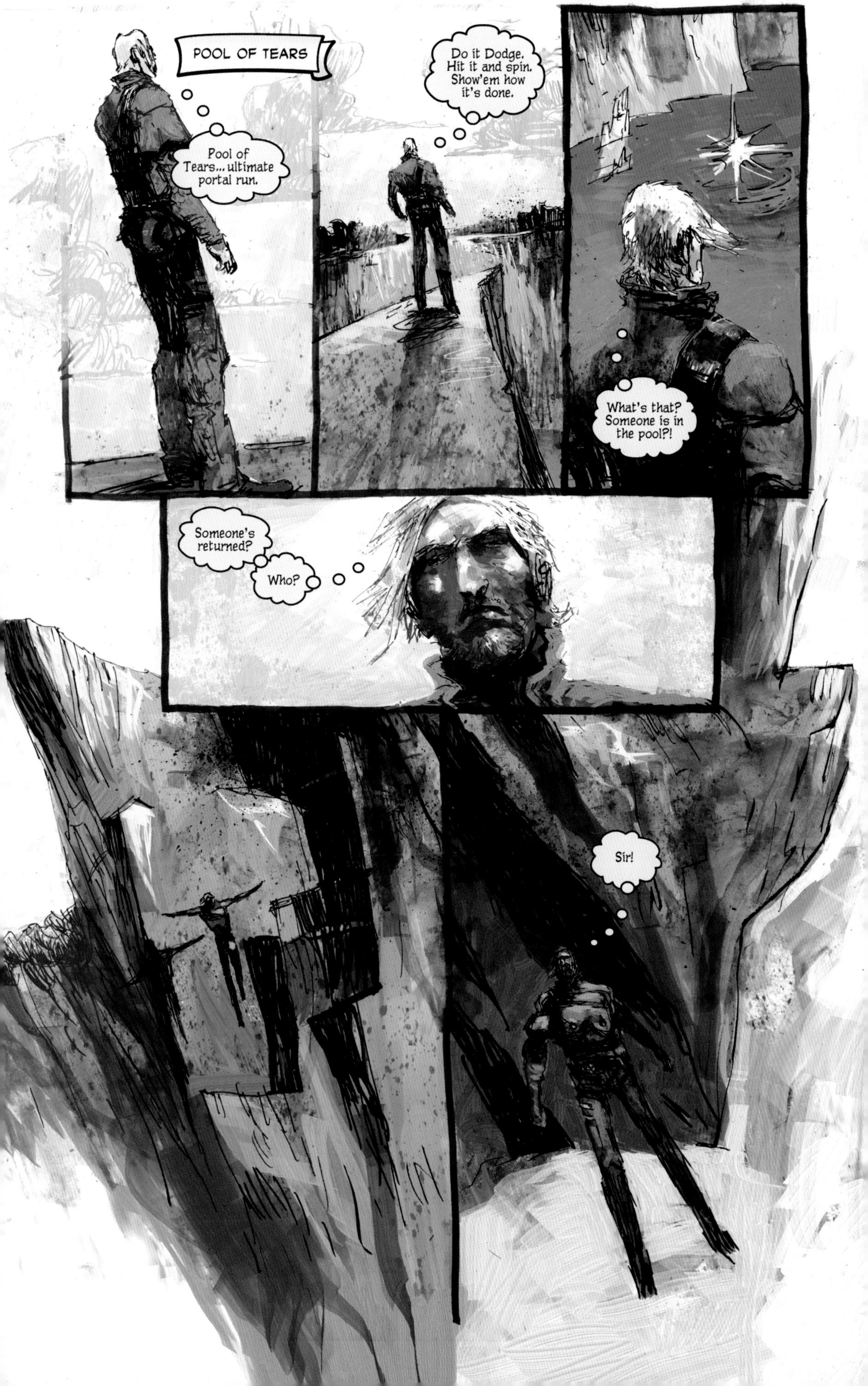
POOL OF TEARS
Pool of Tears... ultimate portal run.
Do it Dodge. Hit it and spin. Show'em how it's done.
What's that? Someone is in the pool?!
Someone's returned?
Who?
Sir!

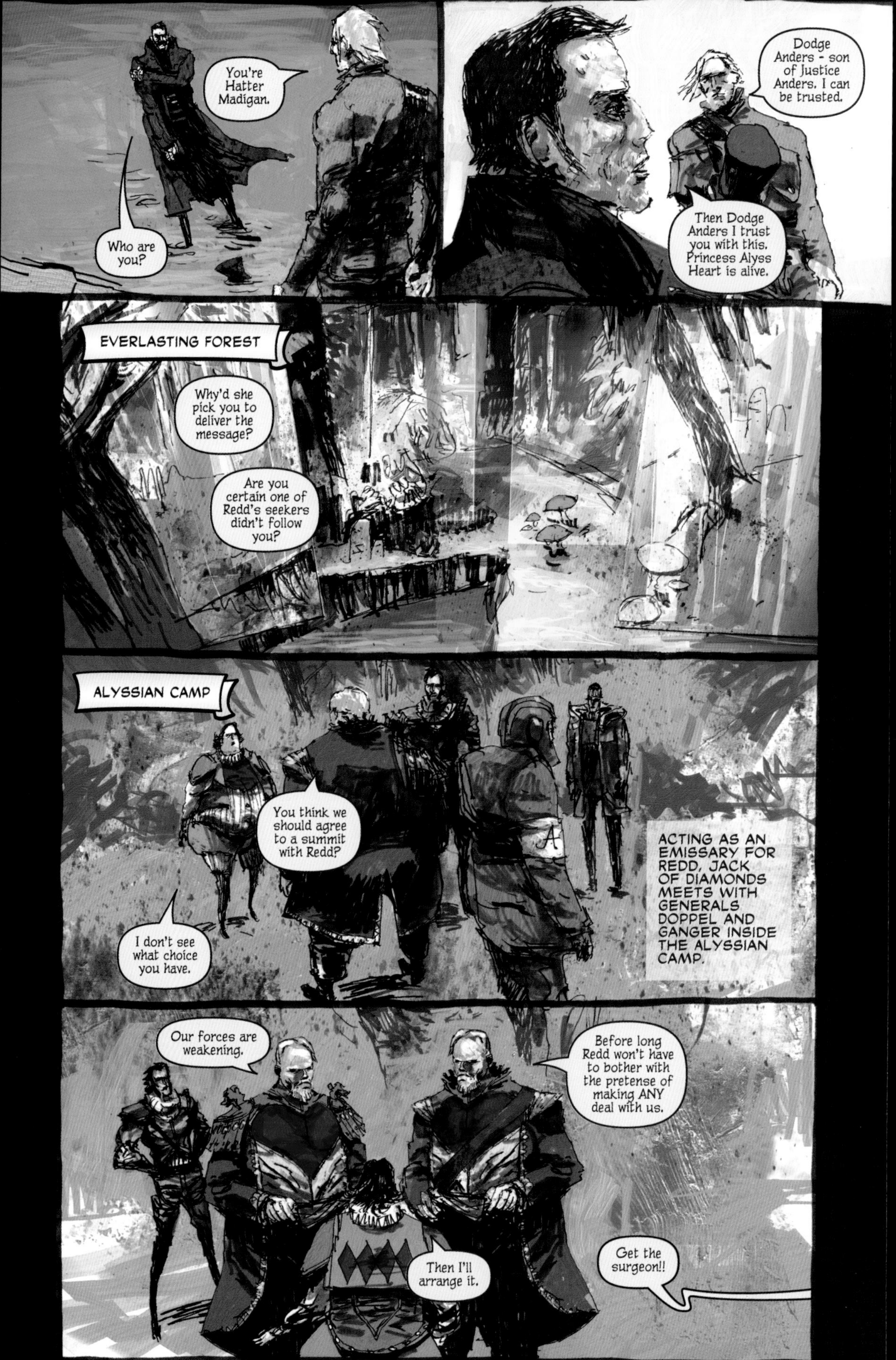
You're Hatter Madigan.
Who are you?
Dodge Anders - son of Justice Anders. I can be trusted.
Then Dodge Anders I trust you with this. Princess Alyss Heart is alive.
EVERLASTING FOREST
Why'd she pick you to deliver the message?
Are you certain one of Redd's seekers didn't follow you?
ALYSSIAN CAMP
You think we should agree to a summit with Redd?
I don't see what choice you have.
ACTING AS AN EMISSARY FOR REDD, JACK OF DIAMONDS MEETS WITH GENERALS DOPPEL AND GANGER INSIDE THE ALYSSIAN CAMP.
Our forces are weakening.
Before long Redd won't have to bother with the pretense of making ANY deal with us.
Then I'll arrange it.
Get the surgeon!!

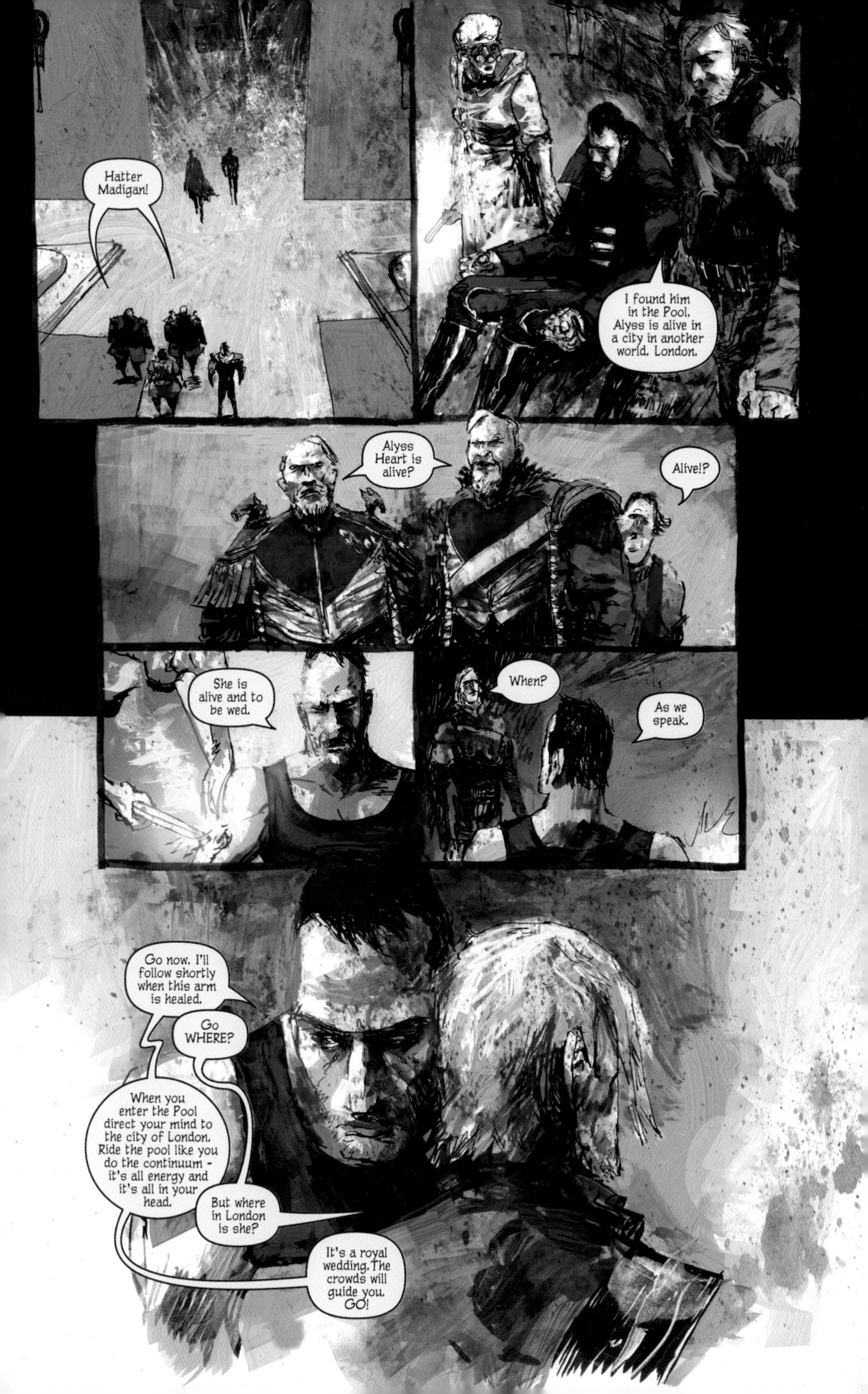
Hatter Madigan!
I found him in the Pool. Alyss is alive in a city in another world. London.
Alyss Heart is alive?
Alive!?
She is alive and to be wed.
When?
As we speak.
Go now. I'll follow shortly when this arm is healed.
Go WHERE?
When you enter the Pool direct your mind to the city of London. Ride the pool like you do the continuum - it's all energy and it's all in your head.
But where in London is she?
It's a royal wedding. The crowds will guide you. GO!

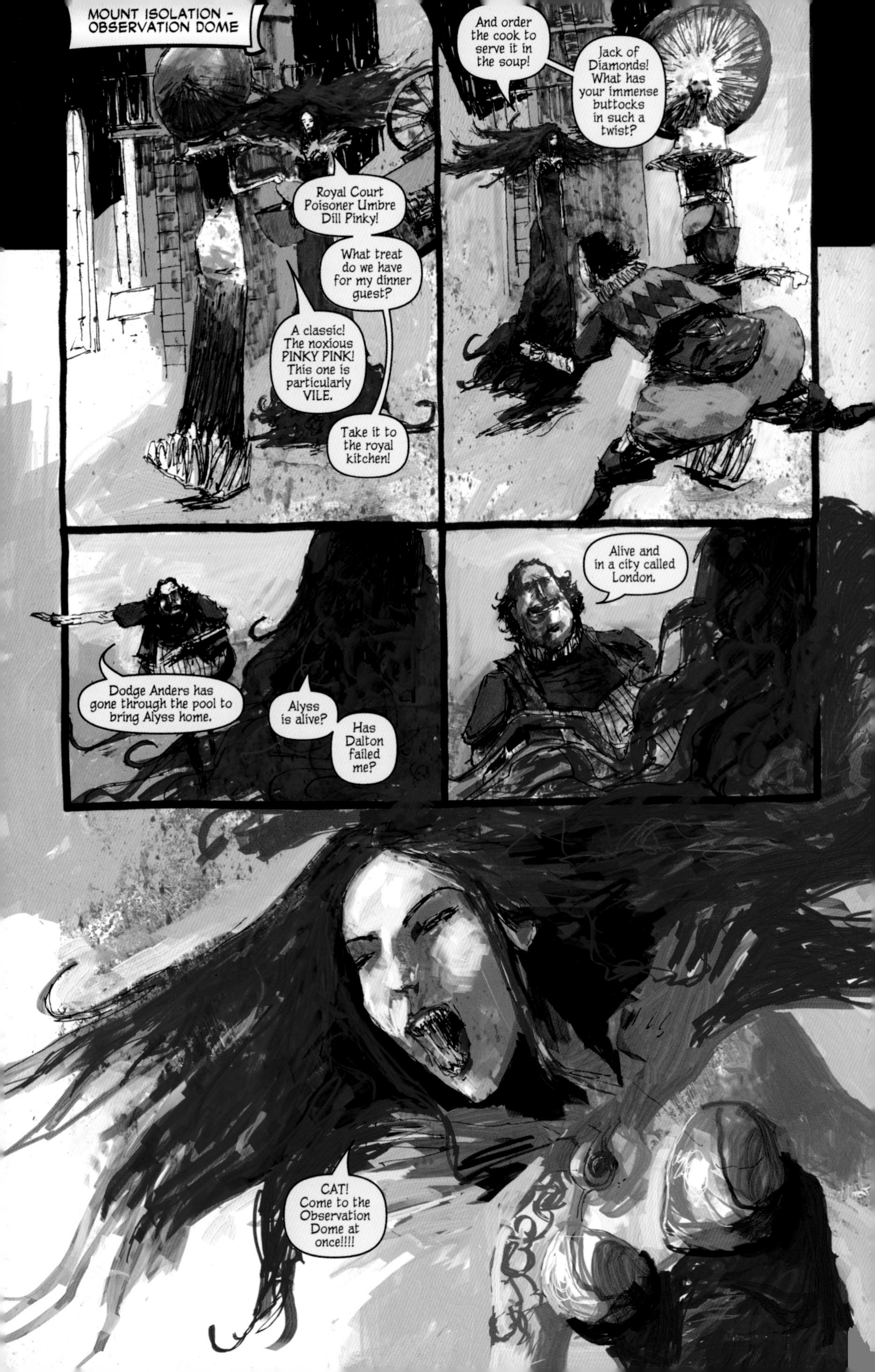
MOUNT ISOLATION - OBSERVATION DOME
Royal Court Poisoner Umbre Dill Pinky!
What treat do we have for my dinner guest?
A classic! The noxious PINKY PINK! This one is particularly VILE.
Take it to the royal kitchen!
And order the cook to serve it in the soup!
Jack of Diamonds! What has your immense buttocks in such a twist?
Dodge Anders has gone through the pool to bring Alyss home.
Alyss is alive?
Has Dalton failed me?
Alive and in a city called London.
CAT! Come to the Observation Dome at once!!!!

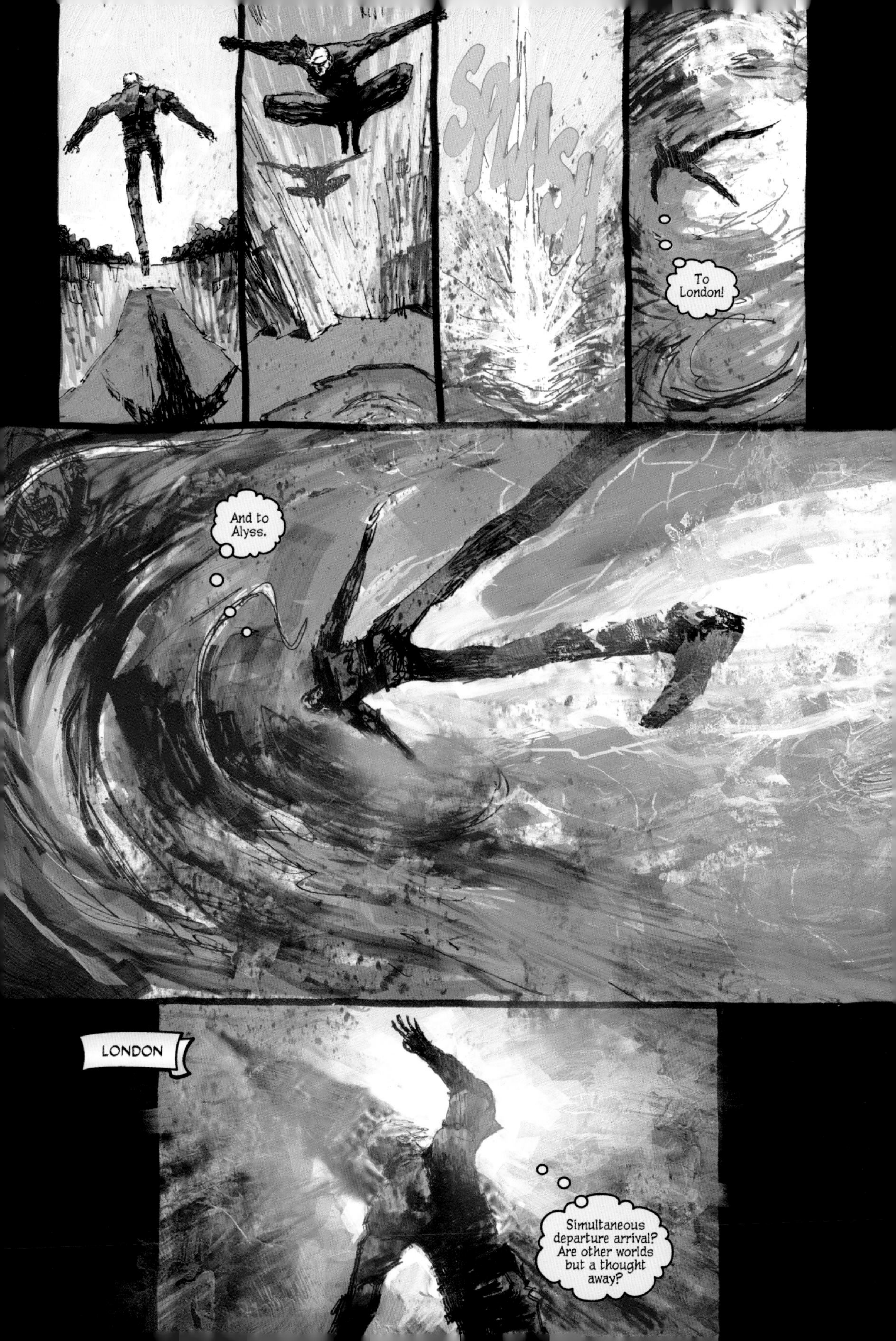
SPLASH
To London!
And to Alyss.
LONDON
Simultaneous departure arrival? Are other worlds but a thought away?

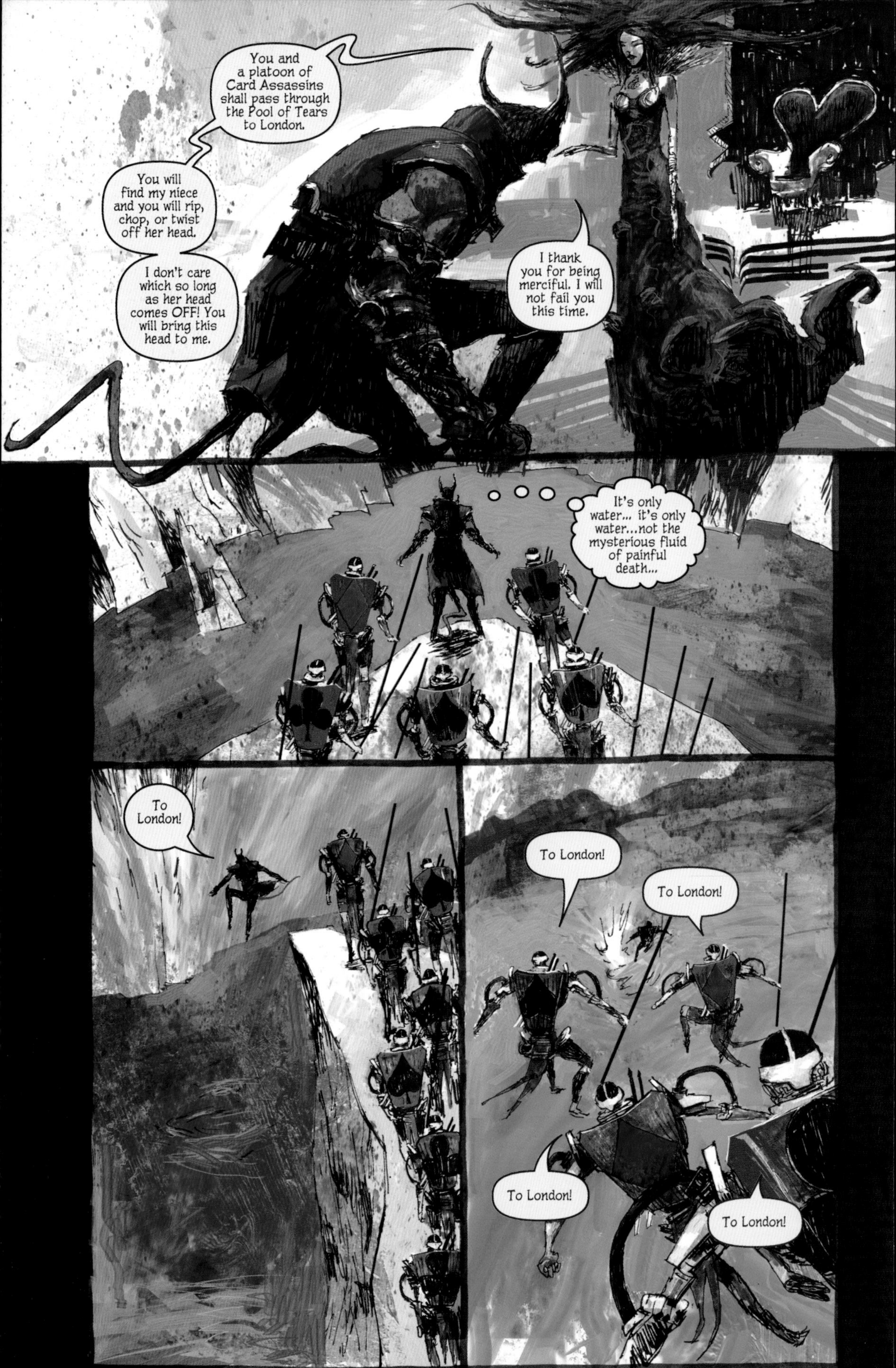
You and a platoon of Card Assassins shall pass through the Pool of Tears to London.
You will find my niece and you will rip, chop, or twist off her head.
I don't care which so long as her head comes OFF! You will bring this head to me.
I thank you for being merciful. I will not fail you this time.
It's only water... it's only water...not the mysterious fluid of painful death...
To London!
To London!
To London!
To London!
To London!

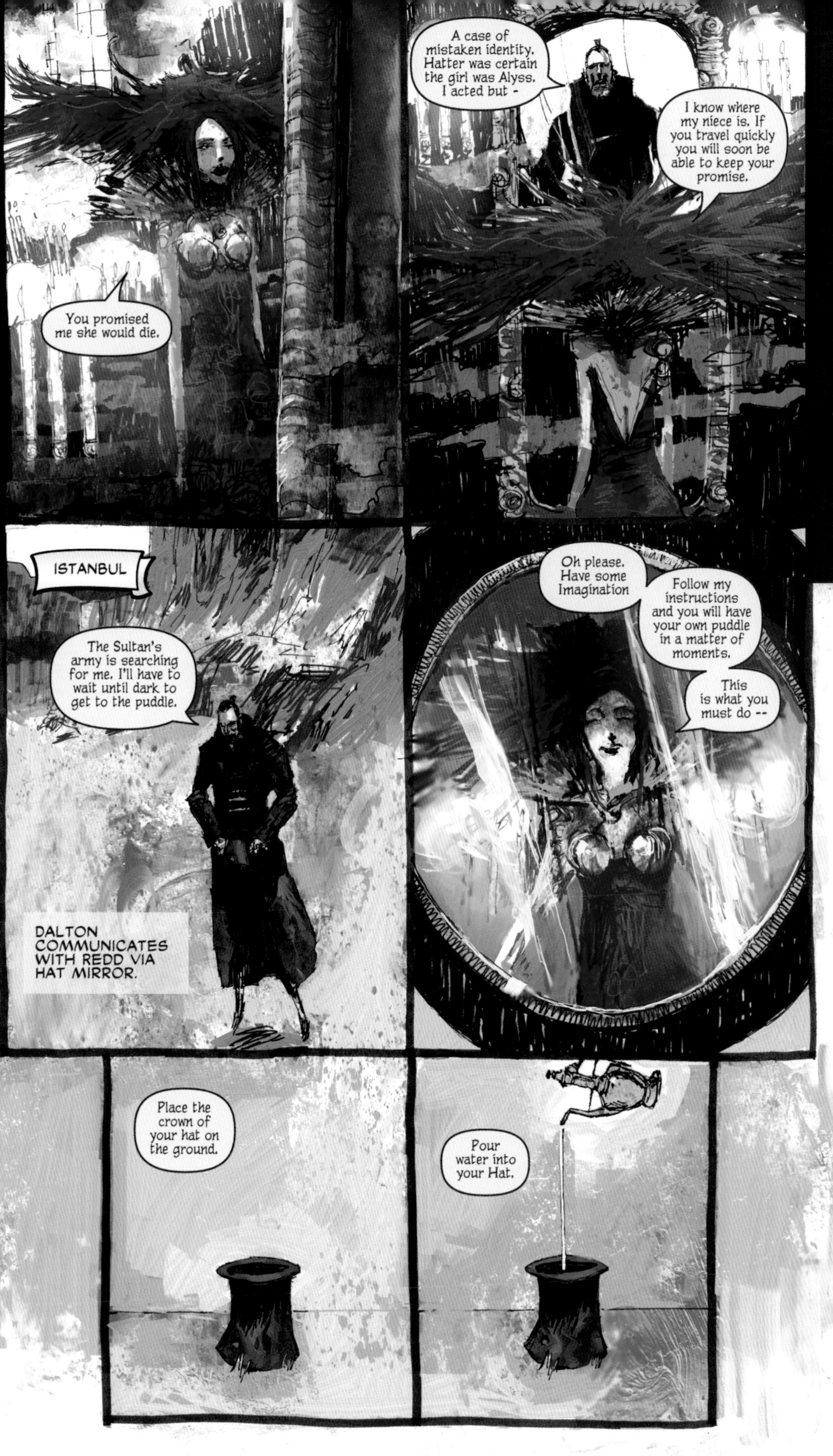
You promised me she would die.
A case of mistaken identity. Hatter was certain the girl was Alyss. I acted but -
I know where my niece is. If you travel quickly you will soon be able to keep your promise.
ISTANBUL
The Sultan's army is searching for me. I'll have to wait until dark to get to the puddle.
DALTON COMMUNICATES WITH REDD VIA HAT MIRROR.
Oh please. Have some Imagination
Follow my instructions and you will have your own puddle in a matter of moments.
This is what you must do --
Place the crown of your hat on the ground.
Pour water into your Hat.

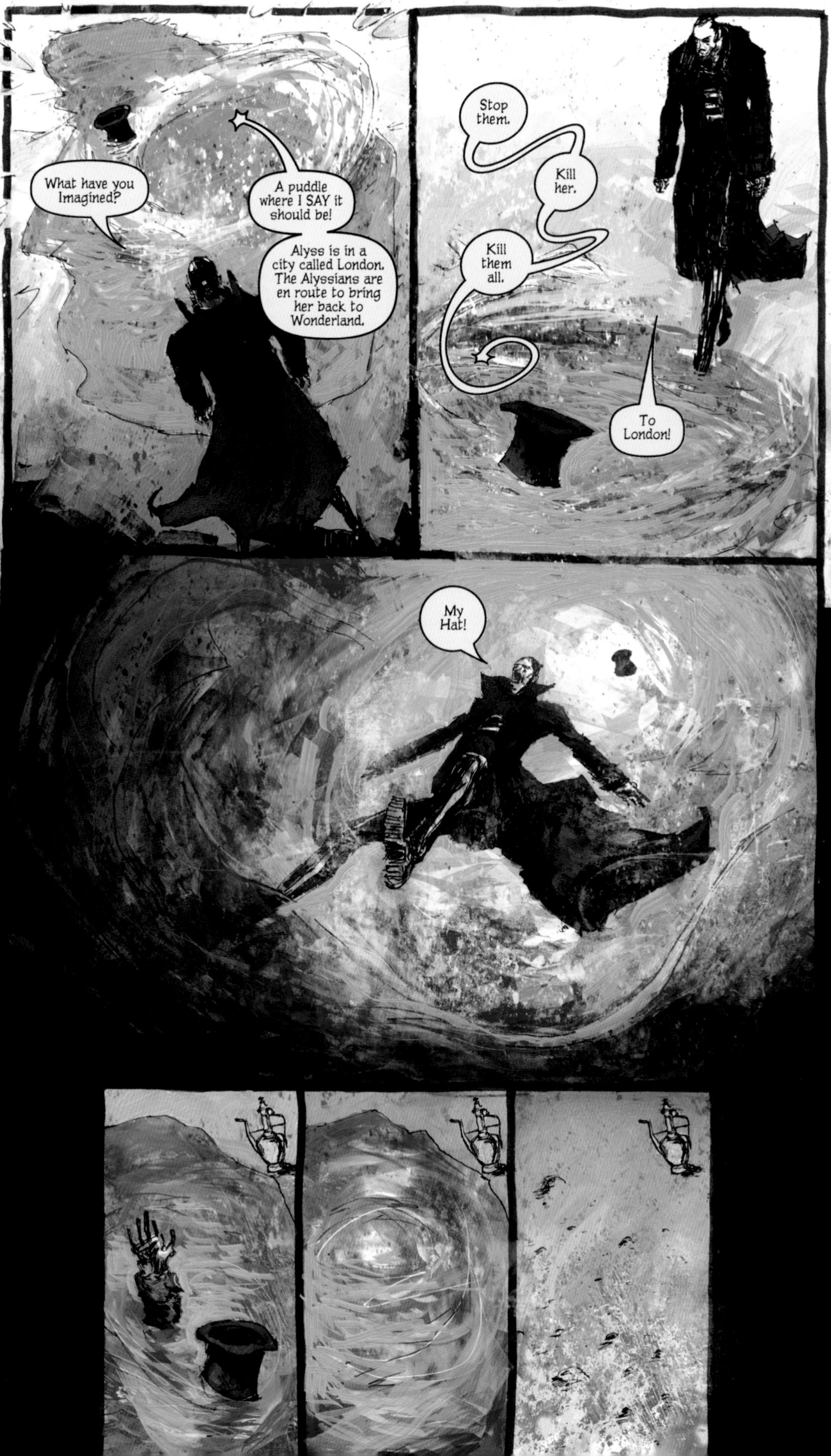
What have you Imagined?
A puddle where I SAY it should be!
Alyss is in a city called London. The Alyssians are en route to bring her back to Wonderland.
Stop them.
Kill her.
Kill them all.
To London!
My Hat!

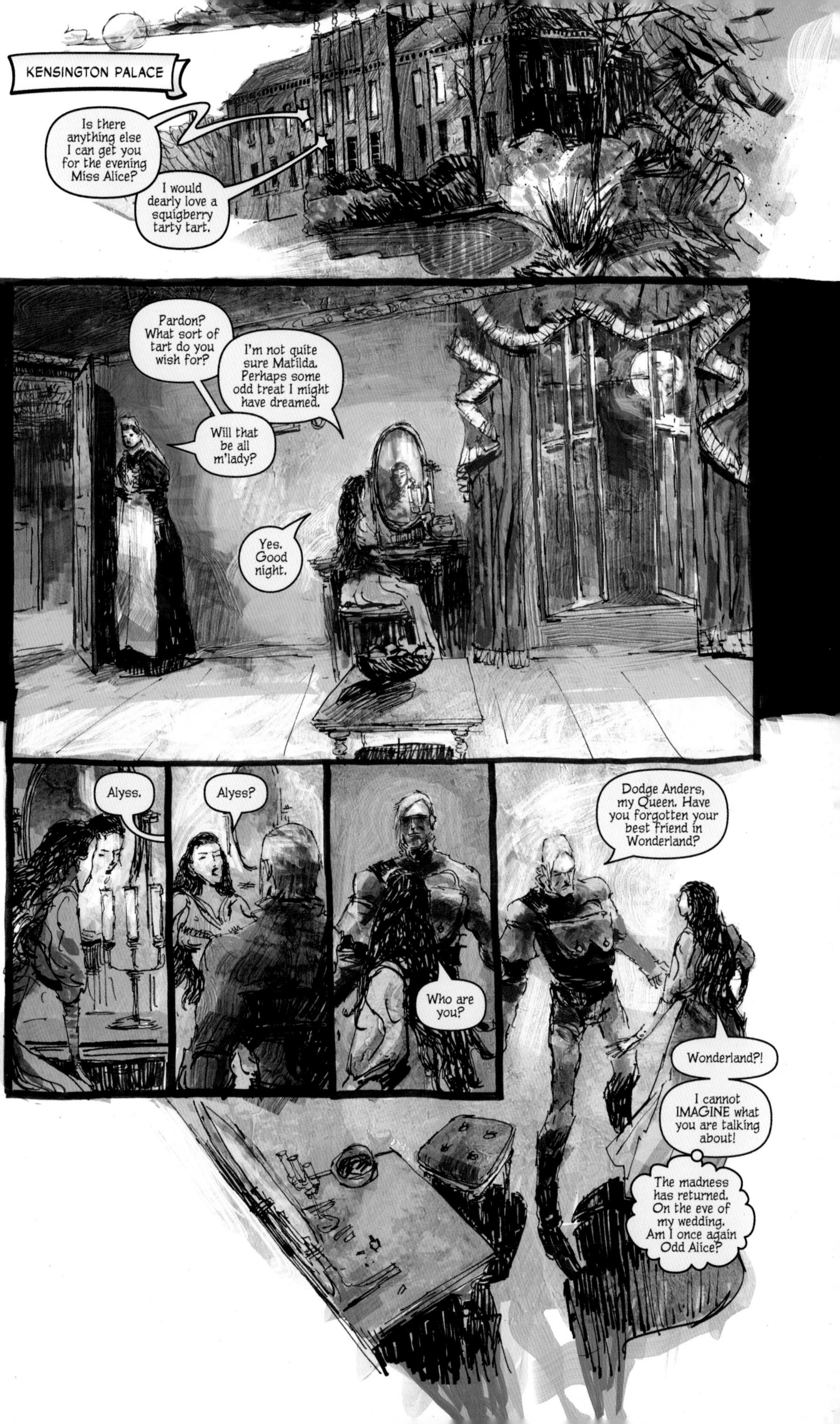
KENSINGTON PALACE
Is there anything else I can get you for the evening Miss Alice?
I would dearly love a squigberry tarty tart.
Pardon? What sort of tart do you wish for?
I'm not quite sure Matilda. Perhaps some odd treat I might have dreamed.
Will that be all m'lady?
Yes. Good night.
Alyss.
Alyss?
Who are you?
Dodge Anders, my Queen. Have you forgotten your best friend in Wonderland?
Wonderland?!
I cannot IMAGINE what you are talking about!
The madness has returned. On the eve of my wedding. Am I once again Odd Alice?

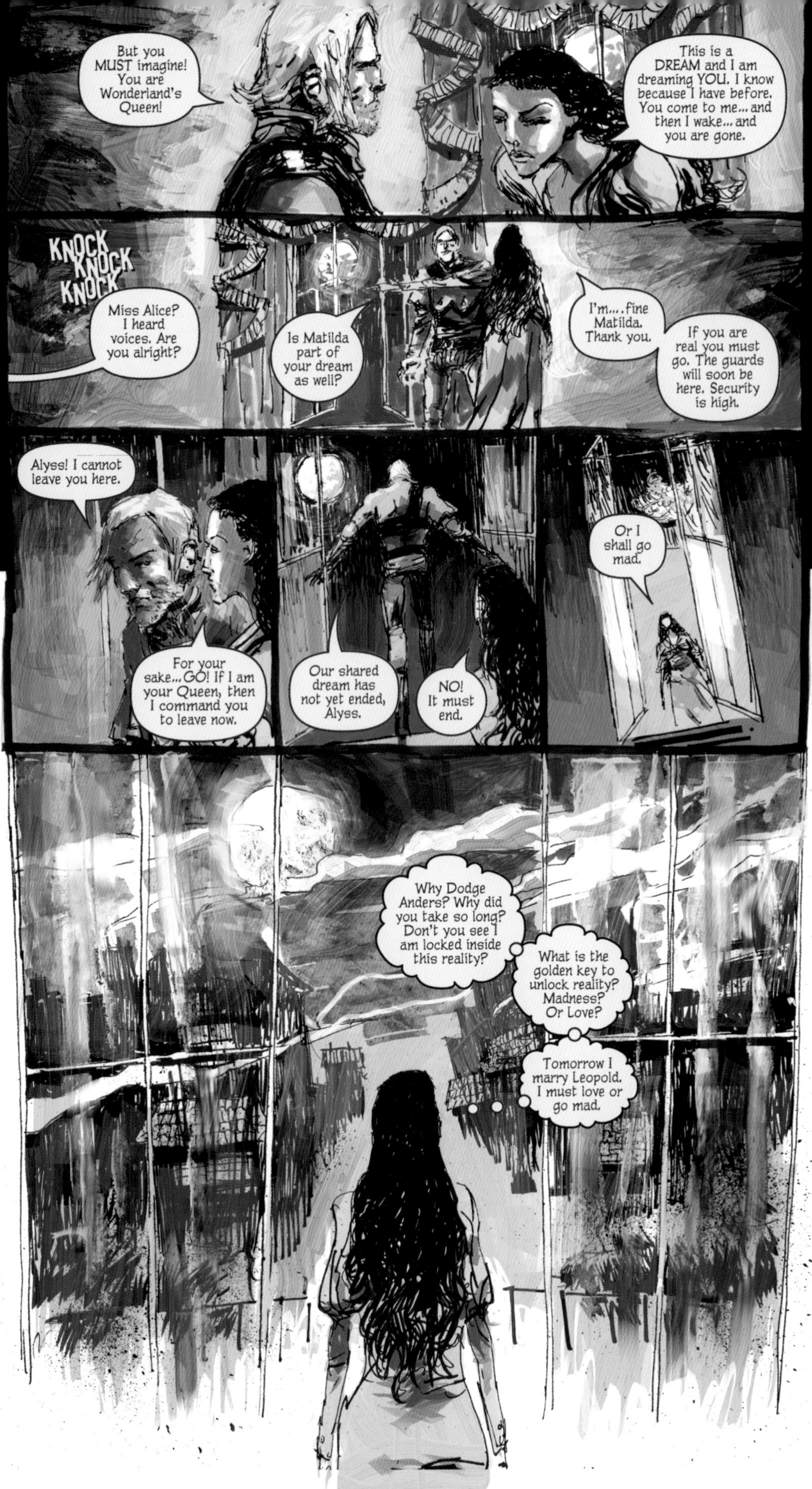
But you MUST imagine! You are Wonderland's Queen!
This is a DREAM and I am dreaming YOU. I know because I have before. You come to me... and then I wake... and you are gone.
KNOCK KNOCK KNOCK
Miss Alice? I heard voices. Are you alright?
Is Matilda part of your dream as well?
I'm.... fine Matilda. Thank you.
If you are real you must go. The guards will soon be here. Security is high.
Alyss! I cannot leave you here.
For your sake... GO! If I am your Queen, then I command you to leave now.
Our shared dream has not yet ended, Alyss.
NO! It must end.
Or I shall go mad.
Why Dodge Anders? Why did you take so long? Don't you see I am locked inside this reality?
What is the golden key to unlock reality? Madness? Or Love?
Tomorrow I marry Leopold. I must love or go mad.

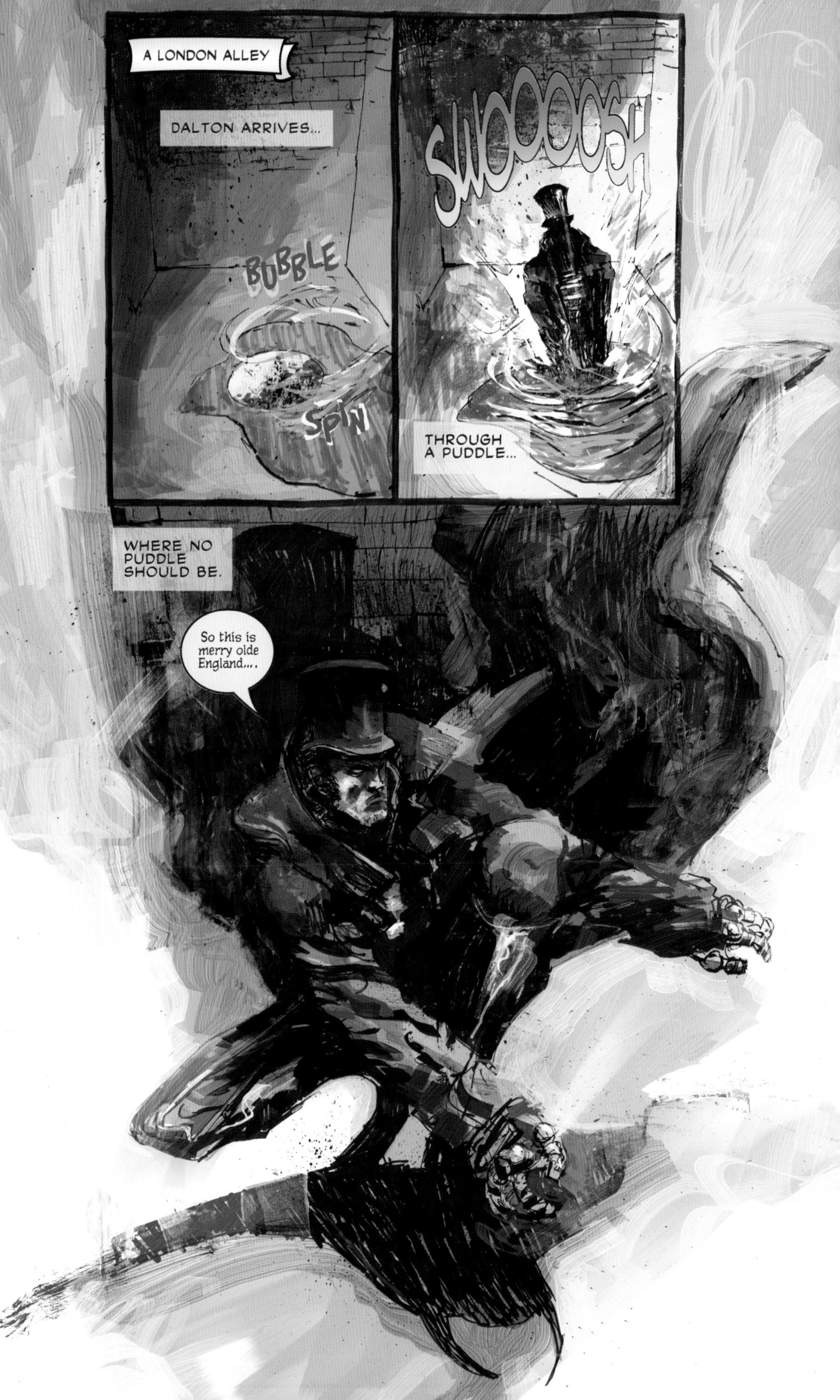

A LONDON ALLEY
DALTON ARRIVES...
BUBBLE
SPIN
SWOOOOSH
THROUGH A PUDDLE...
WHERE NO PUDDLE SHOULD BE.
So this is merry olde England....

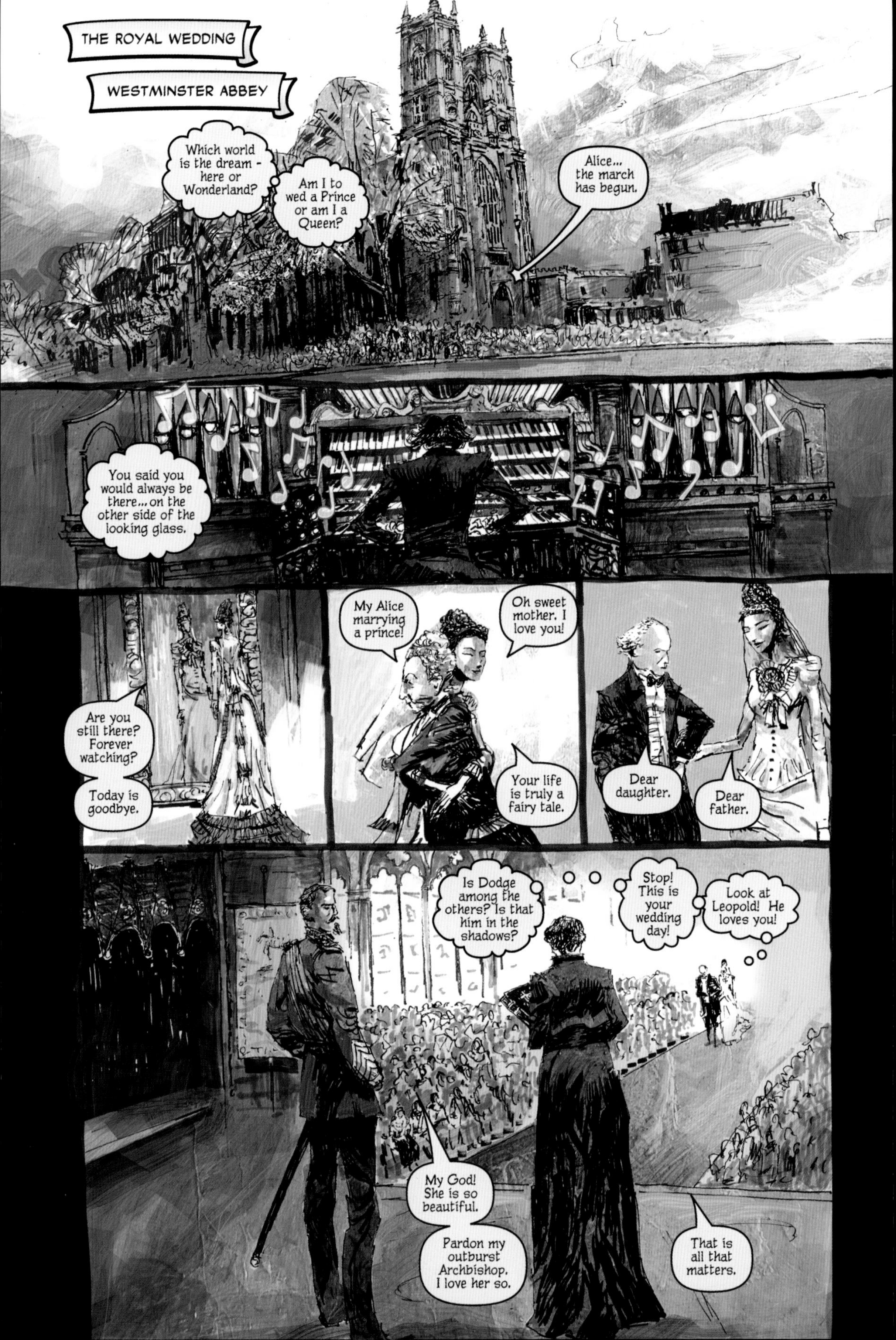
THE ROYAL WEDDING
WESTMINSTER ABBEY
Which world is the dream - here or Wonderland?
Am I to wed a Prince or am I a Queen?
Alice... the march has begun.
You said you would always be there... on the other side of the looking glass.
Are you still there? Forever watching?
Today is goodbye.
My Alice marrying a prince!
Oh sweet mother. I love you!
Your life is truly a fairy tale.
Dear daughter.
Dear father.
Is Dodge among the others? Is that him in the shadows?
Stop! This is your wedding day!
Look at Leopold! He loves you!
My God! She is so beautiful.
Pardon my outburst Archbishop. I love her so.
That is all that matters.

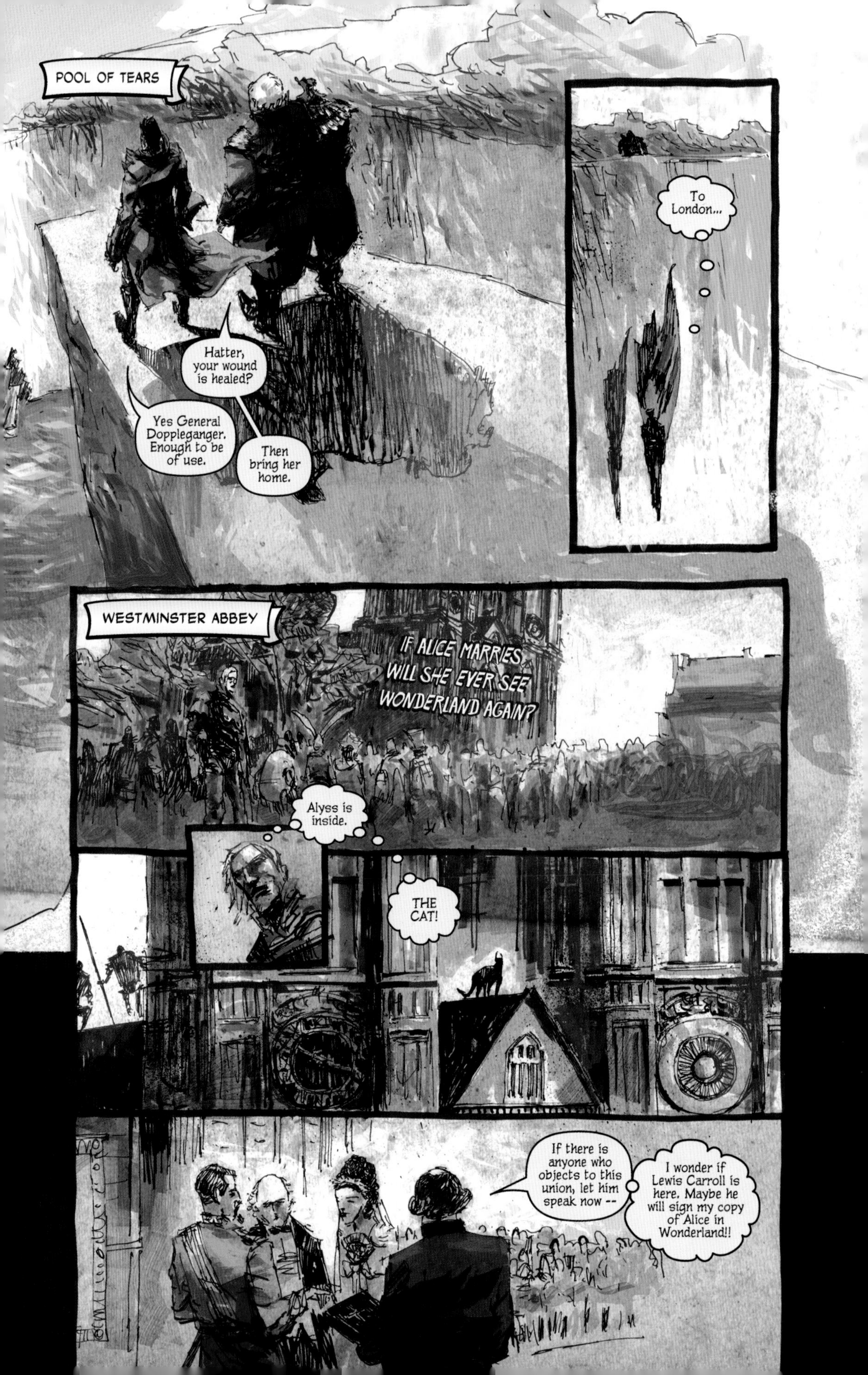

POOL OF TEARS
Hatter, your wound is healed?
Yes General Doppleganger. Enough to be of use.
Then bring her home.
To London...
WESTMINSTER ABBEY
IF ALICE MARRIES, WILL SHE EVER SEE WONDERLAND AGAIN?
Alyss is inside.
THE CAT!
If there is anyone who objects to this union, let him speak now --
I wonder if Lewis Carroll is here. Maybe he will sign my copy of Alice in Wonderland!!

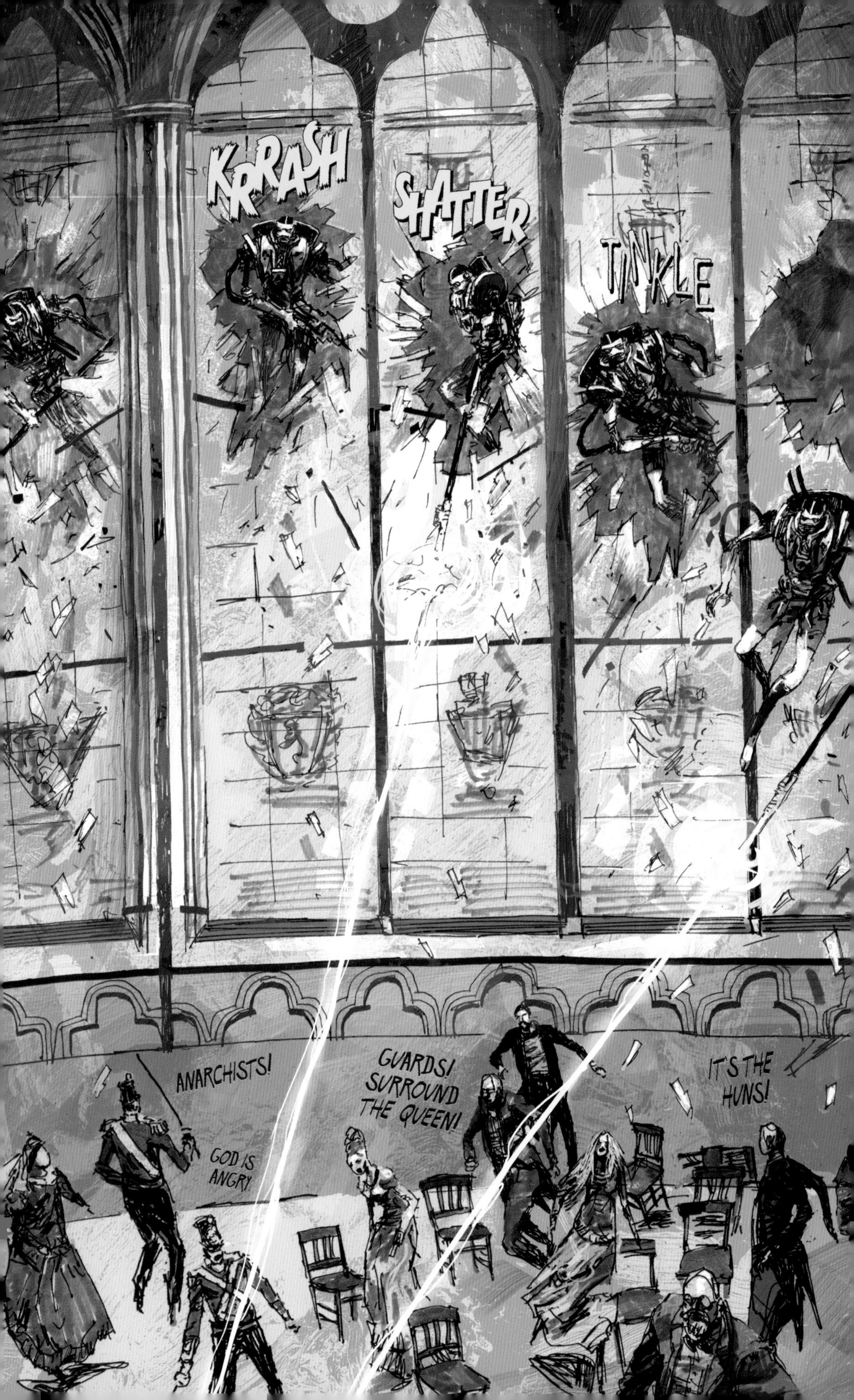
KRRASH
SHATTER
TINKLE
ANARCHISTS!
GOD IS ANGRY
GUARDS! SURROUND THE QUEEN!
IT'S THE HUNS!

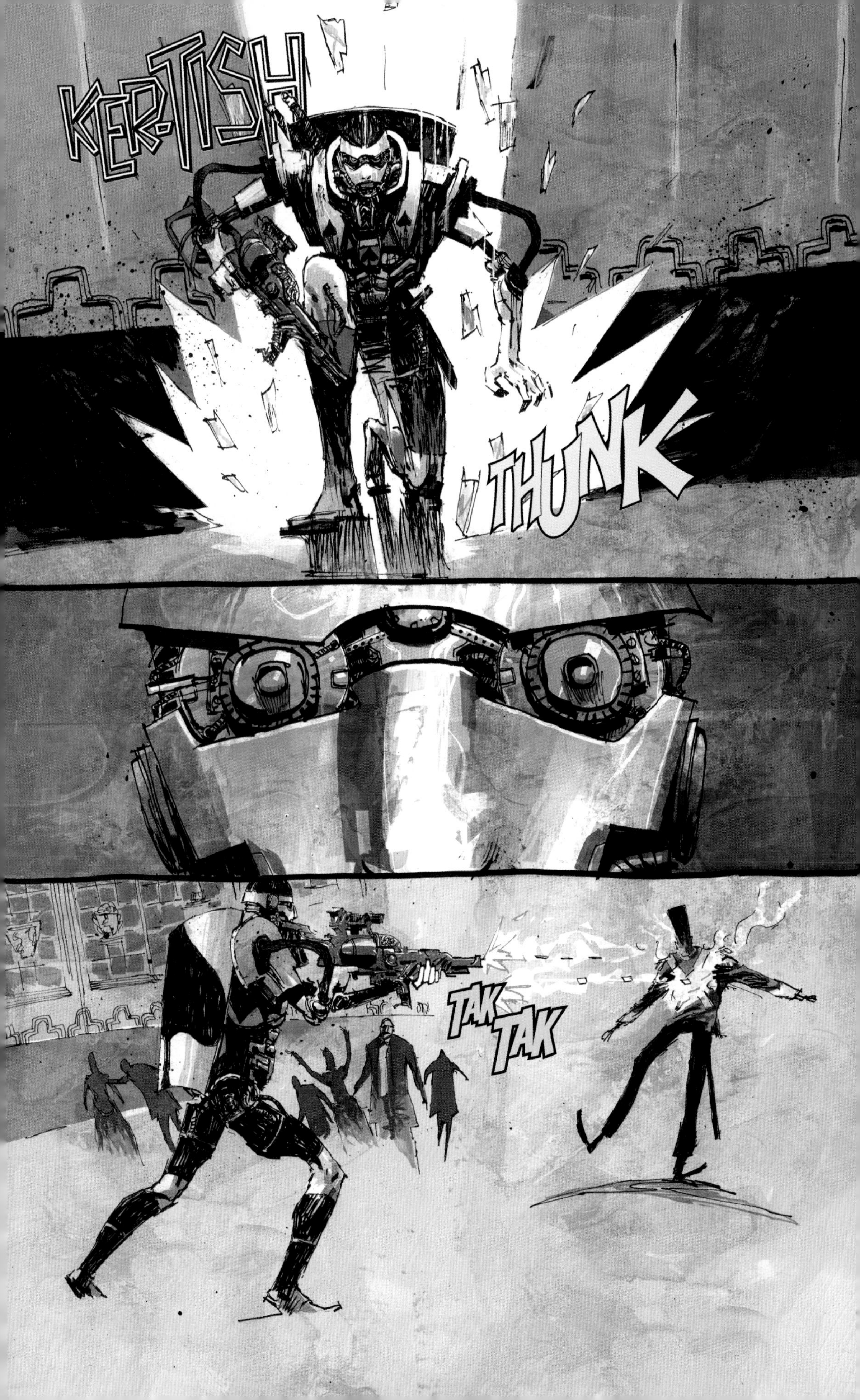
KER-TISH
THUNK
TAK
TAK

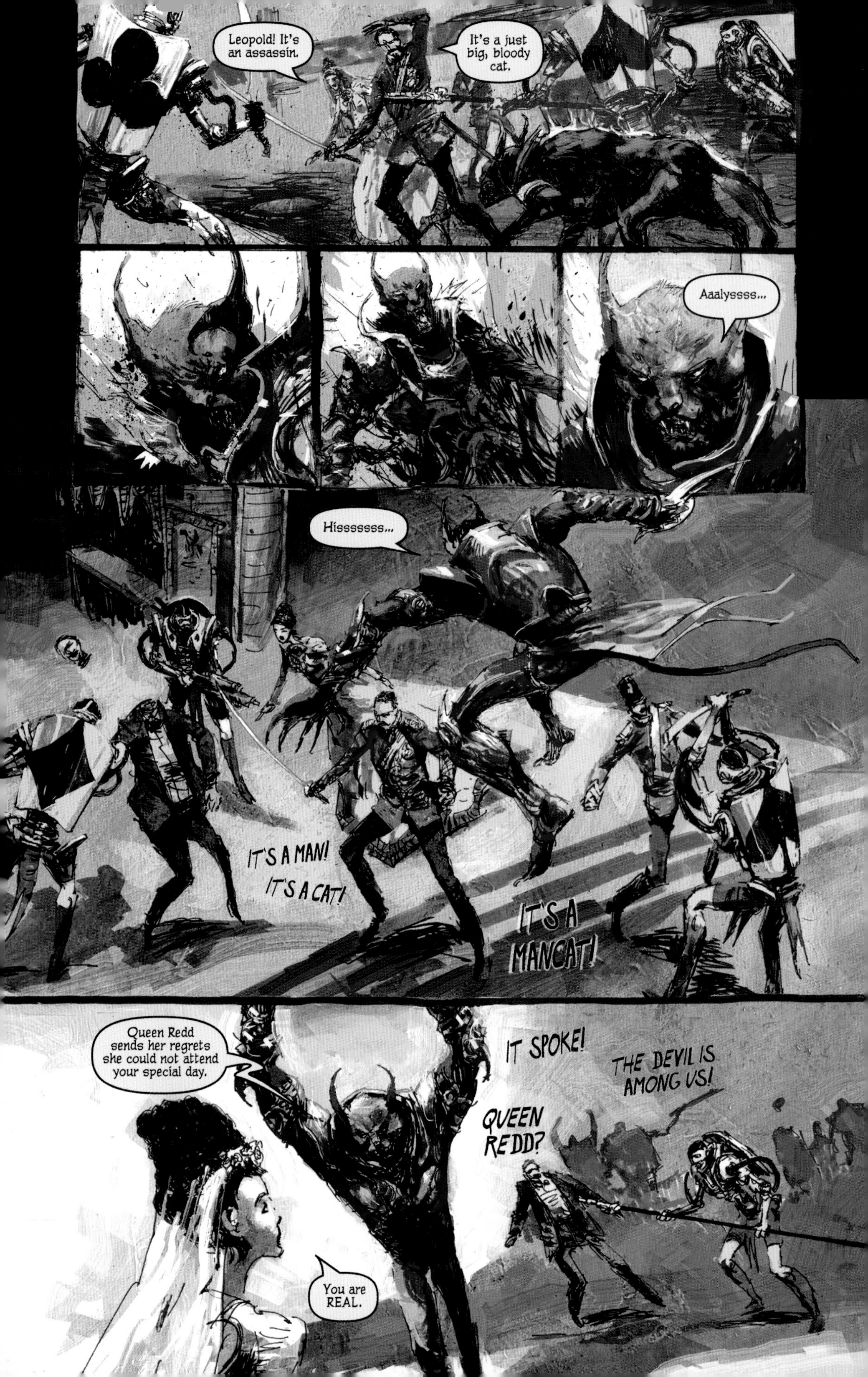
Leopold! It's an assassin.
It's a just big, bloody cat.
Aaalyssss...
Hissssssss...
IT'S A MAN!
IT'S A CAT!
IT'S A MANCAT!
Queen Redd sends her regrets she could not attend your special day.
IT SPOKE!
THE DEVIL IS AMONG US!
QUEEN REDD?
You are REAL.

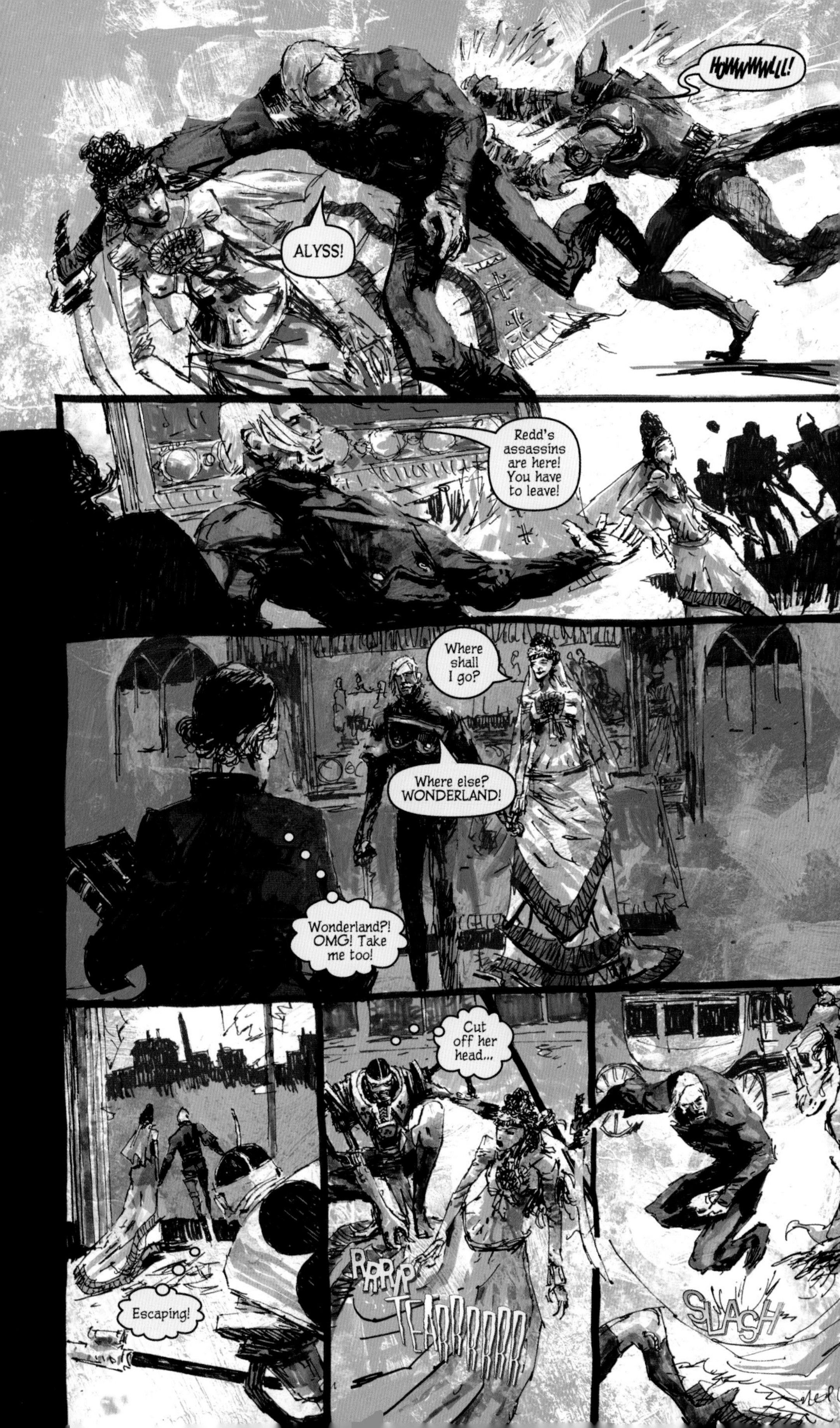
HOWWWWLL!
ALYSS!
Redd's assassins are here! You have to leave!
Where shall I go?
Where else? WONDERLAND!
Wonderland?! OMG! Take me too!
Escaping!
Cut off her head...
RRRRIP
TEARRRRRR
SLASH

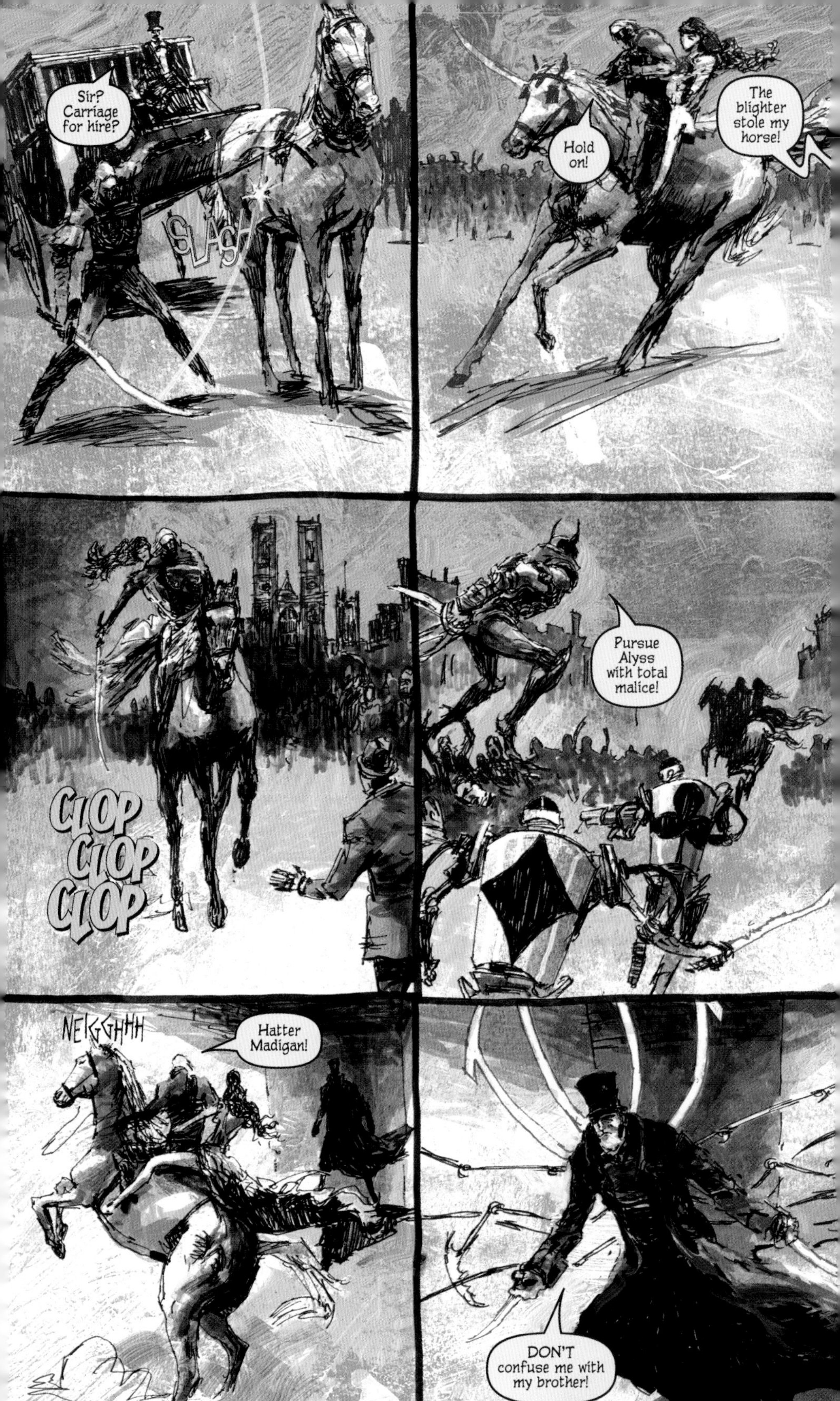

Sir? Carriage for hire?
SLASH
Hold on!
The blighter stole my horse!
CLOP CLOP CLOP
Pursue Alyss with total malice!
NEIGGHHH
Hatter Madigan!
DON'T confuse me with my brother!

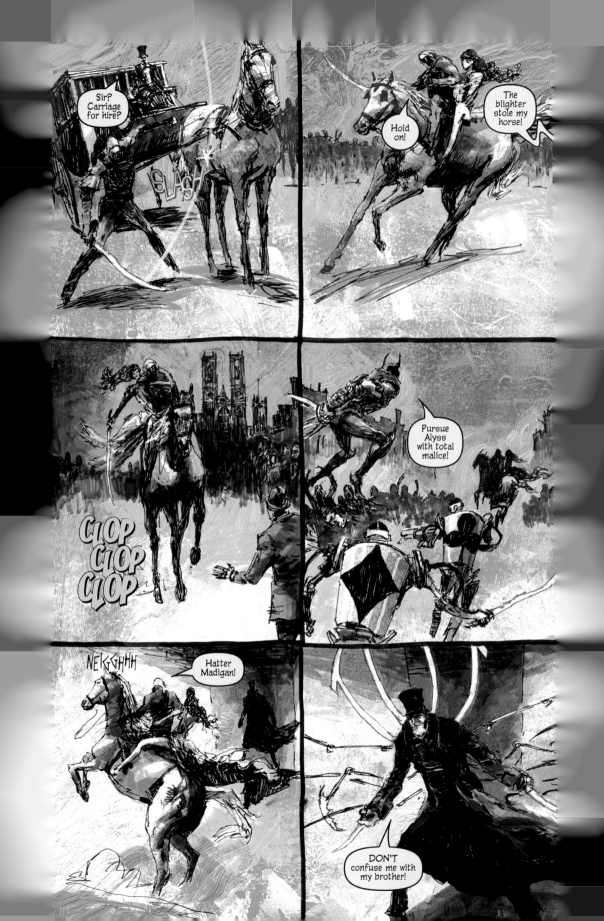

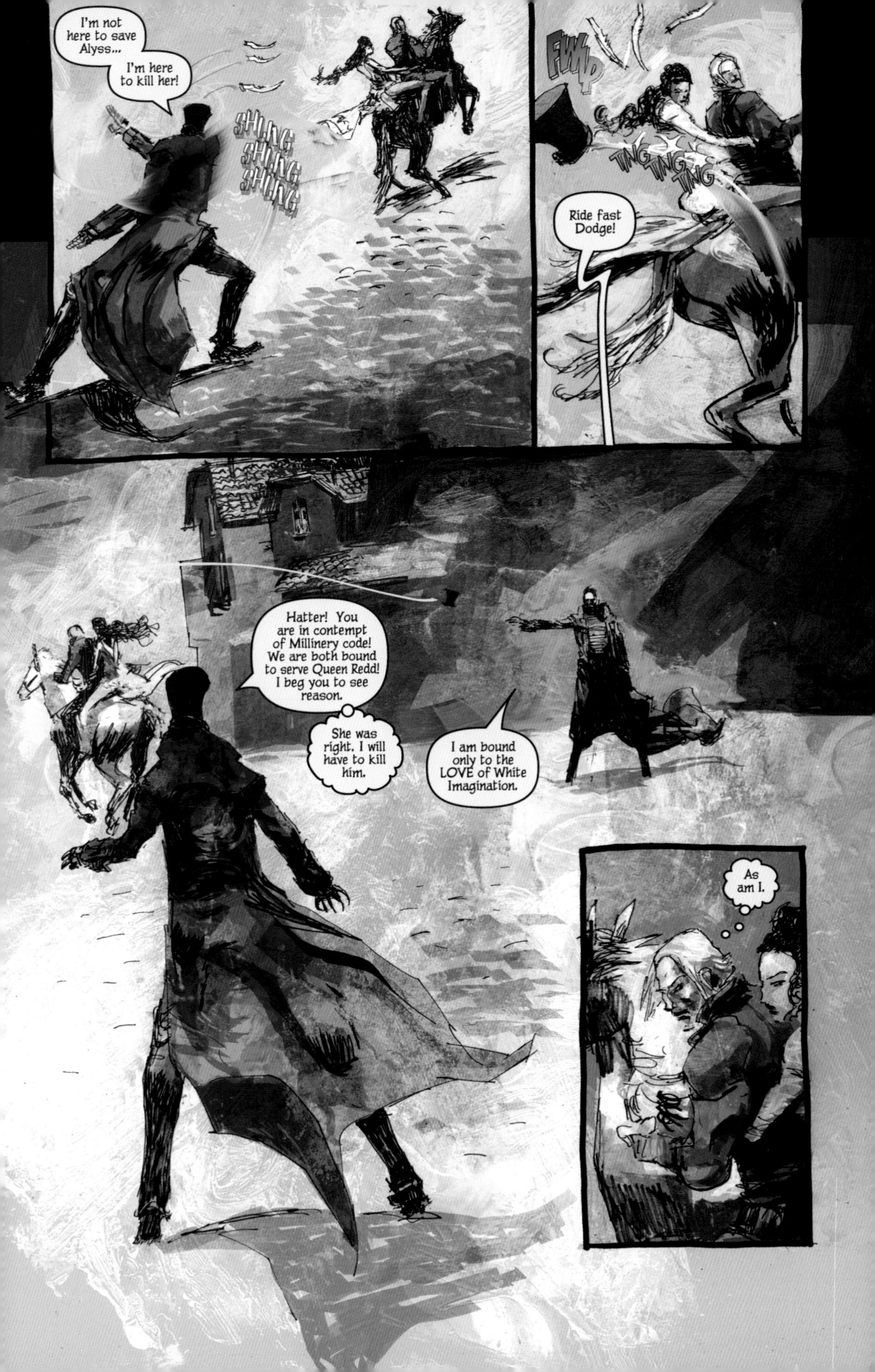
I'm not here to save Alyss...
I'm here to kill her!
SHING SHING SHING
FWAP
TING TING TING
Ride fast Dodge!
Hatter! You are in contempt of Millinery code! We are both bound to serve Queen Redd! I beg you to see reason.
She was right. I will have to kill him.
I am bound only to the LOVE of White Imagination.
As am I.

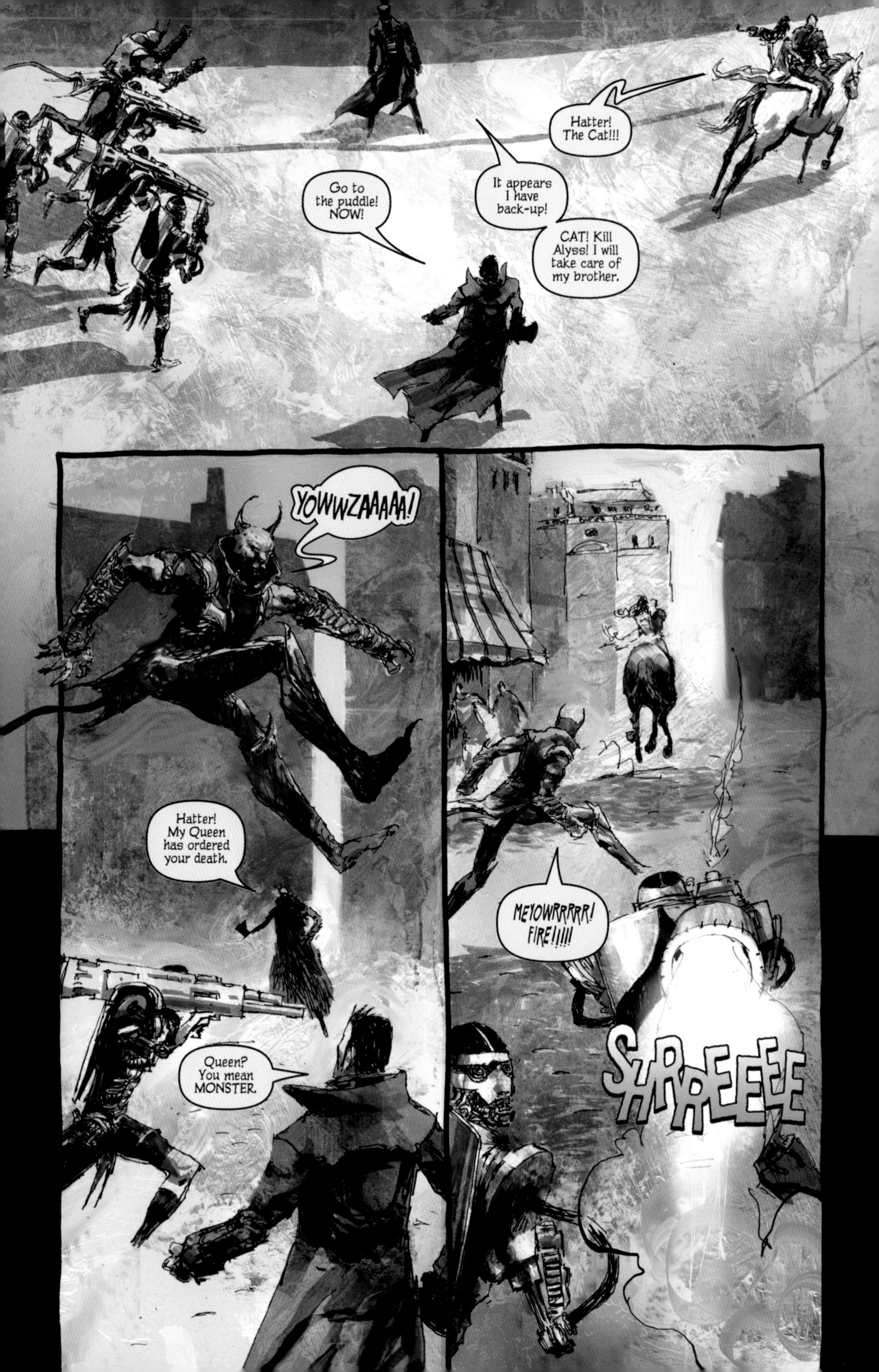
Hatter! The Cat!!!
It appears I have back-up!
Go to the puddle! NOW!
CAT! Kill Alyss! I will take care of my brother.
YOWWZAAAAA!
Hatter! My Queen has ordered your death.
Queen? You mean MONSTER.
MEYOWRRRRR! FIRE!!!!!
SHRREEEE

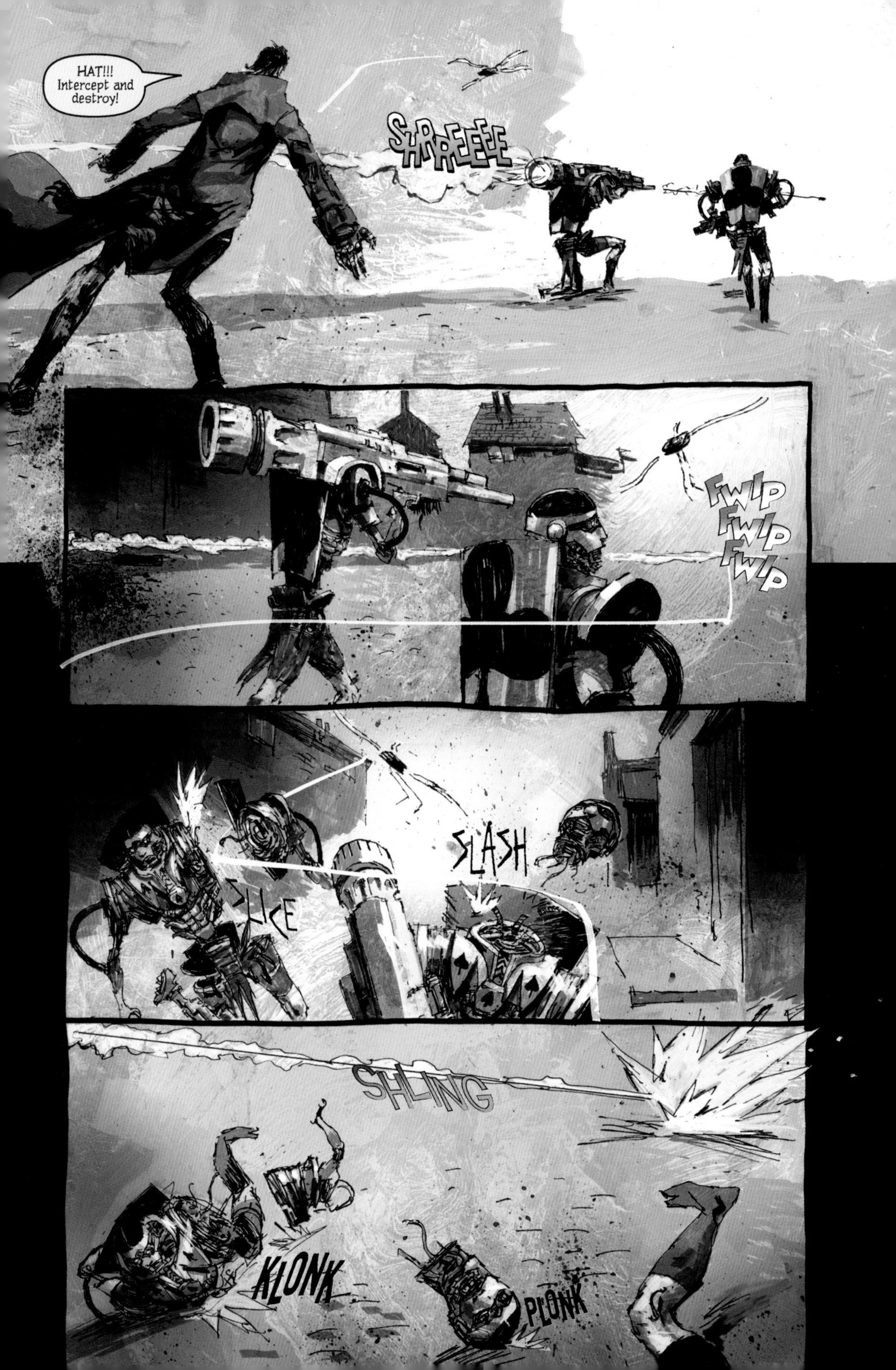
HAT!!! Intercept and destroy!
SHRREEEE
FWIP FWIP FWIP
SLASH
SLICE
SHLING
KLONK
PLONK

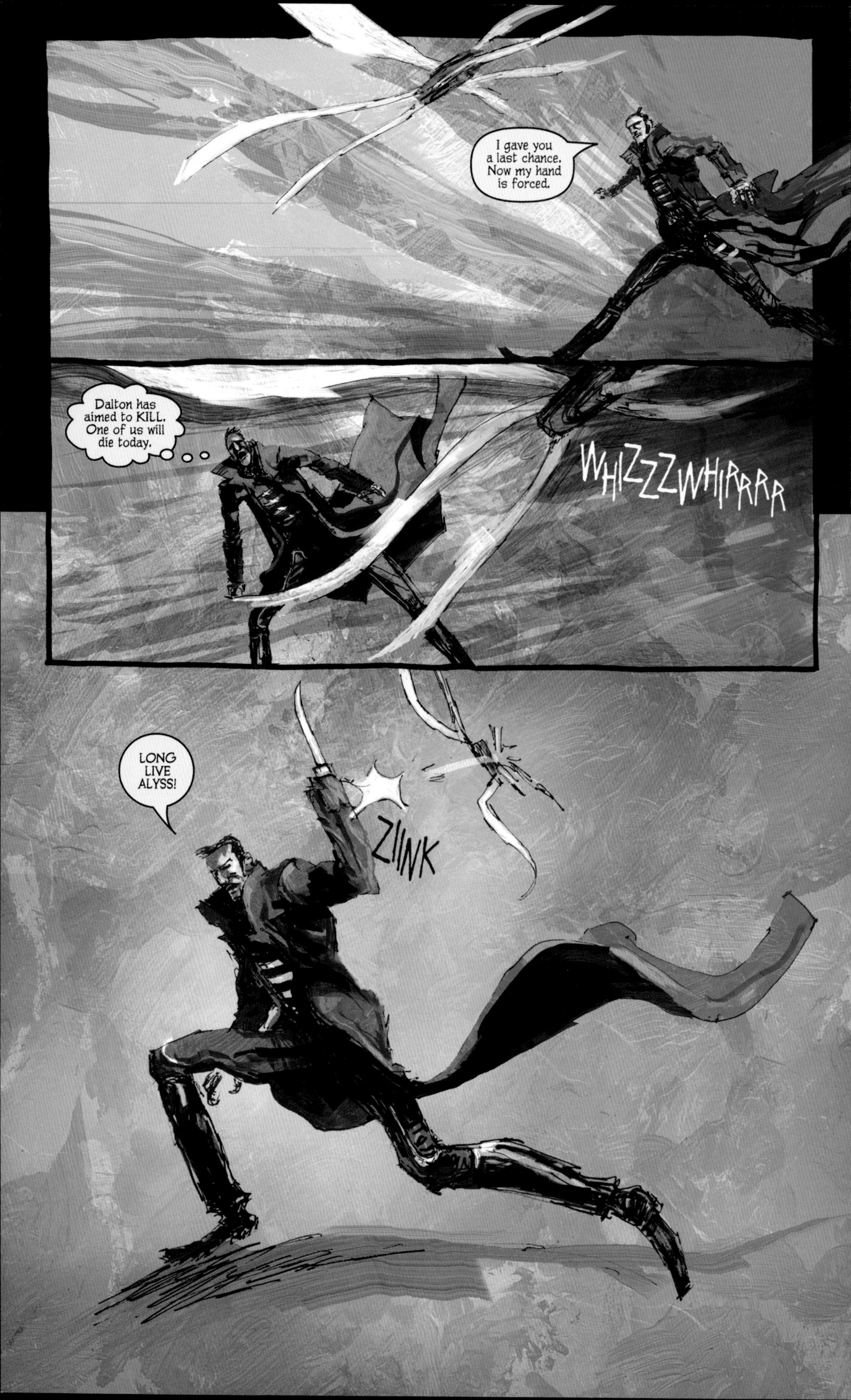
I gave you a last chance. Now my hand is forced.
Dalton has aimed to KILL. One of us will die today.
WHIZZZWHIRRRR
LONG LIVE ALYSS!
ZIINK

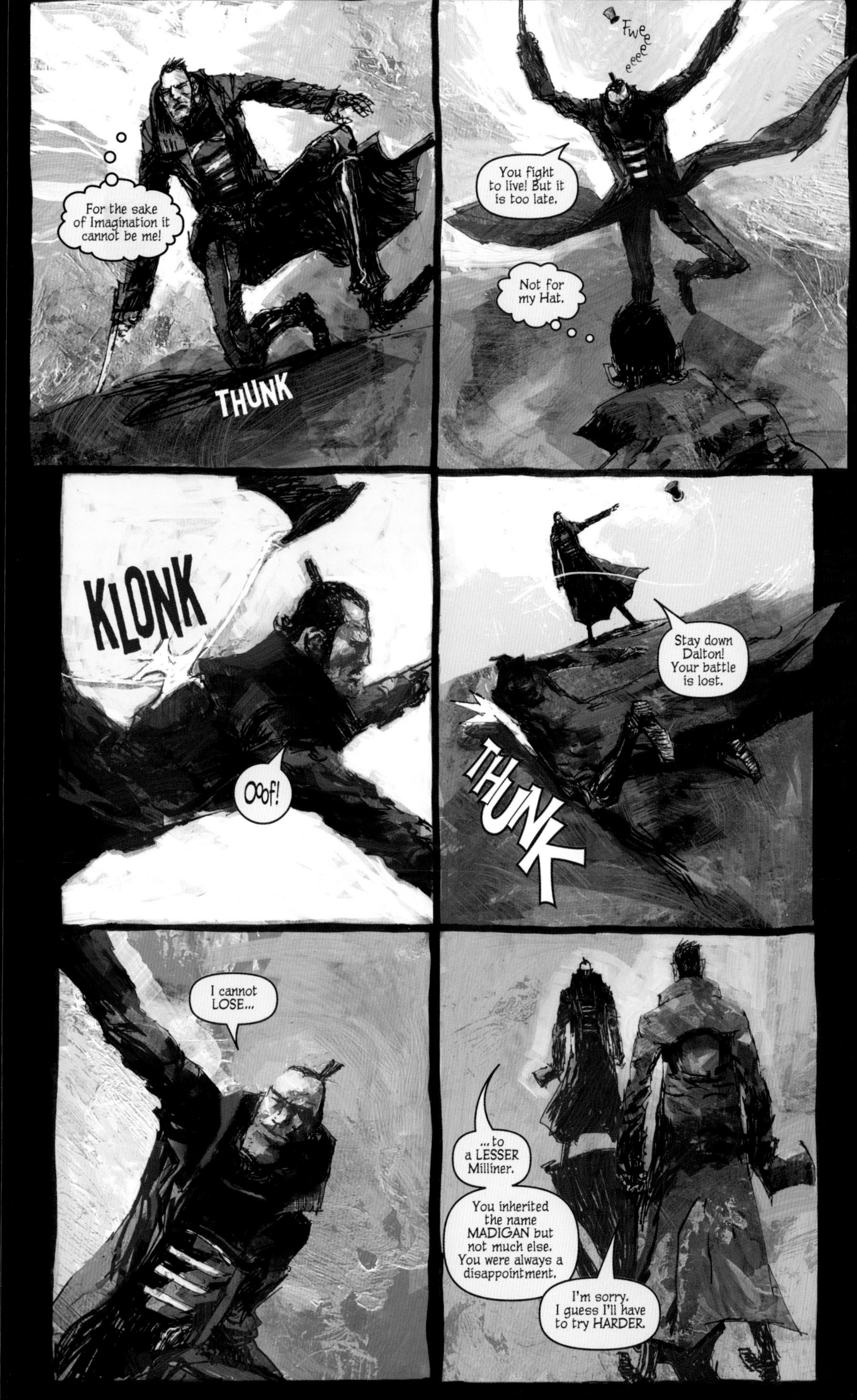

For the sake of Imagination it cannot be me!
THUNK
Fweeeeee
You fight to live! But it is too late.
Not for my Hat.
KLONK
Ooof!
Stay down Dalton! Your battle is lost.
THUNK
I cannot LOSE...
...to a LESSER Milliner.
You inherited the name MADIGAN but not much else. You were always a disappointment.
I'm sorry. I guess I'll have to try HARDER.

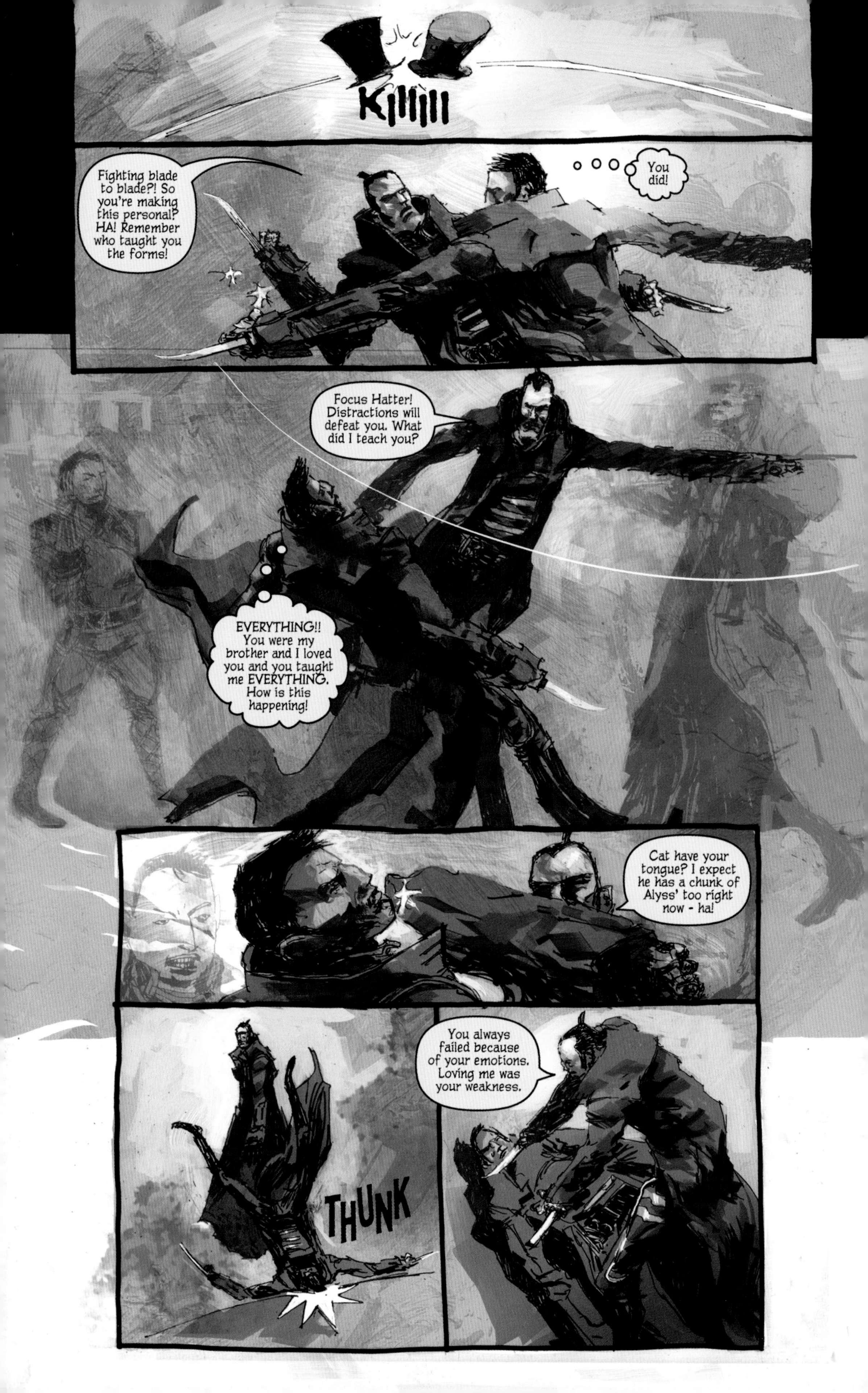
KIIIIII
Fighting blade to blade?! So you're making this personal? HA! Remember who taught you the forms!
You did!
Focus Hatter! Distractions will defeat you. What did I teach you?
EVERYTHING!! You were my brother and I loved you and you taught me EVERYTHING. How is this happening!
Cat have your tongue? I expect he has a chunk of Alyss' too right now - ha!
THUNK
You always failed because of your emotions. Loving me was your weakness.

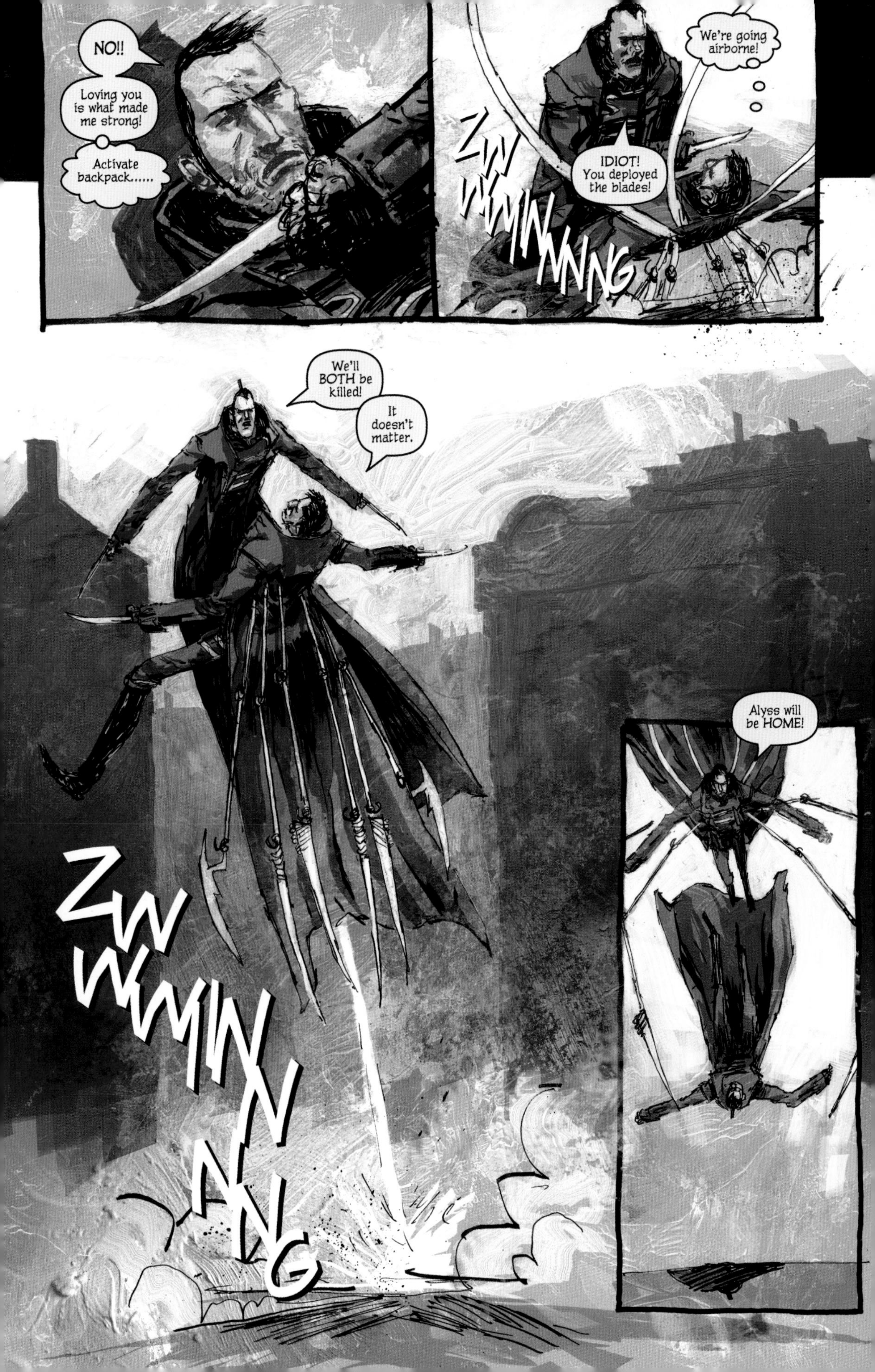
NO!!
Loving you is what made me strong!
Activate backpack......
ZWWMMMWWNNG
We're going airborne!
IDIOT! You deployed the blades!
We'll BOTH be killed!
It doesn't matter.
ZWWMMMWWNNANG
Alyss will be HOME!

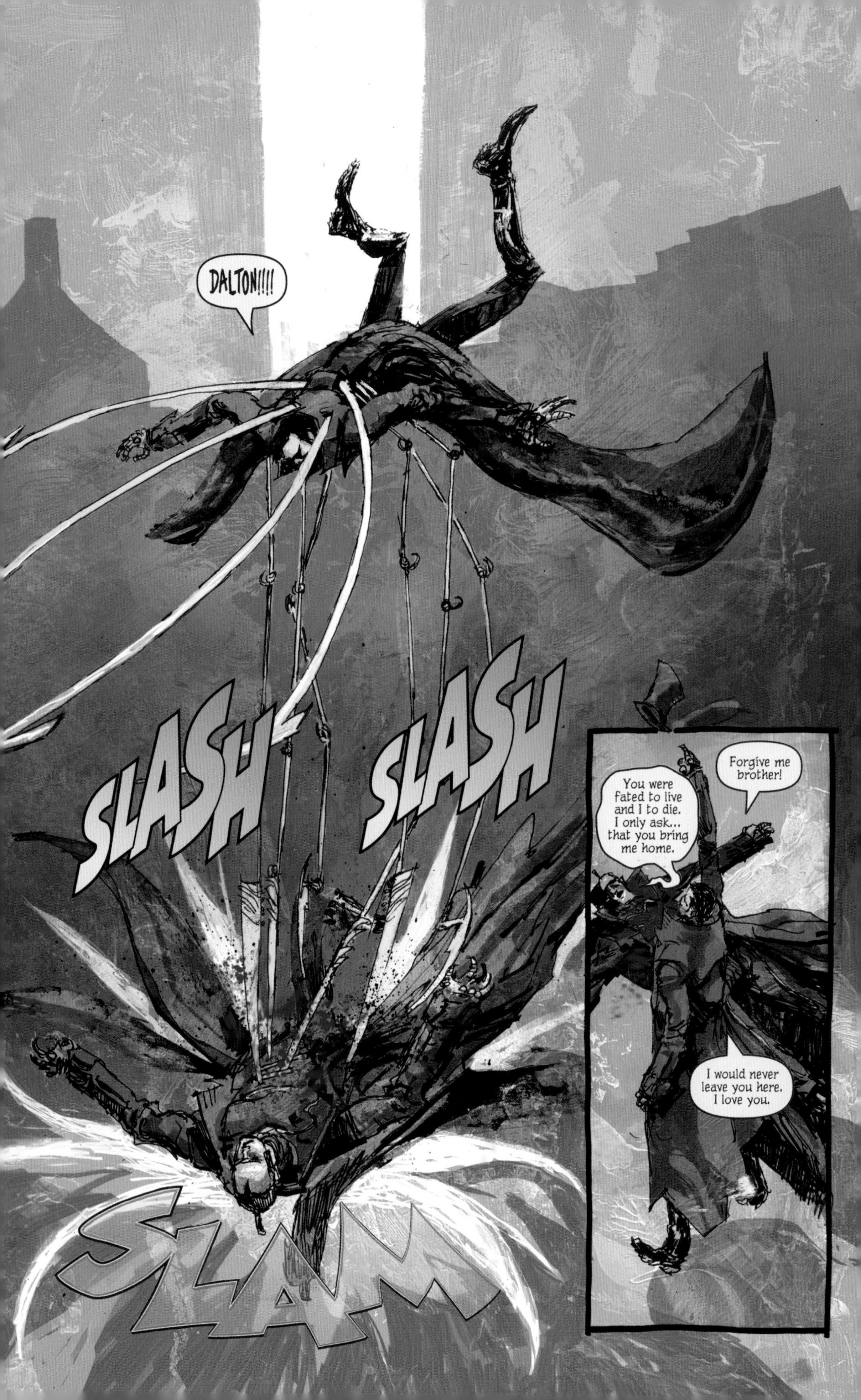
DALTON!!!!
SLASH
SLASH
SLAM
Forgive me brother!
You were fated to live and I to die. I only ask... that you bring me home.
I would never leave you here. I love you.

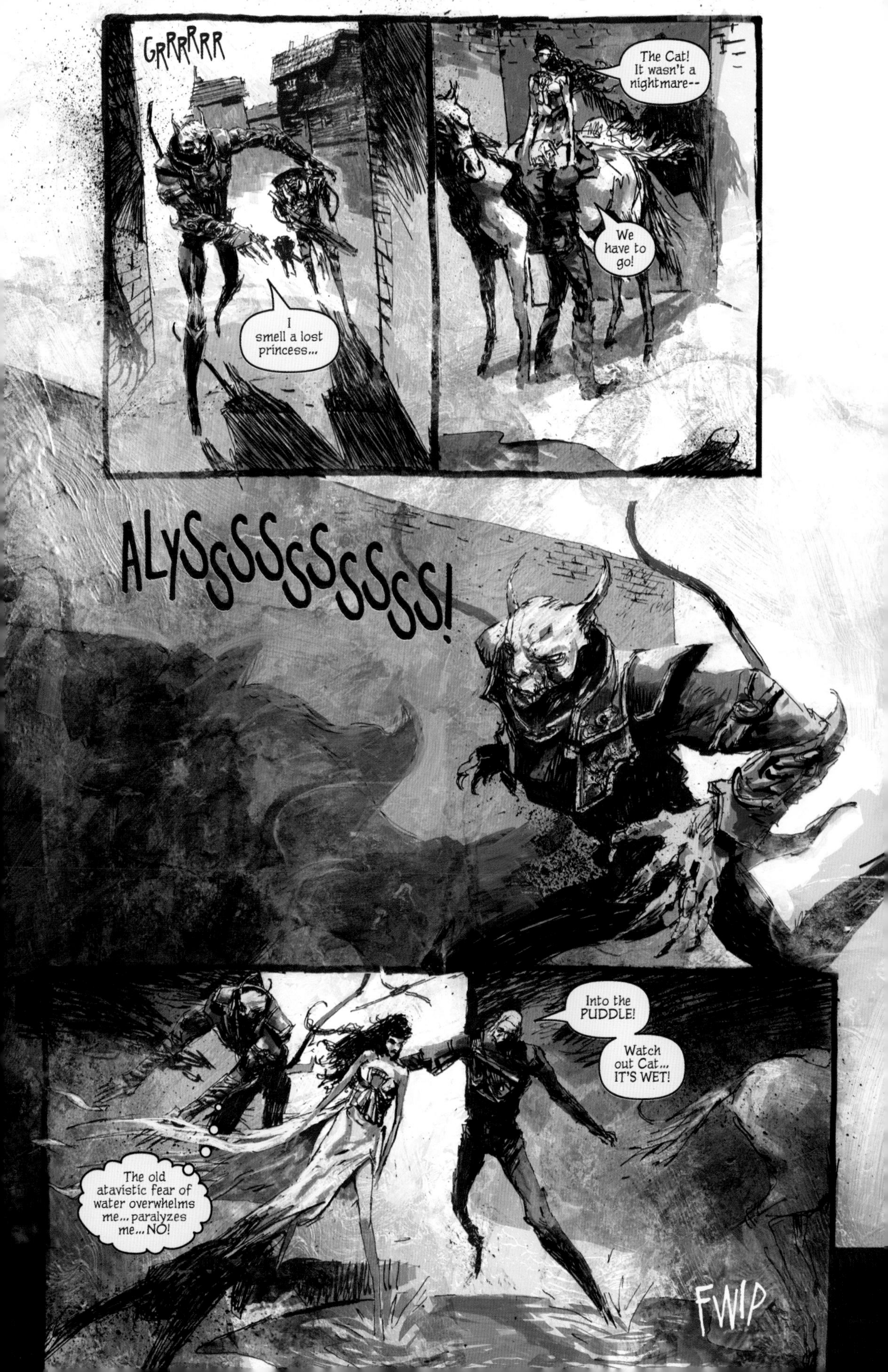
GRRRRRR
I smell a lost princess...
The Cat! It wasn't a nightmare--
We have to go!
ALYSSSSSSSSSSS!
Into the PUDDLE!
Watch out Cat... IT'S WET!
The old atavistic fear of water overwhelms me... paralyzes me... NO!
FWIP

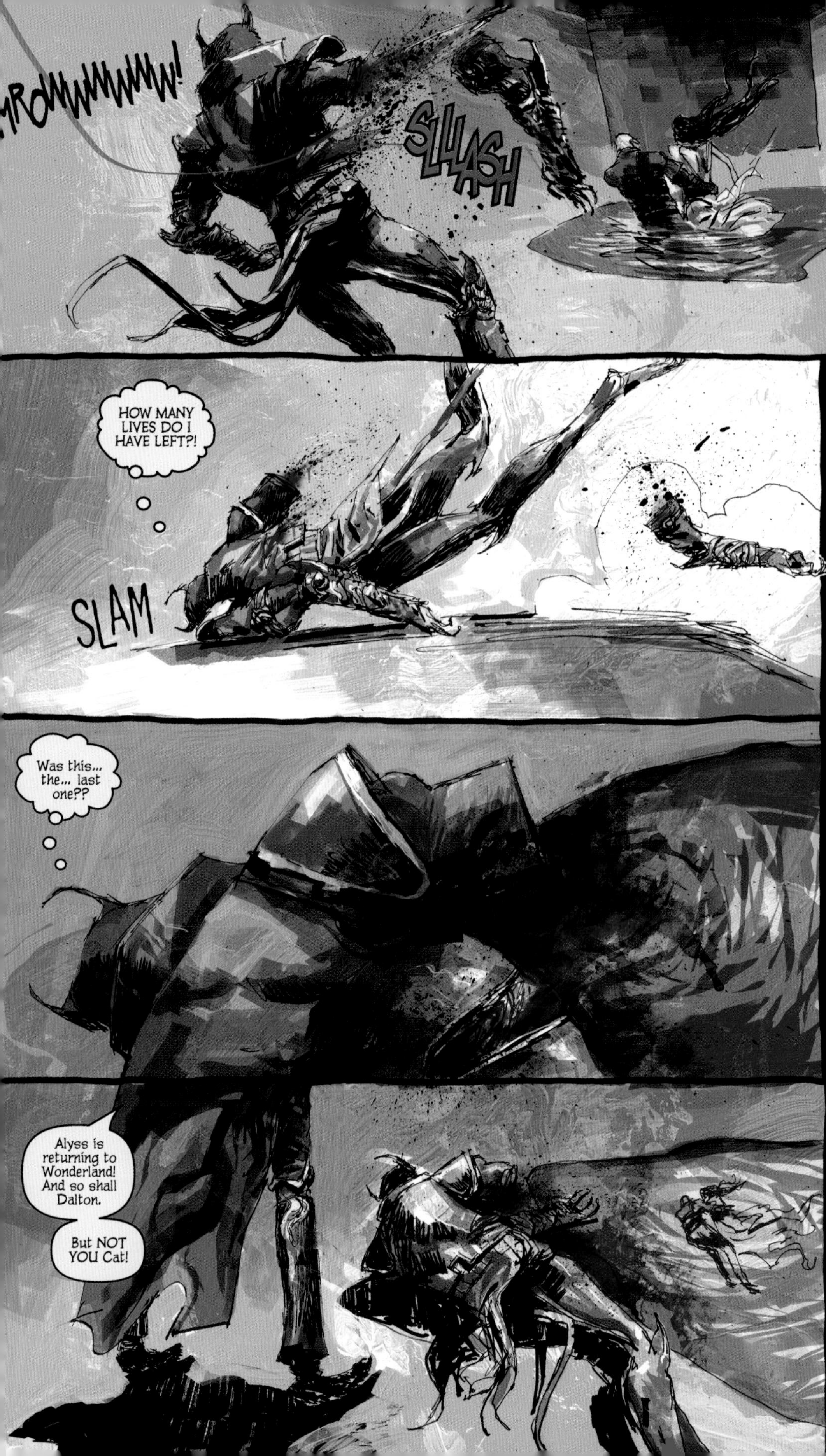
MROWWWWWW!
SLLLASH
HOW MANY LIVES DO I HAVE LEFT?!
SLAM
Was this... the... last one??
Alyss is returning to Wonderland! And so shall Dalton.
But NOT YOU Cat!

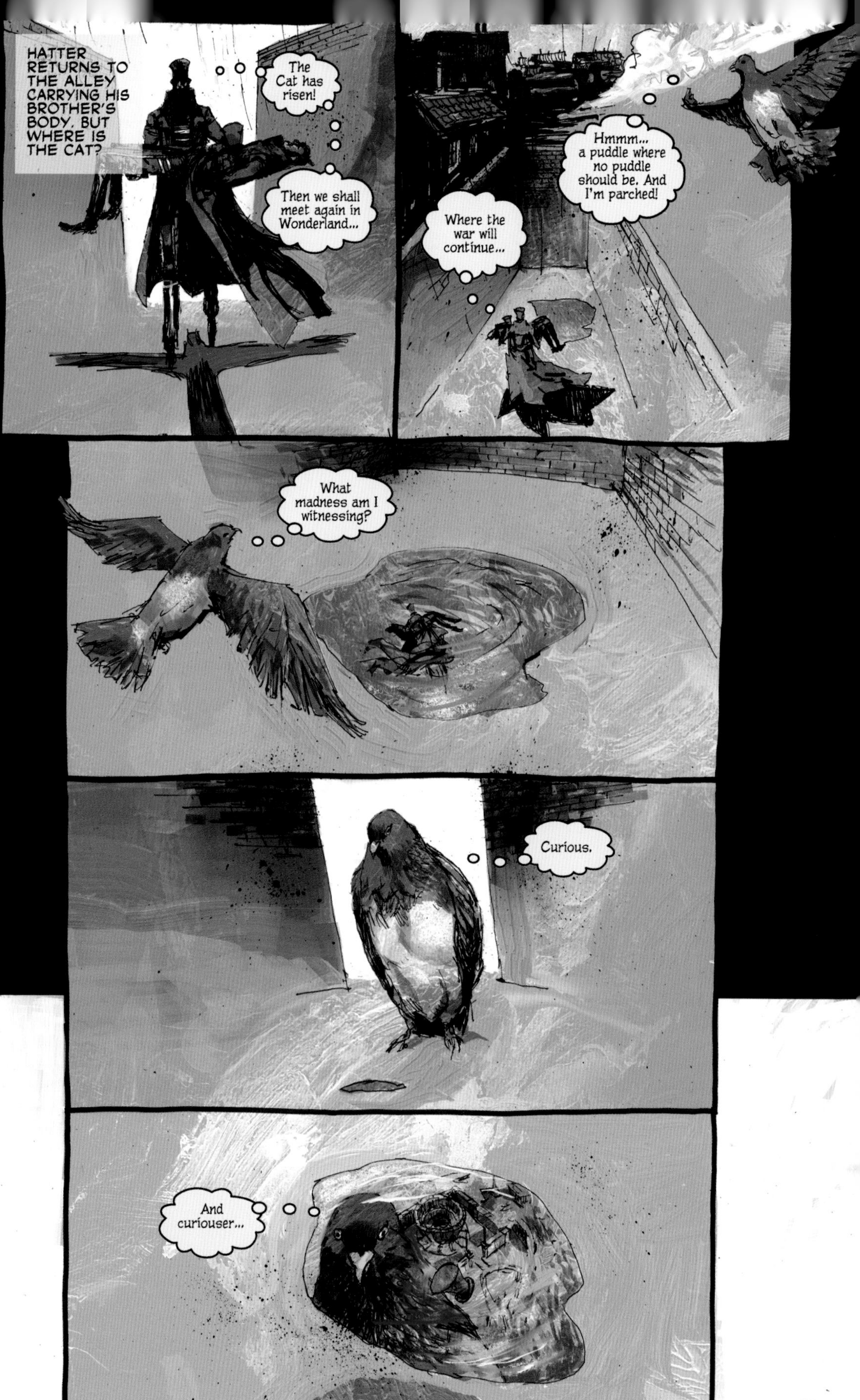
HATTER RETURNS TO THE ALLEY CARRYING HIS BROTHER'S BODY. BUT WHERE IS THE CAT?
The Cat has risen!
Then we shall meet again in Wonderland...
Hmmm... a puddle where no puddle should be. And I'm parched!
Where the war will continue...
What madness am I witnessing?
Curious.
And curiouser...

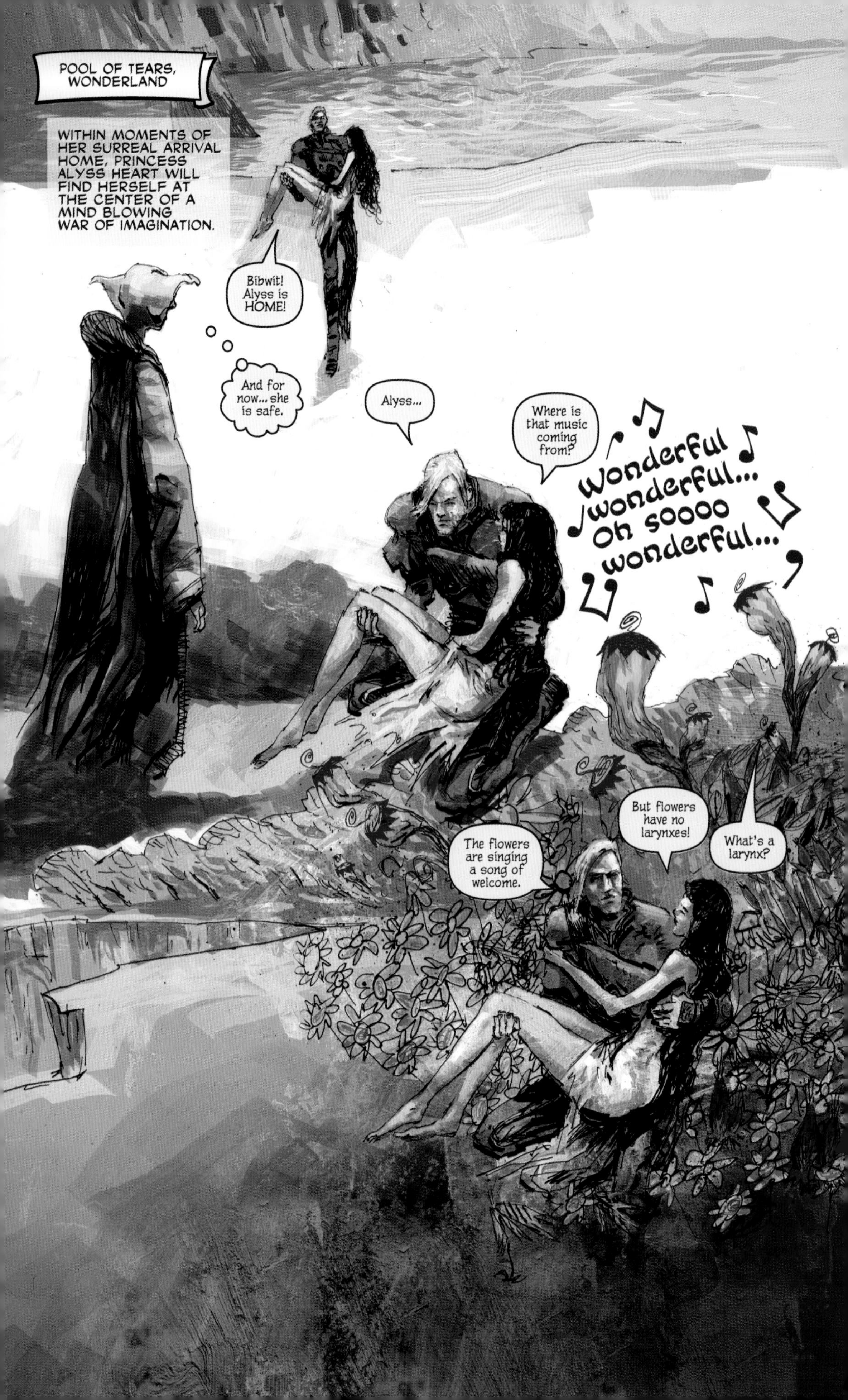
POOL OF TEARS, WONDERLAND
WITHIN MOMENTS OF HER SURREAL ARRIVAL HOME, PRINCESS ALYSS HEART WILL FIND HERSELF AT THE CENTER OF A MIND BLOWING WAR OF IMAGINATION.
Bibwit! Alyss is HOME!
And for now... she is safe.
Alyss...
Where is that music coming from?
Wonderful wonderful... Oh soooo wonderful...
The flowers are singing a song of welcome.
But flowers have no larynxes!
What's a larynx?

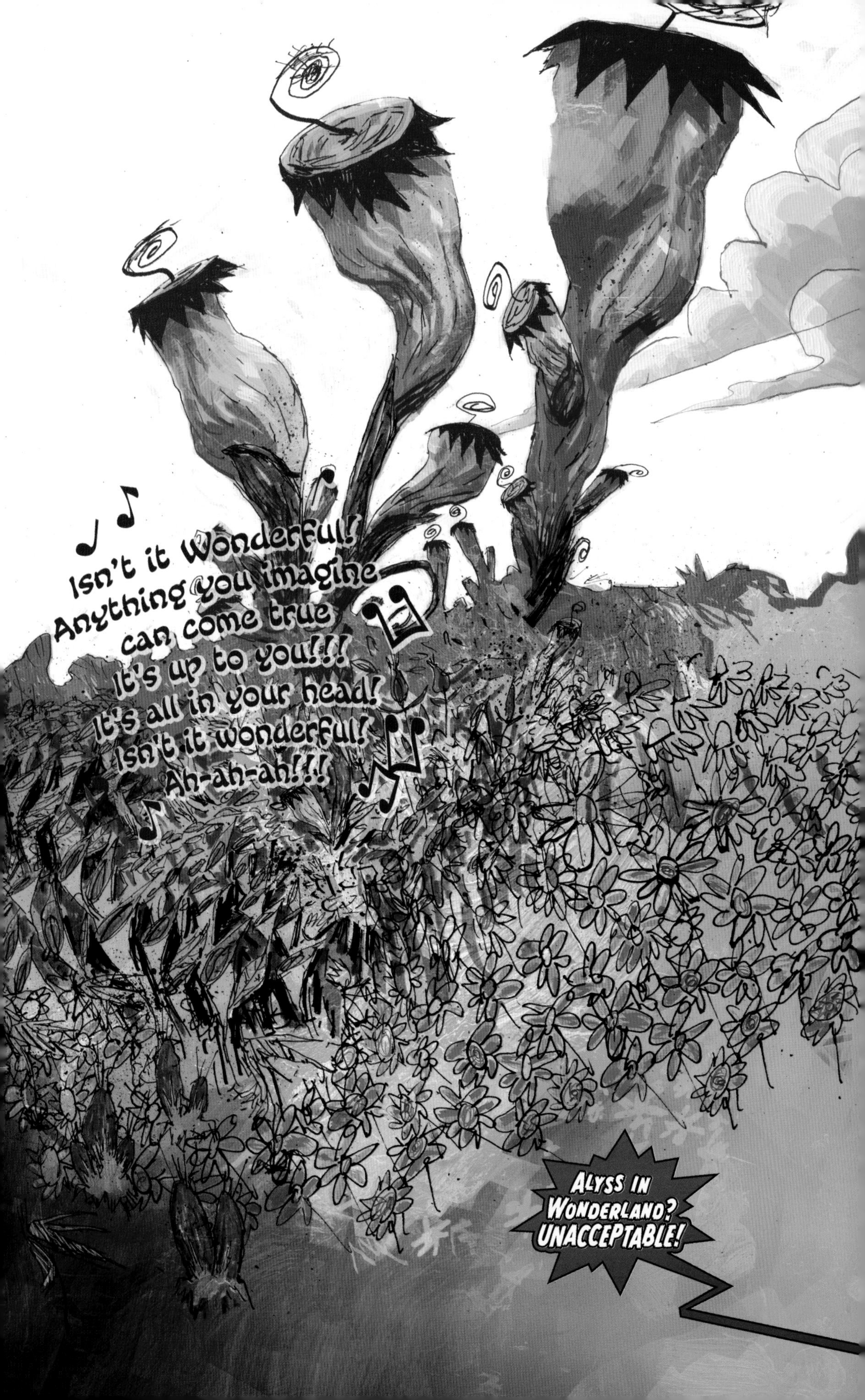
Isn't it Wonderful!
Anything you imagine
can come true
It's up to you!!!
It's all in your head!
Isn't it wonderful!
Ah-ah-ah!!!
ALYSS IN WONDERLAND? UNACCEPTABLE!

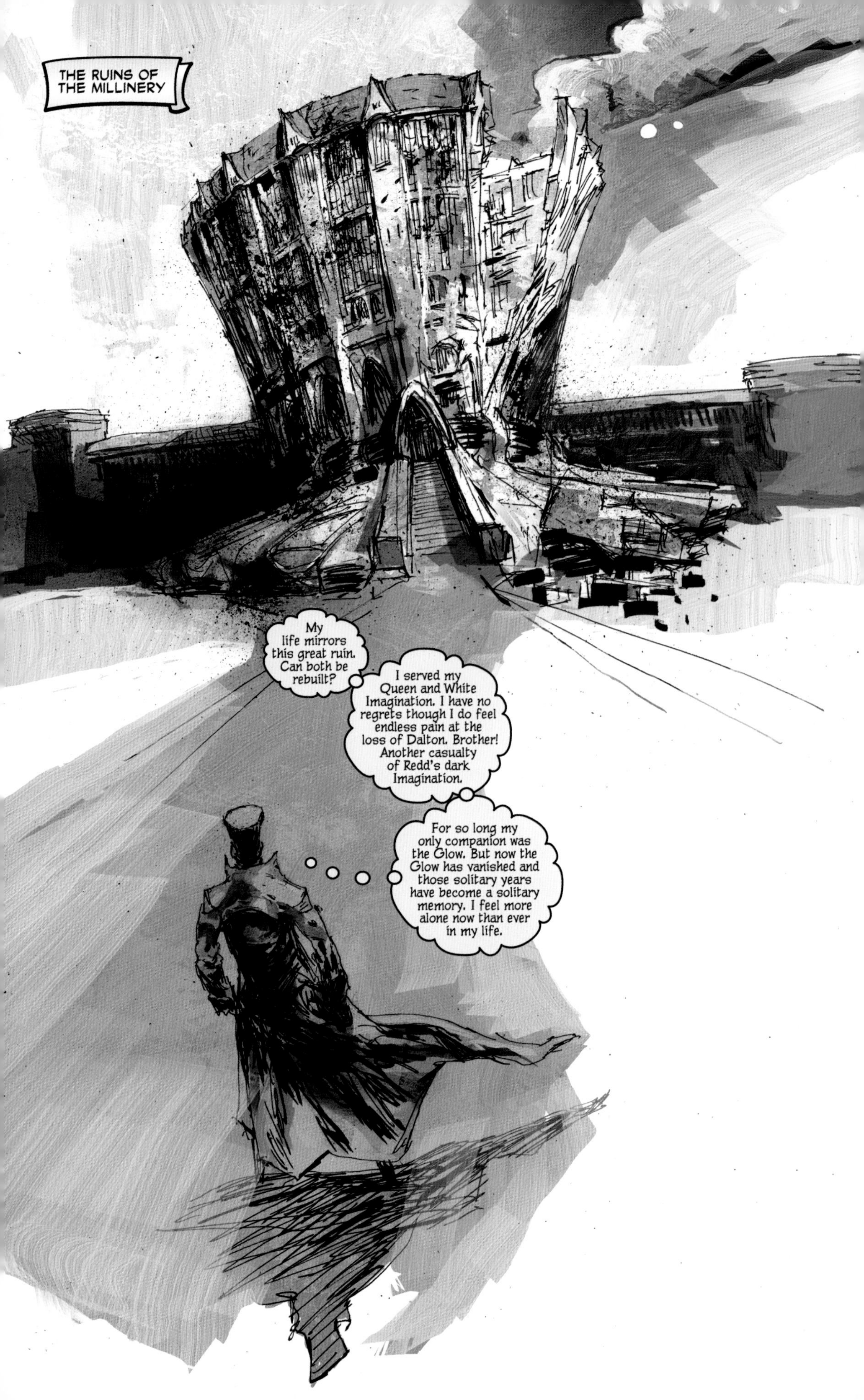
THE RUINS OF THE MILLINERY
My life mirrors this great ruin. Can both be rebuilt?
I served my Queen and White Imagination. I have no regrets though I do feel endless pain at the loss of Dalton. Brother! Another casualty of Redd's dark Imagination.
For so long my only companion was the Glow. But now the Glow has vanished and those solitary years have become a solitary memory. I feel more alone now than ever in my life.

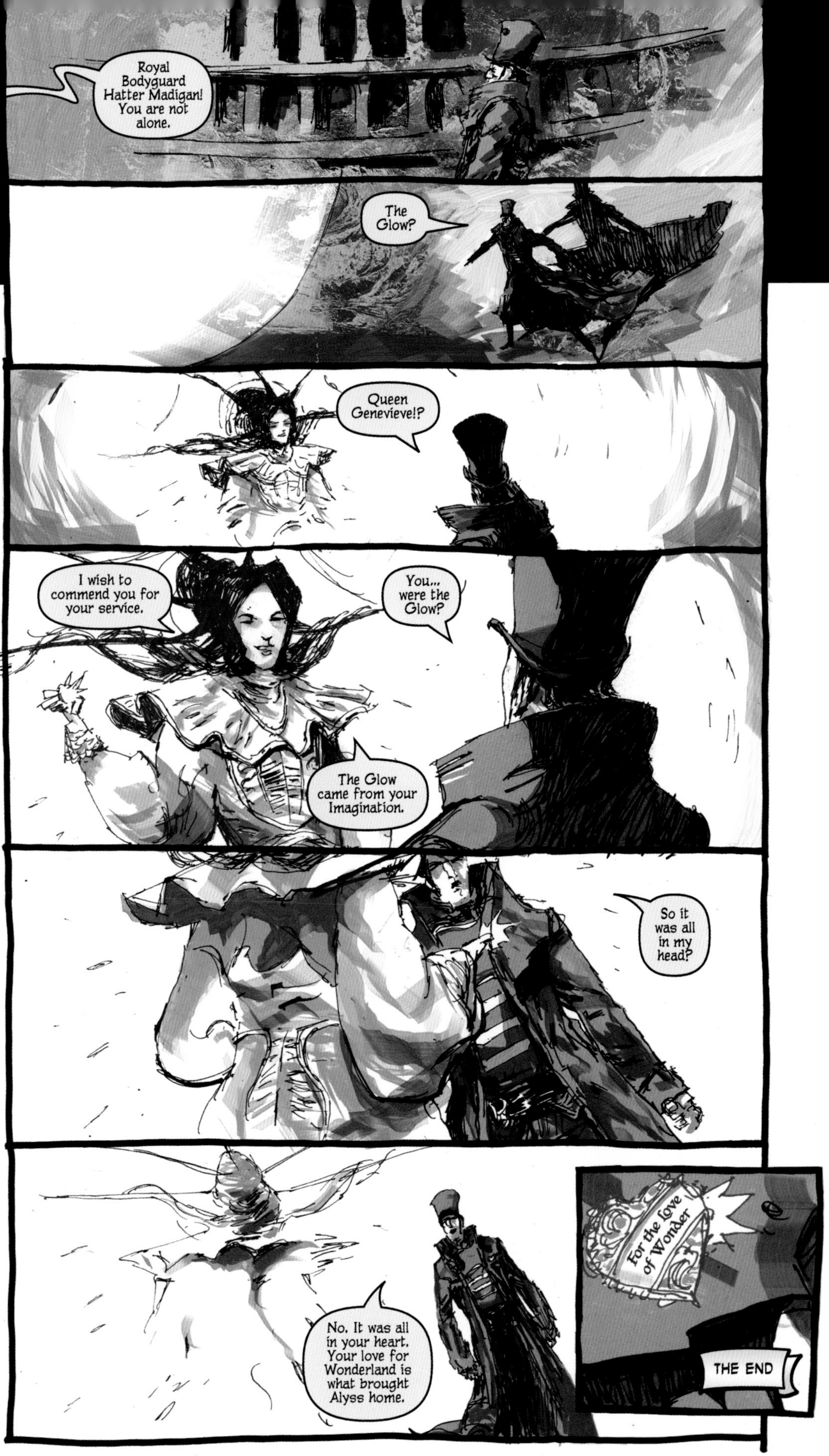

Royal Bodyguard Hatter Madigan! You are not alone.
The Glow?
Queen Genevieve!?
I wish to commend you for your service.
You... were the Glow?
The Glow came from your Imagination.
So it was all in my head?
No. It was all in your heart. Your love for Wonderland is what brought Alyss home.
For the love of Wonder
THE END

"Whenever you are confronted with an opponent. Conquer him with love." –Mahatma Gandhi

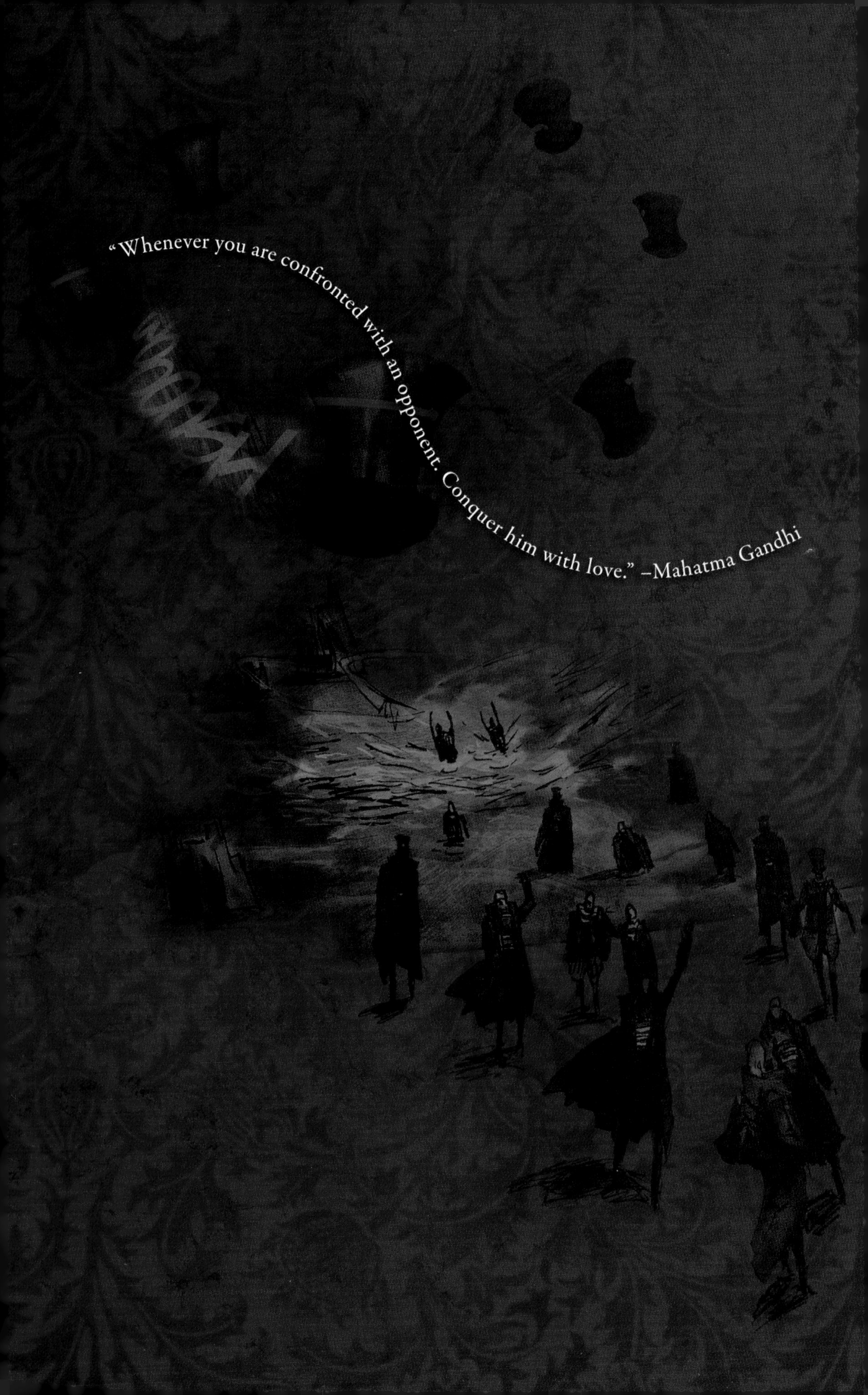

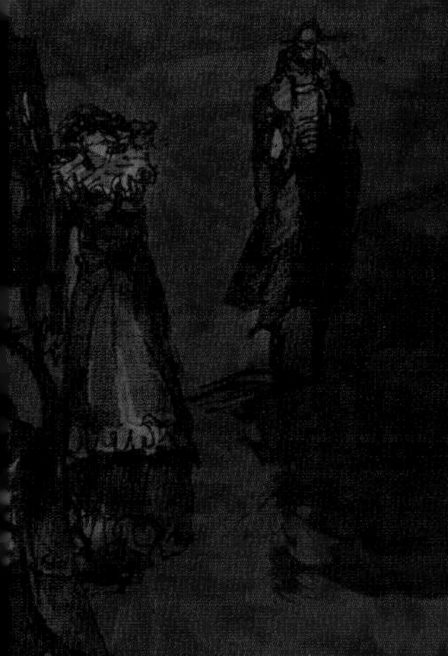

Epilogue

"If a thing loves, it is infinite." –William Blake

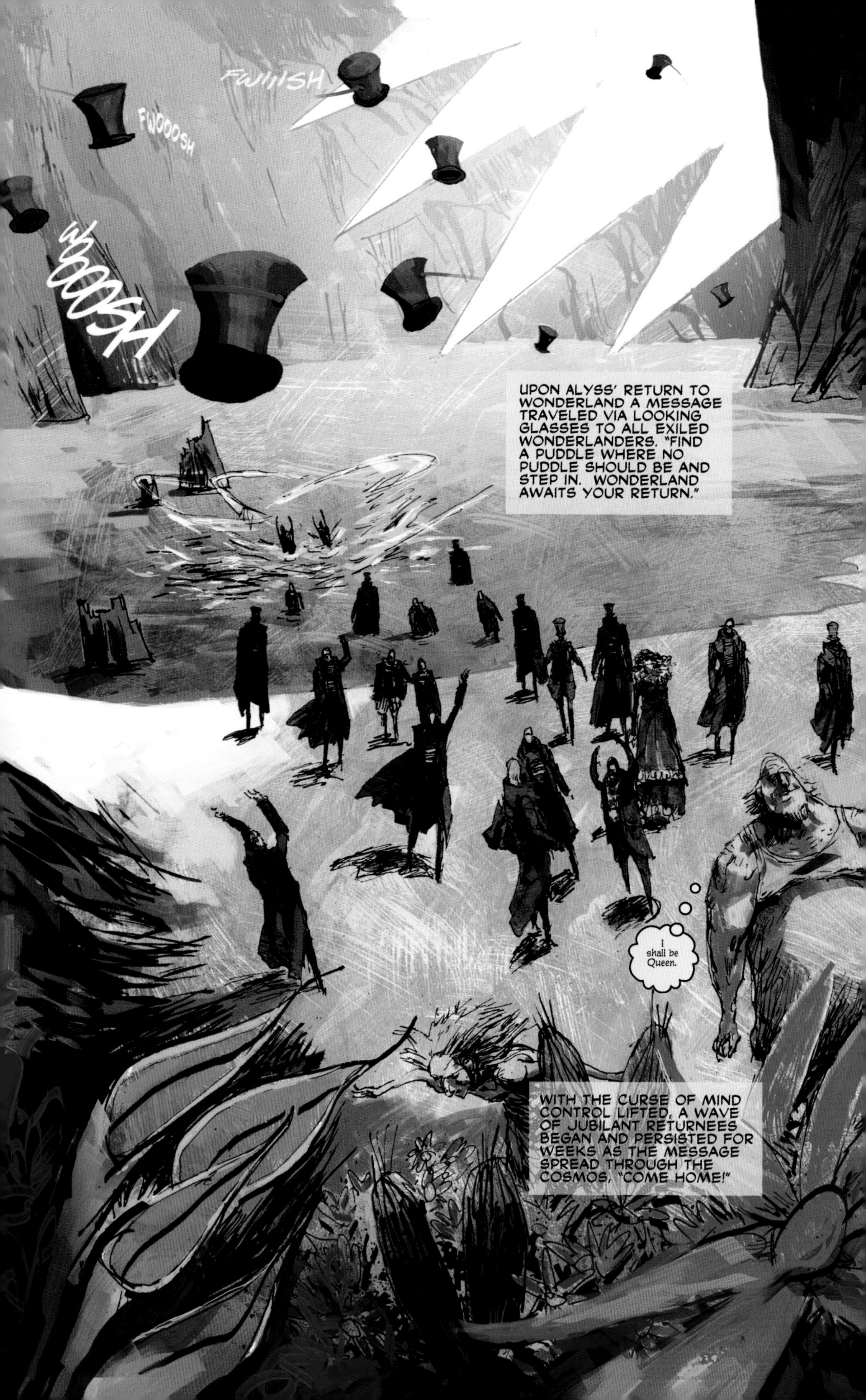
FWIIISH
FWOOOSH
WOOOSH
UPON ALYSS' RETURN TO WONDERLAND A MESSAGE TRAVELED VIA LOOKING GLASSES TO ALL EXILED WONDERLANDERS. "FIND A PUDDLE WHERE NO PUDDLE SHOULD BE AND STEP IN. WONDERLAND AWAITS YOUR RETURN."
I shall be Queen.
WITH THE CURSE OF MIND CONTROL LIFTED, A WAVE OF JUBILANT RETURNEES BEGAN AND PERSISTED FOR WEEKS AS THE MESSAGE SPREAD THROUGH THE COSMOS, "COME HOME!"

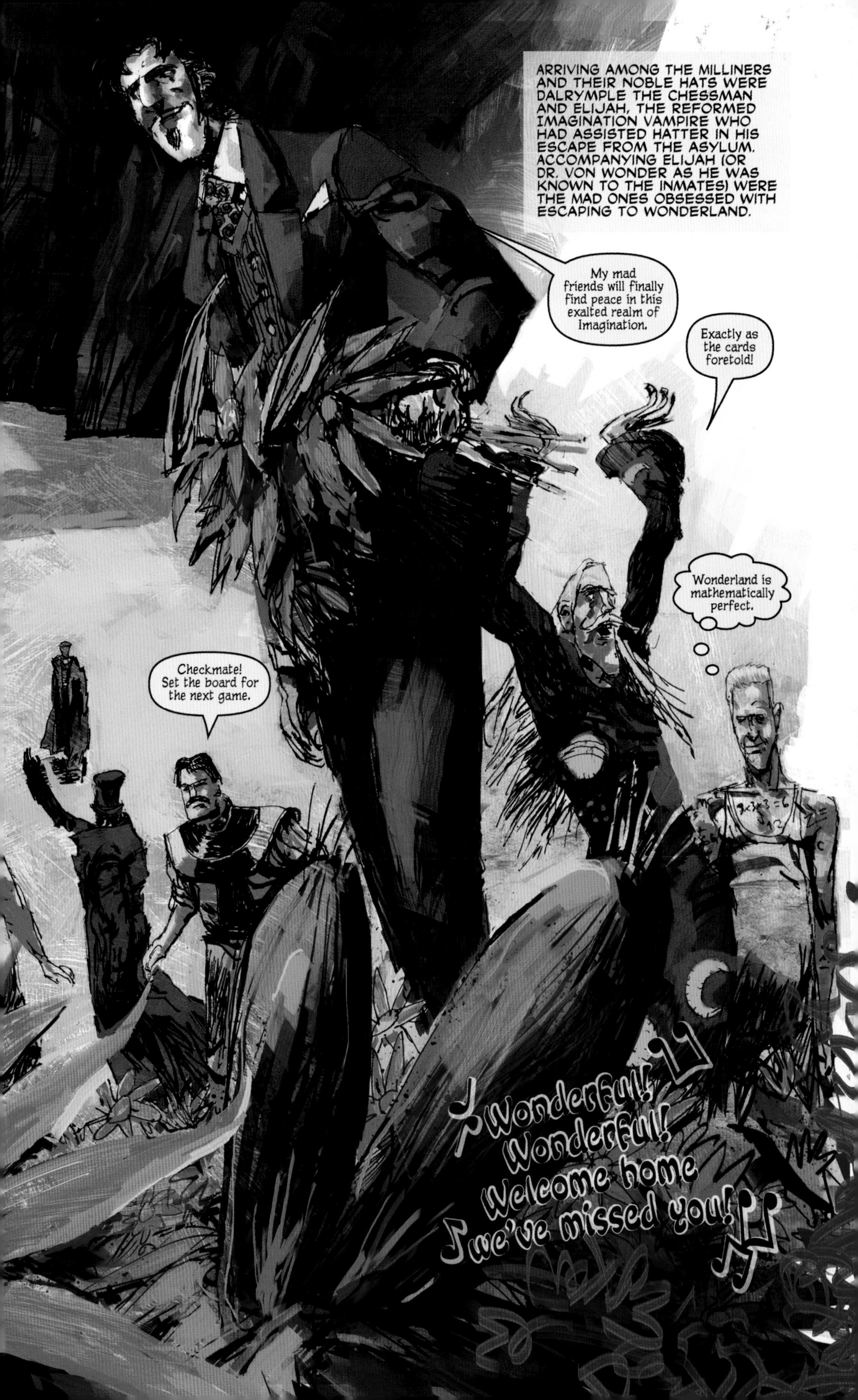

ARRIVING AMONG THE MILLINERS AND THEIR NOBLE HATS WERE DALRYMPLE THE CHESSMAN AND ELIJAH, THE REFORMED IMAGINATION VAMPIRE WHO HAD ASSISTED HATTER IN HIS ESCAPE FROM THE ASYLUM. ACCOMPANYING ELIJAH (OR DR. VON WONDER AS HE WAS KNOWN TO THE INMATES) WERE THE MAD ONES OBSESSED WITH ESCAPING TO WONDERLAND.
My mad friends will finally find peace in this exalted realm of Imagination.
Exactly as the cards foretold!
Wonderland is mathematically perfect.
Checkmate! Set the board for the next game.
Wonderful! Wonderful! Welcome home we've missed you!

Being deeply loved by someone gives you strength, while loving someone deeply gives you courage. —Lao Tzu

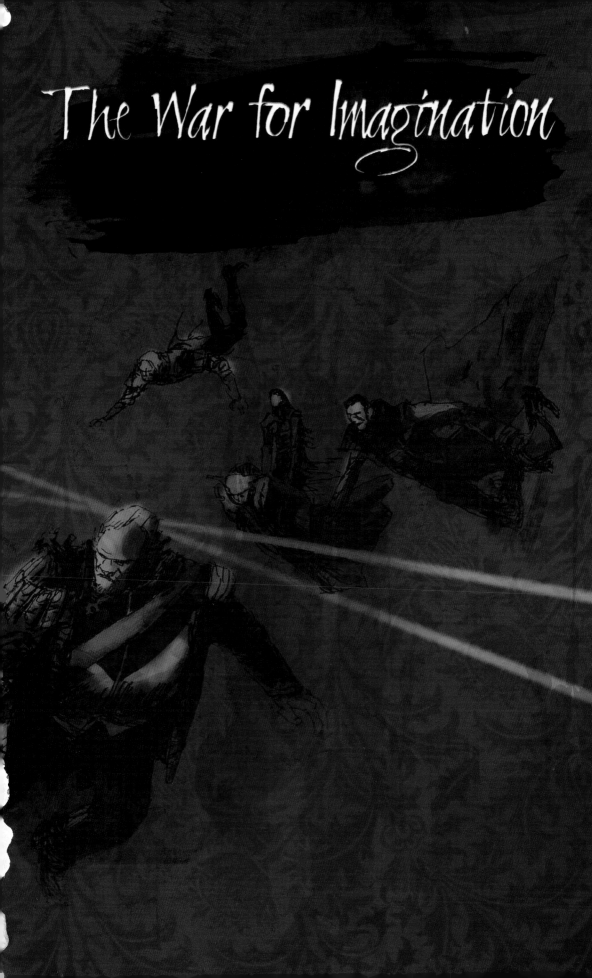

The War for Imagination

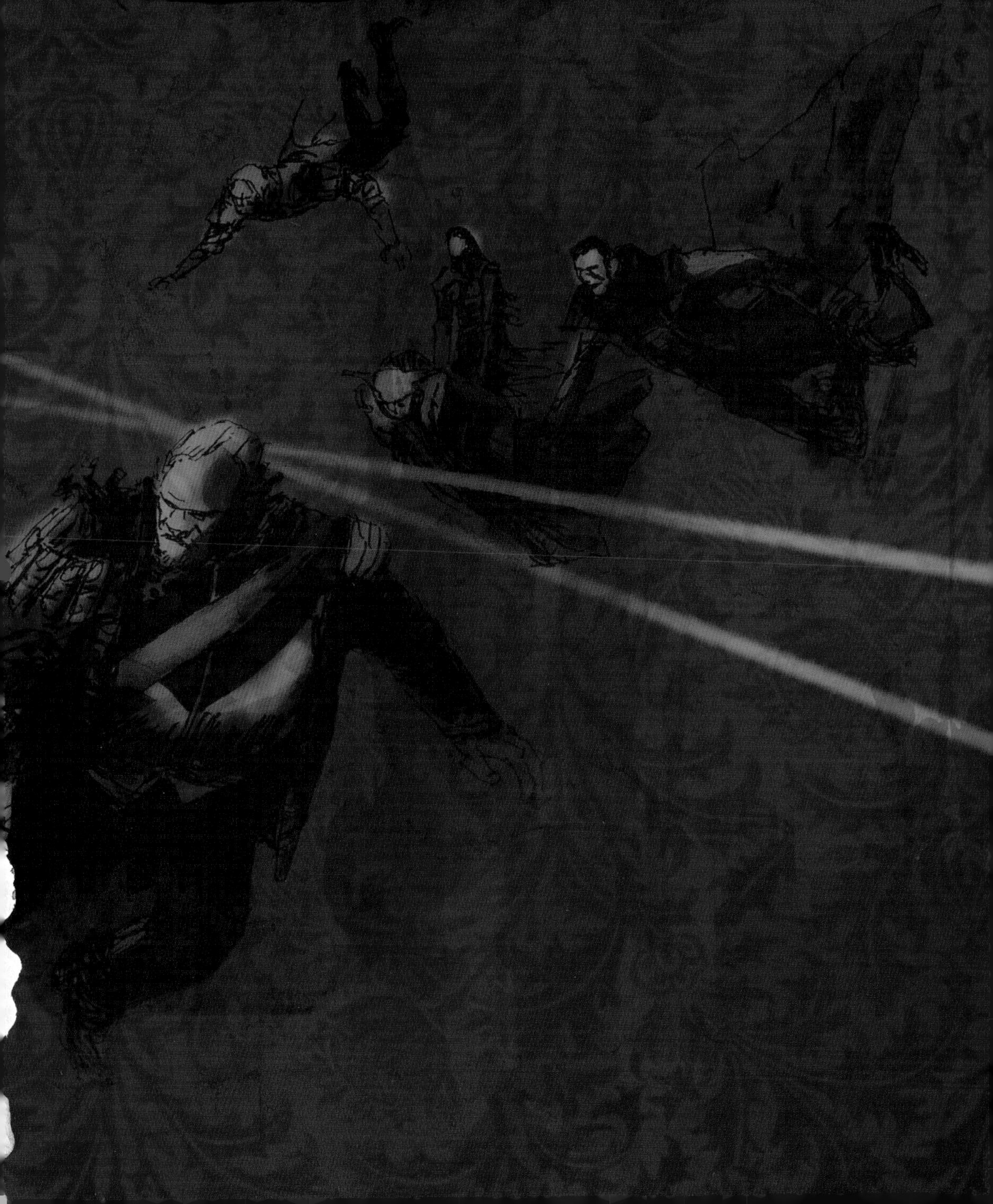

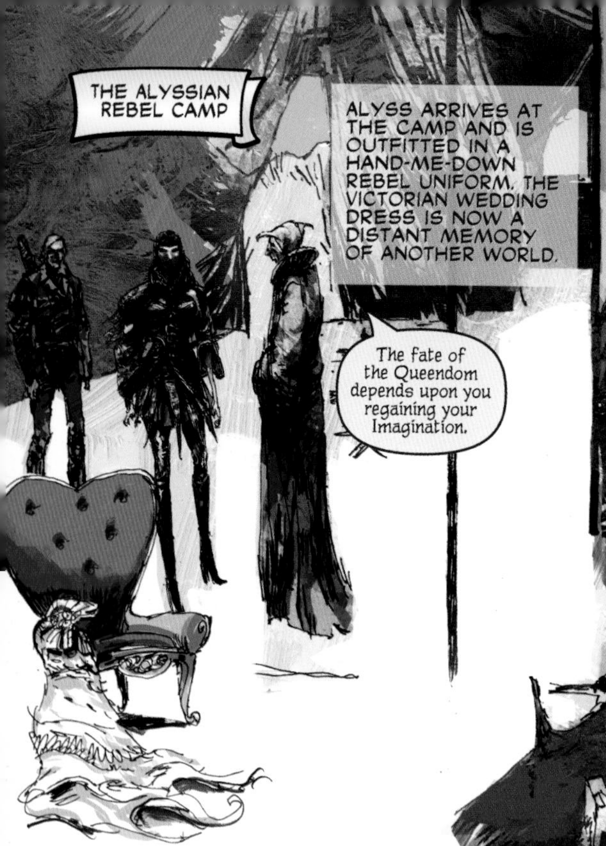
THE ALYSSIAN REBEL CAMP
ALYSS ARRIVES AT THE CAMP AND IS OUTFITTED IN A HAND-ME-DOWN REBEL UNIFORM. THE VICTORIAN WEDDING DRESS IS NOW A DISTANT MEMORY OF ANOTHER WORLD.
The fate of the Queendom depends upon you regaining your Imagination.

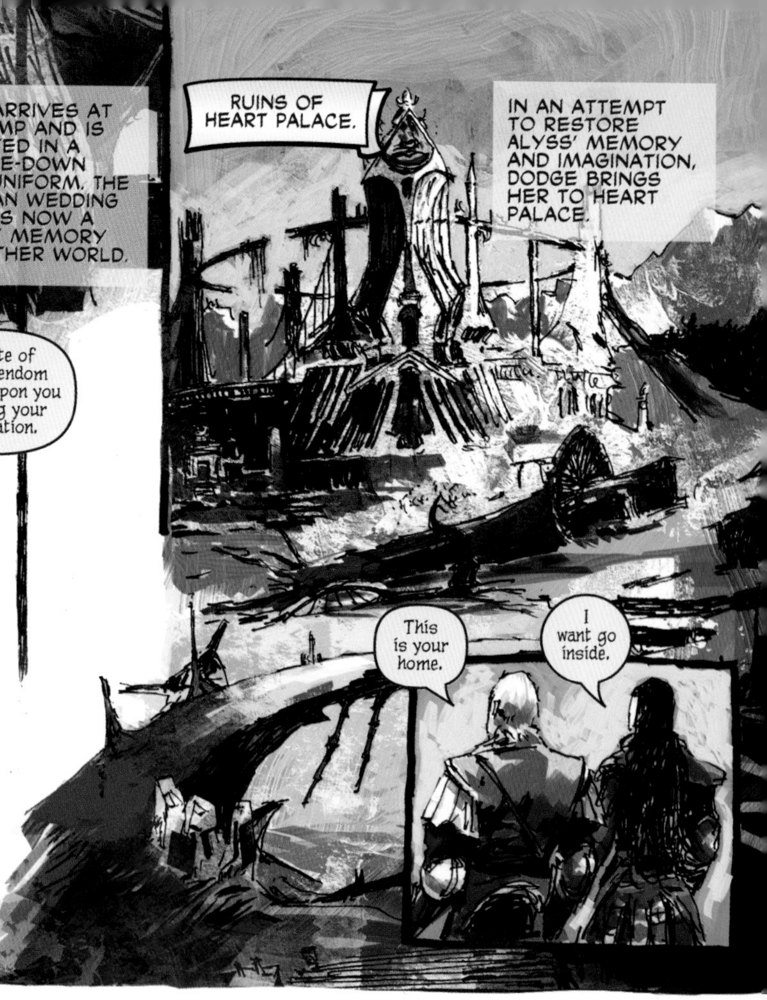
RUINS OF HEART PALACE.
IN AN ATTEMPT TO RESTORE ALYSS' MEMORY AND IMAGINATION, DODGE BRINGS HER TO HEART PALACE.
This is your home.
I want go inside.

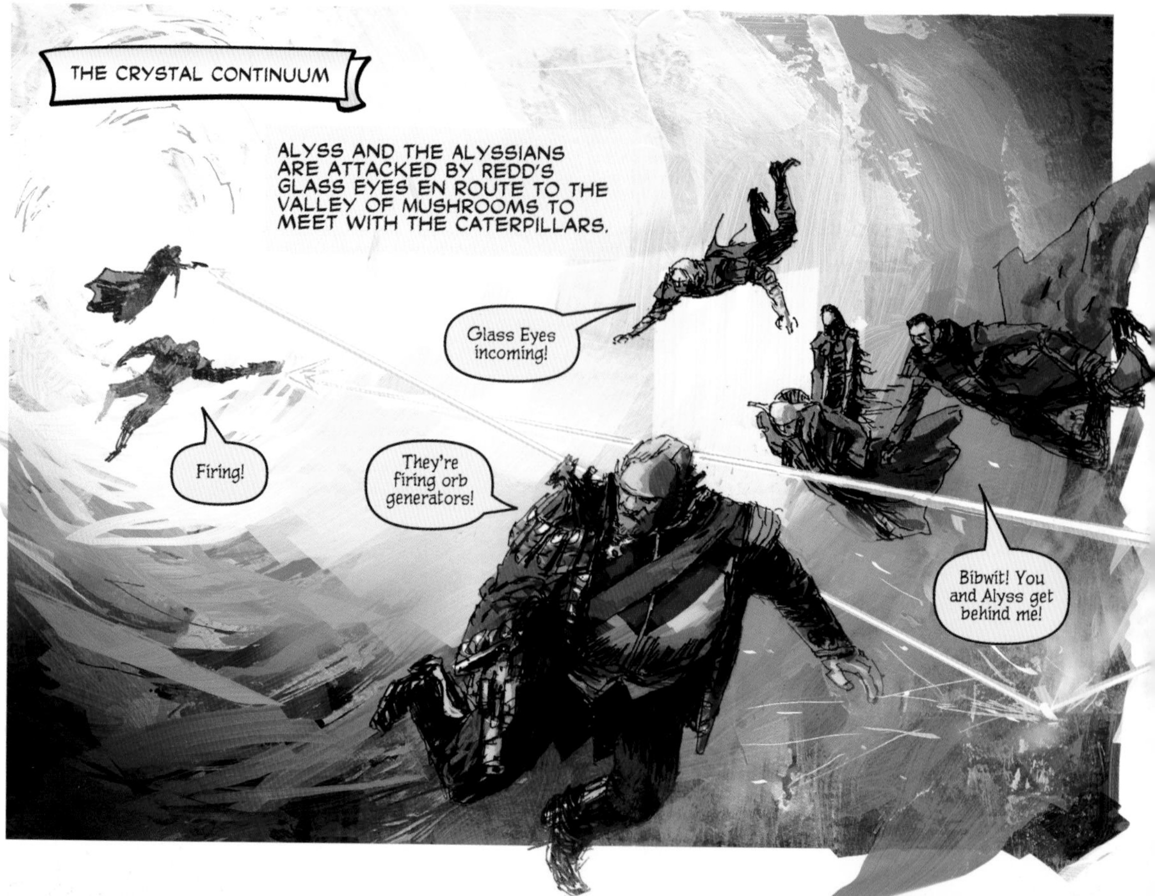
THE CRYSTAL CONTINUUM
ALYSS AND THE ALYSSIANS ARE ATTACKED BY REDD'S GLASS EYES EN ROUTE TO THE VALLEY OF MUSHROOMS TO MEET WITH THE CATERPILLARS.
Glass Eyes incoming!
Firing!
They're firing orb generators!
Bibwit! You and Alyss get behind me!

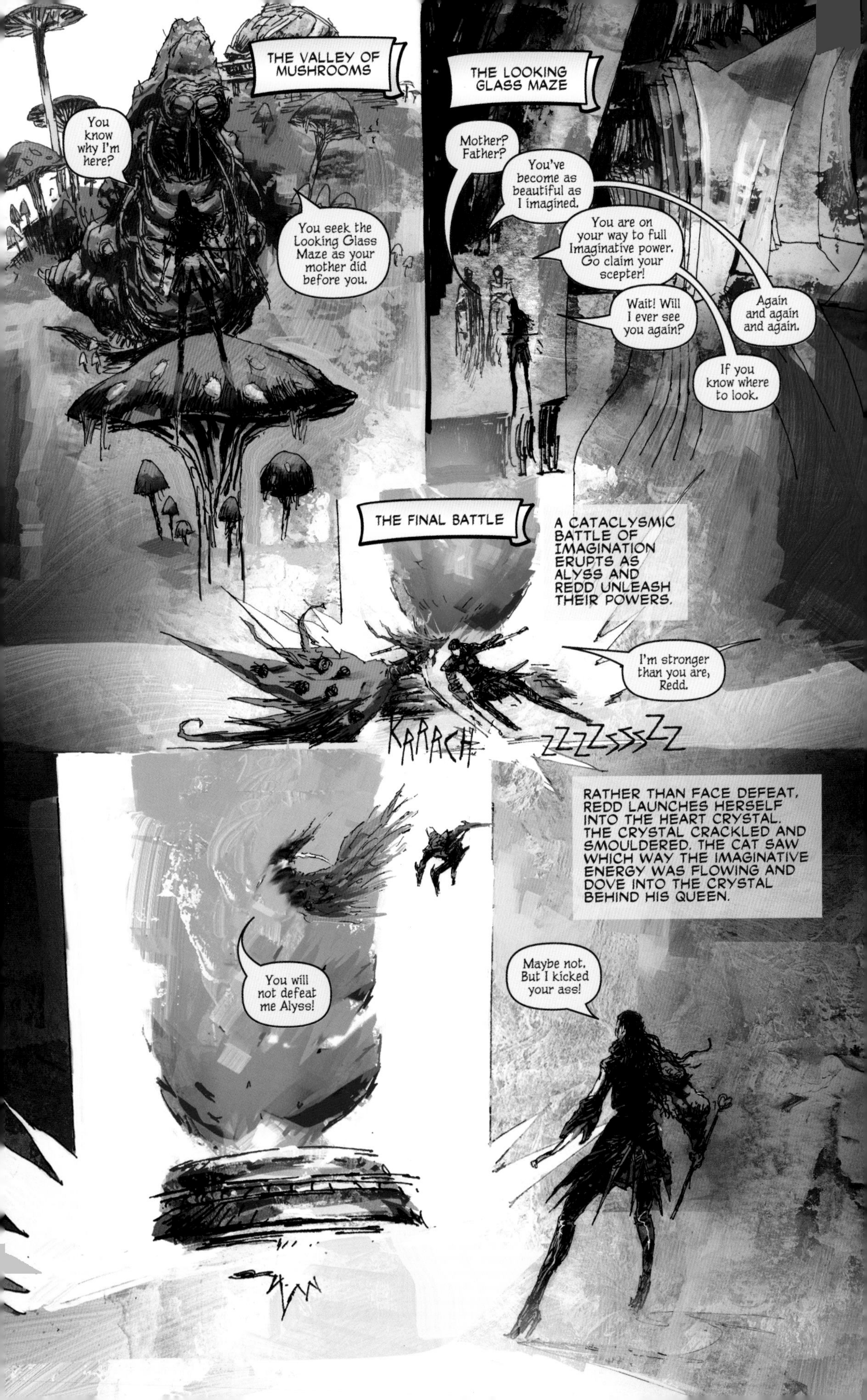
THE VALLEY OF MUSHROOMS
You know why I'm here?
You seek the Looking Glass Maze as your mother did before you.
THE LOOKING GLASS MAZE
Mother? Father?
You've become as beautiful as I imagined.
You are on your way to full Imaginative power. Go claim your scepter!
Wait! Will I ever see you again?
Again and again and again.
If you know where to look.
THE FINAL BATTLE
A CATACLYSMIC BATTLE OF IMAGINATION ERUPTS AS ALYSS AND REDD UNLEASH THEIR POWERS.
I'm stronger than you are, Redd.
KRRACH
ZZZZSSSZZ
RATHER THAN FACE DEFEAT, REDD LAUNCHES HERSELF INTO THE HEART CRYSTAL. THE CRYSTAL CRACKLED AND SMOULDERED. THE CAT SAW WHICH WAY THE IMAGINATIVE ENERGY WAS FLOWING AND DOVE INTO THE CRYSTAL BEHIND HIS QUEEN.
You will not defeat me Alyss!
Maybe not. But I kicked your ass!

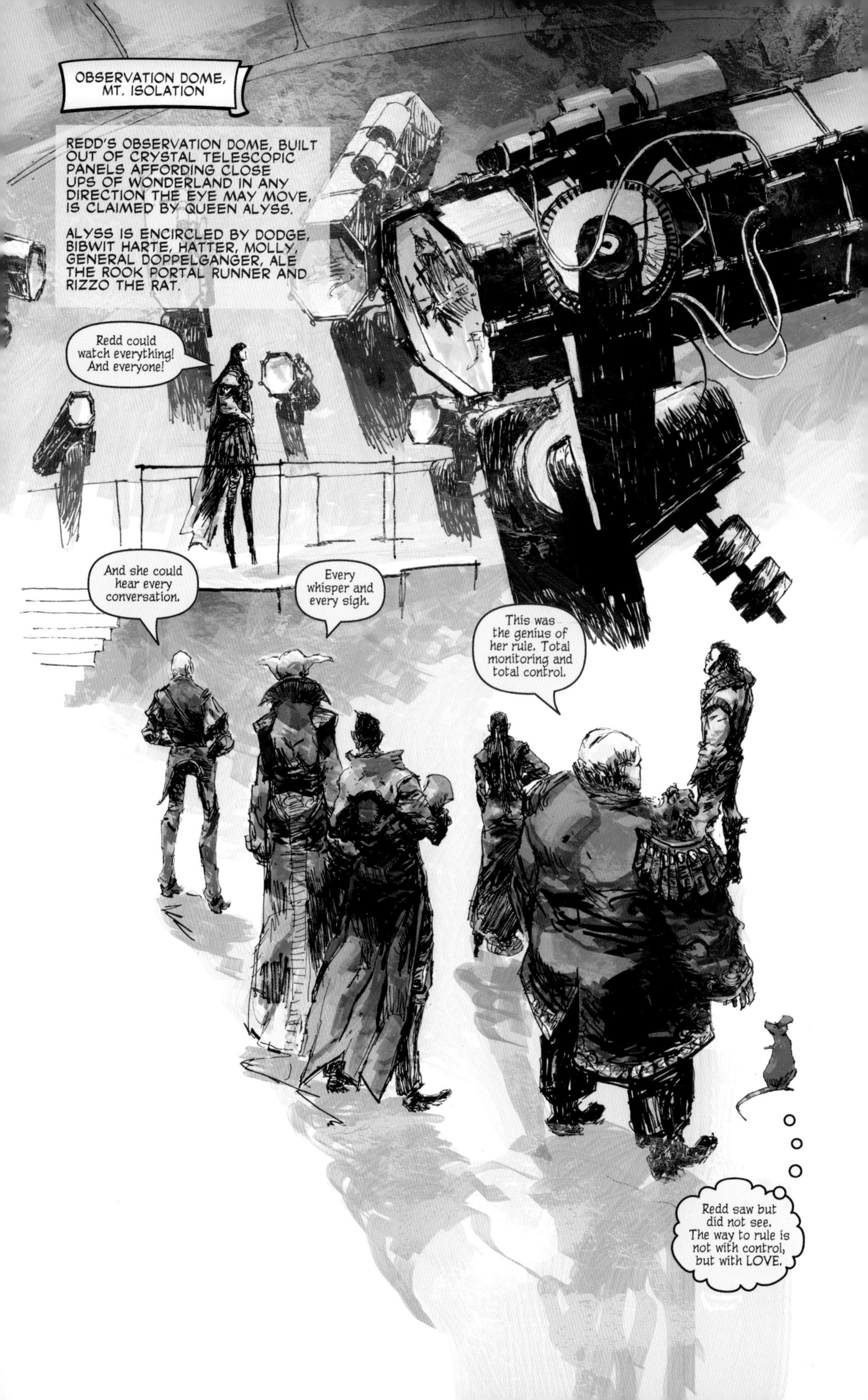

OBSERVATION DOME, MT. ISOLATION
REDD'S OBSERVATION DOME, BUILT OUT OF CRYSTAL TELESCOPIC PANELS AFFORDING CLOSE UPS OF WONDERLAND IN ANY DIRECTION THE EYE MAY MOVE, IS CLAIMED BY QUEEN ALYSS.
ALYSS IS ENCIRCLED BY DODGE, BIBWIT HARTE, HATTER, MOLLY, GENERAL DOPPELGANGER, ALE THE ROOK PORTAL RUNNER AND RIZZO THE RAT.
Redd could watch everything! And everyone!
And she could hear every conversation.
Every whisper and every sigh.
This was the genius of her rule. Total monitoring and total control.
Redd saw but did not see. The way to rule is not with control, but with LOVE.

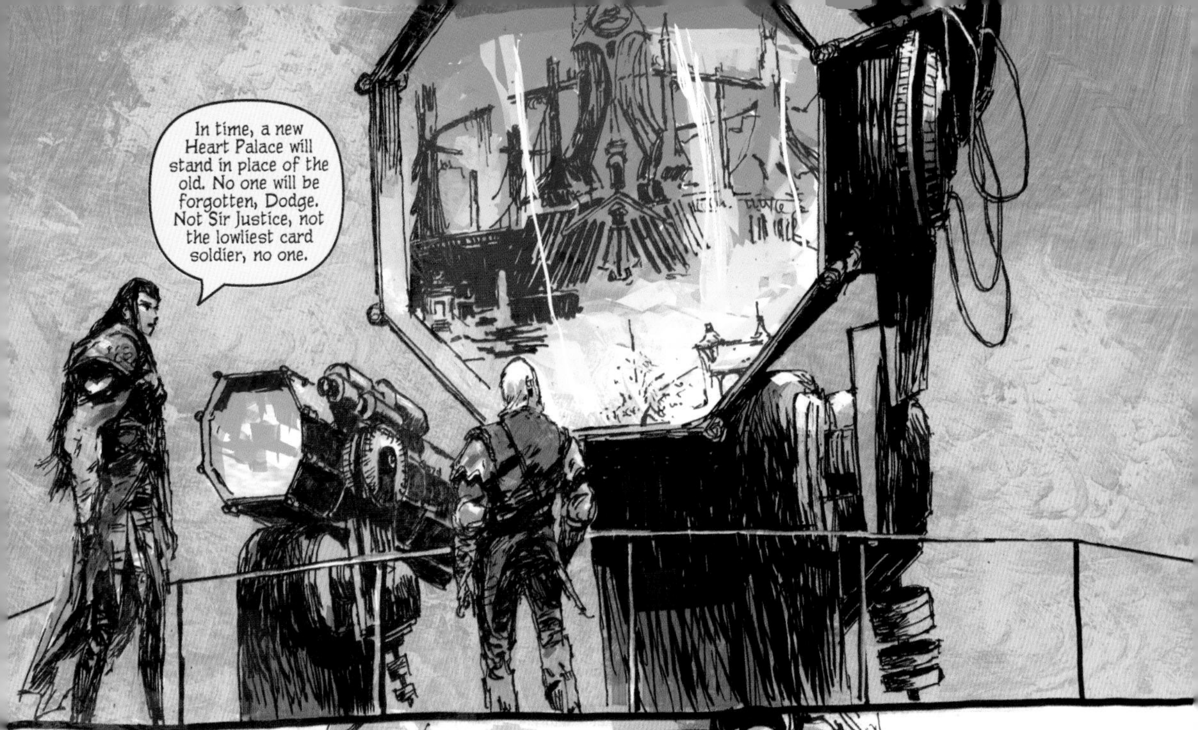
In time, a new Heart Palace will stand in place of the old. No one will be forgotten, Dodge. Not Sir Justice, not the lowliest card soldier, no one.

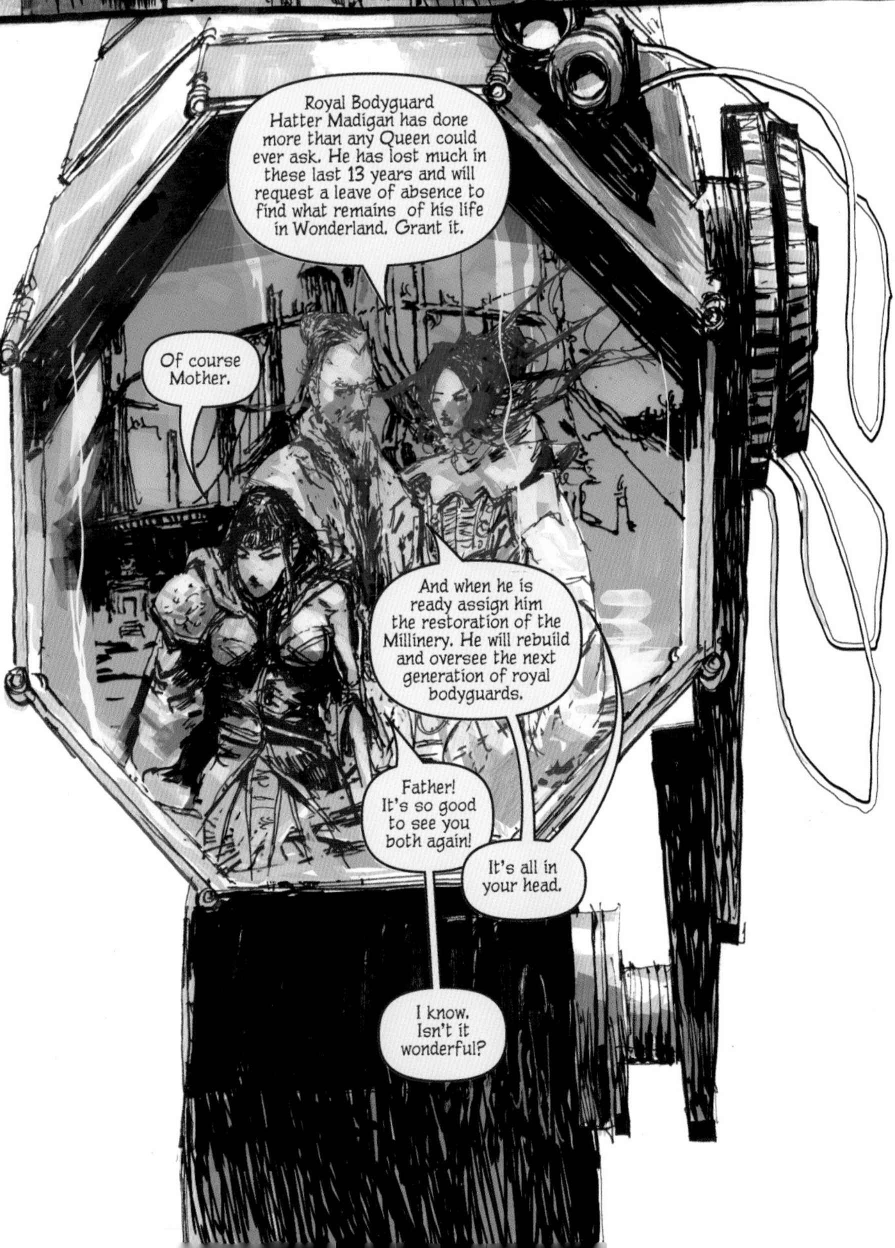
Royal Bodyguard Hatter Madigan has done more than any Queen could ever ask. He has lost much in these last 13 years and will request a leave of absence to find what remains of his life in Wonderland. Grant it.
Of course Mother.
And when he is ready assign him the restoration of the Millinery. He will rebuild and oversee the next generation of royal bodyguards.
Father! It's so good to see you both again!
It's all in your head.
I know. Isn't it wonderful?

For Those Who Know

Included in Volume 5 were the anagrammed identities of four hidden benefactors. Much good is accomplished in the shadows away from the glare of self-promotion. A tip of the Hat to these anagrammed angels. They alone know who they are.

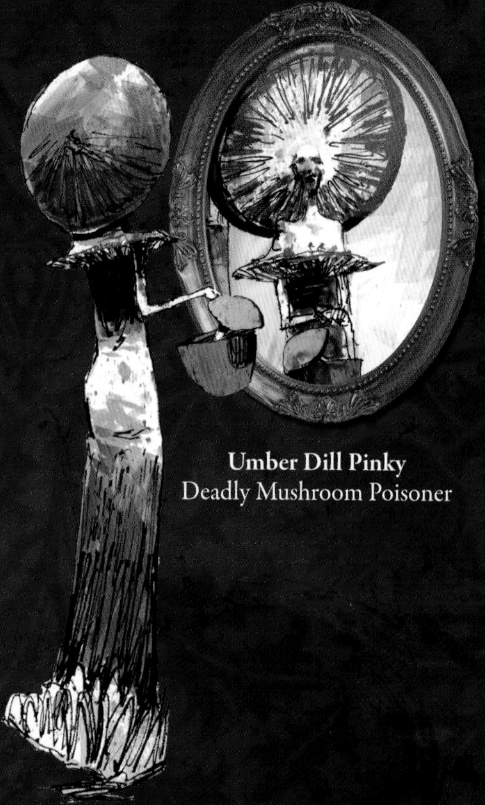

Umber Dill Pinky
Deadly Mushroom Poisoner

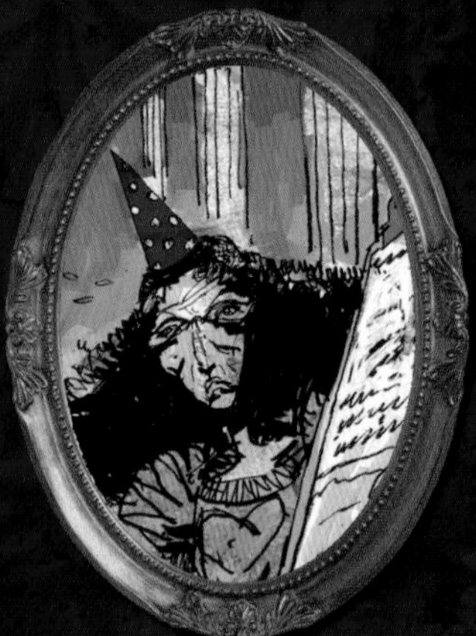

Gala Ilia In Nut
Jubilee Planner for Redd

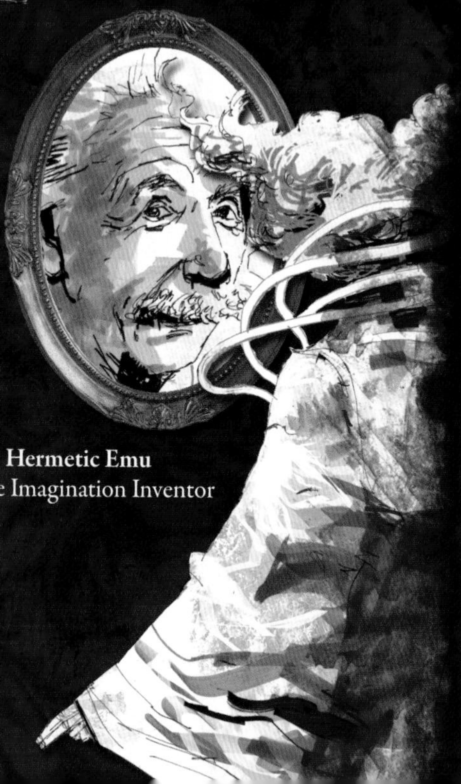

Hermetic Emu
White Imagination Inventor

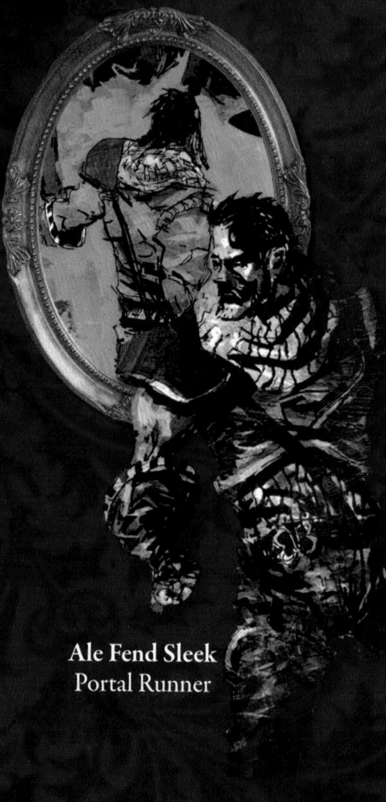

Ale Fend Sleek
Portal Runner

Altered States and Reflected Spirits

Among the Followers of the Glow were two dramatic entities who commissioned the Institute to research their Wonderland reflections. Their impulse to discover who they were on the other side of the looking glass revealed exceptional characters who chose to follow Redd's Dark Imagination. Perhaps their dark reflections in Wonderland are the shadow side of their powerful Glow in our world.

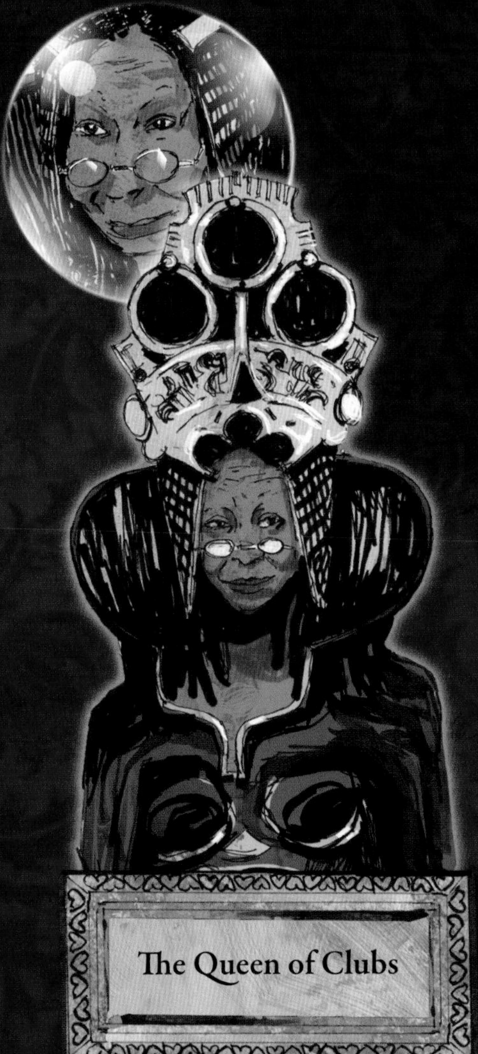
The Queen of Clubs

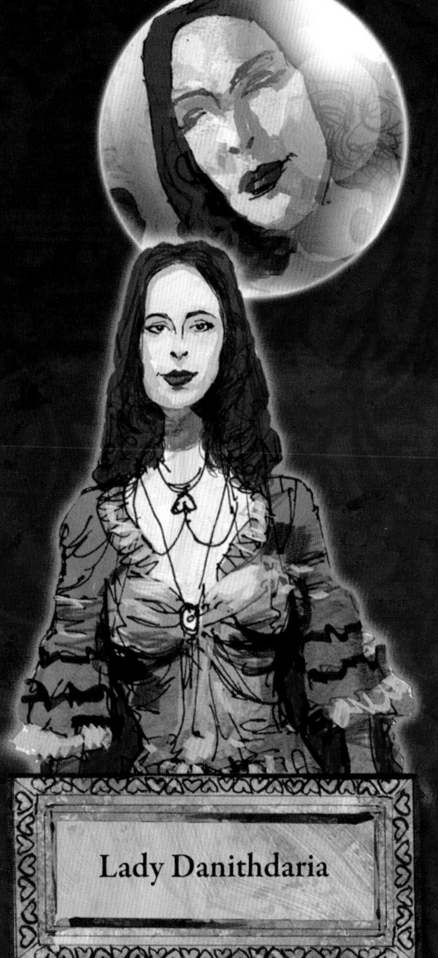
Lady Danithdaria

Hatter's Circle of Friends

Volume 1 – Far From Wonder

Crazy Girl #42
She goes to Wonderland when she dreams
in color and recognizes the Man in the Hat
as the one who will save the orphans
from Imagination Draining.

Intrepid Russian Journalist Magda Pushikin
Stop the presses!
This story is big, a careermaker!

Volume 2 - Mad with Wonder

Sir George Lucius Oliphant Wellesley
Timbromaniac and financier of Hatter's travels.

Elijah the Imagination Vampire
Exile from Wonderland and Savior to the Mad

As we well know it is difficult, if not impossible, to accomplish anything of worth ALONE. We humans are a psychically integrated species who operate at top levels only when we cooperate and help each other. And so it was for Hatter Madigan during the 13 years he searched our world. In every volume Hatter met and shared chivalry, nobility and love with the few extraordinary beings who were able to grasp the power of his origin and mission.

Volume 3 – Nature of Wonder

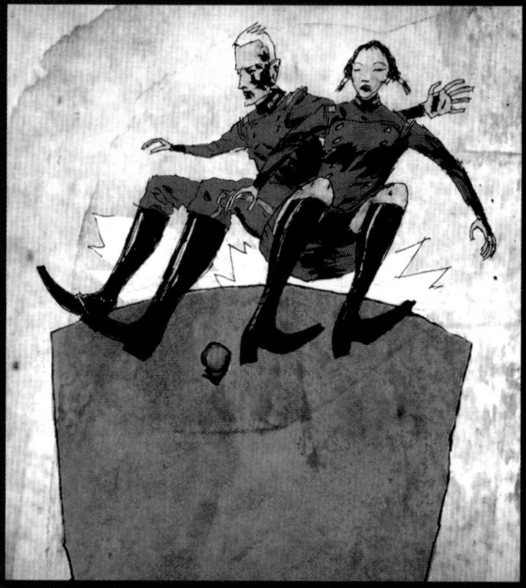

The Bureau of Illuminated Forces (IF)
Agent Horatio Alabaster
Agent Philomena Ark

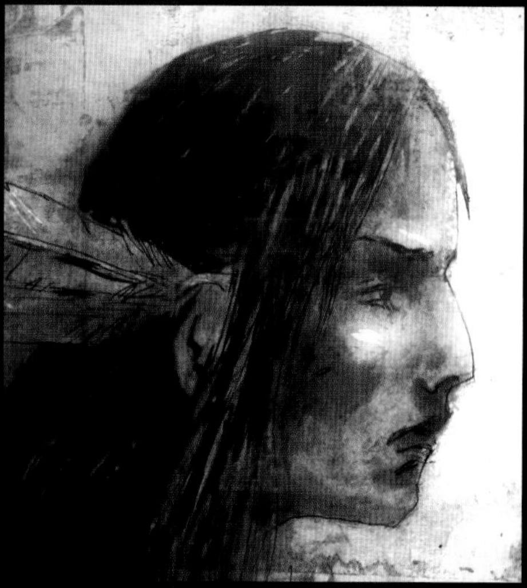

Realm – White Flower Shaman
Protector of the antidote to Dark Imagination

Volume 4 – Zen of Wonder

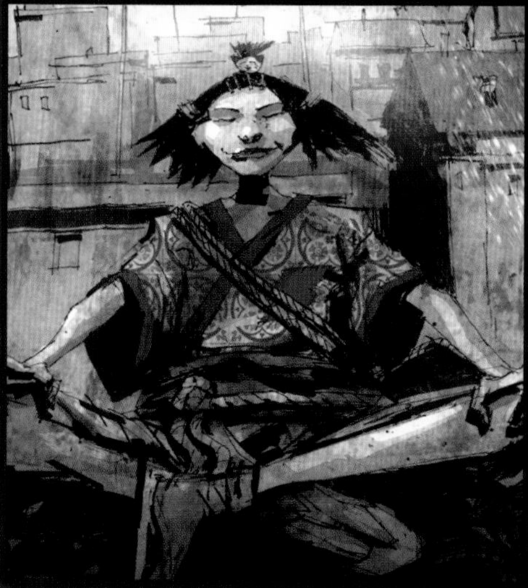

Nekko the Zen Guide
Not a problem! An adventure!

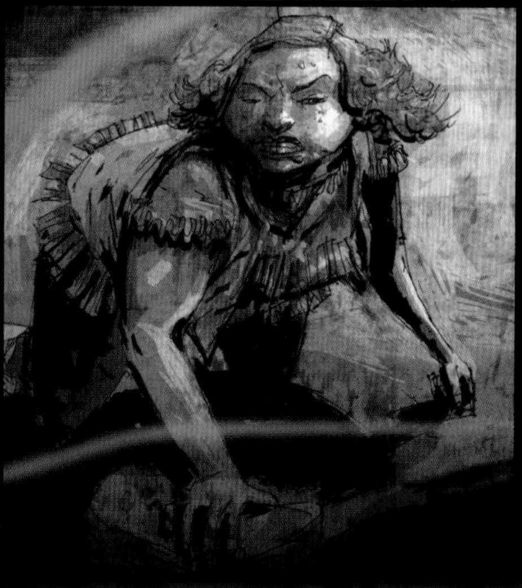

Lil' Dick
American as a can of beans with a heart like a big gold nugget.

The Last Friend

In this final volume Hatter encountered an equally mysterious traveler in chrononaut, Jet Seer. She is a woman claiming to be from the future and time traveling back to collect the DNA of the mighty and magical who had come before. The clock wound down and she had to return but a promise was made to meet again. Where? When? Stay tuned.

Jet Seer
Chrononaut

Thank You
Followers of the Glow!

see
you
in the
other
side...

"Ever has it been that love knows not its own depth until the hour of separation." –Khalil Gibran

Where to Find Wonder in the 3D World

facebook.com/frankbeddor

facebook.com/seekingalyss

frankbeddor.com

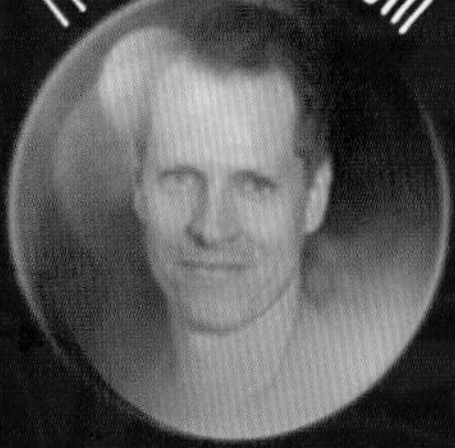

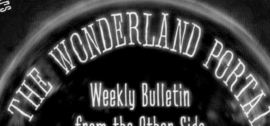

facebook.com/thelookingglasswars

lookingglasswarsportal.tumblr.com

THE WONDERLAND PORTAL

Weekly Bulletin
from the Other Side
of the Looking Glass
News, Art and
Alternative Reality

Sign up at frankbeddor.com/wonderland-portal

pinterest.com/lookingglasswar

samimakkonen.com

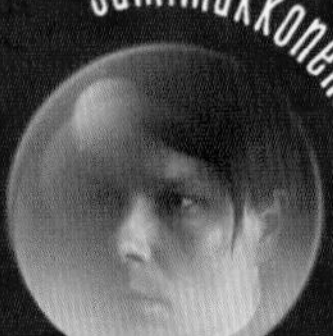

vincentproce.com

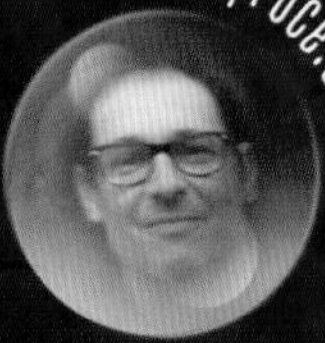

samimakkonen.tumblr.com

instagram.com/hatter_m

youtube.com/user/automaticpictures

twitter.com/wonderlandtimes

twitter.com/SamiMakkonen

ENEMIES UNITE IN A WAR FOR WONDERLAND

IN THE THRILLING FINALE OF THE LOOKING GLASS WARS TRILOGY.

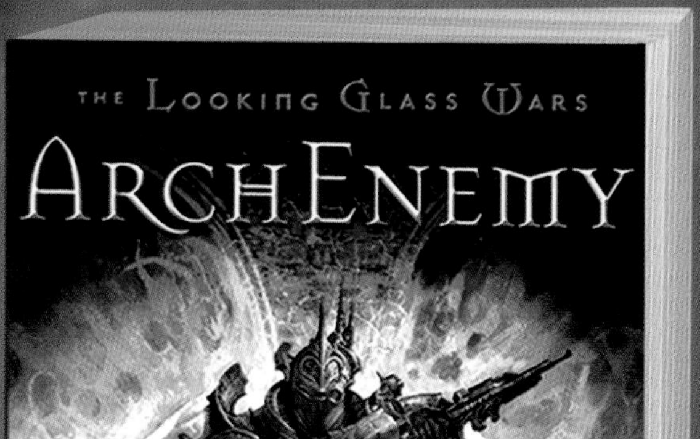
THE LOOKING GLASS WARS
ARCHENEMY
FRANK BEDDOR

"Don't enter *The Looking Glass Wars* lightly. Once you're there, you can't turn back. Frank Beddor makes sure of that."

—*Teenreads.com*

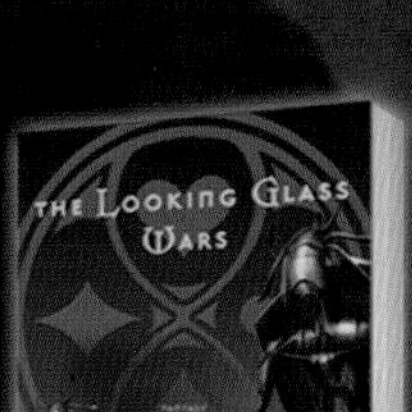
THE LOOKING GLASS WARS
FRANK BEDDOR

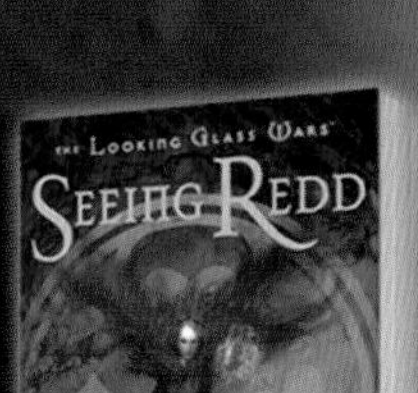
THE LOOKING GLASS WARS
SEEING REDD
FRANK BEDDOR

LOOKINGGLASSWARS.COM

DIAL BOOKS

A DIVISION OF PENGUIN YOUNG READERS GROUP

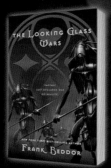

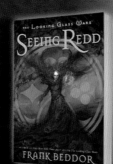

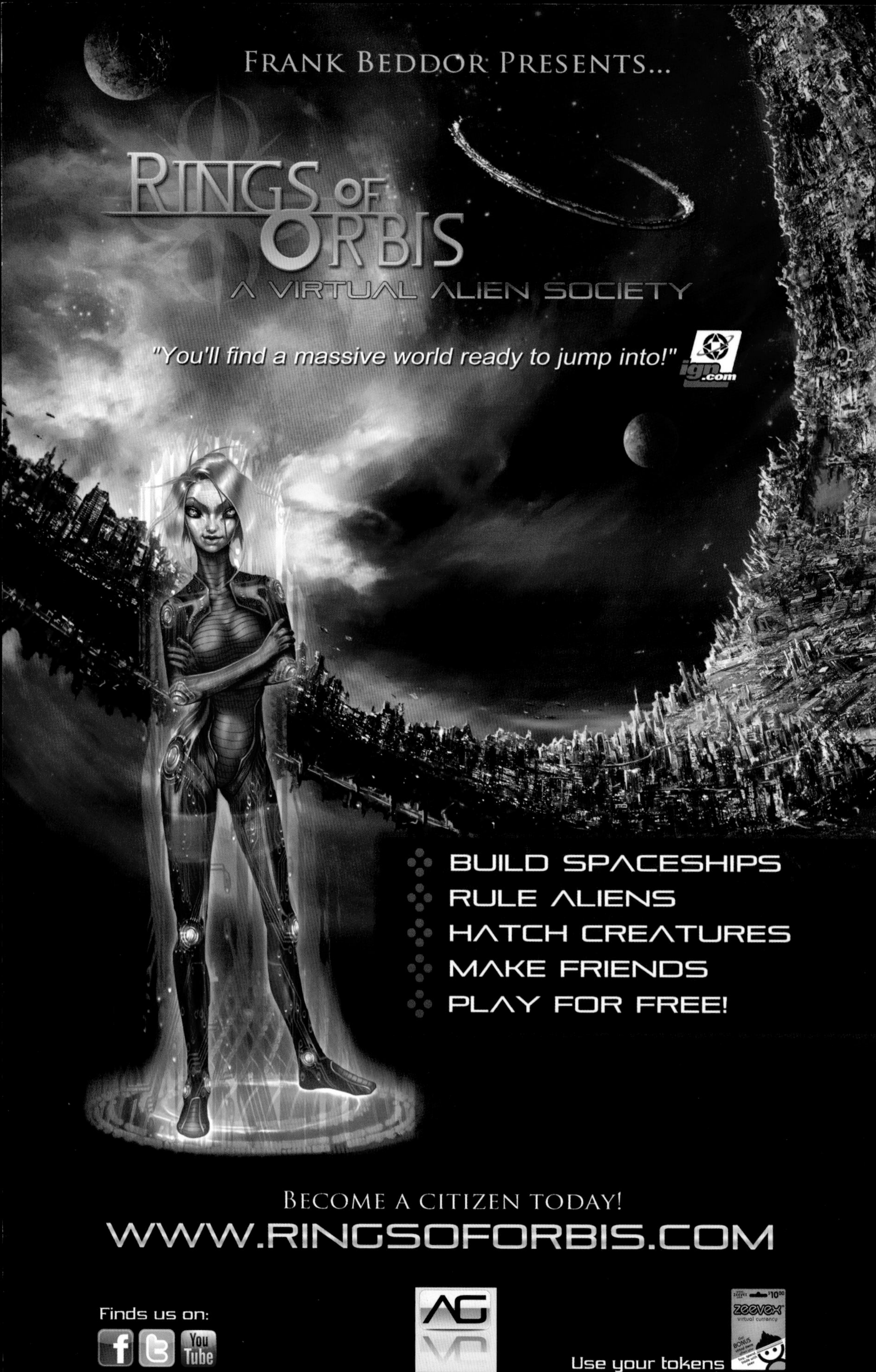

FRANK BEDDOR PRESENTS...
RINGS OF ORBIS
A VIRTUAL ALIEN SOCIETY
"You'll find a massive world ready to jump into!" ign.com
BUILD SPACESHIPS
RULE ALIENS
HATCH CREATURES
MAKE FRIENDS
PLAY FOR FREE!
BECOME A CITIZEN TODAY!
WWW.RINGSOFORBIS.COM
Finds us on:
You Tube
Use your tokens

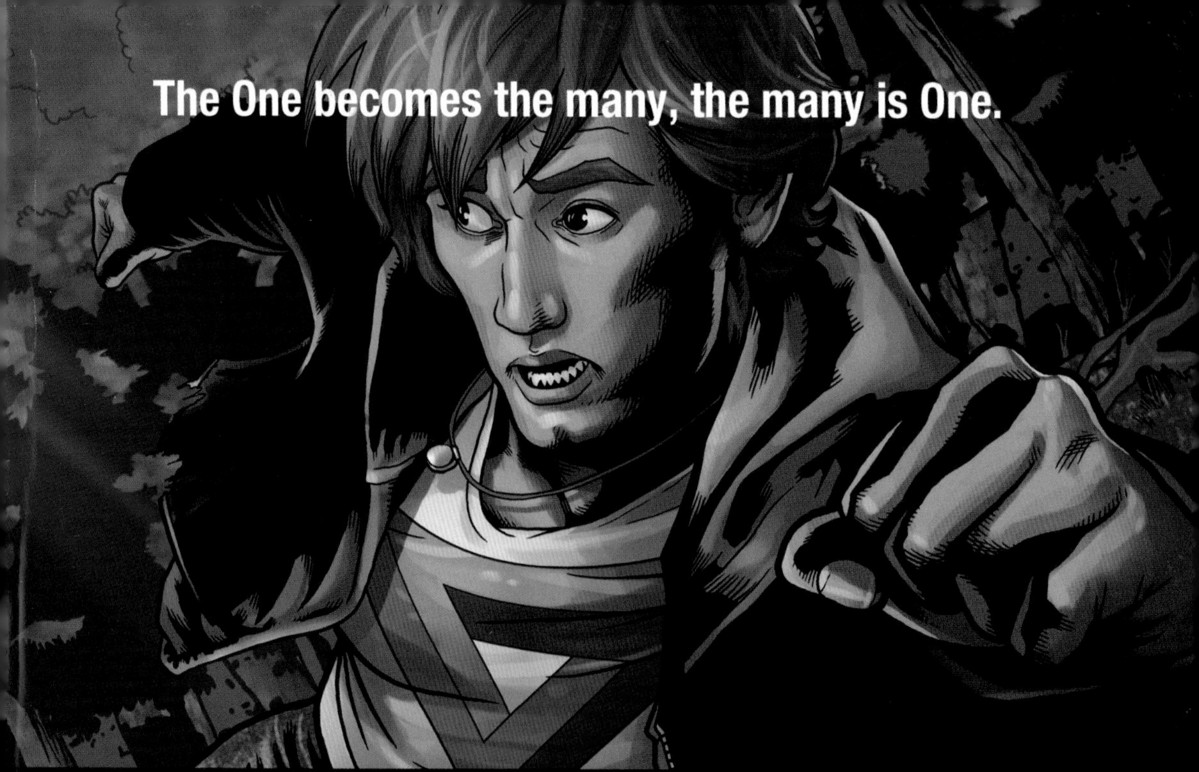
The One becomes the many, the many is One.

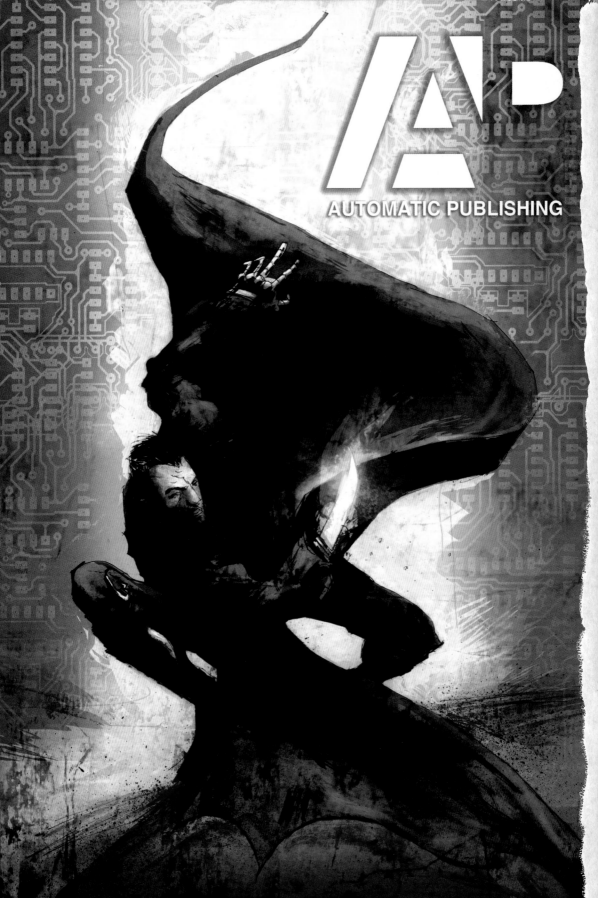

AUTOMATIC PUBLISHING

If you have any probing questions that you would like answered,
please email automaticstudio@gmail.com